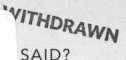

WITHDRAWN

SAID?

Ad... ...56. He has writ... ...collections of poetry and nine works of fiction. His first novel, *Ulverton*, was published in 1992; his most recent, *Between Each Breath*, appeared in 2007. He lives in France with his wife and three children.

ALSO BY ADAM THORPE

Fiction

Ulverton

Still

Pieces of Light

Shifts

Nineteen Twenty-One

No Telling

The Rules of Perspective

Between Each Breath

Poetry

Mornings in the Baltic

Meeting Montaigne

From the Neanderthal

Nine Lessons from the Dark

Birds with a Broken Wing

ADAM THORPE

Is This The Way You Said?

VINTAGE BOOKS
London

Published by Vintage 2007

2 4 6 8 10 9 7 5 3 1

First published in Great Britain in 2006 by
Jonathan Cape
Random House, 20 Vauxhall Bridge Road,
London SW1V 2SA

www.vintage-books.co.uk

Addresses for companies within The Random House Group Limited can be
found at: www.randomhouse.co.uk/offices.htm

The Random House Group Limited Reg. No. 954009

A CIP catalogue record for this book
is available from the British Library

ISBN 9780099479895

The Random House Group Limited makes every effort to ensure that
the papers used in its books are made from trees that have been
legally sourced from well-managed and credibly certified forests. Our
paper procurement policy can be found at:
www.randomhouse.co.uk/paper.htm

Mixed Sources
Product group from well-managed
forests and other controlled sources
www.fsc.org Cert no. TT-COC-2139
© 1996 Forest Stewardship Council
FSC

Typeset in Sabon by Palimpsest Book Production Limited,
Grangemouth, Stirlingshire
Printed in the UK by CPI Bookmarque, Croydon, CR0 4TD

Often you meet your destiny on the very path you took to avoid it.

Jean de La Fontaine

CONTENTS

HEAVY SHOPPING

He was on a high-intensity bash in Stirling when the news came through. Phil McAllister, the operations manager, found him in the corridor.

'I'm a father,' Alan said, blowing his nose. 'She's in an incubator. She's OK.'

'That's cracking, Alan,' said Phil, in his dull Dumfries voice.

'She's two months wotsits — premature.'

'It'll be alright, Alan. They can do anything, these days. You don't need a womb.'

Sophie had called him in the middle of the pre-breakfast induction meeting, twenty minutes ago, and Alan had excused himself because it was Sofe, though he'd pretended it was business. Sophie hadn't phoned him at work since the end of their unfortunate little fling three years back.

Roger Unwin had been in the middle of one of his lectures, grinding on about establishing an organisation culture in an era of flat management while Hairy Mary took notes. It was easy to slip out. It was a relief, frankly: the air was full of his colleagues' pre-breakfast flatulence, unwashed mouths, overdone roll-on deodorants.

Sophie was phoning from the hospital. He had a little girl.

He couldn't believe it. He'd had a few too many in the bar on arrival last night and didn't feel one hundred per cent. The unbelieving part of him was watching him from the outside, with folded arms, cool as a cucumber.

He had a little girl.

'Why?' he asked, like a kid.

'It happens.'

'That's a little bit of a surprise.'

He was amazed at how calm he was being. It wasn't normal. It wasn't even a good thing. The reception was lousy and made Sofe sound breathless. Or maybe she *was* breathless.

'Look, how's Jill?'

'Jill's just fine,' said his wife's best friend.

'And my little girl?'

'Alan, she's two months premature but they're very good.'

'I know she's two months premature.'

'They've put her in an incubator. They're very good.'

'She's going to be alright, obviously,' he said.

'They're very good.'

'Nothing wrong with her?'

Sophie sighed. 'They know what they're doing, Alan.'

'Beautiful, is she, obviously?'

'She's very—'

The line fuzzed and drowned Sophie out, but he thought he'd heard 'tiny'. She's very tiny. All babies are tiny. He walked along the corridor with the mobile pressed to his ear and the fuzz died down in front of a Greek bust that Brian Wallis had said looked like Pat Ryan after the latest sales figures had been posted. A brass plaque on the base said: *Athene Ergane, Working Athena. The Premiere Company Working for You.* He wished life could be simpler.

'Sophie? Hello? Hello? Fuck. Hello?'

She came back on line again.

'Sophie, hiya, sorry about the reception. I'm in this bloody conference centre way up in Stirling. Where're you phoning from?'

'The hospital.'

'And mother and baby – they're OK?'

'I said, they're OK, Alan. Keep calm.'

'Right. That's good.'

How could she be telling him to keep calm? He was

amazingly calm. He knew deep down that everything would be A-plus.

'She's very little,' said Sophie, her voice cracking.

He nodded.

'Obviously. When was she born?'

'At 5.50.'

His heart took a quick breath as if he'd fallen deeply in love. Then it was slamming again.

'In the morning, obviously.'

'Sorry?

'In the early hours.'

'It felt like the night.'

'Why didn't you phone earlier?'

'It wasn't our first thought, Alan. Our first thought was Jill and the baby.'

'They're OK?'

'Yes, Alan.'

'I mean, you know, they're not in danger, obviously?'

'They're in very good hands, Alan. I think Jill would like you to be here. I've got to go now.'

'Of course I'll be there,' he said. 'Of course I will. We'll sort it. Tell her to keep her pecker up and she gets a *very* sloppy kiss from me.'

He didn't know whether to be over the moon or gutted. So he was neither. He was empty where he should have been full. He was watching himself as people do on operating tables. He was acting, he was actually *acting* alarmed. In fact, a large part of him just wanted to get back into the meeting and have Roger Unwin bore the knickers off him again.

The baby had been born way too early. Over two months early. Was that dangerously early? Maybe it wasn't. Maybe they whacked them all into incubators, just to be sure. Premature. His little girl. The cheeky little scrog couldn't wait to get out, she was obviously going to be precocious. Precocious. A better concept than premature. He'd wanted to talk to Jill herself but Sophie had told him she was too tired. She wasn't asleep, she was too tired, and her mobile was switched off. He could always try texting her.

Well done you I love you both very much xxxxxxx

I'll bet she's on an oxygen mask, he thought, sending the message off and immediately thinking how pathetic it was. Bloody oxygen mask — that's why she can't talk. Sophie's protecting his feelings. Or maybe Jill doesn't want to talk to him because he's a man and these are two women working together as women do, shutting him out.

He phoned Sophie again and told her he very much wanted to talk to Jill, she didn't have to talk back, and Sofe asked him why he was sounding angry and he denied sounding angry. He could hear voices behind her voice, and distant metallic crashes and bangs. He said it sounded as if she was on a building site and Sofe said they were at the Hull General, or whatever it was called, but they weren't allowed to use mobiles in the wards so she was walking down the corridor towards the lifts.

'Kingston General,' he said, 'on Beverley Road? You sure? Not the Royal Infirmary?'

'I'm sure, Alan.'

'Our local hospital's the Royal Infirmary.'

'They took her to the nearest one. She was out shopping in the Prospect Centre.'

'Shopping? You mean she wasn't at home?'

The Greek bust glared at him under very wavy hair with what looked like a pair of Ray-bans on the top of its head: it was a Grecian hair-clasp.

'She's not always at home, Alan.'

'What happened exactly, Sophie?'

'In the Prospect Centre.'

'Give us the gen, Sofe. Please.'

His neck started to hurt, twisted over the mobile. His shoulders were raised like a hunchback's.

'She was out shopping late yesterday,' said Sophie, 'in the

4

Prospect. It's late closing on Fridays. She felt all faint at about seven o'clock. Basically, her waters broke in front of Foot Locker and she went into labour. They called the ambulance. They were very good, the paramedics. Saved the baby's life, though it wasn't delivered until about ten hours later. It ought to've been a miscarriage, they said. Everyone's being very good, here.'

He lowered his shoulders with difficulty.

'I phoned her yesterday,' he pointed out. 'At about five. She was full of beans. She was watching a re-run of *Falcon Crest*. She didn't say anything about a shopping trip.'

Sophie didn't reply.

'Was she carrying something heavy? Lots of bags or something?'

'Just her own shopping basket. The jute one with bamboo handles that she really likes. It only had a few things in. I'll take it back and feed Benji at the same time. Does he need taking out?'

'No. Just the biccies, the beef ones, in the big bowl that says *Simply the Finest* or he'll go all daft. I can't understand why you didn't call me last night, Sofe.'

'I didn't know where you were. We thought you were in Stockport.'

'Jill knew it was Stirling this year. Anyway, what about the mobile?'

'You've just changed the number,' she said.

'I gave her the new number. I was very careful to give her that, obviously. It was on a Post-It by the knife-rack. I can hardly remember it myself.'

'She was a little bit out of it, Alan.'

She sounded annoyed.

'I'm worried,' he said, as if instructing himself. 'In fact, I'm extremely bloody worried. I'm so far away.'

'It's not that far, Alan. It's not right up in the Highlands, is it?'

'A good five hours. You've got to get round Edinburgh.

I came up in Brian Wallis's new Mondeo, with a couple of the others. I haven't even got the bloody car, Sophie.'

She said her credit was about to run out and it did so just as she was giving him the number of the hospital, having taken about five minutes to find the bit of paper. That was Sofe all over. Then he'd suddenly found himself crying. He'd been staring at the mobile, his thumb hovering, wondering about trains from Stirling to Hull, wondering how Roger Unwin would take his early departure before the key meeting tomorrow on strategic management for personnel planning, at which he was supposed to spout forth wonders and generally polish the apple, when his nose had filled up and he'd found himself with tears on his hands. It was dramatic. He hadn't done that since his best friend Steve Barratt had got himself killed on the back of a motorbike just before their joint twenty-first. Seventeen, eighteen years ago? Christ. Steve Barratt and the little sprog were the same thing.

He could still hear the Great White Chief groaning on through the closed door. He couldn't go back into the meeting in this state. He'd have to find out about trains. He wanted to see his brand-new daughter, born at 5.50 a.m.

He couldn't face phoning his mum. His fancy mobile was wet from his salty tears, it would probably rust, he had to wipe the keyboard on his tie. The little critter was the envy of the whole department, a Handspring Treo 180 that wickedly combined a PDA with a phone and web access. You can practically wash your smalls in it, he'd joked. Now the company was to install Blackberry software and they'd all have to have a bloody Blackberry in their shirt pockets, by order of the Yanks.

He tried to access the train timetable for Stirling, having not the faintest what rail company it was, but all he got was window-spam and something that looked like a gherkin from Stirling Sex Products Inc. He kept at it, though, walking up and down the corridor with both thumbs pecking away until a timetable came up for Stirling with a cartoon picture of a bear. Change at Lethbridge for Medicine Hat, Swift Current and Moose Jaw. He stared for a moment, perplexed. Where the hell in Scotland was Moose Jaw?

OK, there was a Stirling in Alberta, Canada. With this train you could head off up into the Northwest Territories, alight on Great Slave Lake at Hay River or cross up into the Yukon. He'd love to cross up into the Yukon and paddle through the ice floes, he could think of nothing nicer. There was also a Stirling in Australia, in New Zealand and in California, where of course it was Stirling City. The Scottish Stirling sites he finally scrolled down to had nothing as straightforward and simple as a railway timetable. He could hire a car. He should never have agreed to the share drive thing with Brian Wallis and co. This is what happened when you thought about the environment.

He snapped the Treo shut and shoved it into his jacket and took a deep breath, wiping his eyes and nose on his cuff. Because his suit had been to the dry-cleaner's, he'd got no tissues on him. Sod's law. His bottom shirt buttons were undone over his stomach: he did them up again with difficulty, feeling fat and sorrowful. What the hell was he crying like this for? Because Steve Barratt and his daughter were the same thing. Life could be so simple.

It was at this point, then, that Phil McAllister emerged, looking for him. Alan pretended to have an allergy to the carpets, at first. Phil told him that Roger was keen he be there for the end of the discussion, to give the personnel angle, before breaking for breakfast.

That's when, instead of saying, 'Roger can go hang on his tits,' he said: 'I'm a father. She's in an incubator. She's OK.'

After Phil had said, 'You don't need a womb,' Alan had tried to take control of himself.

'Kristen.'

'Kristen?'

'That's my baby's name.'

And he started cracking up again.

'I'm sorry, Phil,' he said, in a high, pansy voice, wiping stuff off his upper lip. 'Don't know whether to laugh or cry. Everything was going A-plus, too. A bloody wonderful pregnancy. We'd just bought a nice blue pram with a wotsit – a carry cot.'

Phil, a very steady teetotal Scotsman with a deep and tedious voice, gave him a clean man-size tissue and offered to let Roger Unwin know. This was exactly the kind of help Alan needed. For the first time in ten years at Northcott Jackson he felt an urge to hug one of his colleagues. He was glad Phil hadn't asked how mother and child were, but come straight to the point.

Phil went back inside the room, closing the door behind him. Alan heard a muffled interchange of voices, including Roger Unwin's.

Phil's tissue smelt of mints. It made Alan feel sick.

He could picture Roger's face, receiving the news. Slow handclap for Roger Unwin, Man with a Heart of Tungsten. This was the bloke who'd sent round a self-assessment form in the name of career development, then placed those who assessed their performance as 'poor' at the top of the redundancy list. This was not someone who would understand about an incubator. The bastard may well refuse him permission to leave.

They'd be going back day after tomorrow, anyway, after the morning wrap-up. If the baby was OK in the incubator then one or two days was not going to make a lot of difference. He'd have his daughter for the rest of his life, barring catastrophe. Jill didn't even feel like talking to him. Forty-eight hours or so was not going to make a lot of difference, not with a modern incubator in the frame.

His shoes trod the soft plush of the corridor.

If they'd phoned him last night, then things might have been easier. He might even have been there for the birth. But now it was born, he might as well act steady.

If you hadn't gone out and purchased the Treo 180 last week,

8

wise-arse, they'd have had your number and you might have been there for the birth.

He couldn't help it if they'd got in touch only when the ball was rolling. Unless it was the girls deliberately freezing him out.

He was a dad. A real live one. They'd got a sprog at last. Kristen. A name with class. Sounds like an Anglepoise lamp from IKEA, he'd joked, at first. But he'd come round to it.

He cleared his throat as if to speak. He fished out his mobile again and tried Jill's, just in case Sophie had got it wrong. Jill's mobile was switched off. He scrolled through his address book: he should be phoning all his mates, Jill's mother, his own mum, but he couldn't face it. He couldn't even face texting, not until he knew how things were going to pan out.

He had to get down to Kingston General. Right away.

He could almost hear the ripping sound of his own legs. Nobody, but nobody in the whole history of western civilisation had ever contemplated bunking the Northcott Jackson Three-Day Away Fixture. You weren't even supposed to phone home. Brian Wallis called it the Convocation of Cardinals. He was a lapsed Catholic, of course.

That's why they were talking so much, in there: it was called a moral dilemma. They were adjusting to this new universe in which a manager might have to be released early. Short of cardiac arrest, nothing justified it. The whole point was human contact – part of the group's drive to remind employees that they and their colleagues were not numbers but feeling people whose armpits you had to love and understand. Also, they had some hired gun lined up for tomorrow morning, some expert in flat management who'd been sent from Seattle by the Great Gaffers Above at enormous cost to get them to crawl about the floor or hold hands and hum or whatever in the eternal search for improved personnel relations – which meant that the personnel manager's presence was a total requisite. Really, of course, it was all about restructuring. Removing hierarchies was the accountancy boys' latest wheeze to slim without too much squealing. Improving the bottom line. The corporation was over-extended: the Northcott Jackson Group was just a speck in Antron's wide American sky. There was even talk of demerging.

If he were to scarper straight after the meeting tomorrow morning, you'd be talking about thirty hours, the big three o between now and the off. Thirty-one, to be precise.

Not much more than a day.

It was five hours max straight down the A68 and A19 to York and then that last little stretch to Hull. Piece of cake. Getting round Edinburgh would be a pain. He'd check it for size on the GPRS on his laptop. It might well have happened, this crisis, when he was abroad – in Moscow, for instance, when they were slugging it out with BAE Systems and Meggitt for the air force deal. On the other hand, Stirling did feel like bloody abroad. The air, for example. Full of sheep and pine trees. It was Phil the Tartan's bloody fault they were up here in the first place; the pow-wow was usually in Stockport – that much nearer to Hull. But everyone decided they needed a change, this year. Stockport wasn't enough. Fresh air. Hills. Clears the brain.

Thirty-one hours. That was a helluva lot of hours when your daughter was entirely dependent on an incubator.

He needed a mirror, his eyes felt ugly.

The Harcourt had a lot of ferns and Greek busts and lampshades and heavy dark-red curtains and fancy artsy pictures but no mirrors. His room was on the third floor at the other end of the complex and he had no idea where the Gents were here; there were five doors along the corridor and they were all locked.

He tried to see how he looked in the glass of a picture, but the embedded lights in the ceiling made a shadow of everything but his hooter. The picture was a drawing of a very scrummy female with her hands behind her hair, dressed in a sort of shift. One day, he thought, my daughter will grow up and look like that. He imagined her tiny form in the incubator, but could only picture a kind of shrivelled grape.

Then the voices grew and the door opened and they all came out, finding him skulking about there in the corridor like a hoodie.

Some of them gave him very tight little smiles and nods of either congratulation or sympathy, he wasn't sure which. He nodded back, not sure how to look under his puffed-up eyes, then opting for anxious. Phil would have mentioned the incubator. Some of them – close colleagues like Brian Wallis or Simon Milner – knew the baby wasn't due for another two months. Only one of them, Tony Malpas, was aware of the smelly history with Sophie and the current situation with Jill. That's because Tony Malpas was Sophie's half-brother and lived, like her, in a des res in Beverley (though not in the same street). He also drove a 1978 Porsche with leather fittings, the bastard. Now, coming out of the meeting, Tony Malpas didn't even look at him. Malpas was nattering away to Brian Wallis, laughing like a pillock at the latest Wallis crack. Alan couldn't believe it.

And there was Jon S. Volkman, the spy who came in from Seattle: Antron's man, keeping an eye on the Brit hood-lums. He thought it was English to wear white socks and carry an umbrella on his wrist and say 'bloody', but still asked for pork rinds or the AAA. To keep him brushed the right way, Alan played golf with Jon S. once a month and let him win. That way, Alan reckoned he still smelt sweet in Seattle. Now Jon S. didn't even notice him, or pretended not to.

Roger Unwin put his hand on Alan's back; that was always a bad sign.

They walked away from the others, who were filing down the stairs to the Harcourt Buttery for haggis and marmalade.

Alan was all but being pushed along; the pressure on his back was infinitesimal, but it was there. He resisted it by moving faster than the hand, but the hand kept up.

Roger Unwin was tall. He stooped as if the underlings had tiny voices. He had a headmaster's metal-rimmed glasses and (in Brian Wallis's words) 'illogical' hair. He waited until the others had gone before opening his mouth.

'How are mother and child doing, Alan?'

He didn't want to tell.

'She's in an incubator.'

This was a term he'd get to know very well, he thought.

'In good hands, I imagine.'

'In an incubator, Roger. In Kingston General.'

'Not the Royal?'

'No. Jill collapsed in the Prospect Centre, in front of Foot Locker. Her waters broke. A close-run thing. Extremely serious, obviously.'

The managing director of Northcott Jackson studied the bust of Working Athena for a moment, his mouth pursing in thought.

'You know you're the kernel of that people-meeting tomorrow. Kernel as in nut, not military.'

'Roger, you've got to let me go. Phil or Trevor Smith can do the necessaries, take notes—'

'The snag is they can't, Alan. I have to make a report for Seattle, never mind Volkman on the hotline every day.'

'I play golf with Jon S. I let him beat me.'

'They've sent this big shot expressly for the heads of personnel in all their UK subsidiaries.'

'For the leadership team as a whole.'

'It's not one whit whole if you're not there, Alan.'

When Roger Unwin started using dated, headmasterly expressions, you needed cooked conkers for balls.

'It's two months premature,' said Alan.

'It?'

He was being studied over the metal-rimmed glasses.

'My daughter. Kirsten. Kristen, I mean.'

'I expect she's in very good hands at Kingston General. It almost met its targets last year. As I'm sure is the mother.'

'It met its targets by calling trolleys "mobile beds" and shipping the worst cases off to Calais, Roger. Or Belgrade. Or maybe that's where they get the nurses from. "The mother" is Jill, by the way.'

Unwin nodded.

'I didn't doubt it.'

Each year, at the company drinks, Jill and Roger Unwin talked about books; Jill would look forward to it. She'd joined a reading group and would read these fictional works in bed, by torchlight, long after Alan had nodded off over audit reports or *Formula One Through the Lens*. Sometimes she'd cry. He couldn't understand the point of it.

'Novels expand your horizons,' she'd said, a few weeks ago, after he'd not been able to see the point of it again. 'They're about people's dramas and tragedies and joys.'

He'd pointed to the photograph showing Ronnie Peterson's fatal crash.

'That's drama and tragedy, Jill.'

Then he'd turned to one of Colin Chapman jumping about after a Lotus victory. 'And that's joy.'

Now he pressed his shoulders back, trying to feel less of a limp-dick.

'Seriously, and it's nothing to do with skiving, Roger: I'm too bloody gutted to concentrate. I know it's unheard of, but I'm going to have to beg compassionate leave. I'm a feeling human being.'

'And what am I to say to Seattle? Or to Volkman if he asks me?'

Go toss, Yanks.

'My daughter's in an incubator. She's very tiny. Jill had to be rushed to A&E from outside Foot Locker. I don't see the problem, Roger.'

The man kept quiet.

'I thought flat management was all about flexibility and being auto-responsible,' Alan added, foolishly.

Unwin crossed his arms and gave a little, headmasterly chuckle. Alan caught a whiff of expensive cologne. His own upper lip smelt of gone-off peach yoghurt from one of the hotel's complimentary 'Made on Iona' natural shower gels.

'The problem isn't mine, Alan. The problem's yours. They're casting a cold eye over their UK operations.'

'Is that a veiled threat? I thought I was Wonderboy.'

'Nobody's Wonderboy these days. Unless you speak Chinese.'

'Chinese?'

'Start taking a course in Chinese. That's what I advise. As someone who keeps his ear to the future.'

A girl in a black boob tube came down the corridor holding some files under her arm – probably a PA from the Kingfisher bash in the smarter, bigger conference room. Or maybe she was French – Kingfisher had just bought up Castorama, the bastards. Oo-la-la. Her high heels made hardly a sound on the soft red plush. Both men acknowledged her with a discreet nod, making room for her to pass. She was a knockout. Alan felt himself stirring, despite everything. Jill had been off sex for months.

Until three nights ago. Three nights ago she'd put an arm across him while he was reading Simon Milner's report on the Philips-Dell deal, which ended up getting very creased. She told him, wiping herself afterwards, that he'd been a bit rough. He reckoned that was unfair. She'd enjoyed being thrown about a bit. He wouldn't have been rough if she hadn't wanted it rough. (It was the roughest they'd ever been, in fact. It made all the previous times feel very timid. Even those times with Sophie, Alan had thought secretly, because Sofe liked to be in control and she was not sexually adventurous.) Whatever, it had got him dangerously out of breath, like that charity marathon for the lung machine last year, only the marathon was less enjoyable.

Then Jill had rubbed her swollen belly and started worrying about the baby, as if he'd bashed it! She started crying quietly next to him. He craved a cigarette for the first time in months. He took her hand but she snatched it away, turning her back to him under the duvet and sobbing quietly while he bit his lip in the darkness, feeling unjustly treated as well as ashamed of what they'd done together – or of the way they'd done it. He wondered why they'd done it like that, why they couldn't have behaved like responsible adults. Why Jill couldn't have taken some of the responsibility on herself. Why it was always the bloke who carried the guilt.

Roger Unwin sighed as the girl disappeared down the stairs. 'Shirley lost hers moving a cupboard,' he said.

'Come again?'

'It was a boy. Thomas. As you know we have four delightful girls. She moved a cupboard on her own, while I was in the States for twenty-four hours. 1972, it was. He'd be thirty, now. Can't remember why she felt she had to move a cupboard. Maybe to retrieve something behind. Or to vacuum. Women in pregnancy have odd quirks and desires, of course.'

He quoted something old and literary about apricots. Roger Unwin liked to remind everybody that he'd read English at Oxford. It made him insurmountable, somehow, like his tailor-made pinstripes and MCC tie. (All Alan remembered of his psychology degree at Southampton was the ale. And he bought his suits at Harvey Nichols and hated cricket.)

'Yeah, Jill liked to watch *Falcon Crest* re-runs,' said Alan, pulling a face. 'It wasn't vacuuming behind cupboards, anyway. Quite the opposite, in fact.'

He was absolutely certain that she'd not once told him to be careful; she'd oohed and aahed, oohed and aahed with pleasure as he'd thrown her about on the bed.

Roger Unwin was looking at him, eyebrows raised.

Alan blushed. Alan Hurst actually blushed. Among the chief executive's many weapons was the ability to make you think he was telepathic.

'She was out shopping,' Alan said. 'I think she must have carried some heavy shopping. I mean, that's what strained it, obviously. You know our Jill,' he added, too chummily.

Of course Roger Unwin didn't know Jill, beyond their annual book-shag over the company fizz.

His boss nodded in slow motion. With each nod, Alan had the impression of being clobbered by a giant mallet.

The truth was, Roger despised him. It was nothing personal: Roger Unwin despised all his colleagues and employees. He despised the job, that was the trouble. He should have been a don. Life had begun for Alan as a graduate management trainee with Unilever; life ended for Unwin the day he left Oxford, when he'd inherited James Northcott Ltd from his maternal uncle. That's how Alan saw it. Roger Unwin lived for only two things: his koi fish and his 1934 Riley Roadster, into which he fitted with difficulty.

This attitude made Roger Unwin very powerful, at any rate. It was the secret of his power. He'd only survived three mergers and the Antron takeover by despising it all. Even the Great Gaffers Above didn't dare touch him.

'I think,' said Roger, lifting his chin slightly, 'you should assume the consequences of your decision, Alan. I can't protect you, and I won't protect you. I'm not convinced you've altogether understood the recent changes, or will ever understand them. We're no longer on the same field of play. They've shifted the ground-plan, while keeping the objectives. That's why we're all feeling a bit seasick, Alan. It's a question of finding your sea legs and fixing your eye on the horizon. I'm not sure you'll ever be willing to understand that.'

Alan was looking down at his shoes. He moved his head up towards the horizon, feeling a surge of panic. His pulse and breathing started to accelerate. The horizon was some fancy writing in a gilt frame hung above the fire extinguisher: *Every free man shall have the eyries of hawks, falcons, eagles and herons in his woods, and likewise honey found in his woods.*

'Furthermore,' continued the boss, looking at him almost sorrowfully, 'you have no intention whatsoever of learning Chinese.'

Things were getting out of hand. Roger Unwin was threatening him. In one last salvaging effort, Alan suggested that he hire a car and drive back to Hull tonight, to return in the morning. The man pulled a face.

'Alan, act sensible. You'll fall asleep at the wheel. Either you sod off early, or you don't.'

'"Sodding off" isn't my usual style, Roger.'

'Precisely.' Roger Unwin bent his head towards Alan in an awkward stab at intimacy. 'We're enslaved, Alan. All of us. We're chasing the money merely to fill the debt hole. If we don't fill that hole we'll be swallowed up by it. It's slavery. I never saw my girls from one damn week to the next.'

'You played Monopoly with your grandson,' Alan remarked, contentiously. 'You told me that last week.'

Unwin straightened up. 'It was his birthday. Margaret put a gun to my head.'

'I know the feeling,' Alan pointed out, raising a finger. 'The little cold O on the temple.'

He fished out his mobile and twitched his thumb over it under one of those famous psychopathic stares. 'Need to find the number of the hospital, if you'll excuse me, Roger. I'll tell you what I'm going to do. I'm going to leave straight after this hired gun's told us how to change our own nappies from a win/win perspective. It's called meeting the enemy halfway. Not that you're my enemy, Roger, obviously. Not all the time.'

Alan would often dream of meeting that famous stare. Roger Unwin didn't stare at you, that was the trouble; he stared through you and out the other side as if your brain was perspex. Once, way back, when Roger Unwin was giving Brian Wallis the Stare during a management meeting, Brian stuck a bullet-holes windscreen decal on his own forehead. Brian Wallis would melt the corporate hearts in Seattle, he was that sort of bloke. Alan Hurst was not. He was Wonderboy past his sell-by date. There was always something in life to pay for. Sun and rain.

His thumb went spastic under the Stare, it kept slipping off the pimple-size keys. He used both thumbs again and felt like a little kid with a PlayStation in front of his dad.

Eventually, Roger Unwin peeled his ice-blue eyes away and nodded, saying, 'I'll run with that, Alan.'

'Thank you. Most grateful.'

The managing director tapped the glass over the fancy writing on the wall: 'Magna Carta. Now what the hell's *that* doing in Scotland?'

The hotel and conference centre felt uncomfortably new, smelling of gloss paint, the faint burnt-rubber of sealants, the body odour of interior decorators. It was done up as a cross between something cool and Japanese and a country home for geriatrics, and was part of a large sleek 'prestige' development (with 'heart-stopping views', as the brochure rather unwisely put it) that included a multi-screen cinema, a bowling alley, a replica Paris brasserie (closed, or not yet open), a swimming pool called the Cascade Club with waves and slides, and a museum devoted to the History of Ice Cream, all interlaced with a labyrinth of toy roads (max speed 10 mph), gravel paths and wooden signs carefully placed to cause maximum bewilderment.

Alan's room, in old colonial style with an eTV Interactive and pay-view porn, looked out on a roof with heating stacks and chimneys; the others had the heart-stopping view (including Brian, who was on his second bypass). Although it was well into April, the wind was biting and the rain kept up in chronic spurts, flinging itself against the window glass of the unheated conference room as if telling them to shut up. Moody photographs of Tibetan villagers were hung, for some reason Alan was too preoccupied to fathom, against the bare concrete of the conference room's walls. Since the *raison d'être* of these annual bashes was to remove the management team from all domestic ties for seventy-two hours, Alan had to get special permission to leave his Treo switched on during the head-banging sessions. Roger Unwin made it clear that he was being all soft and stupid, granting this.

The speeded-up opening bars of *Oh mio rimorso!* from *La Traviata* (it was Owen Jenkins, the opera-buff retail manager, who'd identified it yesterday) chipped in with monotonous regularity, but it was never the hospital or Sophie. His mother rang five times from Aylesbury, Jill's brother twice from a train calling at all stations between Barnet and Addis Ababa. Reception was terrible, anyway. Tense as hell, waiting for a possible call, he held the mobile in his hand with his thumb hovering as if he was changing channels on the on-screen flip-chart. Old Verdi rarely got beyond the fifth note. Yet everyone up and down the table turned and looked each time, and Roger Unwin (at the head of it) sighed – or would have sighed if he'd been human. Some years back the boss had come out of the office and found the silver-pearl body finish on his Lexus LS400 in the management car park looking as if it had been dragged through a rap concert backwards. Local yobbos or a personal vendetta; either way, his reaction was amazing: he sank to his knees and started blubbering. And it wasn't even his Riley Roadster. That was the only proof they had, as Brian Wallis had pointed out, that Roger Unwin was not constructed from rubber, steel, plastic and the brain of a Great White floating in formaldehyde.

Alan felt exhausted during the morning session. The Full Scottish Breakfast (over which his closer colleagues had been very upbeat about incubators) had somehow got held up in traffic in his diaphragm and his nerves were strung taut. Everyone knew that he had been made an exception of; his Domestic Tie was a huge great pink bow in his hair, that's how it felt. Like a Playboy bunny in drag, he was. And then

Unwin's or a colleague's drone would surface among the flotsam of his thoughts and he'd realise he'd not been listening to a single word. Perhaps he was past it, at thirty-nine. A lot of the blokes (not the three women present, he hoped) were balding; one or two had shaved it all off to the skull to hide the fact. He was not balding, being a strawberry blond. That was lucky.

'Any comments, Alan?'

Whoops.

He would give a little start, as if just woken up, and his chest would burn. Then his improvising skill, his ability to talk sense in bollocks-sized chunks, came into its own. He was also blessed, despite appearances, with a deep and reassuring voice which Jill had once called (in the good old days) 'velvety'.

'Yeah, I'm completely in agreement, Roger. When you fly high you need a pressure-suit. So that determining your own development and sense of responsibility requires a heightened sense of co-ordination. It's like Brian's vicar joke, last night. If the traffic warden and the vicar had agreed on the basic synthesis, to use Roger's term, then there'd have been no joke and Brian would've resorted to those vampires in the pub.'

Everyone laughed, even the green-gilled juniors who didn't know Brian's outrageously disgusting vampire joke. These were cosy internal references and it worked every time (although Roger's term had been 'synergy', not 'synthesis'). In truth, though, sliding a dip-stick into Alan's cerebral tank for a record of what had just been discussed would have drawn a gleaming clean blank. He was not sure Roger Unwin was altogether fooled, of course, up there at the head of the table. And the brilliant early-thirties finance director with the billiard-table haircut, Geoff Soames, was looking at him as if he'd just sneezed messily over the laptops; while Jon S. Volkman wore his cleanest hallelujah smile, sending the usual shivers up the spine.

Alan thanked God yet again that he and Geoff Soames were members of the same Rotary Club (against all the rules). Manning the stall together on Mental Health Day was worth a thousand brown-nose reports.

Having established from a nurse in the maternity unit that neither mother nor baby were in any immediate danger, Alan had relaxed on that front for about ten seconds. Basically, an incubator was an artificial womb. Even safer than a real womb, because it wasn't being lugged about Hull through mad old ladies with sharpened elbows or between psychopaths in white vans. Then worries started seeping through. A power-cut would render the incubator helpless, if the emergency generator failed to kick in. Or some git could kick the plug out of its power point. The nurse would've been trained in customer relations, these days: you couldn't believe a word she said. Of course you couldn't believe her. It was service with a smile. *Don't ever talk on the phone without physically smiling.* Rule number one in customer relations. Rule number two: *Don't ever give anything away.*

It didn't help when Steve Norris from Marketing kept talking about 'incubating' this list and 'incubating' that diagram during the 11.30 session after the Nescaff pause; Alan wasn't even sure what 'incubating' meant, in this context. Amazingly, no one else noticed, but just kept staring at the on-screen flip-chart. He fiddled with his tartan shortbread wrapper from the break and thought: That's how much they care.

He couldn't face speaking to Sophie, and the nurse had said she'd pass on his message to Jill when she was awake. The doctor would be in on Monday, and now it was Saturday. There were no doctors he could speak to over the weekend. He didn't realise people stopped being ill from Friday evening to Monday morning. On top of everything else, the nurse'd had a strong foreign accent, probably Serb; she was obviously hired from an agency, with one day's training in catheter management, full stop. The more he gave it thought, the worse it got.

He shouldn't be *here*, but *there*. Right now.

He should be holding his daughter's tiny hand, not this tiny phone. Would he be allowed to hold her hand, if she was lying in an incubator? Maybe not. Maybe Jill, even, hadn't held her hand. There was the risk of infection. He'd got beyond the shrivelled grape in his imagination; now he saw a doll with tubes everywhere and an assisted-breathing mask the size of her face.

The Tibetan villagers in the moody black-and-white photographs stared at him, as if they felt sorry for him. They didn't need incubators. They just died, left out on the mountain or in the clouds or whatever for the snow leopards and the snow eagles. Buddhists. The Dalai Lama.

'Alan? You might come in at this point, please, with the human angle.'

Whoops.

He phoned the hospital at lunchtime, standing in the porch of the ice-cream museum. Apparently, this was the best spot for reception. The rain spat at his shoes, the wind sneaking in through his coat and getting very fresh with the unbuttonable bit over his stomach. The museum was open, but empty of visitors. He could make out a vintage ice-cream van with *Rossi's* painted on it in the main hall, which reminded him of long summer days in Aylesbury and rushing out with his five pence when the Mr Whippy jingle sounded.

He didn't feel at all tip-top.

Jill's mobile was still off. She'd never liked mobiles; in some ways she was a bit old-fashioned. She went to patchwork classes. Waiting to be put through to the cordless in the maternity unit, he pictured his daughter in a few years' time, rushing out with her one pound when the jingle sounded. She wouldn't have a pretty skirt, he corrected himself, she'd have jeans and trainers. She'd have an authentic Hull accent, too, picked up at school: trendier than nasal Bucks. Unless he won the lottery and they moved in next to Cliff Richard on the Bahamas. He supposed the museum did better when it was hot, which it probably never was in Stirling.

A nurse came on.

'Wait a second, darlin'. I've got to transfer you to the cordless, see. OK, darlin'? Just hang on there, don't go away . . .'

Liverpudlian, he could tell it a mile off. A Liver bird. A Scouse. An angel. There was silence, a buzz, then some knocking noises and distant baby-wails and the sound of someone taking the receiver.

'Hello,' Jill said, very faintly.

'Hiya, sweetheart.'

'Hello, Alan.'

'Hiya! How are you, my love? How are things? Still feeling a bit wobbly?'

'OK.'

'Look, nice one! Eh? You did it all without me. How's our little—?'

'Where are you? Are you phoning from the train?'

'Stirling. Wilds of bloody Scotland.'

'Still up there? I thought you were on your way back, Alan. I thought you were phoning from the train.'

She sounded absolutely knackered.

'Sophie didn't tell you? I can't get away until tomorrow lunchtime, obviously. I moved heaven and earth and Roger bloody Unwin to get—'

Jill started talking away from the receiver to someone about her tray and lunch. She came back on.

'You can't even eat it. Beef curry with mushy peas. I want you here,' she said.

'Mushy peas, yum yum! You are so lucky!' She didn't laugh. 'Listen, sweetheart. I'm gonna be there. Just as fast as I can. Soon as it's all sorted, OK? I'm really happy things are OK. I was a little bit worried. Is she beautiful?'

'You should be here,' she said.

'I know, I hate not being there, not being with you. It's

horrible, sweetheart. Look, why don't you switch on your mobile? Then it's easier to be with you.'

'It's broken. It doesn't work.'

He tried to find out what was wrong with it technically, step by step, but she wasn't interested. Anyway, she wasn't allowed it in the ward, she said. He was gazing from the porch through the sharp, blowy rain at the toy roads, the gravel paths, the thin new lawns between the stone and steel cladding of the prestige buildings. The guttering was making totally exaggerated drip sounds, as if trying to torture him. There was no one, not anywhere. The mobile would screw up all those shiny medical machines that gave him the heebie-jeebies, he supposed.

'I hate not being there,' he repeated. 'But listen, miracles happen: I've got out of the last two sessions tomorrow.'

'Tomorrow?'

'You know how this is Roger Unwin's big moment of the year, and the Yanks are watching closely? Jon S. Volkman breathing over my shoulder like bloody Goebbels? Well, I've got out of the last two sessions. A miracle. After some nifty footwork on my part. I'll be right next to you, sweetheart, and holding your hand this time tomorrow,' he lied, looking at his watch. If he hired a Jaguar jet. 'Is Kristen next to you? Can you see her? Tell me—'

'Who?'

'Kristen. Kirsten. Kristen.'

'Who?'

'Our little daughter.'

There was a short silence. Alan felt his neck seize up again.

'Samantha,' she said.

'What?'

'She's called Samantha.'

'Samantha? You're joking.'

'What's wrong?'

'It's a bit – I thought we'd finally decided on Kristen, Jill. Not Kirsten.'

'I prayed to God that if she came out alive, I'd name her

after the paramedic who saved us both in front of Foot Locker. Samantha Williams.'

'God? But you don't believe in God.'

'Alan, do you have to get at me? Not when I'm in this state.'

'Samantha's fine. It's really great.'

What a truly terrible name, he thought. Samanfa. He pictured a flat-faced secretary with huge artificial eyelashes, not a strapping paramedic.

'You weren't there to discuss it with, anyway.'

'No, Jill. We didn't exactly know it was going to happen. The whole thing was a bit of a surprise, obviously.'

'Not really.'

'What?'

'Not really, Alan.'

'What d'you mean?'

'Not really that surprising, was it? If you cast your mind back a bit, Alan.'

Her tone was very loaded.

He wanted to talk about heavy shopping, but couldn't bring himself to.

'Did you feel something beforehand, then?' It came out all feeble and uncertain.

There was a sigh in his ear, like the sea. Jill had snorted. He was forcing himself to breathe slowly, nodding like one of those stupid toy dogs people used to have in the backs of their cars. He must not get narked. He must keep smiling.

'Anyway, I want to give you and – Samantha a big wet kiss. Eh? Distance is no object. Here it comes.'

He regretted saying that. He felt like a perv, suddenly.

'You haven't asked what she weighed.'

His lips were pursed, ready to transmit the kiss.

'Eh?'

'What she weighed. That's what everyone else has asked. Your mother phoned and it was the first thing she asked. Even your brother.'

'OK, what does she weigh?' he asked, not believing her for an instant: his brother was a boffin, didn't know a baby from an enzyme catalyst.

'You're not interested, are you?'

'I'm basically interested in whether she's fit and well and is going to make it, sweetheart,' he said, too forcefully. He turned his back on the prestige development, having spotted some cheery colleagues mounting one of the gravel paths by the Cascade Club, their raincoats flapping. The *Rossi's* ice-cream van – probably a Morris from the look of the radiator – sat like a giant wasp beyond the plate glass at his nose. Then it slowly vanished, his breath fogging up the glass between. 'You mean I'm not interested in her weight? Or in the whole thing?'

There was a silence. He thought he could hear her breathing. Distant crashes and beep-beeps in time with the drips from the guttering.

'Jill?'

'You're such a shit,' she said, but very wearily.

I know what's happened, he thought. Sophie's spilt the beans. Raked up the past. Women do stupid things like that. They run on emotion. It empowers them.

'Jill, if I leave right away, right now, I'd be out on my ear. OK? Lose my job, get the sack, the big R. OK? I'd be laying myself wide open. They're firing people left and centre. It's the slump. Antron are wobbly at the moment, which means Northcott Jackson are extremely wobbly, especially after losing the Saudi air force contract. Everyone has to behave, Jill, keep their noses clean and their hair greased. I'm thinking of the future. The three of us.'

'I understand.'

'I know you do, really.'

He heard voices in the background.

'Is that the doctors?'

'The proper doctors haven't seen me yet. It's the weekend. It's just the young duty one.'

'But you're both right on track.'

'What?'

'On track. Obviously. Is she beautiful?'

'The doctor?'

Alan laughed. She must be on morphine, he thought.

'She has a bare midriff,' Jill said. 'She doesn't wear a white coat.'

'Jesus. Is she English?'

'I think so. There'll be the proper one on Monday.'

'Is she alright? I mean, our little girl? What does the doc say?'

He couldn't say 'Samantha'.

'She demands a lot of attention,' Jill said. 'That's how the nurse put it.'

'I see.'

He knew, then. She was in danger. His own little girl. In the incubator.

'Sweetheart, I think you'd better have a rest. Could you put me onto the sister?'

'I don't know which one she is, they keep changing.'

'The Liverpudlian. She'll do. Is Sophie there?'

'No. She had to go home and sleep. She hadn't slept.'

'Obviously, yeah.' He felt a pang of remorse that irritated him. 'I'll call you this evening, lovey.'

'They're moving me, for a bit. They're replacing a radiator. It's leaking. There's a sort of flood.'

For a horrible moment, he thought she was saying she had to have an operation. His brow was wet with self-imposed sweat.

'Jesus. I don't believe it. When? I hope it's not far. I hope it's on the same floor.'

'This afternoon, I think. They've got big lifts.' She sounded very weak, now. 'God, I dunno.'

A sigh filled Alan's ear again. There were knocking noises and the jolly Scouser came on, reassuring Alan that mother and baby were doing 'fine'. He wasn't convinced; he imagined that she'd say the same about someone in the last stages of Ebola and go on saying it in the same jolly, call-centre way until the sheet was pulled over the face. They weren't sure where Jill was being moved to, it was a bit full this week, but they'd give him the number at reception. He didn't like the sound of any of it. Not any of it and not at all.

He shut the clamshell top on the Treo with an angry flick of his hand but it came open again, like a car boot. He wanted to yell, really scream his nut off.

The museum receptionist was watching him; he'd not noticed her before. She was next to the Morris van. He nodded, embarrassed, and she came up to the door and opened it.

'We're not closed,' she said, in a thick Scottish accent that surprised him because he'd forgotten. 'We stay open over lunch on Saturdays.'

'Is there anything in there?' he asked, still embarrassed.

'Oh aye. All sorts. It's pretty interesting, in fact.'

She stood there like a flirtatious schoolgirl, leaning against the door to keep it open. *Lord, let my daughter live.*

He had to visit the ice-cream museum, it was meant. It was part of the deal. Life had no multiple-undo facilities: you reaped what you sowed. But sometimes you got given this little open door in which to do something unexpected, change rails, take your fate by surprise. He had twenty minutes before the next meeting. Now he believed in God. Or someone very powerful and wise, maybe even a kind of huge, supremely intelligent CCTV operator.

So he went in. It was a deal. A blown-up photograph of a bowler-hatted man selling ice creams from a barrow took up one whole wall; young men in flat caps and baggy trousers were eating cornets in front of it. *Pure Vanilla Ice Cream Guaranteed* was painted in fancy lettering on the cart.

'Life was simpler in those days,' he remarked.

It was very hot in here: overheated. Micro-climate.

The girl shrugged. Her desk was shaped to look like a wafer ice.

28

'That's four pounds fifty, please.'

'I get a complimentary Sky Ray for that, do I?'

'Eh, sorry?'

'A free Sky Ray?'

She had no idea what he was talking about. Not a single one.

They were supposed to relax in the hotel bar, after the meal. The unwritten rule was that, however much they drank, they must be on sparkling form for the 8 a.m. session. There were two bars, in fact, with Italian names; one was cosy and the other cool. Brian, Simon Milner, Phil McAllister and Alan went for the cosy. Alan had wanted to keep a phone vigil in his room, in front of the idiot box, but Brian reckoned that sounded like penance and insisted he join them.

'I think we should celebrate,' Brian had said, dumping his napkin on the remains of his strawberry sundae.

'Could be a bit premature, as it were.'

'Look, Alan, they're going to be fine. You'll be tucking them in this time tomorrow. Get on the hotel blower now, upstairs, in the privacy of your room, and then come down and relax with Uncle Brian. Press nine for the outside line. The rate per minute's the equivalent of Chad's GNP but never mind, just do it. You know they've got Merryweather on draught?'

Hospital reception took ages to find Jill's new ward. At first the woman, who sounded to Alan as though English was her third language, let alone second, claimed Jill wasn't even in the hospital – neither she nor the baby. There was no Jill Hurst in this hospital. Alan had difficulty understanding what she was saying, and wondered whether the cleaner had picked up the phone. Then he had stupid thoughts: if someone kicked the bucket, did their name get erased immediately from the reception's computer? Another voice came on sounding like Ali G and put him through to the maternity desk.

He sat on the end of the bed, getting ready for the bedside manner.

The phone rang for ages but he hung in there, chewing his lip and swearing and checking his watch. He hadn't heard anything for five hours. He should have phoned every hour, but he didn't want to keep disturbing Jill and the hours slipped by very fast. At last a nursing assistant – Polish, Alan reckoned – put him through to the right ward after a long and earnest discussion with someone else. It was as if Jill had temporarily left this life. The nursing assistant sounded breathless, as if she'd been running. They were searching for an extension number, which should have been pinned up on the board. What British hospitals need, thought Alan, is for people to stop falling ill, not health co-ordinators and governmental targets.

He finally got there and the nurse – male, a friendly bloke, quite posh – said they were both doing fine. Jill was asleep. Alan felt very grateful. 'Thanks so much, mate.' The nurse had his new mobile number, yes, and his hotel number. The nurse's name was Helen and she'd be there until four in the morning. Alan had been sure it was a bloke and realised he'd dropped a clanger but the nurse was nice enough not to care. Maybe it *was* a bloke, who'd played Doctors and Nurses one time too many with his brother.

He took the lift down feeling ready to relax, double-checking the mobile and punching the new extension number into the PDA three times, just in case. The lift announced the floors in French and as he went out the most beautiful bird he'd ever seen in his life went in, probably on her way to some Russian mafioso in the top suite.

Roger Unwin always made a point of joining someone for a symbolic hour after the first full day and there the bastard was – in the cool bar with Geoff Soames, Tony Malpas and Jon S. Volkman. Hairy Mary and her two colleagues were by themselves under a model of a gondola. They were all laughing with their hands to their mouths, as if spitting out stones.

Amazingly, the less-cool, cosier bar was, if not seething, at least lively. People came from all around, the barman told them. Reproductions of old scenes of Rome, complete with cracks in the paint, were hung beneath gallery-type brass spots. The seats were black leather.

'This is very swanky,' said Brian.

'Why Rome?' Simon Milner asked.

'The Harcourt's part of the Premiere chain,' said Phil.

'So?'

'Bought up last year by Mediaset, Berlusconi's outfit. Makes the Emperor of Europe feel at home on his royal visits to Stirling.'

'Is it really? Premiere? Part of Mediaset?'

'Yes, Brian.'

'I think I'll stick to halves. I'll be his one-man loss-making division. Isn't the gyp trying to take control of Kirch, now?'

They settled next to a seven-foot rubber plant with phallic red flowers that turned out to be plastic, but very well done.

Alan shook its leaves. 'The Day of the Triffids, look.'

'Warn me if it starts to move,' Phil said.

'That's what you said when you first saw Pat Ryan,' Brian joked.

He went on cracking jokes about the chief executive and the chairman and the managing director and then about George W. Bush, stuff mostly pulled off the Internet that the others had read too, but forgotten. Otherwise they talked shop and old TV programmes and the latest dashboard navigation gizmos. There was a motor museum in Stirling, apparently. Brian told them at great length about the Bealieu Autojumble a few years back when he'd bumped into Roger Unwin beating some poor old bugger down for a couple of Riley camshafts: they'd all heard it before and many times.

Alan let it roll; no one talked incubators. The mobile stayed silent. He was getting slowly and pleasantly plastered on Laphroaig, its burn gripping his testicles, it felt like. Everything would be fine.

He made them chuckle with his account of the ice-cream museum and then felt he shouldn't have told them, that he'd broken the deal with God.

Phil said, out of the blue, 'I think we should raise a glass to Alan and Jill and the new baby. Eh, wet the baby's head, as they say.'

They raised their glasses and looked at Alan. He raised his malt and smiled and said, 'Snap.' They drank and then he said, 'Jill's a great girl.'

It was his shout; he went to the bar and had to squeeze his way through to find a point of vantage. The barman, who hailed from Slovenia, had two rings in his nose and a pale, artsy-crafty face that made Alan feel stupid, middle-aged and fat.

Alan returned with the drinks and told them about the trendy barman from Slovenia.

'You're not fat, you're thickset,' said Phil.

'Tell that to Jill.'

The conversation slid onto wives, then sex. Timid Simon Milner said nothing but was very interested. The sex talk was not dirty, it was vague and humorous. Alan told them about the smasher he'd seen going into the lift, but petered out when he realised that it wasn't very interesting. Phil mentioned the retail manager who'd died of a heart attack while screwing his secretary. Ah, said Brian, that was in the days when their company was still a family enterprise. Heart-stopping views, Alan joked, but no one got it. Brian tended to hog the humour. He said he would stop screwing Sandra, his secretary, immediately. Sandra was forty-nine with hairs on her chin, nicknamed 'Jaws'. Brian tapped his ticker, which was a genuine worry for him, in fact. Alan told them he had a high cholesterol count, but didn't make a funny of it because it did, in fact, worry him. Brian said the answer, as they all knew, was straight Scotch and Viagra. Alan felt left out when the others nodded sagely. Brian went on to crack a few new Viagra jokes; the last one, about a bloke with a dick so large he had to use a golf-bag and then hire a caddie-car when he got excited, had them all weeping. They knew they were being looked at by colleagues on other tables, were scoring points and provoking envy.

After their recovery, Phil told them in his deep and steady voice about his teenage daughter's low-life boyfriends and how he was regarded as a grouchy puritan for keeping tabs on their movements.

'You're no grouchy puritan, Phil,' Brian said, in a Billy Connolly voice. 'I mean, you're from Dumfries, mon!'

They discussed the voracious sexual appetite of modern teenagers, quoting statistics from radio and newspaper features and a recent BBC Two documentary which, amazingly, three of them had watched – only Simon could recall it in any useful detail, talking as usual like a PowerPoint. The subject was deflected for a moment by Phil, who wondered if they'd seen a documentary in the same series about the Big Bang.

'I never watch pornography, Phil,' Brian joked.

After a serious quarter of an hour discussing the origins of the universe and the size of galaxies and the mystery of their creation, they paused as if for a breather. Simon Milner had said it was all mathematics.

'No smoke without fire,' said Brian, with a sigh, and drained his pint.

After a moment Phil said, very steadily, 'Well, it makes me feel that what I have done in my life is very small potatoes.'

'You on about your bollocks again, Phil? I dunno. What shall we do with him, lads?'

They laughed, Brian clapping Phil on the shoulder. They all felt good.

Then Alan (who'd been very quiet) said: 'In my opinion, that's all marketing hype, that teenage sex stuff. Sex improves with age.'

'He's taking the Michael again,' said Brian, who was fifty-three with a close-cropped, grey beard.

'I think we're all too well behaved,' Alan went on. He

leant forward, so they could hear him even when he spoke quietly. His words felt liquid and warm and honest to him. 'That's why marriages go wrong. The older you get, the more interesting and varied you have to be.'

'You're hardly old,' said Phil.

'For example, Jill and I had a very good time the other night, after a long time off.'

'It's the single malt that talks,' Brian said, lifting his finger on high.

'It was the best time ever,' said Alan, staring at a Carlsberg beer mat on the table. 'And not just because she was very pregnant, I might add. Three, four nights ago. It was a bit rough.' He swallowed. He used to collect beer mats as a kid, stick them up on the Grand Prix wallpaper by his bed. 'I threw her about a bit, in fact. She liked it, obviously. We were a bit rough. But she wanted it like that, obviously.'

There was a silence between them. The music beat away through the general jabber of the others in the bar.

Brian frowned. 'You what? You threw her about, Alan?'

'Never done that before. Never been so rough. It was safe, though. We had a really cracking time.'

'Would you like to give us more details?' Brian said, winking, but half to himself as if he was unsure.

'Nothing to be ashamed of, obviously,' Alan said. 'A natural phenomenon.'

'That's what they said about Krakatoa,' Brian quipped.

There was a silence which accumulated embarrassment like an inane giggle getting louder and louder.

'Was that, er, was that really such a good idea?' Phil asked, slowly and carefully.

'What?'

Phil moved his head about like a wobbly toy, unable to formulate the words.

'In the – circumstances,' he said, at last, tripping a bit over the word.

'It wasn't an idea, good or otherwise,' Alan replied, his face serious. 'It was poetry in motion.'

The others cracked up at that and had a good honest laff, but then didn't say anything more for a few minutes. Brian went off to the toilet. Simon Milner stared at his glass. Phil pretended to look around him at the other drinkers. Alan felt much better now that he'd told them about his personal life, though his decks were fairly awash: he wasn't used to malt, these days. It was very clean and relaxing. It covered everything – the noise, faces, everything – in a soft velvety fur.

There was nothing to be ashamed of.

And then he said, when they were all settled again over a fresh round: 'If only she hadn't carried that heavy shopping.'

But no one responded.

Phil's mobile – bagpipes, for God's sake – sounded and he was on it for ages, very loud and dull: 'Good stuff . . . good stuff . . . good stuff . . . fantastic . . . what's his response on the back of it . . . it'll all go down on his HR file . . .'

'Those sex-calls are a guinea a minute, Phil,' joked Brian.

'Good stuff,' Phil went on, oblivious. 'Absolutely right, John . . . fantastic . . . good stuff . . . excellent . . .'

When he came off, all he said was: 'John Harvey. He's fluffed it. Again.'

Just before midnight, two floozies in very short skirts and what looked like fishnet tops, their black bras visible, appeared at their table and spent half an hour talking dirty. They weren't Scottish. They were exceedingly pissed and came from Southampton. They turned out not to be whores but sales-girls at the Kingfisher conference, which they seemed not to be appreciating. The title of their conference was People First. They worked for a subsidiary of Kingfisher's called Sparrowcom. It was in the DIY public relations field. One of them was as black as the other was pasty-white.

'We came here for some fun,' the white girl said, wriggling

in her chair. 'Ain't that what you're here for, gents? Ooh, my skirt's getting caught in my arsehole. I don't bother with panties. I stopped seeing my doctor when he started taking my temperature the French way, y'know? Only he was using his finger instead of a barometer.'

'Thermometer,' said the black girl, who was on her seventh Bacardi. 'Vanessa here is a thick slag.'

'I don't mind a big dick, though,' said Vanessa, 'because that's not got a fingernail on the end, has it?'

She roared with laughter, as did the black girl. They were almost shouting, but then the other people were yelling and guffawing and the music filled in the gaps. The men were too polite, or maybe excited, to tell them to go away. Alan wasn't excited. He watched everything from a distance, like a sociologist, wondering if these two girls had ever been helpless little newborns. Well, they'd had to have been. They weren't *born* in fishnet tops. The heavy, repetitive music was like an evil slow handclap. He hadn't meant to get plastered, which is why he'd kept off the beer. Also, he was trying to reduce his belly to proportions that Jill would look at without wincing. Phil was right – he wasn't fat, but he did have this belly. At one point, in about the fourth month, he and Jill had exactly the same shape. XXL. It was surprising, it had crept up on him via beer and Mars bars. He'd eat at least three Mars bars a day, to keep himself going. With a couple of non-light Pepsis at lunchtime. Then a few beers to round the day off. He was by no means over the average office weight, though. Nor was he the heaviest drinker, far from it – in fact, he hardly ever got completely and absolutely scrambled on Friday and Saturday nights, like a lot of the others, and he'd kicked the coke habit when he was still with Jonson & Jonson. But he was getting too old for it, at thirty-nine. The drinking lark. Now he was a father, he'd start to behave. He would love Jill and – Samantha – to bits, he would. He'd be a very good boy. At least Samantha didn't sound like an Anglepoise from IKEA. More like a – a sex-call bit, with

digits instead of a surname. No. Shut it. Samantha Hurst.
Middle name could be his mother's: Doreen. What's in a
name?

Sweat was trickling down the edge of his jaw, straight out
of his shaved sideburns. The white one, Vanessa, was on about
fox-hunting, now, for some unknown reason. She was screwing
her face up and saying how sorry she felt for the poor little
fox. It's so crooel, she was saying. Torn to bits like that.

'Keep Britain Friday,' said her friend, adjusting her enormous ear-bangle and leaning drunkenly against Simon
Milner, who was smirking twerpishly.

'They eat its googlies raw,' said Vanessa, wrinkling her nose.

'That's A–rabs, stupid.'

'I feel like eating blokes' googlies raw, when they get on
my wick.'

'I just nibble 'em,' said her friend, showing large white
teeth through her crimson lips. 'I like to take 'em whole in
my gob and suck.'

'Both at once?' asked Brian, with his eyebrows up.

'Flipping it with my tongue, you know what I mean?' she
said, too squiffy to notice. 'It's called good team-work and
flexible working practice, guys!'

It was a relief when they'd gone. Even Brian's jokes had
been feeble. They'd had this great power, those females, talking
dirty like that. Alan wondered whether they'd be any good
in bed, or whether it was all mouth. Jill, who never talked
dirty, was probably a lot better than them in bed. Subtlety
was important. Anyway, those girls were probably extremely
well-behaved, back in the sales office, legs crossed under the
desk and looking up with a *Can I help you, sir? Certainly, sir.
He'll be available in about a year.*

Simon Milner went up for the next shout and claimed
he'd got his bum pinched by a teeny-bopper. They expressed
their disbelief; he was the most unlikely candidate. His chief
thrill was flying model gliders with his son and handing out
Lib Dem leaflets in front of Waitrose.

They looked around them.

The bar was now getting filled up with thickset young blokes with tight T-shirts and shaven heads, accompanied by their giggling underage birds dressed in what would have passed as mail-order lacy underwear a few years ago, leaving their midriffs bare. It made the lads feel old, in their corner. Studs winked in navels like gold sweat-drops.

'Oh look,' said Brian, 'it's the Security Guard Social's night out. Let's rob a sweetshop.'

Alan wanted to tell them what Jill had said about the duty doctor's midriff, but Simon got in first: he said he never thought he'd sit in a bar full of skinheads.

'They're not skinheads,' Brian said, as if forgetting what he'd just said. 'They're just normal young twenty-first century blokes. And their girlfriends are not prossies, they're normal too. It's the same every Friday and Saturday night, round us.' Brian lived in the country, about an hour's commute from Hull. He had thirty sheep. 'As a result, there are bouncers manning every pub and restaurant in the nicest market towns in England. Beverley, for instance. Big bruisers with folded arms. It's *Clockwork Orange* crossed with bloody *Trumpington*.'

'How normal is normal?' Phil asked.

'Normal is letting anti-social elements terrorise society,' said Brian, getting political. When Brian got political, you could see the jackboots growing up his legs. 'Fear. We're all in fear. You recall, coming up the motorway, we kept seeing people chucking litter out of their windows? Cigarette packets and sweet papers and so on?'

'We did and all, Brian,' said Phil, who enjoyed goading Brian Wallis when he went like this after a few drinks.

'Well, I'd dismember them, publicly dismember them. No, seriously. Dead serious, lads. Because after years and years of Keep Britain Tidy, there are still selfish bastards who spread their shit for someone else to clear up.'

'Even the children?'

'It's their parents' responsibility. I'd publicly dismember

their parents. With tractors instead of horses. Anyway, the problem wouldn't come up. Two or three televised executions and litterbugs would never be heard of again. Seriously. Fear, that's what they need. Boot on the other foot.'

'Just like traitors, pickpockets and Highland crofters in the old days were never heard of again, Brian,' said Phil.

'It's stitch in time,' Brian went on. 'It's getting rid of the rotten apple. Instead, we allow ourselves to be overrun. Well, it's your lookout. Don't come running to me when you're drowning in litter and woofters and bloody left-wing yobbos. Remember Enoch? He was a prophet in his own time. Spoke eleven bloody languages.'

The weird thing about Brian, Alan thought, was that he was at his most serious when he sounded most comic.

Alan sat back in the soft black leather couch, hiding his smile. Brian swayed off to the toilet yet again. Maybe he had cancer of the bladder. Their managerial colleagues were likewise spread about, unwinding on the orders of the company, talking and grinning and guffawing and draining their glasses: Alan eased into the comfortableness of it all, not minding the din. It was life. It was human. You weren't just a number. And he was a dad. Tomorrow at this time he'd be gazing down at his little scrog, his very own and no one else's. He shook his head, unable to believe it. He was so happy. He'd get the work-life balance sorted. He'd do his bit. Jill and he had their difficulties but he'd do his bit and they'd keep on track. He'd paint the spare room pink with a frieze of teddy bears. Noah's ark.

A distant mobile went off.

It was his, *La Traviata*. He'd put the bastard in the inside pocket of his jacket because the outside one was too small, and he had to flap about a bit, finding it. He couldn't hear a thing. He pushed his way outside, shouting into the mobile ('Hang on a minute, just hang on'), and one of the shaven-headed lads swore nastily at him, calling him a 'Ginger Prick'. He wasn't ginger, he was strawberry blond.

He trotted outside, into the chill night.

It was his mother, who kept cutting out. She wanted to know why he was so out of breath.

He got rid of her and wondered whether to phone the hospital again. He could phone from the ice-cream museum's porch. He wiped his sideburns with his handkerchief, wheezing. His heart was still hot-rodding in his chest, from the shock of the ring.

He took a turn outside, anyway, for the fresh air, his breathing tubes sticky with smoke. The toy roads were brightly lit, idiots cruising them at about five times the permitted speed. A CCTV camera on the top of a fancy wrought-iron column was moving about drunkenly. He raised his hand to it when the lens pointed down at him. It was very nippy without his coat, but the Laphroaig glowed inside him. Groups of young blokes and their floozies stood about, dressed for summer. Three of the floozies ran past him on their high heels suddenly and his bum was grabbed very near the balls – given more of a squeeze than a pinch.

'Evenin', gorgeous,' the girl squealed, the others laughing.

He had frozen in surprise. She looked about sixteen with a bare midriff that had not yet seen too many chip kebabs. She and her two friends joined a group of about twenty of the security-guard types across the road and he walked on, thinking how easy it would be to get beaten up. The place she'd grabbed and squeezed glowed, it was definitely pleasurable, he could still feel the pressure of the young fingers. It must be a kind of local game. Maybe they only chose men who were beyond the pale, who were the last word in old and fat and ugly. Simon Milner was definitely beyond the pale; a nice bloke, but one didn't quite know how he'd made his son, who was called Dominick and had something a bit wrong with him medically, no one knew the details. Certainly, Simon Milner did a lot of work for disadvantaged kids through Rotary. Alan hoped there was nothing wrong with his own kid, medically.

His own kid.

This place reminded him, at night, of Bickersteth Business Park, where the Northcott Jackson plant was now situated.

He came up to the ice-cream museum, awash with security lights. It was way past midnight. He stood in the porch and keyed in the hospital number after a few slips and Nurse Helen replied immediately, bright as a button, as if night didn't exist in hospitals. She still sounded like a bloke, keeping her voice quieter so Alan had to press the Treo hard against his ear to hear properly – his ears were still ringing from the bar. Everything was fine, mother and baby were sleeping.

'Helen, be a love, tell me,' he said. 'Does it matter if I can only make it by around teatime tomorrow? I mean, should I be worrying that I can't make it earlier? I'm away on business, you see, and it'd be very hard for me to get off earlier, obviously. I'm very worried. I'm dying of worry, in fact.'

The whisky and the tiredness slurred his words, but Helen was as bright as ever.

'Well, it wouldn't do to die of worry, would it? It does no one any good, worrying.'

'No, but listen, is there any reason for me to worry, mate?'

Ouch. He couldn't imagine this voice as a bird's.

'Look, Mr Hurst, you make it when you can. If you can't make it earlier, you can't. We can't always arrange things for the best, can we? They're both in good hands.'

'How's my daughter doing, exactly?'

'It's not for me to say, Mr Hurst, because I'm not the consultant.'

'Give me a general picture, please, my love.'

There was a pause, as if she was taking a breath before plunging. Alan didn't take a breath at all. He thought he heard papers being shuffled. Drug charts, doctor's reports, all that guff. Cold and medical.

'Well,' she said, 'little Samantha's quite poorly, but stable. Your wife has a suspected liver infection.'

'Say that again, slowly.'

She did so.

'*Quite* poorly,' he repeated.

'But stable.'

'And a liver infection.'

He couldn't believe this. It was like a door had opened onto Hell. He'd been walking next to Hell all day without suspecting because he was the right side of the paper-thin wall.

'I thought you said she was doing fine?'

'Who?'

'My wife. Both of them, obviously.'

'Fine, considering. The baby's two months premature, Mr Hurst. Your wife's liver infection will be dealt with on Monday, when the consultant comes back. But she's in very good hands in High Dependency. It's what we're all here for.'

'High Dependency? What does that mean? Is that Intensive Care?'

'No, it's the High Dependency Unit. It means we keep a very close eye on her, as the staff do with Samantha in the Premature Unit.'

He took as deep a breath as he could manage, five feet under in his own panic.

'Why not before? Why can't the consultant come before? Why can't you deal with it now?'

'The nursing staff haven't got the authority to prescribe more than the basics.'

He squeezed sweat out of his eyes, blinked them clear.

'Listen, tell my wife I was goosed. By a teenager. That'll make her smile.'

'Goosed?'

'Yeah, just now, on the street. Well, not street, these little toy, these – toy – road things. No, no, leave it out. Don't worry, mate. Just give her my love.'

He heard the faint sound of an emergency bleeper. Maybe it was Jill's or Samantha's. No, Samantha was somewhere else.

Nurse Helen didn't even say goodbye. Alan pressed his forehead to the glass of the ice-cream museum. The *Rossi's* van was dimly lit; it looked like a faint memory of something happy.

He felt betrayed. He'd gone round the dullest museum in the universe in order to ensure his wife and daughter's lives. It was a metaphysical deal. Only Marks and Sparks on a Sunday night could be duller. Now he felt as if he was back to where he was at lunchtime. Only it was night, and all was blackness and loneliness and fear.

High Dependency meant highly dependent. Tubes and drips and masks. It meant that things were not very good, medically. It meant that things could slip very easily into a worse scenario. Obviously.

He hurried back to the hotel, avoiding the louts, trying to recall the exact words he – she – Helen, the bloke-sounding nurse, had used.

Poorly but stable.

Quite poorly.

Liver infection.

What the hell did *poorly* mean? His grandmother used to say she was feeling poorly when she had indigestion. His grandfather had been 'very poorly' in the Agecare Unit three years ago which meant he was nearly dead. Was he sure that Helen didn't say 'rather' rather than 'quite'? Quite or rather poorly could mean very poorly or not very poorly; it was ambiguous, that one. What a stupid language. His loved ones weren't doing fine at all, they were very sick; they were highly dependent; they were possibly deteriorating hour by hour and every known consultant was on his yacht or shagging his mistress because it was the weekend. He couldn't believe it. You only had one liver, for Christ's sake. Two kidneys, one liver. One heart. Livers were vital. She *had* said liver, hadn't she? Not kidney? How could he confuse the two? They didn't even sound the same and the taste was entirely different. And now he couldn't even walk back a

43

couple of hundred yards to his hotel without fearing for his life. This was England.

OK, he was in Scotland, but it was the same in England, as Brian had pointed out. This was Great Britain, then. The U of K. And Unwin had forced him to stay on and betray his loved ones. He'd kill Roger for that, if anything happened to his loved ones. A crime de passion. Shoot him dead.

His foot found a sleeping policeman where a streetlamp wasn't working and he flew into deep shadow that stopped abruptly against his hands and body. The nearest group of shaven-heads laughed. He'd met the ground with surprising force, in fact; he had to sit there for a few moments, nursing his hands and feeling his ribs and waiting for the air to come back fully. The louts were catcalling him, now; they'd probably kick him to death if he stayed where he was. The most basic human sympathies had disappeared from the world. Even the girls were laughing. He'd have to tell them, if they went for him, that his wife had strained herself with some heavy shopping and given birth way too early. Maybe they wouldn't care, even then.

He stood up, still winded, and wanted to yell at them. He brushed grit from his lips. A law-abiding plumber had been beaten into a vegetable coma a few months ago because he'd gently ticked off some lads for hurling obscenities at his wife: it was a small column in the *Telegraph*. It was always happening. It happened, and then it was forgotten. The waters swallowed it up. Anything could happen. He could lose his wife, his daughter. He could be beaten to a vegetable. He felt he'd entered a new realm of possibilities, and they were all bloody terrible.

He limped back past the Cascade Club and made it safely to the hotel, the palms of his hands and his lips stinging and various parts of him aching. Lady Luck was juggling with him, it could fall either side. Life could turn out wonderful or very, very bad. He went straight up to his room via the emergency stairs, which avoided going past the bar. The stairs were murder; he felt about ninety, his heart beating in his ears. He kept having to pause on the bare, cold landings. He thought of his dad, whose heart stopped in the post office when Alan was nine. Without warning.

The swipe card would not open his door. He was putting the card in upside-down. The green light flashed and the soft little click sounded and he entered his room.

He washed the light grazes on his palms and ran his lips under the bathroom tap, wondering about pain. There was a sharp pain on his hands and lips and a dull pain in his chest. It was a signal that all was not right: a survival mechanism. An alarm. He looked terrible in the bright mirror-light: his skin was greasier than usual and he had even more of those tiny red veins on his cheeks. There was a polite notice about towels in three languages, how if you were a selfish git and really wanted them cleaned each day you had to throw them on the floor and they'd be taken away to foul up the environment, except that it wasn't put like that. It reminded him of Jon S. Volkman's smile. He read it in French and German, too, understanding about three words and wishing he could cross into the Yukon Territory and light out for the endless northern snows on a decent pair of snowshoes. Life could be so clean and simple. He'd often thought that. The human instinct is to complicate. His left arm felt stiff.

He sat on the bed and leant back against its giant cushions in the darkness. He could hear the clicking of cutlery through the open window: knives against plates in the big hotel kitchens below, slicing whole bulls for the carvery. Everyone was somewhere else and far away; he wasn't near anyone. He was completely and utterly on his tod. He'd had to open the window in the middle of the previous night, suffocating in heat and dryness and thick fabrics. He didn't know what to do. He didn't know what to do. The eTV Interactive winked a red eye at him; he thought about surfing or retrieving emails but it was too much effort, it required such a great and ongoing effort. He wondered if his daughter could see, or whether her eyelids were still tight shut.

He shut his own eyes, resting there in the darkness with a hand on his chest. He nodded off and dreamt that the world was being taken over by intelligent plants, the kind of plants you find in hotels and offices and conference rooms; that small red tongues uncurled from their flowers and spat millions of red spores against walls, that these rooted in the walls and brought them down within hours and so whole buildings – office blocks and skyscrapers and ice-cream museums – were cracking like old skin and would soon disintegrate into dust. He saw his daughter running towards him across a town square. It was empty of people. He was closing the boot of his small, plump, old-fashioned car, but the boot would not close as she ran towards him on her little legs, in her pretty black dress. His jacket was buttoned too tight over his chest, he could hardly breathe, but he didn't have time to fiddle about. A wall on one side of the square – high and windowless and right next to her – was covered in lots of tiny cracks. It was ready to fall. The boot would not close, something was getting in the way. He kept slamming it down and up it came again, slowly on its spring.

Slam.

Slam.

Slam.

Only he and his daughter knew the secret of the clever plants. Their evil intent.

'Hurry up,' he called out to her. 'Hurry up, my little peppercorn.'

And she came nearer. And the slamming went on inside him.

And she was coming nearer.

IN THE AUTHOR'S FOOTSTEPS

David's hobby was a statement, of course; Gillian knew that. If anyone asked, Gillian would say he was a hiker, that hiking was his hobby. Really, what she wanted to say was that he was an awkward sod.

Neither of them had ever had an affair. Their marriage, to outsiders, was rock-solid. They'd both spent their lives in adult education and Gillian was a lay preacher. Devout ecologists, they knew their birds. But if David's hobby got much worse, Gillian would have to up sticks. Or, with a bit of luck, he might get properly arrested and put away for a bit, instead of being cautioned and an embarrassment in some local rag. That would shock him out of it.

The rot started, to Gillian's mind, when David took early retirement once the kids had flown. Ludlow was too quiet, after Bracknell. Lives of *quiet desperation*, as Pink Floyd had put it. Gillian played a lot of her ancient vinyl numbers while David pored over old maps in the kitchen. She wondered how she had ended up like this. Distance Learning for the Open University. No colleagues. Rain spattering the picture window and David becoming an awkward sod. She had even started smoking again, and David had banned her to the garden. One morning there was a tussle, and Gillian threw one of *those* books at him. It missed, but landed with a splat and a few of the pages flew out and David smacked her across the face. Or would have done, if she hadn't ducked.

Everything at sixes and sevens, as her mother would say.

'Why can't you just hike normally, like everyone else?'

she'd asked him, one day, when he was strapping on his horrible little snot-green knapsack with those chocolate stains, bound for Telford.

'I *am* hiking normally. It's the world that isn't normal,' he replied.

'Change is totally normal,' she said. 'Look at us.'

'I can choose to live the life I want, Gillian,' he said.

'Well, at this rate you'll live it without me, soon.'

The climax came when he brought back yet another one of *those* books. He'd got enough of them, now, to cram three shelves. There were a couple of local second-hand book-shops nearby: one was neat and expensive with an ex-stock-broker behind the desk, the other chaotic and cheap with Mike and his one-eared cat staring at you from the shadows. If you were prepared to spend a whole morning truffling under his gaze, the cheap one could yield some treasures. Today it had yielded David's type of treasure.

He waved it under Gillian's nose, ever so pleased with himself. She could smell the shop off his cagoule: pipe-smoke and bodily decay.

'Found it,' he said. 'At last.'

'Don't tell me. *The Himalayan Trail, 1914.* Maybe I'll get rid of you for a few months and then you'll fall down some post-1914 crevasse.'

'Do you have to smoke in the kitchen?'

'Bloody hell, David, you don't mind filling your lungs with it in the bookshop, do you?'

He sat down, opening the book.

'Wonderful,' he murmured. 'This is the crown jewel.'

'Looks just like all the others. Old and sad.'

'*Buckinghamshire Footpaths* by J. H. B. Peel, published 1949.'

'Exactly. Just like all the others. *Walking in Warwickshire, London's Countryside, See England First—*'

He took out a reddish leaf that someone had pressed between the pages.

'Fifty years old, this could be. Wych elm. Look. Tragic.'

It crumbled in his fingers like dried tobacco.

'David, that's the last damn book or it's divorce.'

'I could say the same about your cigarette.'

She hesitated. She felt the smoke in her chest.

'Alright. We'll do a deal. Fags versus those books.'

He looked at her over his glasses for a moment, then at the book open in front of him.

'OK,' he said. 'I don't need any more. This is the ne plus ultra, this is.'

'Why?'

'Listen.'

He put a bit more distance between the book and his glasses (another sign of age) and read.

'*Milton Keynes is a homely place. Fields encroach upon the dusty by-lane, and brim over the scattered cottages. There is nothing here of the conventional beauty spot, for indeed no one seems to have heard of the place, save the handful of its inhabitants; and these think so well of it they rarely leave it. I have known and loved Milton Keynes since I was a boy, but at no time in my legion pilgrimages thither have I met a stranger. The church at Milton Keynes, which is among the finest—*'

'I think you've made your point. You're not going to do your thing at Milton Keynes, are you?'

'Of course. A circular walk from Newport Pagnell via Milton Keynes, Woughton and the – I quote – "delightful hamlets" of Little Woolstone and Willen, with a detour to Bradwell Abbey and then on to Great Linford, with its single-branch railway back to Newport Pagnell. In the author's footsteps.'

'Oh dear.'

'It's England,' he said. 'I've every right. Listen. *The church is approached through a line of small trees, having a farm that reaches to the church wall itself, so that cows sometimes browse upon the backs of unsuspecting worshippers who have stopped to discuss the result of the Crimean War, or whatever else passes for news in this most blessed haven of pristine sanity.*'

'Then you won't be wanted there, dearest. If it's a haven of sanity.'

David smiled.

'The cows are concrete cows now, aren't they?'

He almost made it to the end, too; he was only arrested while trying to enter the grounds of the Gyosei Japanese boarding school in Willen.

'*Willen is unspoiled because it is unknown,*' he shouted, waving the book about. '*The cottages here wear an air of permanence; the oaks have a great girth; and old men are hale.*'

The policemen had received about a hundred calls relating to this bloke with his tatty green rucksack, and hauled him unceremoniously across the cycle way to the van. The fun had started when he'd crossed the MI near Junction 14, where Mr Peel had admired the view of 'innumerable drowsy villages cupped within the trees'. A lorry had swerved onto the hard shoulder because David liked to think of the MI as a phantom. He was surprised – disappointed, even – to find the village of Milton Keynes intact. The photographs of Milton Keynes in the book, showing thatched cottages humped like natural grass mounds off a dusty lane, with a church tower in the distance beyond grand elms, had nothing much to do with the clipped suburban verges and Lawson cypresses of the present incarnation, but at least it wasn't under a Tesco storage depot as that ancient wood had been on the last hike.

'*At the inn you will strike a footpath south-west to Woughton-on-the-Green.*'

Days over old maps had established this footpath, as well as the inn. He crossed a few executive gardens and ended up inside the Asda superstore, where the route went up the Prepared Meals aisle. With the help of a compass, he followed the path with its primroses and snowdrops under oaks and elms (it was early spring) through the Chilled Foods section and on via a goods delivery bay into Dixons, which had a special offer on Toshiba laptops. He got into a bit of trouble in Topshop, because the footpath curved into the back area where an off-duty cashier was snogging with a deputy manager. But he wasn't arrested: when he explained what he was doing, producing the book from his knapsack, they just thought he was a daftie.

Bradwell Abbey was in the grounds of the City Discovery Centre, and he ate his picnic in peace. He had a spot of bother when the footpath, after crossing twenty mini-round-abouts, eight Redways and a multiplex car park, wound its delightful way through several offices and the gents' toilets of Mercury Communications. They thought he was one of the Albanian field workers at first, until he opened his mouth. By now, he'd been tracked by a total of 243 CCTV tilt-and-zoom cameras – a brief, shadowy figure doing odd things: he was saved only by the difficulty of someone watching all 10,000 or so tapes on the go at any one time in the local CCTV centre.

Once he'd climbed his way over the sea of parked cars and reached the nearest executive estate, he was again in the realm of private householder security. An alarm rang some-where while he was crossing a neat lawn with a whirly brick feature in the middle, and the cops picked him up as he was scaling the wall of the Gyosei Japanese boarding school a few minutes later. In fact, the alarm was in the form of a member of the Milton Keynes Development Corporation, who thought he was her estranged husband come back to do her harm. He did not resist the police, he only quoted Mr Peel, but they arrested him anyway. Reports of a tres-passer had come in thick and fast over the last hour. Several people had phoned the police from their mobiles when he'd climbed on their cars, which had been in the line of the footpath. He'd even been roughed up by the owner of a Mazda MX-5 convertible, and lost his bobble hat. The police had got fed up: they were sick of alternative theatre at Milton Keynes, all these arty bods down from London littering the public space with their Lottery-aided wank, high on wacky backy or whatever. So they hauled him in.

But they decided he was a genuine nut, going on about primroses and elms and meandering, drowsy streams.

'I just want to get to Great Linford,' he kept saying, 'down the winding English lane and its high-banked bend, the fields studded with hedgerows. Look!'

And he'd flash the book at them, which they finally confiscated.

'Jesus,' said one of the coppers, 'what are you on, mate? Bang him up for the night, will you?'

When they let him go in the morning, he was not charged. Gillian stopped smoking and got very crotchety. David went quiet for a while and watched a lot of television. Gillian was almost relieved when he came back one day with *Rambles through Middlesex*, published in 1929. She went straight out and bought ten packets of Marlboro.

'At least he's not a drunk, at least he doesn't hit the old bottle,' she murmured to herself, as he plotted the next hike with his old maps, his finger cutting clean across the slumbering hamlet of Heath Row.

THE PROBLEM

He wondered if it had started long before he thought it had started, so he spent a few days rummaging in his childhood for signs. True, he'd had an unusual number of old school chums dying young, but he couldn't find any indication of his Problem in the days preceding their deaths. The whole point, he thought, is that it's related to pleasure, which is incoherent – no, illogical. Pleasure is definitely not logical. At least, it's not logical when it's at the level that stirs the gods, that sets off the bastards' bleepers.

One incident, however, gave him a kind of clue, a shiver of recognition. A scrap of the victim's clothing, as it were.

In those days – up to the age of twenty-three, in actual fact – he lived with his parents on Princedale Avenue, on the outskirts of Latham (about twenty minutes on foot from where he was living now, well into his fifties). Princedale Avenue was a very steep road, lined with thirties houses of the semi-detached, bay-window, pebbledash variety, and it made straight for the summit by Broad Hill Farm (now the Tech College) with only a few shallow bends in concession to the slope. It was the kind of road people got vertigo on, especially where, at one point, it gave a view of Latham and the Chiltern beech woods beyond.

The bus he took to and from the local grammar in neighbouring Bellridge – the 361, which was a green RT double-decker with a rear open platform on which the usual conductor would stand daringly close to the edge and only lean against the pole with his shoulder, not holding on tight, the road surface a blur beyond his shoes – would always have a job getting up that hill. It would huff and puff, spewing out diesel fumes and shuddering at each shift of gear until first was reached and some kind of massive, mysterious equilibrium was arrived at between the 9.6 litre diesel and the natural force of gravity.

There was one hitch: he had to get off halfway up, at the stop opposite his house. As a small kid, looking through his bedroom window, Ted would move his head until his eyes were at the same angle as the road – and the bus stop's sign looked as if it had been bent over in a strong wind. It was a weird place to put a bus stop, because even to wait there you had to sort of brace yourself against the slope, one foot lower than the other, like one of those blokes on the wing of a biplane in an old film.

And he was, in fact, the only person who ever got off at that stop.

It must have felt pretty hairy for everyone else inside. Ted would watch from the kerb as the bus, releasing its air brakes with a hiss, settled back a bit until enough power was accumulated and the engine hauled it up again, away from catastrophe, and off it throbbed, labouring up out of sight beyond the spindly ornamental cherries that lined the road. Sometimes it stalled, and the application of the hand-brake made it bounce. There was a pause, like a bomb about to explode, and then the six massive cylinders were fired again and off it chugged, tall as a house, wobbling from side to side. Or so it seemed.

One very cold day, when he was about thirteen and flourishing with spots, the bus had sounded a bit rough as it approached his stop, the whole interior juddering so much that you could hold your nail against the window glass and get a machine-gun effect, or fantasise that you were doing a fab solo roll with Ringo Starr. He'd grown out of the thrill of the top deck, which anyway tended to get the yobbo smokers from the Secondary Modern these days, and stuck with the old folk in the lower saloon, generally choosing the transverse seats over the rear wheel arches to get the fresh air and some decent elbow room.

The conductor looked at him, as he got up from his seat, with the usual Here's-the-swot-in-glasses-as-wants-to-get-off-at-the-bloody-Princedale-Avenue-Request-Stop look. Ted even felt bad about pulling on the cord and sending that little *ping* ringing through the saloon up to the driver sitting high in his glassed-off cab – the faceless driver one never knew, apart from the back of his head, unless you remembered to look in the near-side window over the radiator as the bus slowed down on arrival. Who knows, maybe it had always been the same driver, all these years?

The conductor had gloves cut off at the top knuckle and a Latham Rovers scarf today, on account of the cold. He was pretty young – in his late twenties, probably – but to Ted at thirteen he seemed middle-aged, or as if he had always been that age, and Ted was vaguely frightened of him. His name was Ron, that much Ted knew, and he had bright red hair with long sideburns shaved off at an angle. He leant against the pole and the juddering made the handle on his ticket-machine revolve on its own. He leant out to look forward, one foot swinging away from the platform like a sailor, then gripped the pole and swung even further out. He started to sing, his breath making a big cloud in front of his face.

Have you seen your mother, baby, sta-anding in the shadow . . .

Ted's elder brother, Mike, a Stones fan, had bought the single a few months back.

'There's bloody ice on the hill,' Ron said, swinging back in again, his money satchel bouncing on his hip.

He'd sung the song as if he was making fun of it, harshly, but then that's how Mick Jagger sounded.

Ted nodded. He scrunched up his ticket and popped it into the used-ticket holder at the bottom of the stairs, but fluffed it. Litter. The wind caught the ball and blew it out.

'Ice,' Ron the conductor repeated, raising his eyebrows under his cap. 'That ain't nice.'

Ron was looking at Ted while he said this, which Ted found unpleasant. Then the bus juddered to a stop, as Ted had ordered. Thinking back to this incident, now, forty-odd years later – trying to see when the Problem started – Ted realised with a flush of shame that he should have said, 'We'd better not stop then. I don't mind getting off at the top, by Broad Hill Farm.' But he didn't say that, either because he was too shy or because it hadn't occurred to him.

So the bus stopped and he alighted and he watched open-mouthed from the pavement as the vehicle, instead of slipping back a few feet as the driver revved – the semi-automatic preselector transmission doing its job, trying to do its job, not quite doing its job, the thrust and weight ratio audibly out of sync – slipped back a few feet more and then a few feet more and then some more. In fact, the bus passed Ted on the pavement and carried on going downhill, but backwards – Ron the conductor not saying a word from the back but just looking down at the ground passing by with his mouth open. Looking quite scared, in fact.

The driver took evasive action and yanked the wheel, so the big bus ended up sideways on, its back wheels bumped up on the pavement and giving those on the transverse seats a bit of a shock. If there'd been a car behind or if a mum with a pushchair, say, had been passing by at that moment it would, Ted realised afterwards, have been more than a little scary incident. The bus didn't topple over, either, despite the fact that it was sideways on to the slope and looking as if it was drunk. In fact, all it did do was get started again, the engine revving madly, and avoid the stretch of ice in front of the stop as it throbbed its way back up.

'Nice one, kid!' shouted Ron, as the bus passed Ted on the kerb – the back advert still demanding, as if nothing had happened, *Have you MACLEANed your teeth today?*

Ted felt like shouting, 'Piece of cake!' Or was that what his older self invented, in memory? One couldn't be sure.

One thing he knew: he was more embarrassed and ashamed than he'd ever been in his life before.

As if in proof of this, Ted was told by Ron, the next time, that the Princedale Avenue Request Stop was no longer in use, non-functional, out of service – kaput. There was no sign that it was no longer in use, but that's what Ron told him, and added, 'You'll have to jump off, kid. If you ring the bell he'll slow down for you. OK?'

The bus was always going slowly at that point anyway, but when Ted rang the bell, blushing furiously, the bus slowed down to less than a walking pace.

'Go on, then,' said Ron. 'Hop off.'

Ted felt a bit like a parachutist waiting to jump – more because he didn't want to draw attention to himself than from nerves. He'd seen loads of people jumping on and off when the bus was moving, but had been told by his mum never to try it as she knew the son of a friend of Marjorie Nield's who had done just that and hit his head and gone funny. He'd been a clever, hard-working boy; now he just picked up cigarette butts from the gutter. But Ted hopped off, because he had to.

Surprisingly, the ground rushed away under his feet and he all but lost his balance. Ron laughed from the retreating platform.

Bastard, thought Ted. I ought to ask for my thruppence back.

Ted's voice broke, he started to shave, he kissed his first girl, Gillian Knowles, behind the youth club where he went to play pool and drink Tizer and feed the juke-box every Wednesday night. He got shoved about by the black-leather Rockers one evening up Watercress Lane and was left with a fractured rib (which, although very painful, he told no one about because he didn't know it was fractured until an X-ray for suspected colon cancer when he was in his mid-forties revealed the fact, and he remembered those days of gritting his teeth that seemed like last week).

All through this time he would wait for the 361 to slow down every weekday up Princedale Avenue, and jump off. Ron was replaced by others, including a long-haired blonde conductress, Phyllis, with green mascara and a big bust, whom Ted and most of the other males on the bus fancied a great deal as her machine, bouncing above her groin, rasped out their tickets or as her arm stretched over their heads to pluck the cord accompanied by a 'Sorry, darlin,' or a 'Mind yer 'ead, duckie' – her leather satchel so close to your nose you could smell it over her sweat.

But the bus still refused to stop at Princedale Avenue Request, as if the incident had gone down in legend, like the misty legends Ted was into at the time: Fantasy literature to go with his penchant for Fantasy board games.

And he did actually dream of it, now and again: appearing out of swirls of fog, it was a phantom spot that only he and some cackling skeletons would alight at, surrounded by a bubbling, evil-smelling marsh. The marsh would gradually creep nearer the little concrete island, its bus sign leaning like a dinghy's mast in a storm, until it crept over his knees and he would wake up, sweating. His house had been nowhere in sight.

But Ted no longer feared the hopping off. In fact, with the years of practice, he had become an expert. He did it with style. The faceless driver would hardly slow down, now: Ted would ring the bell, nevertheless (sometimes Phyllis anticipated him, giving him a knowing smile, and he would say 'Ta,' and try to swagger a bit behind his blush), and you could hear the engine soften a little, clearing its throat – but the change in speed could be measured only by an extremely sensitive instrument. Ted would nod his cheerio and swing right out, gripping the pole, and just take the ground running up to him by running in turn to meet it, his school satchel bouncing on his full-grown spine. He felt like Dean Martin, or John Wayne, especially when there was a girl or two on board – maybe one of those pretty, dark-haired types from one of the posh old houses on Broad Hill Lane. It was very like riding into town and slipping off his horse before it had stopped — *yeehaa* in a cloud of dust — and all the townsfolk scratching their foreheads and wondering who this goddamn good-lookin' stranger was.

Yeehaa!

He'd never once take a look after the bus as it strained up the hill and out of sight, leaving that weird silence behind it, that delicious quiet in which, for a few seconds, he was alone and life was complete and full of promise, his whole body relaxing, in repose for a moment and the birdsong that had begun again seeming to be inside him, coming from inside him. No, he would never once look back before striding over for tea and a chocolate Bandit with his mum and Mike. The passengers' eyes were upon him through the bus windows (certainly the pretty girls' eyes), and he would gaze into the mountainous desert ahead, his eyes narrowed, his shoulders squared, a rifle on his back instead of a school satchel, about to embark on some great and perilous quest rather than tea and bloody homework. The Dr Malliner's Grammar School shield on his blazer was like a deadly target, by now, inviting bullets of ridicule. But just for a moment, when he hopped off the 361 at Princedale Avenue Request, he was a hero, an athlete, bold and true. He surprised people. He took it running, swinging right out and just letting go. No one else, in all those years, ever got off there or hailed the bus down anxiously with an arm stuck straight out. He was, therefore, unique.

That was it. That was the first manifestation of the Problem.

Because, the day before he fell off (or fell over, as he was always correcting his mum to her dotage), he remembered being aware, for the first time, of how happy he was to have this special moment in his life; it was like a gift, a gift from God. (He was still religious at this time, singing in the church choir and helping at Communion.) Probably owing to the presence of the pretty girls of Broad Hill Lane — one, in particular, who was only about fifteen with very dark eyes and a shy smile, from Latham High, but whose name he never got to know – this moment of jumping off the moving bus gave him a glow in his life that was almost, well, sexual. That's how he judged it now, over forty years on: sexual. *Love, love me do, I'll always be true* . . . It was all about letting go, wasn't it? Your hand slipping from the pole with its white, slightly roughened surface for a better grip, slipping away and into danger and freedom.

He had no memory, in fact, of the fall itself. He woke up in hospital just a second or two, it seemed, after the bus crossed Bodwell Road by Latham Town Library to go up the hill and he was still sitting down at that point. It was a damp day in March and the windows were fogged up with everyone's breath and damp coats. He was seventeen, in his last year at Dr Malliner's. Because he'd shot up, the inside of the bus seemed smaller. Cramped, even. His back rolled against the hand-rail if he leant back. He had no girl for the moment – but that was OK because he had to study. He wanted to be a sound engineer and work in radio or television. He fancied, if that wasn't too strong a word, commuting from Latham to London, as Latham was one of the last stops on the Tube, thanks to the Metropolitan Line – that weird phenomenon that swaps darkness and sooty brick for daylight and fresh air, like a fantasy journey.

When he woke up in hospital he thought he was on the Met Line at Paddington, funnily enough, just pulling out. He tried to get up but nothing happened. There was his mum, asleep in the chair. There were lights flashing, and bleeps. There was a nurse and voices that were echoes. The nurse wasn't looking at him, but dealing with someone in a bed with bandages around his head. This turned out to be himself.

'Can – you – hear – me? I think he's coming round, Mrs Rainer. His eyes are beginning to open.'

They're fully open, you twerp.

Love, love me do.

Hop it.

'Mrs Rainer, your son's coming round. I'll see if the doctor's here.'

'Ted, dear? Ted?'

He hated this name, frankly. It was old-fashioned. Geoff would've been ideal. But lovely Uncle Ted had been killed in the last month of the war and as the nephew arrived a few years later all but on the same date, Ted it was. Ted it always will be.

'Mum, what happened?'

'Ted, can you hear me? It's your mum.'

'What happened, Mum?'

'It's your mum, Ted. Ted?'

'I know it's my mum, you pranny. What happened? What the heck am I doing here? *Mum?*'

'I don't think he can hear me, Doctor. He's not saying anything. Oh dear.'

Eventually, of course, he recovered, but it was touch and go. His brain had been bruised by the impact of the pavement kerb on his skull and it was only his youth and his desire to live that had pulled him out of an irreversible coma. But all this, he thought (some four decades on), is irrelevant: the point is, I was definitely conscious, just before, of — I know, the word is *appreciation*. I *appreciated* it. So it was taken away from me. The gods took it away from me.

Aha, they said: Ted Rainer (Edward to you, please) is *appreciating* something.

Yes, he thought, so very long away from it in time: that was the first occasion on which their bleepers bleeped.

'You fell off the bus, dear,' said his mum, once he was talking coherently.

'I didn't.'

'You did. You fell off because they didn't stop.'

'It was wet, Mum. I slipped.'

'We've been advised to take them to court, because you definitely rang the bell.'

'Signalled the request to stop,' said his dad, who had taken time off work at the depot to support Mum.

'At any rate, you shouldn't have tried to jump off,' said his mum. 'You should have told the conductor.'

Phyllis. Love, love me do.

'They don't stop if it's too delayed,' said his dad. 'The request signal. There has to be fair warning, for deceleration purposes.'

'Listen, they ought to know by now, he's been taking that bus for – how many years?'

'Twenty-three,' said Ted.

His mum laughed. 'You're not even eighteen yet, dear.'

'I'm eighty-eight.'

'Stop ticking him off all the time,' said his dad. 'Let him be.'

That was the first time. The second time, of course, blurred into the third and fourth because he wasn't yet recognisant of the Problem. And everyone has trivial disappointments. But his early life, following the accident, was definitely spotted with like incidents of a lighter nature. There was a glow of appreciation, and the gods were always listening. No, their bleepers warned them. It was probably done by some electromagnetic impulse on a plane we know nothing about. Undetectable to the human ear.

What was clear as day was that, even back then, he had the power of destruction. That is to say, it wasn't just personal disappointment or disaster. He could affect the lives of millions.

When he was in his twenties and training at the BBC as a studio engineer (on *Dr Who*, just then, perfecting the Cybermen's terrifying beeps), he went for a long walk one weekend. He was already a keen bird-watcher, by this stage, recording their songs on a reel-to-reel. He looked out on Grailsham Valley, a few miles from Latham, and experienced an intense appreciation of its natural beauty. He was with Gale, but not married, and they got down to it in the woods there and then (the one and only time outside – *al fresco* as it were). The very next day, he read in the local paper about the plans for a major chalk-pit in Grailsham Valley, which naturally went ahead despite local opposition.

Not long afterwards, there was the building of the office block with concrete cladding like a lot of kitchen sponges, just days after he had stood with Gale one golden autumn evening and admired the view of Latham there.

'Fancy having such a nice view just five minutes from your doorstep,' she'd said.

'I'm a bit of a lucky bloke,' he'd replied, and for the first time in his life he'd looked out on Latham, bathed in evening sunlight with the golden woods beyond, and thought it the most beautiful view possible. He'd felt this glow inside him. Mind you, he was still head over heels with Gale, back then.

And on the Tuesday after, the cranes had moved in, the concrete walls like sponges had gone up.

They had a boy, Simon. God, he'd looked at him one day and thought he was amazing. Simon was five, five and a half. Gale couldn't have any more, for some reason.

Ted had thought, playing sandcastles with his little lad in the homemade sandpit (they were in Chorley Avenue, by then, and Gale was working part-time as a receptionist at the dental surgery), that Simon was the most beautiful, perfect creation possible. The bleepers had bleeped. The bastards up there had cocked their heads, they had stirred in their pool loungers and said, *Oho, Ted Rainer's appreciating something.*

Hit the ground running.

OK, it wasn't death or mutilation, but the glass door that the gust slammed on Simon the following day sorted that perfection out. Simon's a session musician, these days, and one of the reasons he keeps to the shadows instead of being out there on stage is no doubt due to the scars, faded though they've become with time.

It was around then that the father started to realise his powers. Or his curse. He'd slogged up the hill (for the exercise) to visit his mum and dad, and realised how his dissatisfaction with life might well stem from the angle of the road in front of his childhood home. Everything on a slope. Kinking his head, he saw the house as raised up on one side. Earthquake effect. But dissatisfaction was safe. When he found himself appreciating Gale, he knew her time was up. He was still head over heels with her, that was the trouble. She was even prettier, to him, than that pretty, dark-eyed girl on the 361. After the trauma with Simon, it was bound to happen. He felt the glow when they were cuddling on the sofa in front of *Tomorrow's World*: I'm a lucky bastard, he thought, having Gale to myself. I'm born with the sun in my mouth.

'I don't understand it,' his mum said, three days later. 'Except I never quite trusted her. I said to your dad, she's not—'

'Shut up, Mum.'

'It's never the fault of the man, is it?' said his dad, unexpectedly. They were watching *Mastermind*, if he remembered rightly.

'What are you talking about, dear?'

'Never trust a dentist, I say. Nasty taste, they have.'

It was almost a joke, to his dad.

'Nebuchadnezzar,' he added. Because that was the answer to the question on the TV. 'Though I couldn't spell it for love nor money.'

Ted, looking at his dad, had glowed inside. Even through his grief and anger. His dad had always been there, solid, a little cack-handed with emotional matters, but solid. Never getting in a strop. Not ever. Watching forklift trucks all day at the depot, and reading his *Time-Life* encyclopaedias for education, and never getting in a strop. His war limp. His admiration for his son, working at the BBC, meeting famous people like Dick Emery, knowing all about bafflers and birds.

And the bleepers went and they took his dad off. Stomach

cancer. Within three weeks, not even leaving him alone for the grand final of *Mastermind* — won by the bloke who couldn't get Nebuchadnezzar. It was a bad year and Ted started slipping at work, coming in late, splicing the wrong bits of tape. He had to go freelance, mostly applying his sound skills on stuff like *Inspector Morse* at Carlton TV.

He was careful, after that. People would say he was a bit glum, try to find him a new partner. He found Sandra himself, but never glowed inside, looking at her. He was careful about that. Once, one time, he did slip up. He appreciated the birds. Trying to drop off to sleep one night over the teenage yobbos' sozzled shouts (Latham had lost most of its old shops to the chains — and it was no longer all that safe at night, so Latham itself wasn't in danger of being appreciated, of being destroyed by a nuke strike, say), he thought how lucky he was to be in England, to be able to listen to the birds through his portable hi-tech audio equipment (more sensitive than the naked ear), to rejoice in the lark, in the movement of swifts, in the swish and sway of crows over a ploughed field seen from on high.

It was Mike who showed him the article in the *Telegraph*, at work, the next morning. The latest shock-survey, the figures, the catastrophic decline in numbers. The imminent end of the British songbird: pesticides and all that.

The gods had done a major job, that time.

Oh, he was very careful, these days. And that's why he was so cross and upset with himself, now. Simon had come over for Christmas Day in his latest (a flash Toyota with a stitched-leather gearstick), Sandra had gone all out with the goose, Mum had been picked up from the Home and sat there in the corner, ticking everyone off. And he'd settled onto the sofa, a bit sloshed on the lager (he never drank wine, though Simon had brought along some Aussie plonk), and Simon had said, 'You know where we're going to go next year, for Christmas?'

'Tahiti?'

'Almost. Thailand. The band are booked for one of those posh hotels on the beach.'

Simon's band played New Orleans-style jazz, electro-acoustic. Ted liked it.

'We'll come along,' Ted had said, and Sandra had laughed, her chins wobbling.

Hit the ground running.

And he'd leant back in the sofa and imagined the beach, the palms, the blue sea, the warmth. And he'd thought, *We'll book a package early. I'll surprise her. We'll all be out there. Mum, too. Maybe not Mum. Just us three. And Mum if at all possible. It'll be paradise.*

And he'd felt it: that glow, that warm glow. Thailand, Christmas 2005. That's us.

And then, the very next day – Boxing Day – they were listening to the radio over breakfast, planning a bird walk up in Ashley Woods, when the news came through. It didn't even sound that serious, at first. But by the end of the day, he knew. He knew the gods had truly carved the joint, this time, gravy and bones and all.

Ted's glowing again, they'd said. *I think he needs to be taught a strong lesson.*

And he would never make amends for it. For moving the earth itself, the earth's crust, for shifting its spin. For all that death and suffering. It was beyond him to make amends. All he could do was crouch and stay alert, very very alert. Their bleepers would never go off again, he'd sworn that, watching the TV news: the wailing people, the drowned corpses, the little bloke running in front of the wave, the destruction. That was so very careless, Ted.

Never again.

He'd stay glum. He'd watch, as it were, the Request Stop pass by from the driver-only single-decker (about three a day, if you were lucky), and he'd get off at Broad Hill Farm (now the Tech), though it was a walk down. He'd button up his cardie and stay glum, walking down, as it were. Or the next thing you know, he'll be appreciating the universe. All its lovely stars and symmetry and silence.

THE SILENCE

The robbery went badly. At least, it went badly for us. This was in 1959, in Calcutta. The thieves took my mum's engagement ring along with the rest of her jewellery which was in a box on a shelf above her bed. She was fast asleep. They took it without disturbing her. That's what she said.

She woke up in the morning and found the rest of the bed empty. She called out for my father because she thought he was in the loo. Then she went in search of my father in the big living room and noticed the door to the spare bedroom was open. It was too early for the servants: even the sweeper, who had a long white beard and was an untouchable, hadn't yet turned up. She thought my father was in the spare bedroom having a smoke because she didn't like him smoking in bed. She pushed the door open, but it stopped halfway, blocked by something which turned out to be my father's legs.

What I remember is waking up to my mother's screams over the rumble of my air-conditioner.

Westinghouse, it said, in silvery letters.

My next memory is of my *ayah*, with very red eyes, taking me out into the garden. Our garden was one huge lawn with thick shrubs growing all round it, and the grass was almost soft. You couldn't sit on the grass without getting bitten. I wanted to sit on the steps; they were as wide as the house and that's the way you went in. I would sit on the steps for hours playing with my Dinky toys, the stone cool on my bottom.

My *ayah* said I couldn't sit on the steps today. I noticed there were men coming in and out of the house. They had white trousers and white helmets like the policemen who waved at the traffic with sticks.

'You stay here, Andrew,' she said. 'With me, please. At the bottom of the garden.'

She threw a shuttlecock at me and I tried to hit it back with my plastic tennis racquet, over and over. She had never played with me like this before and so it was a special day. The heat made me sweat more than usual because I was concentrating and running about. The grass made my feet sting a bit through my rubber sandals, but I didn't care. My *ayah* had shiny black hair and a missing tooth at the side which you could only see when she smiled. Her sari smelt of perfume and of her underarms. She sat on her heels with her sari tucked between her knees and chucked the shuttlecock with a little twist of her wrist, again and again, putting a fold of her sari over her face sometimes so I'd have to wait. Ramji the untouchable sweeper came out and watched us, leaning on his broom and not laughing. He was my favourite and would ruffle my hair and I'd have to guess where he was hiding behind the bamboo curtain in the living room. No one else was allowed to be touched by him but he was always laughing.

Then I was walking on my own into the huge empty living room with the fans turning round and round. The shutters were closed but the sun had found its way in through the slats, making stripes. The big grandfather clock ticked and ticked and ticked and I thought: *This is death.*

This seems a ridiculous thought for a boy of five, but my father had died and I knew that by now, although I didn't yet know he had been killed in the spare bedroom.

At some point later, in England, I learnt how it must have happened: my father was crossing the living room and saw the spare-bedroom door wide open and went to close it. The robber was waiting behind the door with a long curved sword in his hands. We had bought it on a trip to Katmandu and it was used to slice heads off special cows in one go. It was called a *kukri*. My father had hung our *kukri* on the living-room wall. 'Our *kukri*, who art in heaven,' he joked. I remember that. Our *kukri* was very sharp and the robber showed no mercy.

These robbers never did, my mother reported the police as saying. Our *kukri* had disappeared, so that must have been the weapon. They had cut through the wire netting on the veranda with bolt shears.

We arrived in England a few weeks later and lived with Gran and Gramp in Whitstable. I went to school in a blazer that made my neck itch. Gramp was retired and had a big white moustache and spent his whole time gardening with a cigarette stuck to his bottom lip. He put chicken-wire like tubes around the plants to stop the rabbits, though I never saw any rabbits. The house was in the middle of a lot of other houses and there were no rabbits, but Gramp was sure there were rabbits and that they nibbled everything unless you took precautions. I kept the borders neat with a clipper that was too tall for me, so I had to hold it halfway down the shafts. Gramp always said I did a better job than anyone else, ruffling my hair, and I wondered whether I should offer to clip the edges in the neighbours' gardens for money – but not for Bob-a-Job and charity. I never had the courage, though.

One day Mr Majhi turned up from Calcutta.

I was ten, and Calcutta seemed so far in the past that it was as if it had belonged to another person's life. Mr Majhi had worked for my father in B.O.A.C. and had come to pay his respects while visiting his cousins in London. I got back from school and Mr Majhi was amazed at how I'd grown, but I had no memory of Mr Majhi.

My mother was poorly with her problems by now and wasn't at home, so she missed Mr Majhi. Her problems arose, I was told, from the shock of seeing my father on the spare-bedroom floor. It had taken years for this shock to come through properly and now it was coming through and she had to stay in a special place where it was quiet and soothing.

I was pretty sure he'd had no head when she'd seen him there. Every time I saw Gramp prune the heads of the roses I thought of my father and our *kukri* from Katmandu sweeping down in one long stroke. Now I wanted to ask Mr Majhi about this head business, but didn't dare.

We all went out into the garden after tea and Gran sat in her usual chair, watching Gramp mow the lawn, though he was getting a bit too long in the tooth, she said, to push the mower.

Mr Majhi stood very respectfully, watching Gramp work, and he kept calling out, 'I'm sure I should be giving you a hand with that, you know, Mr Lindsay.'

Gran just sat there and said, 'He will have his way, Mr Majhi,' each time Mr Majhi offered to help. 'He's always been ever so stubborn.'

'Like Terence,' said Mr Majhi. 'But in the nicest possible way, you see.'

Gran didn't say anything back because she was my father's mother and talking about Terence upset her. She went very pale, that was all. That might have been the sunshine reflecting off her skin, which she'd rub cream into to keep it soft and tender. It was because of the sunshine that we'd all gone out into the garden: it must remind Mr Majhi of Calcutta, I thought. The taste of the jam sponge cake was still in my mouth.

I never wanted to go back to Calcutta, though. My mother said there had been a corpse outside the house for two weeks before the police moved it. It was not my father's corpse but a beggar's. Calcutta was full of beggars who just died like that. You'd pass them when you went out shopping and step over them and it upset my mother. Even telling me about the beggars upset her.

I wanted to ask Mr Majhi whether he was a member of the Tollygunge Club, which had a swimming pool and a bar with bamboo walls. Then I remembered my mother saying that it was British Only.

'There's a rough patch over there,' Mr Majhi called out, smiling and pointing to a bit of the lawn that was completely neat. 'What very nice grass you have here in the old country, by the way,' he said to Gran. 'Just like a bowling green.'

Gran said thank you, as if it was her doing.

I wondered whether I should tell Mr Majhi about the dream I kept having. I'd had it for years.

In this dream I'd wake up because of a funny noise and call out for some water. I was sweating and it was dark. My father popped his head round the door and I could tell he was in his striped pyjamas. I told him how thirsty I was and he said he'd get me a glass of water. Then I'd really wake up, trying to stop him going but not being able to move.

I wanted to ask Mr Majhi if my father had been found with a broken glass and a puddle of water next to him. I stood there in the garden watching Gramp push the lawn mower over the grass that didn't need cutting anyway and tried to pluck up courage to ask Mr Majhi but Gran would have heard because she was between Mr Majhi and me and anyway maybe it would be better not to know. The robbers had been very quiet and they had tiptoed in and taken the jewellery box from right above my mother's head and tiptoed out again. But I was always a light sleeper, Gran would say. She wouldn't say this because I'd told her about my dream, she'd say it anyway. Sometimes it's better to roll over and just close your eyes, even if you hear a noise. But it's very hard to sleep if you're thirsty. It's what Gramp would always say about flowers: all flowers need water. You can tell by how they look whether they need a bit extra in the summer, or in any dry patch. Spring, summer or autumn. You just need to look.

Mr Majhi stood with his back to the garden wall and he

was paying us his respects, as if we were a gravestone. Gramp was pushing the mower. I was wondering whether to ask Mr Majhi about the broken glass and the puddle of water.

Then Gran said, as if she'd been thinking hard about it: 'Yes, you're right, Terence was just the same, Mr Majhi. Stubborn as an ox.'

'He certainly was, Mrs Lindsay. But oxen are sacred in our country, you know. Very special.'

He gave a little chuckle. He had made a clever joke. I already knew about cows being sacred in India. Gran just sat there, watching Gramp. She hardly ever mentioned my father. I couldn't think of him as 'Terence', in fact. My mother always said, 'Your dad'.

And then I realised that Mr Majhi was secretly telling me about this head business. Our *kukri* had been used for slicing the heads off special cows in Katmandu and that's what he meant.

And my thirst grew and is still growing and still no one has brought the water because they are all cut down. Sometimes it's better to roll over and forget all about it, but I'm a stubborn person and I like things neat. Even now I'm like that. Even now I like things neat when I shouldn't really worry at all. I was hoping Gramp would ask me to clip the edges so that Mr Majhi could ruffle my hair and say I was better than any gardener in Calcutta . . . but Gramp didn't ask me, he just went on mowing as if he was giving a demonstration while we all watched without saying one thing more.

DEAD BOLT

They were stacking the chairs in the Community Hall. The chairs were grey plastic bucket types with little metal grips each side so they could be attached to each other in rows and the helpers were having problems ungrappling them. But they were laughing about it. The concert had been a success and everyone was high. Maybe the drinks after the concert had helped; there had been Kir Royale provided by Nolan's wife, Andrea, and Duncan had brought along some bottles of Sainsbury's green cider with brown-paper labels that made it look locally brewed. The younger chaps all wanted beer or lager, and Nolan asked Duncan why he hadn't brought any along. Duncan had felt that beer or lager wasn't right after a classical music concert, but he didn't say this. He wasn't sure of his ground.

'If they want a piss-up,' he said, 'they can go to The Granary.'

Those who hadn't gone home were pitching in to help, now: there wasn't even a broom free. They were all keen to do their bit. Duncan had some dirty glasses in his hand and he was waiting to get into the kitchen. A kid he didn't know, about eight or nine, was blocking the door, trying to stack a chair. It was like *It's a Knockout*. The kid was leaning back holding the chair and trying to get the metal legs to slide into the right place over the other two chairs already stacked together. Duncan watched. He was exhausted, almost hung over. Then someone else old enough to be the kid's grandfather appeared in the kitchen door and helped him slide the chair into the one below.

There was a trio of silver-haired women in the kitchen, tall county types in flowery dresses whose names he could never get right. And Marjorie, who cleaned the hall. People who used the hall had to clean up after themselves and then Marjorie came along and complained that they hadn't done a proper job, although she was paid by the Community Hall Association to do the job. She was a thin woman with over-size feet and hands, and teeth that didn't fit properly inside her mouth. The posh trio were wiping stem glasses and being over-nice to Marjorie, who was telling them something – complaining about something, it sounded like – in her raucous voice, the strong local country accent grating on Duncan's nerves. The posh trio were responding but it sounded as if they were talking over her. It sounded as if everyone was talking at once, in there.

Duncan slipped the glasses carefully onto the furred wood surface next to the old sink without anyone noticing him. Or they chose not to notice him. He caught a whiff of Marjorie – sweat, old dishcloths, stale Avon perfume. Always keep the right side of Marjorie. Then he went out again. A couple he knew only as Rob and Gillie or Julie or Gillian thanked him very much and said goodbye, backing away in their snazzy coats from the clearing-up. They were thanking him because Nolan wasn't there. They were rich and lived in a manor house, that was all he knew about them. He had tried to keep in the background, not drawing attention to himself in case people suspected. Maybe it didn't matter if they suspected. It might matter soon, though, if the contract went through – suspicion working backwards as well as forwards. He couldn't see David Wilkes. Maybe the man had left without saying goodbye. Maybe he'd only said goodbye to Nolan. That would have been a crucial moment. Nolan would have rehearsed it.

The chairs made a deafening clatter and crash as they were being stacked. The hall's acoustics were not good. He heard a tall attractive blonde – he'd noticed her in the audience –

talking to the kid in Swedish or possibly Dutch. The only kid up late. Steve Jonson was starting to mop the floor, showing somebody how to make the right sweeping movements with the mop. To and fro, to and fro, in easy curves. Steve the expert in everything except in the way he dressed: always the SAS-style green roll-neck jacket, shapeless jeans, cheap trainers. He was a bird-watcher, too.

Susan had gone home with the girls straight after the concert. They had walked it, taking the torch up the shortcut, the rough track they called the High Street as a joke. It *was* the hamlet's main street, historically speaking; they had fought against it being tarmacked to avoid idiots racing up it. He'd felt very country bumpkin, fighting that battle against the tarmac – Nolan had teased him, he remembered, saying how he ought to don a green bobble hat and wellies. They hadn't brought the car. The hired stem glasses and the drinks had been brought in Nolan's car.

'I'll wait up,' Susan had said.

'Why?'

'I won't sleep until you're back. I can't help it. Don't get at me about it, please, Duncan.'

There were no more dirty glasses on the big table. Duncan roamed around, checking for any on the floor. Steve's mop swept towards him and he had to perform a little hop over it. Sarah Livingstone and Jackie Coops were sweeping just ahead of the mop, and the chairs were getting stacked and dragged across the lino just ahead of the brooms. Duncan thought about saying to Steve, *It's a military operation*, but couldn't be bothered. He was too tired.

'Looking for your bouncy ball, Duncan?'

'Yeah, Steve. You've missed a bit there. I can see it through my microscope.'

'That's your pawmarks, mate.'

Duncan found a dirty glass on a sill, behind the curtain to the right of the back door. He left it there: to get to the kitchen he'd have to cross Steve's shining empire of mopped lino. Next to the curtain was an old framed photograph of the hall's interior, dated 1928. Behind the 1928 Hall Committee (big-nosed and ugly in their silly hats and thick shoes, with the exception of a pretty girl in the front row), the hall looked like a different place, and not just because it was in black-and-white: wooden floor, plaster walls, beamed ceiling, curved wall-lamps under little glass shades burning to gas, probably. Only the doors and the placing of the windows were the same. A stove sat in the middle, with a thick pipe going up, and there were wooden chairs around the edge. Duncan had never noticed this photograph, or never paid it any attention. The interior looked very real, even in black-and-white. You could almost touch it, touch the glass shades or the shiny floorboards or stroke the rim of the chair-backs. For a moment, slightly pissed probably, he seemed to go right into the photograph, right into the past.

'Fancy her, do you?'

'Luverly, Steve.'

'Bit like Nicole Kidman,' said Steve, pretending to study the photograph.

Yes, the hall looked completely different, now. It had been revamped a few years back, just before they'd come to the village. The local builder, a thuggish bloke by the name of Keith Glover, was responsible. False ceilings in agglomero, strip lighting, metal-framed windows, cork tiles on the walls that the youth group had tried to coat recently in pale-green emulsion. It now looked like a social security waiting-room from the 1970s. It looked less real than the old interior in the photograph, in fact.

He slipped outside by the side door and lit his first cigarette of the night. The air was sweet and cool, even through the Marlboro. He let the cigarette tick over for a bit and drew in the country air through his nostrils; damp leaves, mist, something a bit – what was the word? Began with F. Meaning wild, savage, untamed. He searched for it, couldn't find it. Not 'fetid'. Certainly not 'futile'. Or 'flaccid'. Duncan Jolly on *University Challenge*. A bit late for that, though. Very mature student.

It could still surprise him, this country air. Even after five, six years. Bats flittered about the outside lamp above the door. They must be bats, he thought. They were too big to be insects, this wasn't Africa. He was a bit frightened of bats: their Orc faces. Radar ears. The hall had a bit of land, sandy and wet with a lot of birch trees on it, blending into the bigger woods around. These woods petered out up on the bare downland where he and Susan kept meaning to walk more than they did.

It was amazing, that he lived in the countryside. That the countryside was his to live in at all. It was truly amazing. He was one of the people from the countryside. Yet he still felt a Bromley man.

Nicole bloody Kidman. Who did Steve think he was? Sutton Dewey's answer to Ronnie Barker. They hadn't heard of anybody since Ronnie Barker, here. He tried to recall whether Ronnie Barker was dead or not. Amazing, how these things slipped one's mind.

He hardly ever did this. He hardly ever just stood outside doing nothing, appreciating the country air, indulging in a smoke. It made him feel young – in his twenties. Or younger. He wondered if he shouldn't have spent more time in his life just leaning against a wall, smoking, contemplating things, ruminating. Instead of rushing about chasing money and all the rest of it. There was a verse he'd learnt at school that said that. *Take time to stop and stare*, something along those lines. A picture of a clapboard house in a Western, with a stoop and a rocking-chair and a grand view of the desert, came to him. He narrowed his eyes as hard men did in the films he'd watched as a kid; they'd lean on the stoop and look out into the deep dark desert, the canyons and the wotsits and the secret water-holes and the tiny fires of the Indians.

He walked forward gingerly into the darkness until he

was on the edge of the birch trees. He was wasting his life. Forty in two years' time. The Big Four O. Duncan Jolly, forty years old. He breathed in deeply and heard his wheeze, pushed his shoulders back and felt the weight of his frame, his belly pressing against his shirt. He would start to slim on his fortieth. The day after it. No beers. No fried stuff. No Snickers bars. No cigarettes. He'd begun to wheeze a few months back. He'd thought it was a cold, at first. Running to catch the post office before it closed, he had wheezed. A definite wheeze. But when he compared himself with other blokes of his age, he found himself nicely down the middle, weight-wise.

He'd start worrying at forty. Derek Taverner of Elton Electronics dropped dead at forty, jogging. He'd not heard of anyone dropping dead like that at thirty-nine, it was always forty plus. The birch trees' trunks were white enough to look quite bright, now his eyes had adjusted. Death meant you made no more mistakes.

For some reason, the countryside made you think more about death.

He looked up for stars. The sky was clear and dark, but it was a bit muddy, muddy-orange. That'd be the motorway, probably. Or retail parks, lit like prison camps. Or just towns. Something winked, moving slowly across. A satellite, or a plane. No stars visible. He'd read somewhere that only twenty-one per cent of England was dark enough to look up from and see the stars, these days. Funny, how he remembered figures like that.

A few people were leaving the hall and laughing as they said goodnight. He wondered where Nolan had got to. Maybe he was talking to David Wilkes by the cars parked along the lane. Nobody had appreciated the cider. There was a lot of it left, now, to purloin.

Feet scrunched up the track, up the shortcut beyond the hall's wire fence. Pocket torches picked out the route; there was a slight mist that showed up the torch beams, like in a film. Apart from Marjorie, no locals had come along, he realised. By 'locals' he meant people born and bred in Sutton Dewey. That was disappointing. All having sex in the shower, no doubt.

He kept stock-still by the trees, like a poacher, shielding the glow of his cigarette as the torches wavered up the track. He could imagine being a hunted man, the Gestapo or whoever after him with their guns and dogs and torches. He recognised Jackie Coops's high voice in among the others. He'd quite fancied her when they first came but she'd suddenly got past it, letting her hair and knockers go and losing her style. It happened.

The voices sounded pleased with themselves, as if they owned the place. Very pleased with their lot. Very posh. Very superior.

'. . . performed . . . ridiculous . . . really great . . .'

He felt a shiver of pleasure when he heard them; however superior they sounded, he had one thing over them, like the lord of the manor or something. He could just sit back and grin, knowing how this one thing made him superior without a single breath wasted on his part. Not just superior: it actually made him more real.

And it wasn't planned, it had just fallen into his lap. It was fate.

He'd come with Susan to property-crawl; she wanted to live in the proper country, he'd lost his job at Doublegroup Systems and they reckoned, with the extra saved from the price differential between Guildford and here, he'd be able to start something on his own in the consultancy line: there were estates and individual homes sprouting like mushrooms in Berkshire. Also, they wouldn't be too far from his mum in Tring, but not too close, either. They were meant to be having a recce of the prestige development in traditional brick-and-tile but Susan spotted the *For Sale* notice in the window of this long, low cottage and knocked on the door.

The owner was a nervous, arty type of woman in her

fifties. She said, 'In fact, I love it, but as you might have noticed I no longer have a wedding ring. He's in New Zealand. God, that's not far enough as far as I'm concerned.' Her paintings were very sexual, they were all huge thighs and knockers and fannies put on with a trowel. 'Of course, he's just next door when it comes to money. Banks and solicitors, you know. I have to do everything. I could kill him. And his floozy.' She was drunk, but she showed them round. The place smelt of cats and oil paint and woodsmoke and its sloping floors squeaked. Its thatch was green. 'It's all my mother's fault. What do you think of therapy?' The woman had a straight fringe that got in the way of her eyes; she kept shaking it out of her eyes, like a twitch. 'All he's left me of himself are these,' she said, showing them drawers full of men's socks.

It was definitely damp, and lacked central heating. Duncan's heart beat fast through the whole visit. He and Susan didn't talk about it, afterwards. They were late for their appointment and pretended they had got lost. Three of the five brand-new prestige houses at the end of the lane – a private road, apparently – had a new BMW in front. They had shaken hands with the estate agent and left and looked at three more houses in the area without once mentioning the old cottage. Anyway, it was too expensive, and the woman had said the price was already too low, that the cottage was historic, probably the oldest house in the village, the original smithy. Built 1492.

'The year they discovered America,' the woman had said. 'Christopher Columbus.'

'The film's very good,' said Susan.

The woman blinked at her as if she was backward. Then the phone started ringing and she picked it up and shouted down it, swearing.

The oldest house in the village. The original smithy.

They drove back to Guildford on the motorway and it was while they were stuck in a jam – a caravan had hit a tree and smashed to matchwood – that they admitted their feelings about the cottage. They were almost breathless, talking about it; Susan rubbing her swollen stomach and letting her eyes fill with tears of excitement and anticipation.

Now Duncan realised, five – no, six years later, standing there in the dark, that he had never been more content than in that hour, stuck in that jam on the M25. Probably not in his adult life, anyway. Anticipation. Everything still to play for. And somehow they had stepped sideways in buying the place. They had hitched onto someone else's life. Hijacked it. That's how it felt to him. That they didn't really belong to the house, even though it filled him with pleasure, thinking about it. *The oldest house in the village. The original smithy.* They'd expected to change, become different and more interesting, but nothing had changed. In fact, they'd felt less interesting, compared to the house. Susan had got tireder and tireder. The country air, probably. Too pure. A bit ratty, she'd got, on a daily basis.

He wondered if people had noticed that he had slipped out. He headed back through the trees to the hall, but he stayed by the back door. He couldn't face going inside.

The exterior halogen shone on his hands and glowed on the roll of his shirt where it hid his belt. He thought about the girl's hands, the girl who had played the cello. She was known locally, was quite attractive with long straight hair that she allowed to fall down in front of her when she was playing. At least two people said afterwards that they reckoned she was copying Jacqueline du Pré, were almost sniffy about it. The pianist was a teacher from the posh boys' school, Downley College – a Latin teacher, not a music teacher. Nolan had introduced him as a music teacher and had been corrected and Nolan had then made a witty remark which Duncan couldn't recall. That was Nolan all over, part of his Irish charm. The fact that he was also a bloody good clarinet player helped, too. Nolan was potty about music, in fact.

He should have been a musician instead of a businessman – could have been, really. The fact that it was just a hobby increased people's admiration for him. Duncan had once asked him why he hadn't gone professional and Nolan had scoffed at the idea. What, end up boring his knickers off in some two-bit provincial orchestra earning ninety-eight quid a throw? Perhaps Nolan wasn't so good after all, Duncan considered: a big fish in a tiny pool. Like the business.

Why ninety-eight quid? Why not a hundred? Nolan never rounded things off, that's why.

The Latin teacher played excellent piano, according to the experts present. Plump, with wild grey hair like Beethoven. By the name of Colin Skeeton-Ash. Susan had talked to Mr Skeeton-Ash, afterwards, about the fees, how much it cost to send your son or daughter to Downley College, and Mr Skeeton-Ash had looked at her as if the questions were distasteful. When he told Susan how much one might expect to cough up annually to keep a child at Downley – he'd actually used that expression 'cough up', peculiar coming from someone double-barrelled like him – Susan had looked startled. Duncan felt demeaned; not because the amount was pretty well the equivalent of his annual salary, but because Susan had given herself away by looking startled.

Posh-shop, he'd thought. It was Andrea who'd recruited the pianist, of course – she had friends in the college. Contacts, anyway. Nolan gave Mr Skeeton-Ash a bottle of decent Aussie red, afterwards, £15.99 at Oddbins – Duncan had chosen it. Duncan had never actually said thank you to the bloke and had made a point of doing so as he was leaving.

'Thank you very much,' Duncan said (almost adding 'sir'). 'On behalf of everyone present, Mr Skeeton-Ash.'

'Good cause, good cause,' the teacher replied. 'Sorry about the andante in the Schubert.'

'That's quite alright.'

A prime prat's thing to say, he now realised. He didn't even know where the andante was in the Schubert, whether andante meant fast or slow or something else like 'loud'; he knew next to nothing about classical music, although he didn't object to Classic FM on long drives, if he needed to relax. The public-school arsehole of a teacher had smirked, of course, seeing right through Duncan and out the other side. He'd even looked down his nose at the label on the wine and said, 'Oh, Aussie. Oak chips and barbed wire. Well, there's always a first time for anything.' You can't go wrong at sixteen quid, though. Fifteen ninety-nine.

There was laughter behind him, through the varnished wooden door with its old-fashioned latch. They hadn't changed the doors. They were solid originals, from the 1920s, but let in draughts. Duncan thought he detected his business partner's high laugh and found himself stiffening like a rabbit. He'd almost finished his cigarette. The muffled crashing of the chairs had stopped. How many had come, in the end? A hundred and fifty? Two hundred? Packed, anyway. Each one paying seven quid for the privilege. It wasn't Rosterpovitch, but it was quality stuff for the area. And all in a good cause. You can't get a better cause than a children's hospice.

He smiled to himself and flipped his cigarette into the black grass of his shadow. He'd met the director of the hospice, David Wilkes, at the Briar Hotel cocktails six months ago. Wilkes was new to the region, and about the same vintage. Although he was a northerner, they'd got on, mainly because of their mutual ability to parrot whole passages from old episodes of *Only Fools and Horses*. Duncan had been on form that day and established from Wilkes that there was no security system at the hospice. It was a huge rambling Victorian pile, with a couple of naff extensions, and not a dead bolt or an alarm anywhere. There were smoke detectors, and fire extinguishers, but nothing against intruders. It took kids in from a big area – though more kids got mortal illnesses than you realised, said Wilkes, and it all needed a lot of complicated technology.

'Keep mum about that.'

'About what?'

'The technology. These days,' Duncan pointed out, 'being a kid's hospice is no guarantee against a break-in. And then there's the paediatric angle. Peeping toms and stuff.'

'Paedophile, don't you mean? Perish the thought.'

Duncan had physically blushed at his mistake. But he'd told Nolan the next morning that the hospice might be their next big job. They needed a big job; the firm was steering very close to the wind financially, for reasons neither partner could really fathom. They worked seventy-five-hour weeks, not including weekends. Surelock Security Systems had a reasonable rent in the slightly shabbier part of Stourminster. They employed four reliable blokes and a part-time secretary, Sheena, and ran a couple of three-year-old Ford vans. With all the new private estates springing up, their services were in demand. Yet the figures got the accountant shaking his head.

'You need a break,' he'd said, at the last meeting. 'And not break as in holiday. One big job. Too many piddling little alarms for old biddies. The Army, for instance.'

'Already sewn up,' said Nolan. 'They take their own boys, insiders they can trust.'

'Don't tell me, Mr Murphy,' simpered John Wills, the accountant, 'that they don't trust a decent fellow from Londonderry.'

So the hospice break had got them both dreaming. And then, when Nolan was wondering what charity to support for his concert, Duncan had made the kind of suggestion he'd been valued for by his previous employers. He had that sort of mind; it was brighter and faster than he knew, except that he knew that he didn't know. Perhaps there was a section of it, sort of cordoned off, that was better developed than the rest.

What's more, he'd wheedled out of Wilkes the crucial information that the place was going to have its insurance

reassessed in 2003, following new European bloody guide-
lines. Wilkes was worried: the medical equipment was valuable, there were video machines and a couple of Macs. He'd
heard that bedroom doors had to have code-locks on them,
the type where you tapped out a four-digit number. Duncan
had given him his card.

'That's our line of work,' he said, gearing into the prattle.
'Home security systems. Twenty-four-hour monitoring. I can
come and look it over, if you want. Free estimate. I'd recommend swipe cards for the bedrooms and multi-access keypad
entry for the rest. And entrance function, of course.'

'Entrance function?'

'The door stays unlocked from the inside. Useful in case
of fire. Given you've got a lot of kids, who'll maybe be sleepy
and confused in the middle of the night. Of course, you'd
top that up with panic hardware for the main doors. Better
safe than sorry. What's your access control?'

'Sorry?'

'I mean, if your system was networked you could control
up to eight doors at once. Or more if the electronics are
built into the reader itself. You can choose. The technology's
moving all the time, it's incredible, it gets better and better.
And what I can say is that we don't charge for the software,
which is extremely powerful.'

'Fire,' Wilkes had repeated, feebly, as if the possibility had
never occurred to him before.

'What you don't want to be is caught out by the insurance bods, who'll have a hotline, or maybe even be affili-
ated with, the big home-and-business security boys.'

'Is that true? Are they? Jesus.'

Wilkes looked bewildered: there he was, in charge of fifty-
odd dying children, and he knew nothing about the real
world.

Nolan had been tempted to activate Plan X on this one,
but Duncan thought it unnecessary and somehow immoral,
given it was a kids' hospice, and for once Nolan had agreed.

Anyway, to stage a minor break-in was always, to a certain extent, dangerous. Plan X was only to be used in very specific circumstances, like the time Roger Deakin of ATT Computers had just taken over the Thatched Barn in Swinley Beauchamp and reckoned a couple of Yale locks and leaving the radio on would do the job. Plan X – Sheena's glamour-boy with the bad complexion doing his bit – had decided him otherwise, and Nolan was on hand in the saloon bar of the Highfield Hotel at just the appropriate hour, Roger being a man of ingrained habits. That one job alone had saved them for another six months, because a couple of Roger's mates in the business, in equally inappropriate buildings, followed suit.

'Won't the bastards get in by the thatch, now?'

'Roger,' Nolan had replied, leaning on Deakins's Astra and looking up at the picturesque roof, 'eighty per cent of all break-ins are through a door. You've got infra-red access control, motion-detecting outdoor floodlights, an integrated alarm system and twenty-four-hour CCTV showing Andy Warhol's latest.'

'Eh? Andy Warhol's dead, isn't he?'

'But there's one aspect that still worries me, looking at your very attractive place. Fire does not use a door. Fire looks at thatch and goes yummee.'

'You don't happen to do fire security, do you?'

'Roger, we do. It's not our main line, but we're develop-ing it.'

'I lost a year's work in that break-in. My bloody back-ups won't boot.'

'Water sprinklers. That would do it. Like in the films. Prevention is better than cure, when there's no cure, Roger.'

Now and again, worrying about finances, Duncan wondered if Director Murphy was pilfering from the till. He and Andrea had just bought a mill-house somewhere in France, and Nolan's new car was a show-model BMW. Andrea had appeared tonight in a fabulous outfit, all green and sparkling, which had made Susan's maroon two-piece look dowdy. The only element Duncan felt superior about was, of course, his own domicile. Nolan's house was B for Boring – a kind of big Barratt with knobs on: kit conservatory, fold-away pool, huge open windy fireplace they never used. Andrea would come for dinner at the Old Forge and joke about the low beams and sloping floors; she was green with envy underneath, though. You could tell. Susan appreciated this, and would salt the wound by making the place look very romantic – dipping the halogens and relying on candles in the brass sconces she'd got from the Past Times catalogue while Duncan pointed out something new and historical he'd dug up about the house from some old codger or other.

'The oldest habitation in the village,' he'd say, pouring out the Premier Cru. 'Complete with a ghost. A very good nose, this one, Nolan.'

He could hardly believe it himself – about the house. That's how people would sometimes introduce him at village socials: 'Duncan has the oldest place in the village, lucky man.' Nolan was impervious: he couldn't care a toss about history, he was too present in the present and too big about the future. Quite often one got the impression that Nolan was chafing against the ropes, that he was destined for much greater ends. He'd started out, Duncan knew from Andrea, in Aer Lingus, checking over the planes' electricals; had risen to some responsibility, fallen out with the unions and gone his own way without a bean. The story was that he'd spent his first months in England sleeping in a rusty old container in Docklands, before the area was done up. Then it was snow and no picture until Andrea, the nice house and the snazzy suits. Duncan had once asked him, during a boozy conference in Basingstoke, to fill him in on this transitional period, but Nolan had clammed right up.

'I bought new shoelaces and walked across the sea,

Duncan,' was all he'd said, in a sort of ponderous sing-song over-Irish'd way. Which had made Duncan feel even smaller.

We've got the oldest house in the village. The original smithy.

He lit his second cigarette of the evening and took another turn towards the wood. It was very black, the countryside. Business ought to be better than it was.

Susan was permanently frightened, living where they did. The Old Forge looked extremely classy. It must be a target, she said. The floors and beams would creak on their own and she'd wake him up, white-faced.

'There's someone there.'

'No there isn't.'

'Yes there is. What's that noise, then?'

'The fairly disturbed axe man of Sutton Dewey.'

'Go and see, Duncan. Please.'

'We've got an alarm and floodlight system, Susan. Installed by you-know-who.'

'Exactly, Duncan. That's why I'm so bloody worried.'

'Not even a cockroach could get through.'

'Duncan! Please!'

And he'd have to crawl out of bed and investigate. He was a bit frightened himself, but not of burglars. The oldest habitation in the village had a proper ghost. He'd never seen it, but he'd been told about it. It was of a young woman who'd been burnt to death in a fire in the early nineteenth century. The house was so still, in the middle of the night. Full of old crooked corners and shadowy ends of rooms. Waiting for something. For them to get out, probably. She appeared – was supposed to appear – at the bottom of the old stone staircase that led up to the TV room and adjoining guest-room. Stark naked, long hair down to her waist, her skin all purple. How come, he'd scoff, her hair wasn't burnt? Nevertheless he'd stand on that spot and test it, half-jokily. Testing himself, really. Testing his nerves. Because if she appeared, if you saw her, it meant she had your number. It meant you were doomed. It was a warning, a warning from the other side. But he never felt anything. Nothing at all. It was disappointing, because he didn't really believe that stuff about being doomed if you saw her. One man in the nineteen twenties had seen her and then fallen out of a tree a week later, that was why. A certain Mr Wilfred Kingston. He was picking pears, up in the tree. It was all written down in black and white in *Our Lovely Village*, by Esther M. Podleigh, who'd done the sketches, too, back in the sixties. Now Duncan was in one of the sketches, as it were.

The nineteenth century is five minutes ago, to this house, he'd think. And Susan was usually asleep, anyway, by the time he crawled back to bed. She slept a lot, these days. Alice and Molly weren't a valid excuse any longer: they were at school most of the day and didn't disturb them much at night. He wondered if Susan was depressed. Depressed people slept a lot, apparently. There was a programme about it on the radio the other day. She'd get at him. Niggle. As if he was unsatisfactory.

There were little scuffles in the dim shadows of the birch clump. He knew nothing about animals; a bit more about birds through Steve Jonson. A car leaving the other side of the hall, where there was a gravel area next to the road, passed its headlights over the garden. Trees leapt up and died back into darkness. He picked his way further into the trees, getting caught a bit on suckers and thorns. Another mob passed along the track, laughing, their torches bobbing about in front of them. He could almost imagine, skulking there in the trees, the undergrowth tickling his ankles (he hoped it wasn't nettles), the resentment felt by the locals. He could almost feel it in his body. These people owned the nicest places, while the locals skulked on the council estate. These people had upgraded with the proceeds from a London-area sale, and were very pleased with themselves. He drew hard on his cigarette, feeling the damp soil creep up his legs, and realised just how niggling it must be for the local yokels, to hear these people nattering away like that, and laughing as if they owned the world. A little further up the track their voices got lower and more serious, as if they were laying into people, criticising, sniping behind their backs. That's what it sounded like, anyway.

He didn't know why he was picking his way deeper into the clump of birch, the pale trunks catching whatever light came from the night. It had something to do with the fact that he was knackered, that he'd been with over-excited people all day, that this had followed hard on a very stiff week during which Susan had gone all tearful on him when he'd come back from a brief pint in The Granary – alone – on Thursday evening. This was probably why he was venturing now into the darkness of the trees, catching his feet on roots and undergrowth that might as well have been a bottomless lake, they were so black, when he should have been socialising in the hall, winding up the charity concert.

'You never think about me,' she'd wailed. '*I* never even think about me.'

Just because he'd slipped out for a pint or two.

He stood there, trying to adjust his eyes to the blackness under the trees, and thought what a bloody thin cover it really was for a sales pitch, Nolan's charity concert. They might as well have had a banner at the back of the stage, with *SURELOCK SECURITY SYSTEMS* on it. Waitrose had done this for the Netherford Jazz Festival he and Susan had gone along to last year; a lot of blokes drinking beer and jabbering at the back of the tent, where the bar was, acres of empty grass covered in plastic cups and discarded fish-and-chips paper, and these poor bods playing John Coltrane in front of a huge banner saying *WAITROSE WORKS FOR YOU*, or some such. He'd actually laughed: it was a joke. Waitrose'd paid for the marquee, or a bit of it, and got the right to upstage John Coltrane. In fact, the Waitrose symbol was everywhere, you couldn't move without being reminded that this was not a jazz festival but an advertising jamboree. What hurt most was that he and Nolan had made a bid for site security, and Waitrose had provided their own. Local business done in yet again by faceless giant. Duncan was glad when he'd heard through the grapevine that a fifties Selmer saxophone had been nicked and a teenage girl molested during the Big Band jam session: a few Surelock CCTV cameras about and that would not have happened.

He was thinking about work again: blinking in near-total blindness in a nighttime wood, with his hand on a tree trunk, and he was getting stressed out about work. He couldn't help it. This was what Susan failed to understand: if she'd only get a job, even a part-time one, it would be a lot easier. He couldn't believe he was nearly forty. This fact rushed into his head again. His hand gripped the rough birch trunk as if it was steadying him. He'd thought that by forty he'd be rich and famous: not exactly a celebrity, but a bit more famous than he was, which was totally non-famous, unknown, a nobody. His house was quite famous, at least in the village and to local history nutters. Once, in the early days, they'd had a delegation from Reading University – a lot of weirdos in anoraks working on a project to do with the changing role of the blacksmith in the history of rural labour relations. Microhistory, someone called it. 'Site-definite'. They picked their way over the house and scratched around a bit where the actual forge was and hoped nothing was going to be done to that room. It had been the arty woman's studio, cobwebs everywhere on the crumbly brick and freezing in winter.

'The beams are rotten,' Duncan said. 'It's all got to come out and then we're putting in central heating and a damp course. It's going to be the sitting room.'

'Are you sure they're rotten?' the professor had said.

'Yes. A screwdriver goes straight in. Knife through butter.'

'What's keeping up the roof, then?'

'The cobwebs, probably.'

They'd actually made him feel defensive. They went on about specialists pumping the beams with silicon or something to avoid having them replaced. He'd had it costed and of course it was out of the question, but he'd felt guilty when the beams had been pulled out. He might have acquired the biggest antique in the village, but it wasn't Windsor Castle. It certainly wasn't. And Susan wasn't Her Royal Highness, though she sometimes acted like it. She'd bought plum velvet curtains for the lounge, to go with the plum velvet lounge suite, and hung a small chandelier above the dining-room table.

The trouble with the house, he thought, was that it was this overwhelming style statement, and they just weren't up to it. It was the cider making him think this. They weren't up to it. In fact, they were faking it. Cider was lethal, because it was sweet and you didn't realise it rotted the cells. Sweetness was often lethal. Sugar. He almost had a carnal passion for Snickers bars. They just weren't up to it.

Something was rustling in the wood. He turned and crashed his way out of the trees, hurting his ankle on something sharp. Perhaps that's why he'd gone for the cider, he reflected, bent over and rubbing his ankle near the back door. He was wheezing again, just with the effort of bending over, his belly getting in the way, compressed against his belt buckle. The back door opened and it was – God – it was Nolan, standing there like a king in a blaze of light. He had a bucket in his hands and he was looking at it and then he threw its contents over the grass, lifting his head as Duncan jumped out of the way of the shiny arc of dirty water. It hit his shoes, though. Soaked his turn-ups.

'Bloody hell,' Duncan cried out. 'You nearly missed!'

They both had a laugh about it. Everyone else had gone home, in fact. They went into the kitchen and Nolan leafed through the labels on the keys: *Men's Toilet, Women's Toilet, Main Door, Side Door, Outside Shed, Walk-In Cupboard, Kitchen*. The keys were solid and heavy on the thick ring, the ink on the yellowing labels so faint Nolan had to hold up each one to read it in the best light.

'I keep digging keys up in the garden,' Duncan said.

'It's a joke,' Nolan remarked. 'This one must be the broom cupboard.'

It didn't have a label. Nolan picked up the big bunch of keys and rattled it at his hip.

'C'mon, Jolly, visiting time's over.'

'I'm complaining to the director about that water torture,' Duncan joked, in a whiny voice. He was a bit annoyed that Nolan hadn't made more of a fuss over the wetting.

'I am the fucking director,' Nolan said.

'Director, my feet are wet. I've been physically abused.'

Nolan was locking up the broom cupboard.

'I can't help a man who can't piss straight,' he said.

'Where were you, anyway?' Duncan asked. He felt less tired, now everyone had gone. The kitchen smelt of the kitchen at the back of the doctor's where his mother had worked as a receptionist when he was a kid: Vim and dish-cloths and a sweetish, woody smell. He liked it.

'Driving Mrs Parkinson and her ninety-one-year-old sister home.'

'That was nice of you.'

'I sold them a floodlight, a timer and a couple of dead bolts.'

'Seriously?'

Nolan snorted.

'You hard bastard,' was all he said.

Nolan threw the keys on the table and fished out from his leather bag a small flat bottle of cognac.

'One for the road,' he said. 'And to drown our sorrows. David Wilkes has not the means to install so much as a trip wire. He's getting a fucking dog, the clever bastard. He said it'll double as a pet for the poor dying kids. The manager's golden rule: avoid duplication of effort. We've just made a great effort for nothing, Duncan, let alone duplicated it.'

'And fire? I got him white about the gills on the fire angle.'

'Not white enough. Anyway, it turns out they did the once-over a few years back, before his time, and the inspectors are happy.'

'He never told me that.'

'He'd never noticed that the doors were a bit heavy and had bars on. People go through life with their eyes closed, Duncan.'

They drank the cognac out of the stubby hall glasses, the others being dried and packed away in the hire people's boxes. The hall had no stem glasses at all, as if the only beverages it knew were tea, coffee or lemonade. They kept on drinking, talking over the concert and David Wilkes and strategies and future plans and other more personal matters. It was a nice place to talk, the kitchen. That thug Keith Glover hadn't touched it, though the Hall Committee had been discussing its renovation for years. Through the open door the main room spread behind them, empty but still throbbing a bit. There were only the safety lights on, casting a reddish glow over the spotless floor, and Duncan found it amazing that anything had happened there at all that night, even though there was a pleasant lingering smell of perfume and drink and tobacco. He'd think this about a lot of things. Perhaps nothing had happened, and he was in some other dimension. The cognac allowed his thoughts to flow into deeper areas: philosophical, he was getting. It was like that book Susan had got him. But I'm just thick, he decided. An overweight wheezing thickhead.

'It's the pressure,' Nolan was saying. 'It shouldn't do it to one.'

'Life slips past. You're never quite sure—'

'My uncle shot himself,' Nolan interrupted. 'For example. With my father's gun.'

'IRA?' asked Duncan, without really meaning to.

'With respect, you've no right to jump to that conclusion.'

'My brain's in neutral.' Duncan smirked, pulling hard on

his cigarette. 'Deadhead. Deadheading the roses, Susan's been, all week. We have so many shrubs. So much shrubbery.'

Nolan nodded. His big face was flushed red, his pale-ginger sideburns fluffy where he'd been scratching them, his bald patch shining with sweat. Susan reckoned he was handsome, like an old film star. Charlton Heston or someone. Duncan couldn't see this: a farmer's face, that's what he saw.

'That was pressure,' Nolan went on. He rubbed at a mark on the old oilcloth that covered the wooden table; it was an antique cigarette-burn, but Duncan didn't want to tell him. 'That was certainly it. The farm. No money. Disease. You've got to lengthen your vista,' he added, looking up at Duncan suddenly, his eyes sharp.

'Me? Specifically?'

'Tell me about yourself, for once, my friend.'

'Not now,' Duncan said, with a little scoffing noise.

'Exactly what I mean,' said Nolan, pointing at him.

Then he emptied his glass. He recharged it. There was something very pale about him, now, under the strip light.

'Andrea,' Nolan said. But didn't say any more. Duncan served himself, apologetically. Then Nolan said: 'Risk. You calculate the degree of risk, then back off or go forward. D'you know what that girl really does?'

'What girl?'

'The harpist. I mean the cellist. The star of the evening.'

'I thought she was just that. A cellist.'

Nolan shook his head.

'A paramedic.'

Duncan was gazing at the Vim label directly in his sight-line, next to the sink. On the wall next to the Vim was a handwritten notice, in faded red italics: *Please check water urn on ★ and not o!! This is very important!!* The drawing-pins were rusted. Everything's important, he thought. Those drawing-pins were shiny and new, once. The person who wrote that notice is dead, most likely dead.

Sutton Dewey is the centre of the world.

'What d'you think on that, then, Duncan?'

'I'd better have an accident, quick.'

'She's giving it all up, y'know, the cello and that. This was probably her final concert. To be a paramedic. Nice looking, I thought. I think I'll have a heart attack just for her. Kiss of life.'

'You know that fire over in Conholt, the pub there? I know a bloke, a fireman, he had to work around the kids trying to get out of the window, sort of stuck to the window they were, their bodies, completely calcinated or whatever the word is. Black.'

Feral. That's it. A feral cat.

'Purple,' said Nolan.

'Had to work around them, not touch them. Like Pompeii. Those three kids in Conholt.'

'Purple. They call them purples, firemen do. Code for a stiff. Over the walkie-talkie and whatnot.'

Duncan thought about this. Purples. *A purple at Number 13, over.* It gave him some nasty images. That's why the ghost at his place was said to be purple. He'd thought it was all imagination.

'I think it's fucking heroic,' said Nolan. 'To give up music for that.'

We've got three purples at the Old Forge, Sutton Dewey. Two kids and a female. Over.

'Handling stiffs,' said Duncan, wonderingly. 'All cold and horrible.'

'My stiff's not cold and horrible,' said Nolan, tapping the table. But both knew it wasn't very funny.

They talked a bit about the music, the Beethoven and the Schubert. Like pretentious gits on the radio. Duncan mentioned the andante and Nolan agreed as if he hadn't spotted that Duncan didn't have a clue what an andante was. Everything could just go, everything one had built up and loved to pieces during one's whole lifetime. Train crash, for instance. Some git in his Mazda on the level crossing. What could you do about that? Put a security system in, that's what. Perhaps Nolan should organise a train crash next.

'She was very attractive, anyway,' said Duncan. He saw a small, tight, bare arse all of a sudden, knew that Susan would be asleep, wished he could have the cello girl for breakfast, lunch and dinner. Wished he could be her victim. She'd be smashing in paramedic's uniform, without a pair of knickers underneath. 'Nice fingers. Very slender.'

The hall seemed to be theirs for ever. The keys lay fanned out on the table, waiting for orders: they could have been Roman, they were so big and old. I could have taken her on this table, Duncan thought. Engineered it somehow. A bit of gallantry never comes amiss.

'We don't know anything about anyone,' Nolan said, wiping his hand across his mouth. 'Come to that.'

Duncan refused a lift – partly because he knew, even in his own woozy state, that Nolan was not really up to driving. Not that he expected Nolan to crash in the few hundred yards to the house, with Nolan's own home being only half a mile further on, but a little voice told him to walk. He took heed of little voices, now and again: sometimes they were pretend voices, telling him to fly away home, your house is all burnt, your children are gone – but he only knew they were fake after he'd rushed back and found the house and family intact. They'd had difficulties locking the main door of the hall – Nolan was supposed to have repaired it, but the winter's damp had swollen the wood again and the dead bolt wouldn't go home at the top and they were reasonably pissed. All the heaters had been stolen a couple of years back, and the bolt really had to go home. That would be a great advertisement for Surelock Security Systems, Nolan kept saying, if the director couldn't even bloody well lock up the Community Hall properly and there was a break-in. It made Duncan want to laugh. Then they both started laughing, wiggling the handle for all they were worth, pressing themselves against the door. The cool, damp night all around them. The dim trees with their peeling trunks. The cognac was slipping deeper into Duncan's head, taking him by stealth. His hand brushed Nolan's knuckles and they were cold, but his own hands were burning. Duncan studied the poster on the door, finding great import in the fact that it was over, the concert, that the event printed in front of his eyes, with its precise time – *8pm, 23rd October, 2002* – was over, finito, kaput. All things must pass, he thought. Look at that. Won't you look at that. That's time passing, that is.

Nolan ripped the poster off the door and booted it away.

They gave up on the drawing-pins. Who the hell can ever get drawing-pins out of solid wood with their nails, even sober? You need a bloody chisel, Nolan laughed. The car dug gouges out of the verge before it shot away. He may well kill himself, in fact, Duncan thought – but in a resigned, non-worried way.

At the window of the car Nolan had said, his face lit up by the dash lights, all electronic, computerised gizmos: 'Plan X, methinks, pardner.'

'What? On the hospice?'

'I'll have a word with Sheena in the morning. Think of it as a casualty that requires urgent treatment. A paramedic, Duncan, not a fucking cellist.'

Duncan was tapping the roof of the car, ready to express his reservations, when Nolan had shot away, almost taking his partner's toes with him. Duncan was left with his hand in the air, like a prime-time jerk. He needed to get back to the house.

He walked unsteadily down the rough track that was the shortcut that was in the olden days the main street of Sutton Dewey. A survey for the millennium had counted forty-two houses and a pub in Sutton Dewey, not counting the new estate. Sutton Dewey went back to the Domesday Book. It was so tiny no one had noticed it going on and on. He might well die in Sutton Dewey. The security light in the newish house to his right was activated by his passing and bathed him in a blaze of white. It was precisely as if someone had noted him and was now watching what he'd do. That was the mistaken impression it was supposed to give. The Singing Kettle. What kind of a fuckwit name was that, carved into varnished wood? The Old Forge was an excellent name, wrought in iron, solid and simple. But the house wasn't them at all. Even the sloping floors were getting to him. Let alone the low beams. They had paid too much, stretched them-selves, for something that wasn't them. The whole place had needed rewiring and damp-proofing and when they'd removed the ivy, the chimney came with it. He felt less and less interesting each day that passed. Or maybe that was age. Or not being Irish.

He walked on in the new white world of the light, trying to look unsuspicious and steady. He hadn't installed that light. The owner – an accountant with Shell, whose name was currently escaping him – had bought it elsewhere and installed it himself on a ladder. Duncan remembered him on the ladder in his golfing hat, looking like Mr Professional. 'All you have to do is use your loaf,' he'd shouted down, when Duncan had expressed his doubt that something so delicate could be done by an amateur. Duncan now stumbled and almost fell forward onto his face, into the black of his own shadow. The trouble with security lights is that they cast this very black shadow in which bottomless pits might lurk. The light clicked off and his eyes adjusted. He relieved himself into the tangle of the bank, hoping no one would come and then not caring a toss, the piss hissing into the dark tangle of weeds. He was sure his piss didn't shoot out as fast as it did. He could've knocked a tin can off a post with the pressure of it, a few years back. Plan X on the hospice struck him as a step too far. A small step for a man, a huge step for mankind. Where was the moon, these days, anyway?

The kids would scream. It wasn't fair on them. They were on their last little legs.

He rounded the corner between the hedges, passing a couple of bungalows tucked into the long back garden of Jackie Coops's nice little number. His shoes couldn't get a grip on the track. The rough stones kept budging and there were deep ruts. Jackie Coops's security light was not coming on; Surelock Security Systems had installed it. They'd also installed the alarm system and the smoke detectors because the place was the National Gallery of Sutton Dewey: three family Gainsboroughs and a Reynolds, but keep it secret. It was very dark, he couldn't see why there weren't more street-lamps down here. There were loads of them down by the new prestige estate, where the lane went up to and out of the swanky iron gate. He stopped by Jackie Coops's little wooden thumb-latch version and waved his arm over it, trying to get the security light to activate itself. Something was wrong: it was supposed to activate itself in the environs of the gate.

He opened the gate and stepped in. The modest period manor – olde brick and tile, long sash windows, shiny ivy – didn't budge the other side of the white gravel. He walked slowly towards it, his feet scrunching on the gravel in spite of his best efforts to tiptoe. He thought of Susan lying in bed, waiting for him in vain these long hours, and felt free and wicked and peculiar. The security light was not coming on; there was a fault. Or she hadn't armed the system tonight. They'd put in a two-in-one sensor to cover motion and acoustic glass break for the Coops house, he was sure of that. Nothing. The alarm was, if he remembered rightly, a Brinks ninety-decibel, connected to the copshop at Netherford. Pierced you right through. Turned your brain to walnut whip in approximately five minutes of exposure. He'd better not touch the windows, either.

That was a mean sales pitch, that one.

'Cat burglars, Jackie, can cut a round hole in glass without a sound. And no flexing of air pressure, either. But the window vibrates, especially these old sash numbers.'

'Does it now?'

'And vibrations activate the alarm through this little contact, Jackie.'

'I know all about vibrations, Duncan. I'm feeling them right now, looking at you.'

'That may have something to do with your hand being down my trousers, Jackie. Pulping my chestnuts.'

He stood under the front porch and grinned, wishing the sales pitch *had* gone like that. Instead, it was all very well behaved and above board. He was too moral, that was the trouble.

He stared at the door, rocking slightly as the brandy took him from behind. Jackie Coops was a widow. You never knew with widows. The door had an entrance function, he remembered. Never locked on the inside.

He ought really to warn Jackie Coops, sleeping unawares in her big house in her big feather bed in her silken negligée. Still a great figure on her. Gagging for it, probably. A hand, which turned out to be his, made to lift the big brass knocker, his heart thumping in both ears.

Then the light came on and he was shielding his face. The next thing you know, it'll be all ninety decibels of brain-melting alarm.

He trotted back over the drive, like a man in stripes escaping a prison camp, with several shadows spiralling in front of him. The gravel more than scrunched – it screamed, it howled, he was a berk. Either the light was on a delayed timer or it was faulty. Or maybe the infra-red beam had been repositioned by a squirrel or by the wind. Either way, it worked.

He only slowed down halfway up the main track, feeling how thickset he was. Maybe Jackie Coops, in her skimpy negligée, had leant out of the bedroom window and spotted him. She might have been in the shower. Things happen after a Badedas bath. As a kid, he used to stare at that advert and imagine being the bloke visible through the window beyond the towel-wrapped bird – the cool dude down below in his E-type on the sweeping drive somewhere in the country-side. I want to be him when I grow up, he'd thought.

He was somewhat out of breath. Very much out of condi-tion. In Jackie Coops's sitting room, he remembered, was a glass table with Victorian playing cards under the glass, showing a straight flush.

Just as well the light had come on. He would not have been responsible for his actions. He would have placed his hands on her melons and left them there for days.

Nolan's up on the verge this time. You can't do it to a kid's hospice.

He half expected his house to have a blue light flashing over it, like in a film, but it was dark. His house was bloody beautiful. Nolan called it 'The Fab Four', because the thatch on the four dormers was like a Beatles haircut, but Nolan was jealous. You can't imitate an antique house. Duncan walked towards the knotty front door, expecting the outdoor light to beam him up as usual, but there was nothing. The GX-35 Combo Sensor here and at Jackie Coops's was meant to detect any movement of objects with a temperature close to that of the human body, so either he was dreaming he was moving or his body temperature had plummeted. Or he wasn't an object.

He stood inside his house, in the darkness of the sitting room, not putting on the lights, wondering why the place no longer ever smelt of beams and woodsmoke, of genuinely old things. Susan liked her air freshener. She must have gone to bed, was probably as fast asleep as the kids. She'd not armed the system, foolishly, so he wasn't dead, he wasn't a ghost. She would be narked with him for not getting back sooner, come the morning. He was almost swaying, more from tiredness than drink. The motion sensors up in the corners of the low-beamed sitting-room ceiling were detecting him, their red lights coming on every time he moved. He was definitely alive.

He stood very still, seeing how slowly he could move his arm before the sensors' little red lights came on. It was hard, because he was pissed. It was a challenge. If a cat burglar moved slowly and steadily enough, frame by frame as it were, he could get away with it. It would take about twenty minutes to cross the room, in very slow motion, but he could do it. He couldn't keep his balance on one foot without swaying, so he slid over the carpet step by step. The speed of a minute hand. It was a laugh. Like crossing over very thin ice.

He was doing very well now, heading for the corner near the old stone stairs up to the TV room. So far, so good: undetected. No sudden movements. No cracks in the ice. He was trying not to giggle, sliding his feet inch by inch over the carpet. Or shiver, because the air was very cold. He'd never known it quite so cold, in fact.

Then, quite unfairly, the lights started flashing on the motion sensors. He was not moving, but the motion sensors were flashing, on for a while then off, irregularly. The hair was standing up on the back of his neck, the only bit of him stirring. He didn't turn round, he stayed extremely still, his hands by his sides. The red lights in the motion sensors were coming on and going off, exactly as if someone was walking about in the room.

He turned round. There was no one. He turned back and froze again, the room swaying slightly. The sensors must be dicky, though they seemed very certain about it. On. Off. Pause. On.

Swivelling only his eyeballs, he glanced towards the foot of the stairs, where the burnt girl was supposed to appear, purple and naked. Nothing, as usual.

Anyway, he thought (with some relief), she would be undetectable. Her temperature would be nowhere near that of the human body. No way. Nowhere near.

BRIGHT-GREEN TRAINERS

The train groaned as if from some internal pain. Hugo adjusted himself in the seat. He saw flocks of birds rise from the marshes and out of his life as the window took one view away from another. It was, he thought, like a shuffled pack of cards. Life is like this, too; he might have been born a hundred years before he was actually born and fallen in love with Dorothea Tremlett, on whose poetry his dissertation was building itself inch by inch. She was very beautiful in the photographs and her long Edwardian dresses suited her as modern dress might not. He had absorbed the few surviving photographs and could now revive them in his head one by one. He closed his eyes and pictured her. She was in front of shrubs and a low brick wall and he tried to make her lovely profile move round to face him, but her eyes were bloodshot and she had a deathly, white-faced grin. He opened his own eyes and wiped the misted-up glass of the carriage window. He was alone in the carriage.

Much later, when the train eventually pulled into the station at which Hugo had to alight, he woke from a deep and troubled sleep in which flocks of birds were diving one by one onto a corpse. He manhandled his baggage through the narrow carriage door and only just made it onto the platform before the guard's whistle blew for the off and the last door banged shut.

He found a hotel in the village and wandered about, admiring the clapboard houses and the air of brushed cleanliness. Dorothea Tremlett had stayed in Denmark for several

weeks and had spent five days in Harboor. This little spit of
West Jutland had an astonishing light, he decided. Dorothea
had also said that it was astonishing and he wondered if he
was here to confirm or deny, or discover something that she
had not discovered. He stood on the long sandy beach backed
by dunes and let the wind comb his hair back from his large
brow, imagining her doing the same, her dress flapping out
behind her and the parasol ungainly in its awkwardness.

Would she have worn gloves? Would she have known
him as she came towards him on this otherwise empty
beach that stretched out either side under its enormous
sky? Would she have known him for what he was? Would
she have been frightened of his knowledge of her, or
instantly fallen for his intimacy with her private, unpub-
lished verses, her secret letters, her journal? He walked up
and down, covering several miles before the utter emptiness and the continuous salty wind off the North Sea, whose
waves were alternately grey and green as the sun scudded
in and out behind white clouds, tired him and had him
clamouring for a bite to eat.

He ate herring smoked as of old in a low cottage white-
washed like the cottages of small harbour villages in Cornwall
or Brittany. There were tourists speaking in German and
Dutch. He wondered whether there was a lovely place on
earth where, as in Dorothea's day, not a single traveller went
to in their sunglasses and gaudy clothes. He particularly disap-
proved of the cyclists, seeing their bright Lycra apparel as an
affront to the sober air of the village, abandoned by the
busy world on its sandy spit. His own clothes were sober,
deliberately old-fashioned. He bought most of them in
Oxfam, seeking out the sturdy stuff of fifty years ago: tweed
jackets, herringbone coats, ties and cravats. He had so little
money, he was a poor scholar. This was what he said to Julia,
with whom he reckoned he was in love, when she got at
him about his clothes. Really, though, he liked to look old-
fashioned. He had a horror of the present, in some ways.

The lurid shallowness, the noise. That metallic, blinding light off cars.

He looked down at his shoes. They were dark and heavy, fit for a funeral. They had belonged to his father, were almost new when his father died. They felt even heavier here – not the thing for the beach, for Denmark's bright casualness. But something about them reassured him. He had always needed to feel reassured.

His hotel was an ugly redbrick building set a little outside the village in its own garden, but the guest houses in the pastel-coloured fishermen's cottages had long been taken, he was told. He had imagined turning up and being ushered into some old withered lady's back room with tarred floorboards and heavy pine furniture and a smoky peat fire, as if nothing had moved on since Dorothea's time. But everything did move on, unfortunately. He so wished Julia had been able to come. And then he was glad she hadn't. With Julia about, he would not have been able to concentrate on Dorothea.

The hotel turned out to be bright and cheerful. He was offered beer and pork chops off the barbecue and appreciated the solar panels set into the roof, yet this did not move him and he was here to be moved. An anti-nuclear poster dominated the hall, and there were talks advertised that looked ecologically minded, with exclamation marks after the Danish titles.

Dorothea had described the sober, sad darkness of the people, the spiritual depths of loneliness and isolation somewhere so poor that the thatched roofs were patched in places with old pots and pans hammered flat. None of the houses was thatched, Hugo noticed. The people here were well off, large cars cruised about the streets, including the inevitable 4x4s with their mastiff jaws that Hugo particularly reviled for their vulgarity and arrogance. The children were immaculately if sportily dressed, glowing with health.

A large clean supermarket blasted him with its bracing air that was nevertheless different from the air off the sea on the beach; it spoke of sterile things, chilled products, the morgue of capital and profit. He felt quite depressed, wandering up and down the aisles in a search for little luxuries to keep him going at his work in the hotel room, and scarcely chuckled to himself when he saw that a certain brand of bubble gum beside the cash desk was called *Zit*.

He sat at the bedside table in the room and did his best to work, his knees awkwardly set to one side. There was no proper table in the room, as if guests no longer needed a table to write their letters on. No one wrote letters any more, he realised. He was the only person he knew without the Internet, and he wrote with his grandfather's plump, solid pen. His great-grandfather had been killed in the trenches, like Dorothea's nephew. His great-grandfather's mother had refused to eat, after that, because (she explained) how could she eat when her son was not eating? She had wasted away and died. All this must have affected his grandfather deeply, and so perhaps his father, too, long after. Everything leaves its bruise.

He wondered why he was here, what good it might do either to him or to the world. His dissertation was a passport to a higher degree set like a gilded crown upon a mountaintop, from which he might climb down into the valleys of the real world, but passports and crowns were no part of Dorothea's life, for she abhorred all outward badges of success and spent her short life, its thin currency, on verse.

Was it good verse?

Hugo's supervisor had warned him that he might grow disappointed with it after a while, striking endless shallows in a way one never did with Emily Dickinson, whose simplicity yawned to great depths in which one might fight for air and light. Dorothea Tremlett shared many characteristics with Emily Dickinson, his supervisor had intoned, save one: that of profound despair. Tremlett is too contented with her lot, he had said, lighting his cigarette and smiling. And she was not, like Emily Dickinson or Emily Brontë, an inveterate masturbator. This had made Hugo blush. He'd had no idea. It affected him like fall-out, like radiation from some toxic source.

He walked the next day after breakfast. He had never seen land so flat, so enormous. The sea gnawed at the spit either side and he wondered if it might last another hundred years. There were bright fields of mustard or rape and sallow fields of wheat and barley. Trees hugged the farms like a fat wall but otherwise the wind struck nothing on its eastward course. There was the odd bright sail on the inland sea known as Limfjorden and the wind whipped corrugations of foam across its breadth.

He removed his shoes and socks and paddled in the sea, watching wetsuited surfers plunge into breakers whose height was no doubt exaggerated by the general flatness. The sight of these hearty surfers, gleaming like seals, did him no good at all and he again felt a pang of despair in relation to his own work. The terrible word 'cissy' leapt at him from some schoolboy hoard and he sighed heavily, turning on his heel and starting to run in his bare feet, leaving his shoes and socks where they were.

He ran and ran across the shallowest part of the sea, the part that stretches over the sand like molten glass only to retreat with dizzying speed and then to brim up again over itself, sparring with itself, swirling with clusters of bubbles and foam in some elaborate attempt at pattern and meaning. The edge of the sea, the very edge, is always white, Hugo noticed. Effort fluffs up foam. The lace of the dance is very fine. The beautiful lace that finely dances where the herring dies in its throes, the deadly roe of continuance and fate. Lines from Tremlett's one poem concerning her stay in Denmark ran through his mind in strange time with the beat of his feet as they smacked through the glassy water.

He was not fit and the effort had him feeling sick and exhausted. He clambered up the low dunes and lay on the top amongst the marram grass, which was sharp against his face and hands. It was almost hot, but the sun was fitful and the wind chilled him. I am neither warm nor cool, nor do the birds feel chill; we are flung as the foam is flung upon the weather and the wind of ill.

This is awful, Hugo thought to himself: I am depriving my soul in some way.

Yet he knew that if he were to sit up and see, as in a dream, Dorothea standing in her long cream dress below him on the Jutland beach, he would shout out her lines to her and probably run down and fling himself upon her loveliness. He liked the idea of this, and turned it over in his mind, conjuring it from the empty sand of the beach below him, changing the angle of his viewpoint so that the extraordinary scene loomed up very close, his fingers searching for the ribbons and the cloth buttons at the poet's throat, his mouth gnawing at her neck, the breasts appearing through the rent bodice like two treasures he had travelled for years to touch and admire.

He shook his head suddenly and rose. It was disgusting, he thought. I am disgusting.

He explained to himself, buffeted by the wind off the sea as he stood upon the heights of the low scruffy dunes, that it was natural to hate as much as love the subject of one's dissertation.

He would study art and become a painter, he decided, gazing upon the complexity of light and colour that the sky had ushered from the moving surface of the water below and beyond. He would buy a hat with a wide brim, like Augustus John, and paint real pictures as opposed to the rubbish he'd seen on a visit to Tate Modern with Julia, who loved all that childish fakery.

He walked back to his shoes only to find them gone from the place he had imagined them to have been. He could not identify any salient point around him and walked further, judging the distance as too long. The tide had risen and had taken his shoes. His father's shoes.

He laughed, without meaning to. Denmark was a place one could walk in bare feet and not be noticed. Had Dorothea felt the wet touch of the sand on her toes, the swirl of the water graze her ankles? A sober place, where the women are muffled in black crinoline as if the whole coast is in mourning for the lost gods of the fishermen, the lost souls themselves swallowed by the deadly sea and its cold. Letter to Frank Garnett, 1898. The use of the word deadly. Make connections. Spin the web until the fly is caught.

He missed his father. But he did not miss the shoes.

He lay awake that night, wondering if he should indeed become a painter. He imagined himself with a wife and children, a wife vaguely chestnut-haired (not like Julia), and children vaguely dark, running about a daisy-spattered lawn vaguely in the country.

Perhaps he should run an art shop, selling expensive, top-quality oils and brushes and so forth, for the discerning.

The room's heating system seemed to be unseasonably on, ticking quietly in the pipes, the sunlight beating on the glass in the day and running through the pipes into the radiator at night. The window was open and he drew the curtains and leant right out. The moon was almost full. He thought he could hear the sea crashing and booming, but it might have been the wind in the straggly Scotch pines fringing the garden.

He had evidently been born a lifetime too late.

He would never own a car or a television or a computer, although he was conscious how hollow youth's vows are. He wondered if he should try to look up Julia when he got back. She wasn't chestnut, and not as lovely as Dorothea, but that didn't matter. She worked for a foreign publishing house and was, much to his regret, Australian.

He would run to her in his new shoes.

They sat by the door, just there. They were the kind of shoes he would never have bought, in normal circumstances: a pair of fat trainers, bright green, with a silver flash and clashing red laces. They were the only pair of shoes that fitted him in the whole of Harboor. They made him feel odd, but not altogether unpleasantly so. It was preferable to walking about barefoot.

Who was it said about someone that they were very alive from the feet down? Max Beerbohm, probably.

He would run to Julia in his trainers the colour of artificial grass. He would astonish her. Sometimes it was the only way.

The one and only way, Hugo thought, chuckling at himself in the night breeze and in the radiant moon.

THE CONCERT INTERVAL

Rob had had no idea that Madge was at the concert until he saw her in the green room. He was holding his stick caddy, which she'd call his handbag. He didn't like to leave his sticks on the stage, not since Toronto when he'd got back from the interval to find the caddy stolen. He'd left it tucked under one of the tymps' cross-stands, so that to pull it out you'd have to be careful not to send the drum rolling over the stage. He'd all but broken down in tears, bereft of his tymp sticks, but then someone had fished out some xylophone sticks from a cupboard and he'd managed to soften the plastic heads with band-aid and lint from the First Aid box. His solo (it was the *Messiah* that time, too) had sounded like a kid on a primary school kettledrum. Just before the final aria, the band-aid came unstuck and the lint flew off onto his beard. It was the worst moment of his life.

He'd not yet married Madge, back then.

She was with Tonia and Sophie, old school friends of hers he'd never liked. The green room was already crowded but they'd found places at one of the long Formica tables. They must have been sitting in the seats very close to the exit, and been one of the first lot down. As he made his way towards them, pretending to be pleased, Rob thought he heard the second bassoonist, Naomi Wallis, saying rude things about his pitch. Naomi Wallis was quite capable of it, especially talking as she was to first viola – the spitting image of Sean Penn. Rob couldn't picture Sean Penn, in fact, but that was what the rest of the orchestra maintained. It was a game they all played on long coach journeys between venues: finding their twins in the world of the famous. Because of his beard, Rob's twin was Rolf Harris. Rolf Harris back in the sixties, he hoped. It could have been worse: second viola's was Myra Hindley. And second viola was a bloke.

'Surprise surprise,' said Madge, as Rob took the chair they'd saved for him.

'I'm the one who's supposed to say that,' said Rob. 'I thought you were eating at Julia's.'

'Julia's got the flu. Anyway, we wanted to hear ourselves cough on Radio Three.'

'Famous for a second,' said Sophie. 'You look quite nice in black tie, Rob.'

'Thank you, Sophie.'

The other two giggled, of course. They always ganged up on him, these three, that was the trouble. It started subtly, and then got obvious. Madge was thirty-eight, and yet still went puerile in the company of her old school friends. She never did this with anyone else. He asked if they'd used the comps.

'Of course. You don't think we'd *pay* to hear Rob Barlow on drums, do you?'

'Thank you for that one, my love.'

'I thought he did it very well,' said Tonia. '*I* couldn't do it.'

'It would be a bit odd if you could,' said Rob, already irritated. 'I've had years and years of training and practice.'

In fact, he'd only played about a minute before the interval. That was Handel's doing, not his.

'But you just bang 'em,' said Sophie.

'Bang them?'

'Your drums. It can't be that hard to learn.'

'You have to know *when* to bang 'em,' Madge pointed out, raising her painted eyebrows. This feature was a recent thing, to do with her age: she'd plucked each eyebrow and replaced it with a thin line of purple. Rob thought it made her look like Lady Macbeth.

The word 'bang' was gathering colour to it. Rob tried to change the subject.

'Are you interested in attacking the bar? We've got about fifteen minutes.'

'We were hoping for some drinks down here,' Madge said.

'You must be joking.'

'Don't you get free drinks and fancy grub?' asked Tonia, surprised.

Rob pointed out the thermos flasks and plastic sandwich boxes and miniature fruit juice cartons appearing the length of the table.

'It's DIY, for an orchestra. Otherwise it's head down at the bar, with General Public. Even at Christmas.'

Sonia nudged Madge. 'Isn't that the gorgeous hunk who was singing solo?'

Rob looked. It was Silvio Rocchetti, the baritone. He was laughing, as usual, showing large white teeth, his slick black locks bouncing just above his collar. His sung English was a lot better than his spoken, but not perfect enough to convince the orchestra that he had been chosen to do this Handel for any other reason than to draw the crowd. He'd appeared on the empty stage while Rob was tuning up a couple of hours before the concert, and had started on this long and tedious anecdote about the time he'd had a go on Keith Moon's drum-kit in Rome some twenty years back. Rob was adjusting the tuning screws and tapping the calfskin with the hard, 33-mill wood-headed stick, straining his ears through the deep, broken English to get the perfect pitch, the precise colour, bending his head towards the drum like a doctor listening for a heartbeat, the tips of his fingers feeling the vibrations on the membrane, the correct frequencies growing like ripples in a bowl of water until they lapped inside him and he knew it was done.

Rocchetti had gone on talking while Rob was strapping

the protectors onto the heads and pulling the leatherette covers over the two drums, having given the copper on the bowls a final polish, the church interior curved behind his distorted face and Rocchetti converted into a fat dwarf. Rocchetti's stories were famous, the man was a celebrity, he slept with every soprano in sight – but Rob was bored. He was bored by Rocchetti's stories, and yet they made him feel boring and inadequate in turn. They made him feel like a little bearded tympanist who looked like Rolf Harris – when in his heart of hearts, somewhere in the terrific depth and resonance of his soul, he knew he was something else much greater and more startling.

And now the girls – his wife and her two old school chums from Letchworth High – were ogling Rocchetti, mentally goosing him. It made Rob feel sick. He was in a sensitive state, for some reason. The first half of their *Messiah* had not gone terribly well – you could tell this from the way the woodwind bods were now fiddling with their reeds and looking tense. A young, fresh-faced second oboist had opened her case next to him and there again was that smell of pad grease, cork and humid velvet that always conjured up those miserable childhood hours struggling with the flute, his mother standing over him and yelling until the day he fell in love with the tympani during a concert at the Albert Hall.

He was thirsty. He could've sunk a pint, but instead he got out his camper's bottle and took a swig of its lime cordial.

'It's very squashed in here,' said Sophie.

'You should try some other venues,' said Rob. 'Smith Square, for instance.'

'What's Smith Square, when it's at home?'

'St John's Smith Square. The green room's the crypt, it smells of toilets and cooking from the restaurant and it's minuscule. Then to get on stage you have to go up this narrow spiral staircase into the back of the church and walk along right in front of the audience. We all hate this, being musicians. It's OK for experimental actors, I suppose.'

'Oh, you're *so* sensitive,' mocked Tonia, flapping a hand.

She was a high-dependency nurse in Basingstoke, and this always made Rob feel futile. He scratched his beard and ignored her. It was hot and stuffy and the oboes were shrieking in little spurts and everyone was talking too loudly. Rob wanted to be anywhere but here. He was happiest in a big, empty concert hall with a decent acoustic, a chamois-headed stick in each hand, beating out his beautiful sounds. He was happiest when no one was listening but the gods.

His wife was saying hello to Frank Taylor, the principal trumpet. Frank had been in the orchestra even longer than Rob, and Rob had once reckoned that Frank Taylor fancied Madge and vice-versa. He'd even played with the idea that Frank and Madge had had an affair. Rob didn't like Frank Taylor, but was obliged to pretend he did. Now Frank was settling down next to him, in the chair vacated by the oboist. Frank's lips were distorted by forty years of trumpet-playing into a moue, which made him look camp.

'Rob,' he said, winking at the girls, 'has the nicest pair of baroque bowls this side of Watford.'

'Thank you, Frank. I think my wife knows that already.'

'I'm not sure I do, actually,' said Madge, pulling a knowing face.

Rob caught her glance and, for a split-second, saw the ferocity in it. This was unpleasant; this was getting serious. He could do without this in the middle of a big concert, in the middle of the glory of the greatest oratorio in the world.

'I thought little men were the best in bed,' said Frank, patting Rob on the back.

'Little men and fat trumpeters,' Rob smiled, keeping it light, though his heart was pummelling against his throat.

'I did used to wonder,' said Sophie, grinning, her drink problem wafting across the table.

'Wonder what?' asked Madge.

'About you and Rob, the height difference and that.'

Tonia gave a dirty chuckle. Rob shook his head as if he found it all rather sad, which in fact he did. He couldn't ever take on Madge and her two chums from school; together they formed an invincible trio of mockery. His wife sort of crossed to the other side each time and he just had to wait until she was back with him again. It was a matter of sitting it out. She always did come back. It was very hot and crowded, the green room. Even the one Christmas garland looked as if it had been forgotten from last year.

'Oh, I always *sat down* for it,' he heard Madge say, or almost shout, over the hubbub, and this made all of them laugh – laughter which Rob pretended to go along with.

In fact, he was repelled. He looked at Madge across the table, there in the suffocating room crowded with faces too familiar for comfort, and felt repelled. He was repelled by her high, painted eyebrows and her sour mouth. This was his wife, and he felt repulsion. He was sure the repulsion was originating in her, in fact – that he was merely feeling the beat of her repulsion in the air in the same way that he felt the shiver of the membrane in the tips of his fingers, edging towards the precise intonation on his drums. She was repelled by him, seeing him through the eyes of her disappointed, messed-up old school friends. The blurts and squeals of the oboists and bassoonists testing their reeds, unable to relax, soaking their fine reeds in their spittle, started to send out sharp glass-like pieces in his head, scattering the depth and resonance of his inward mind, to which the sounds he made on his drums were always attuned.

'Poor old Rob, it's not fair,' said Tonia. 'Is it?'

'I couldn't care less.'

'That's it,' said Madge, with a fierce edge to her tone. 'As long as he's got his drums, he doesn't care. The drums are his children.'

The drums were to blame. One marriage, no kids. *And unto them no child was born.* Her old refrain.

'It's my job. I care about my job.'

'See how *I* care,' said Madge, producing a turkey roll from a plastic sandwich box. Rob took it with a nod. She handed out chocolate reindeers, bleeding into their wrappers. He was the only one with a turkey roll. He wasn't even hungry. The pre-sliced turkey was dry.

Frank rested his elbow on Rob's shoulder.

'The point about Rob is that he's totally bloody reliable. Without this little man, the orchestra would be bloody amazing.'

'Thank you, Frank. Your solo was terrible in the run-through, by the way.'

'O man of sorrows,' said Frank. 'One can only do one's best. The trumpet shall sound, nevertheless.'

Rob picked at his turkey roll. Frank had now started on his usual loop tape about Moscow. He'd spent three months in Moscow last year, teaching the baroque trumpet. He'd known one of the musicians in the theatre siege. He'd seen amazing things. The Russian male was an endangered species – murder, alcohol and suicide. Yet Russians were so creative! They built their own houses in the country, because the country was so enormous, there was room for everyone. Everyone had to build their own *dacha*, Frank said, with a guttural, cod-Russian accent that was infuriating. Ah yes, so creative! He had seen an experimental theatre piece in which white-gloved gestures emphasised certain themes – love, the family, death – in a ritualistic manner. It was difficult to describe. The actor wore the glove on his left hand. It had been performed in a cellar. And their music was much more emotional, if less precise. Even Handel was fuzzy but superbly emotional, played by the Russians. Passionate, that was the word. Frank was making his own gestures, impressing the girls with his tales of Moscow, his faux accent.

Rob started to feel peculiarly small and enraged. Frank was needling him, under the surface, because the orchestra's tympanist was famous for his precision. He was always precise, yes – but that didn't mean he wasn't also seeking a strong tonal colour. 'Emotion' was a totally meaningless term. It could only be transmuted through the instruments at your disposal. Anyway, Rob loved Russian cinema – at least, he had once attended a Russian film season at the South Bank years ago and been bowled over by a twenty-minute Russian film about two runaway soldiers in the last war, sheltering in a ruin with classical paintings on the shattered walls, like something from a dream.

Frank Taylor had stopped talking. He was looking at Rob. So were the girls. Frank must have asked him what he thought. Rob had crumbs in his beard.

'I like Russian shorts,' he said.

The girls – his wife and her two old school chums – glanced at each other and then started snorting into their hands, shoulders quivering and shaking, tears welling in their eyes. Frank was chortling, too. Silvio Rocchetti was looking over at them and smiling, as if he knew why they were finding Rob Barlow funny. Rob felt his deep and resonant inner mind rising up in a great swell of rage. He had part of the turkey roll in his hand. He raised his hand and hurled the bread at his wife. The bread bounced off her chest and the turkey slice flew out. People were looking, there was a kind of hush around them. The shouting, swearing voice was his own, as if he could hear only the after echo. He rose from the table and shoved his way through the musicians and singers crowding the room until he found the concert hall's fire exit door and burst out into the cool night air. He didn't have his stick caddy with him. He'd left it behind on the table in the green room. He was glad. For once, he was glad. He started walking up the road behind the hall and he kept on walking. He walked until he was in an area he didn't know, with strange houses and unknown streets. His breath showed on the damp air and he didn't have his coat, but he was exhilarated. He kept on walking, swinging his arms and walking. It was ten minutes into the second half of the *Messiah* and Rob Barlow was walking away, further and further away, exhilarated by his madness. He tore off his black bow tie and threw it from him. All his life he had been where he had to be, he had attended and been punctual and had beaten out the precise note at the precise moment at the precise pitch. The whole glorious edifice of the *Messiah* was crumbling behind him, cracking and leaning forward and falling like a building in a bomb raid. His two drums silent amidst the consternation. Silent on stage under their head protectors and leatherette covers, like two pools. His drums silent. Silent the tympani. Silent even where they sounded out in the solo, singing deeply in his mind's ear as he kept on walking through the hammering of his real heart, his membrane of ordinary flesh. Silent the tympani. Silent.

At last they would know him. At last they would know who he really was, in the roar of their consternation.

KARAOKE

He first came across William Pool in a pub.

It was a dark, sleety evening in Redditch. He had given a reading in the local bookshop. At least, he would have given a reading, but he and the poetry festival organiser and the grumpy bookshop owner had sat there until half an hour's grace had been granted and no one had turned up. There wasn't even a man in a bobble hat.

'Can't understand it,' said Gail the festival organiser, whose earrings were copper fish. 'We normally have at least thirty people.'

'It *was* advertised, was it?' said Greg.

He hadn't seen a single indication, anywhere in Redditch, that Gregory Jones and Tabitha Leary were reading tonight until he'd arrived at the bookshop, where there was a notice in the window the size of a flyer. Tabitha Leary had gone down with flu, apparently, but no one would have known that, would they? (He had been looking forward to meeting Tabitha Leary, after a glance at her jacket photo – though these were often ten years out of date.)

'It was very well advertised,' said the bookshop owner, scowling at him.

It was always the writer's fault, Greg knew that. A yellowed clipping on the wall, headlined 'Paul's Passionate for Poetry, Alright', showed the bookshop owner, youthful and grinning, in front of the window, clutching Heaney's *Station Island*.

'I'm obviously not Heaney,' said Greg.

'Oh, they'll come to anything, usually,' said Gail the festival organiser. 'They're often quite lonely people.'

'As long as there's some booze after,' muttered the bookshop owner.

'Talking of which, let's go and sink our sorrows in a pint of local ale,' said Greg, who was shamming nonchalance and good cheer.

The bookshop owner had to deal with stock and the festival organiser had another date. Her copper fish jittered along to her apology. To Greg's annoyance, she left the bookshop clutching a bottle of wine. He was abandoned to the pub opposite, which was housed in a long newish concrete development squeezed out like toothpaste to the end of the street.

'This is all material,' he thought to himself; 'I must not succumb to *Verzweiflung existentiell*.' For some reason, speaking in German always made him feel better. One day he would learn the language.

The pub was part of a chain: *This is a Falstaff Inn* said a discreet sign. The look was, naturally enough, Elizabethan. There were gnarled beams and knotty nooks, slightly more persuasive than their equivalent in California, but somehow more troubling. Old hardback books filled the niches – a job lot from the chain's decor warehouse, he presumed. Instead of taking notes for a poem of which the first two lines ('It doesn't matter much in Redditch/what sanctuary you seek, it is all the same') had jumped on him while he was ordering his pint at the bar, but which had stayed doggedly discontinued, he browsed through the niche behind his head. It was like turning over bodies in a catacomb. Forgotten pre-war thrillers about murders and cricket in that lovely Penguin green, which he felt like nicking, but didn't, were secreted among truly pointless volumes: *Legends of the Cornish Saints; Tap Dancing Made Easy; Annual Report of the Chrysanthemum Society 1952; My Days With the Water Board.*

The last book in the row was warped.

He took it down with the same air of amused futility as

he had the others. Or rather, he prised it off, as it was stuck to the shelf on a film of spilt beer.

The title was in Latin.

In fact, the whole book was in Latin, all five hundred-odd pages, and mottled with damp. It was precisely a hundred years old, published in 1899. A Victorian child had coloured in the portrait of the author, one William Pool, on the frontispiece, turning his huge whiskers blue and his long hair green, though some nursery tantrum had obscured his mouth and chin in wild streaks of crimson.

Greg was about to put the tome back, having dismissed it as some kind of mind-grinding ecclesiastical work, when his attention was drawn to the book's first words. Above the opening Latin sentence was its translation in English, done by a neat hand in pencil, spilling into the margin. The sentence read thus:

The desire for love is no more than a kind of neurasthenia . . . though very good to me, like flowers.

There were no further translations. He checked throughout the book, releasing its odour of mould, of pipe smoke and leadfoot labradors in gloomy, beeswaxed studies looking out onto laurel in vanished counties. Nothing. He wished, not for the first time, that he'd paid more attention during his seven years of school Latin: the text hovered just out of reach, maddeningly intangible. He had, however, established that it was a novel – for it said so, in English, on the title page. And the first sentence intrigued Greg. It more than intrigued him: it had him hooked.

The desire for love is no more than a kind of neurasthenia . . .though very good to me, like flowers.

For there was something odd about the sentence, something slightly 'off'. Teasing, perhaps. The kind of sentence that flows through your head as you wake up. Greg looked again at the author's portrait, a rather crude lithograph taken from an original painting. If that one sentence recalled the prints and paintings of an Aubrey Beardsley, effete and unworldly, its author did not: gruff, jowly, the sensuous lips at odds with the lean nose and suspicious eyes, William Pool was a man to be reckoned with.

Greg reckoned that only Oxbridge dons, Eton school-masters and conservative ecclesiastics wrote in Latin at the end of the nineteenth century – and mostly light verse for High Table. Was William Pool one of these? He doubted it: behind the coloured scribbles the man did not look comfort-able enough. The lighting in the pub was complicated, throwing strange coloured shadows over the furred paper, over the defiant face. It almost seemed to move, to be moving its mouth; certainly by Greg's third pint it was.

The desire for love is no more than a kind of neurasthenia . . . though very good to me, like flowers.

Then the karaoke evening got going, with 'Talkin' Bout a Revolution' shrieked forth by a plump, white-faced woman in a flowery dress. Greg returned William Pool to his niche under a smuggling poster and fled through the nightmare flashes of a stroboscope to catch the train home, feeling hungry and drunk and pointless.

But he did not forget Pool. He had scribbled down that first sentence on a beer mat, and the words haunted him.

An advanced search on the web came up with nothing. He scoured the major London libraries for information about the man: nothing. There wasn't even a copy of Pool's book, not anywhere. He wished he'd nicked it from the pub, now. He phoned Alastair MacGregor, his brother-in-law. Alastair was a classical scholar teaching at Royal Holloway. Greg wondered if the sentence merely reflected the *fin de siècle* manner of the translator. Foolishly, he had not recorded the original Latin.

'What a pity,' Alastair said. 'Between us we might have discovered the English Proust. What was the title?'

'*Animula Vagula Blandula*. Sounds like an internal disease.'

'Far from it. That's Hadrian, his last poem, written on his death-bed. Great emperor, hopeless poet. Except for the very last one. *Little vague* . . . no, *Little fleeting flattering* . . . no, *Little fleeting soft-flattering soul, the guest and comrade of my body, into what regions . . .*'

So the title was *Little Fleeting Soft-Flattering Soul?* That wouldn't have got the Booker, Greg thought. And it sounded ominously religious.

A friend who was an antiquarian books dealer had never heard of William Pool, but made appropriate enquiries. Waiting for the information was worse than waiting for reviews: Greg knew from the outset that there would be none. He sat at home in Kentish Town and watched some terrible TV full of D-list celebrities, imagining William Pool sitting among them and glowering. His eczema came back again and his tiny flat smelt of hydrocortisone cream. His foreign students at the language school grew more and more foreign, somehow, and the awful woman that ran it grew even nosier.

'What's this thousand-yard stare?' she asked, blowing smoke in his face. 'True love thwarted, is it?'

After a few months, during which he found at least thirty William Pools in the Somerset House archives (none of them helpful), he gave up. The true William Pool had vanished from the earth.

The only thing to do was to go back to Redditch.

He did so. It was still sleeting, and in exactly the same manner, as if it had sleeted continually for the past year. *Verzweiflung existentiell*, he murmured. The pub was empty but unchanged, except for a lottery kiosk placed just where he had sat the first time. The niche was hidden behind a poster of a grinning girl in a bikini, a lottery ticket tucked between her grapefruit breasts. The bartender – Azim, if the badge on his lapel was telling the truth – asked Greg how many tickets he wanted.

'Are there still books behind that poster?'

'Eh?'

The background music was in the foreground. He had to shout.

'Books. You know, those weird things you handled at school.'

'Oh, right. Dunno. Hey, Steve, bloke here wants to know about books.'

'You mean the bookshop, sir? Over the road? Next to Thomas Cook's? They've got a great offer on golfing holidays,' he added, winking at Azim.

'Well, the last time I was here, I found this really great book, where the poster now is. I think it might still be there along with other stuff about nasturtiums and so on.'

'Nasturtiums?'

'Doesn't matter, forget the nasturtiums. It was this other book I was wanting.'

Azim and Steve peered at Greg as if he was alien, talking in an alien language. It was at moments like these that Greg fleetingly recognised that he was, in fact, from another galaxy.

'A book,' said Azim.

'Yeah. Just a book.'

'Called?'

'Oh, right. That would have been useful. Its title was *Animula Vagula Blandula.*'

'Chinese, is it?'

'Sounds a bit impolite to me,' said Steve, making a rude gesture with the neck of a Smirnoff bottle.

Greg smiled gamely with the lads. He had planned, of course, to walk out with the book. To steal it. This would now be difficult.

Azim unsellotaped the poster and the girl crackled down

on top of him. The niche was empty, except for a spider and its web and an empty bottle of Thai beer.

'Whoops, management won't like that,' said Azim, removing the bottle. 'No books, though.'

'Who put up the poster? Who removed the books?' Greg's hands were trembling.

'Dunno, I'm only on temporary,' said Azim. He waved his hand at the other niches. 'Those look like books.'

Greg helped him put the girl back up and then leafed through every book in the pub, as if William Pool might have been camouflaged within. The books were mostly novels, by people with names that no longer existed: Herbert, Phyllis, Edgar, Winifred. Novels that go on being squeezed out like toothpaste to the end of time – or the end of humanity, at least. Steve and Azim eyed him suspiciously. He got to the last book, sighed, and looked so sad they offered him a half-pint of Foster's on the house.

'Hang on a minute,' said Steve. 'What about this?'

He bobbed down behind the bar's counter and emerged with something Greg instantly recognised.

'That's it!' Greg all but shrieked. 'That's the one!'

It was even more warped and covered in a crazed Venn diagram of beer-rings – but it was *Little Fleeting Soft-Flattering Soul*, alright.

'Stopped the glass-washer rattling,' Steve explained. 'Just the right width.'

'Can I borrow it? No, I'll buy it. How much?'

Steve looked at Greg with tiny eyes full of sterling.

'Management property. Genuine antique. Let's see now . . .'

Greg was saved by the arrival of the chilled-food lorry from Northampton. While Azim and Steve were distracted by rustling envelopes of Home-Cooked Shepherd's Pie, Greg sneaked out – with William Pool under his coat.

Within hours he was back home and on the phone to Alastair. Alastair would do the literal translation, Greg would turn it into decent prose. They would find a publisher and share the royalties. Greg left the book with Alastair and spent a restless week, teaching his foreign students distractedly, without conviction. Greg's ex-partner, Stephanie, phoned to tell him she was engaged – to the Bolivian actor for whom she had walked out on Greg last year. Greg actually didn't care. A week earlier and he would have wept. Love's sorrow and the greats of English literature no longer seemed to matter.

On Friday an envelope arrived: the first shortish chapter had been done.

Even through Alastair's flat, unworked prose, the chapter made Greg want to run out into the Kentish Town morning and shout very loudly. Instead, he made himself a large coffee and got straight down to work on Alastair's literal translation, trying to come to terms with the enormity of his find. Here was a novel written by an Englishman seemingly soaked in the poetry of Baudelaire, Rimbaud, Mallarmé: the lucid daring, the bizarre imagery, the profane anti-social defiance, the clinical rage, the fevered calm. All this some thirty years before the French avant-garde made it over the Channel in the form of Pound, Eliot, Joyce, Woolf, Lawrence! The language itself reminded Greg of none other than Samuel Beckett – many decades later. Although the novel was set in Tamworth and narrated by a fancy-goods salesman called Oswald Pock on his death-bed – thus the title from Hadrian's poem – the atmosphere was the surgical nihilism, the desperate dark comedy, of *Waiting for Godot* or *Endgame*. And in the process of converting it into ringing English prose, Greg felt a sense of destiny, of a circle completing itself: the novel had been written in Latin, as Beckett's plays had been written in French, precisely in anticipation of this conversion into English. An English unsullied, purified, shorn of its sensuous accretions, somehow distanced from its soiled roots, objectified and therefore able to regard itself freshly. The dry flower of a dead language swelling into life at his touch, more beautiful than the compromised speech of its – or our – present.

Above all, the Victorian constructions of every Victorian novel had vanished: the language was for all time, as modern as he might make it. A language that thought, connecting in limber leaps as it moved through the episodic and quite banal events of the life of a fancy-goods salesman in the English Midlands. And there were passages that sent a shudder through Greg, as if Pool had anticipated everything:

The land seemed dead to him. The very soil of England seemed dead. Poisoned, and by its own people. Was it because he was old that the sky above the fields seemed silent? He asked Charlotte about this, but she only scoffed and said he was deaf. He did not think he was deaf. Barbarous speech lay in the folds of the months and the years. The lilies, the larks, the very waters themselves would be violated and the ancient towns laid waste from within. Charlotte cupped her full breasts and allowed Oswald to kiss them, once, twice, three times. England's breasts would be withered soon, he knew. The invisible oxen would draw barbarian wagons across strange bridges with the trains flowing beneath, and children would be the ransom of the world.

'It's a very clever collage,' said Alastair, a few days later. They had met up in the courtyard of Somerset House to compare notes. Greg had felt that the magnificence of the classical courtyard and its modernist, state-of-the-art fountains would be a suitable place to discuss Pool. They ordered tea and cakes. The tea came in paper mugs. It was windy, despite the bright sun, and the paper mugs blew off and the pages went wild. 'Yes, a very skilful scissors-and-paste job.'

'Er, what on earth do you mean, Alastair?'

'It's made up of thousands of snippets of Latin verse, from Horace to Petronius to Notker the Stammerer. You name it, it's in there, somewhere. I even found Caligula's line about wishing the Roman people had only one neck. I think that about the English, sometimes.'

Alastair was Scottish. Greg found this fact irritating from time to time. His sister, Jill, had called her kids Jeanie and Angus.

'Alastair, what the hell are you on about?'

'A sort of Victorian scholar's parlour game, that's what it is. For instance, that bit about the oxen and barbarian wagons is lifted straight from Ovid; *Perque novos pontes—*'

'But that's the whole damn point,' Greg cried, secretly panicking. 'History's a scrapheap, a pile of rubble. Eliot's fragments. Out of which we make anew. As Rimbaud did, and Baudelaire. And Beckett. It's avant-garde! It's revolutionary!'

The fountains' hundreds of jets emerged and sent spindrift over them, as if they were next to the sea – along with a strong smell of chlorine.

'A very clever pastiche,' Alastair went on, remorselessly. 'By an unknown and sexually frustrated public-school master, I reckon.'

Greg blinked. It was like hearing someone slag off Ivor Gurney or John Clare.

'OK, I admit there's a mildly pornographic and scatological element, a Joycean streak, but that *explains* why it's in Latin.'

'Don't see it.'

'A language open only to the initiated.'

Alastair laughed. Greg had always considered Alastair's laugh to be one of his least attractive characteristics. Even Jill had to admit that. While the rest of his brother-in-law was as civilised as a Roman villa, his laugh was pure barbarian. Pictish, perhaps.

'Schoolboys of that period would have had little problem deciphering it, Greg, or even spotting the references.'

'OK, I know, but if the book had been written initially in English, just imagine what would've happened. Scandal. Look at that brilliant bit about his slippery fish swimming into her and the treacherous evidence of foam and—'

'Ausonius. Wonderful poem on the Moselle river, originally.'

'But – look – what? Hey, pfff, I don't care,' Greg sputtered. 'The point is, it would've been dismissed as a blue book, to be sold in plain brown covers.'

'Blue covers, surely.'

'When in fact . . . Anyway, nothing's new under the sun.'

'If you say so,' said Alastair.

Greg manfully described what he imagined this strangely coloured rivulet, this little prophetic pipe under the Channel, might have done to the moribund English scene – its High Victorian smugness, its stifling bourgeoisified good taste. The dream-like references to the Siege of Paris of 1870 had led him to believe, he went on, that Pool had actually been there as a young man, rubbing shoulders with the likes of Mallarmé, Verlaine . . . perhaps even partaking in the Communards' brief rule that followed, swept along by revolutionary ideas. Alastair was not impressed, however; his interest was in the rubble of the Roman world, not the twentieth century's – in the salvaging operation of Cassiodorus and not the smashing operation of the avant-garde some fifteen hundred years later.

Greg retrieved his mug from the fountain just as the sunken jets reappeared. He had to jump back but got a little wet. Alastair was laughing.

'That's barbarism,' Greg said; 'paper mugs here, of all places.' Deep down, he was angry with Alastair for subverting William Pool, each soft Edinburgh know-it-all syllable like a pebble thrown at porcelain.

The next week he took the train to Paris. He found nothing after a day's search in the archives, but in the city-history museum near the rue des Rosiers he saw, in a glass case devoted to scraps from the Siege, a ration card distributed to one W. S. Poole of 32 rue Trucage. The street had disappeared under an office block. He phoned Alastair that evening, sweating with excitement.

'How many Pools in this particular fish?' was all Alastair said, who'd had a tiring trip back from Egham on a faulty train.

The weeks turned into months and Alastair, who was drowned in administrative duties at Royal Holloway, started to resent Greg's frequent pleas to get a move on. Greg's own muse had vanished: he'd found a three-day job in the local picture-framing shop and the customers drained him with their emotional needs. He spent most of his spare time worrying at his Pool prose, urging Alastair's lifeless literalism into bloom.

'You've drowned in it,' said Alastair.

The book was finally finished early in the following year. Retaining only the title in Latin but explaining the book's origins, Greg sent it off to all the major publishing houses.

Animula Vagula Blandula was rejected twenty-seven times. Greg's publishers' – a specialist poetry press – reckoned it was his own work, a massive folly. Greg eventually brought it out himself, at no small expense, in 2003. The printer had promised endpapers and there were none, but that was the only technical disappointment before the distributors' report.

The problem was not just the crassness of the official chain-bookshop buyers, it was the meanness of the critical reaction. There were, in fact, only three printed reviews: one in the *Good Book Guide*, which was equivalent to having a recipe in *Good Housekeeping*; a tart piece in the *Times Literary Supplement*, mostly devoted to the declension of 'vagus' and declaring, finally, in a great trumpet of intellectual perspicacity, that the book was 'mostly well written'; while the *Literary Review* dismissed it as 'a pastiche of sub-Victorian drivel'. The local Redditch rag ran the story of Greg's discovery, suggesting (in so many words) that Pool was a sex fiend, and accompanying the article with a frighteningly appropriate photograph of Alastair. Through the latter's connections it was considered by the *Front Row* panel on Radio 4, who laughed a lot and reckoned the book was an inept fraud – a claim which incensed Greg to such an extent that, if he'd had any money at all, he would have embroiled himself in a lengthy legal tussle with the BBC.

Twenty-one copies were sold, the rest rearranged as a desk unit and spare bed in Greg's tiny study.

'Pool's day will come,' he said to Alastair, tapping them. This had become Greg's catch-phrase. Alastair's book on Cassiodorus had just received a rave in the *Guardian*, so Alastair couldn't have cared less, either way. 'The thing is, he's still ahead of his day, because his day is our day.'

'Gregory,' Alastair said, annoying his brother-in-law immediately, 'concentrate on your own work.'

'My own work's finished. I'm dried up.'

'As Ovid said, *Caelum non animum mutant qui trans mare currunt.*'

'What the hell does that mean?'

'You should know. You helped translate it.'

Alastair opened the copy on Greg's desk and found the last page.

'*They change their skies but not their souls running over the sea.*'

'It's the last bloody line of the book, Alastair. A beautiful line. Stunning. That's not Ovid, that's William Pool.'

'It was Ovid originally. Word for word. You don't believe me, do you? Scissors and paste, Greg.'

'I *can't* believe you,' Greg said, his head in his hands.

He read the last page to himself while Alastair fetched a couple of beers from the fridge. Greg felt a sense of hopelessness, as if a close friend had betrayed him:

He had not been heavy on the earth, though he was old. He whispered to Charlotte, when she brought him his cocoa with her shoulders bared to the gaslight: 'Let the hard turf cover me tenderly near Aberaeron, where the ocean leans on the land. A clear dawn shall free me from time's age-old laws, and I shall leave on the rushing stream of fortune to find my place, my end, far from fancy goods and the envy of the false—'

'Come on,' Charlotte said, 'your cocoa's getting cold.'

'Like the trails of words,' he murmured; *'like the trails of words themselves, that change their skies but not their souls running over the sea.'*

He had been invited back to Redditch the following day – to read from the book, not his own work. At first he hadn't wanted to go back to Redditch, but then he had perceived it as a symbolic and necessary return to the source. He would read that last page, even if there was no one in the audience, and then he would cross to the pub and place the original copy back in the shelf behind the girl in her bikini, if she was still there. She probably wasn't, because everything changed, everything was built from rubble, there was nothing new under the sun and he didn't care, not now. He didn't care.

'There you go,' said Alastair, returning with the beers. 'Get this down you and cheer up. You've a face like a douchebag. There's life after Pool, you know. Find a girl. Write some verse. Translate some Anglo-Norman stuff. There's lots of it, entirely neglected. The *Roman de Waldef.* The verse of Chardri.'

'I don't know Anglo-Norman.'

'You'll find enough literal versions and you could work them into poetry, produce an anthology. Now there's another undiscovered country. Forget Pool, forget the Latin. I'm throwing out ideas, Greg.'

'I've got this poem about Redditch,' Greg replied, wiping the foam from his upper lip. 'It's only two lines long. Want to hear it?'

TROLLS

The pony was skitty on the rocks as he led it across the stream. The glacier had moved in his dreams and he was no longer sure which outcrop was which. A great nervousness in the sky under the drizzle and the wet moraine field dazzling whenever the sun broke through. It was hell to cross. All those smooth uncertain stones, squealing against each other.

A plume of smoke rose from the tin-roofed house as he picked his way over the trackless moorland, pulling the pony after him, to where the tents still stood under the rocks.

Anthony and Gillian welcomed him as if he had been away days, over-indulgent in their leather boots and expensive jackets. And this irritated him, he saw something mocking in it, as if his desire for solitude was something improper.

'Was it good?'

'I had to go a fair bit round the lake to be totally alone,' he said. 'There was this homemade jetty and a rowing boat and this bloke working on it. But the lake's big. It's right under the glacier, practically. It was good. It was good being alone.'

'Don't mind us,' said Anthony.

'I won't,' said Clive, smiling.

Tobias, who had some tummy problem since they'd drunk from the hot spring the day before, appeared from behind the outcrop and said, 'Clive, you have to go to Fallujah. CNN just called.'

'Very funny,' said Clive, who (like the others) had kept his mobile on message function from the day they had started out.

Steinn was down by the house, chatting with the old woman there.

'Keeping the natives happy,' said Anthony.

They struck camp with the usual minor dust-up over missing pegs and set off, waving to the old woman standing in the doorway – for whom the strangers and their tents had not been the astonishing intrusion they had all imagined it would be. Clive knew this, having met her son by the homemade jetty. The son must already have been in his fifties, with a curiously pale, almost bleached face, like a wraith or a piece of driftwood. He spoke quite good English. He told Clive that they frequently received 'trekkers' – the term his, no doubt borrowed from an American, a borrowing which amused Clive because it was the name Gillian gave to her boots. The man asked Clive what his job was.

'Freelance cameraman. Without his camera.'

'Films?'

'News,' said Clive. 'Dangerous places. I needed a break.'

The son had nodded and carried on fiddling about in the tiny rowing-boat, its oars folded like a dead man's hands. Much later, at dusk, when Clive was cooking his sausages over the fire, he had seen the boat sculling in the distance, a dark spot on the last red bars of water. It had heightened his own loneliness, rather than removed it.

The path wound through the moorland. They disturbed eager little plovers. Chill gusts reminded them where they were, because the sun was burning on their faces. An inordinate amount of lavatory paper was snagged on thorns or bundled under lichen-covered rocks.

'It was the same in the Himalayas,' Clive said. 'It's all those Aussies, I reckon.'

Gillian was Australian, from Melbourne. He had meant it as a joke, but Tobias was shaking his head, taking it seriously. Gillian hadn't heard – she was leading the pony just ahead, and the pony's hooves made quite a lot of noise on the stones.

'This is when I hate the masses,' said Tobias. 'You open

up the land to the people, and this is the result. They should all be hung.'

'Hanged,' said Anthony, who was nineteen years older than his partner. 'Never hung. Unless you're talking testicles.'

Steinn was their guide. He was probably in his mid-thirties and had long hair bunched up under his bobble hat. Clive told him, when they'd paused by a tumbling stream to snack their provisions, the curious fact about the glacier, the way it had moved while he was asleep. He'd gone to sleep on the pebbles with a view of the ice shining in ribbed blue under the moonlit snow, dreamt it was surging slowly towards him, woke up at dawn to find that it was no longer the same shape, that it had shifted, lowered its bulk, like something alive settling into itself, advancing towards its prey. If he had taken a photograph beforehand . . . The others were listening.

'It's between you and the glacier,' said Tobias.

'A fight to the death?' suggested Anthony, without a hint of a smile.

'I don't mean that,' Tobias continued, in his best Etonian drawl; 'one mustn't see everything in terms of conflict. I mean that either Clive's seeing things, or the glacier's moved.'

'Not both at the same time?' suggested Clive.

Gillian snorted. She'd known Clive for years and there was a loyalty. 'I believe glaciers do move,' she said.

'Yes, about an inch a century,' said Tobias.

'They are . . .' Steinn began, searching for the word.

'Vanishing?'

'Enlarging?'

'Very cold?'

'Thank you, Anthony. Melting?'

'Yoh, melting,' said Steinn, jabbing a finger at Gillian. 'Globble warming.'

'Global,' Gillian corrected. 'Sure it wasn't a troll? They're big enough, aren't they?'

Steinn laughed. 'Sure! Maybe!' He pointed at a ridge from which boulders protruded like vertebrae. 'There was being

a troll. It dance at night, then the sun shine and he is freezed.'
He froze himself for a moment, his hands spread, his back
curved over.

'Trolls are seriously large,' said Tobias. 'Large as glaciers.
Now, if you'll excuse me.' He left them, disappearing behind
some rocks.

Steinn stirred and waggled his eyebrows, bleached like a
burn victim's on his copper-red face. '*Huldufolk,*' he said,
pointing to a grey, wind-twisted boulder. 'Hidden people.
My grandmother, he was communicating with the hidden
people. They are very beautiful and clever. Very good at sex,'
he added, with a laugh.

'Good gracious, can't wait,' said Gillian.

'Gnomes,' said Anthony. 'My gran had lots of them in her
garden. The mind boggles.'

'Also *afturganga*, very bad. Not like *huldufolk*, but dead.'

'Zombies,' said Gillian.

'Yoh,' agreed Steinn. 'Zombies, come to take away us all
to dead place. And *Gluggagaegir.*'

Anthony chortled. 'My bath running out?'

'They look in the windows, nighttime. For stealing.'

Steinn put his hands either side of his face and stared
through an imaginary window, with boggling eyes. Clive's
boots shifted on the pebbles with a noise like something
being torn. It was really very quiet and empty, here. The air
smelt of lichen.

'Can't have been a troll, in my case,' said Clive. 'It was dawn.'

'Well, they obey their own rules, do trolls,' Gillian said,
glancing at the ridge, its spine cobbled on the sky-line. A
thrush pranced about over the stream. The pony ignored it.
'Maybe that's why people who plant really provocative things
on the web are called trolls.'

'Are they?' said Anthony.

Clive frowned and looked away. He didn't want to hear
about the web on a trekking expedition in Iceland.

'Y'know, someone who deliberately stirs things up on the

web,' Gillian went on. 'Flaming. To flame is to troll, because it gets people flaming angry. Making us look even more stupid than we already are? It's a kind of trap. Flame bait.'

'*Trep*,' Clive echoed, irritated.

'How did you lose your foot?' asked Anthony, after a few moments of quiet. 'Or does everyone pose that question, at some point or other?'

'At some point,' said Clive.

'Do you mind being posed it?'

'Katmandu. In a riot. Dum–dum bullet.'

'Gosh. How odd. Katmandu.'

'People lose their feet everywhere,' Gillian pointed out.

'I *hope* not everywhere,' said Anthony, curling his long fingers around his bony knees, 'or we'll be tripping over them.' He appeared to be wearing a deerstalker, but it was not: it was merely a designer article from Jermyn Street. 'I thought people were more likely to lose their *equilibrium* in Katmandu, man.'

'Most people express sympathy, and wince,' said Clive.

'Not me,' said Anthony. 'I'm frightful and unfeeling. Aren't I, Tobby?'

'Probably,' Tobias replied. He had reappeared, buckling his trousers. 'Did you see the eagle? Or certainly a falcon. I'll look it up in the bird book.'

'Too late,' said Anthony. 'You have to look it up as you're spotting or you won't know a hawk from a handsaw.'

'I always thought that meant something by Black and Decker,' said Tobias. 'Hamlet's dad's handsaw.'

'The only bird I know is a parakeet,' said Gillian.

Anthony shook his head. 'I don't think we have one of those here, guv.'

'Norwegian blue,' said Tobias.

'Nailin' up the perch!' cried Anthony.

'Nailing up the perch?' Tobias scoffed. 'What are you on about? Get it right.'

'I used to have it word for word,' Anthony admitted.

'That's age,' said Gillian. 'Don't I know it.'

'You are not so much age, Gillian,' said Steinn, gallantly. 'Go friendly with yourself.'

'Easy on yourself,' Gillian corrected, tossing a pebble into the stream.

'You'd better watch him,' said Anthony, raising his eyebrows. His hat, perched too high, looked even sillier. 'Maybe he's one of them there hidden folk.'

'I'm watching – aren't I, Steinn?'

'Yoh,' nodded Steinn. 'I'll tell you many flowers.'

'I don't think our Virgil has quite got the drift,' said Anthony.

'Just as well,' said Tobias, munching from a packet of KP nuts and raisins.

The air was chillier around the stream; Clive hugged himself in his thick sweater and stared at the stones slicked incessantly by the water. He could not stop these people talking, that was the trouble. He could smell the office, the Tube, the deep fry of England rising from their natter: each one of them was like a comic-strip astronaut, encased in a bubble of helmet that shut them off from alien air. He looked about him, barely able to take in the treeless sweeps of green, the mountains, the amazing burn of light. Two days ago he'd watched smoking geysers drift into a cloudless sky while Gillian advised Anthony on the best way to hide grey hairs. That one afternoon and night on his own, lying by the whispering lake, its enormous stretch reminding him of some giant tarn rather than a loch – though it was a loch's breadth – had merely seized up his giving side, his tolerance of the others' awkwardnesses, had made him crave yet more solitude, gallons of it, at the same time as it had frightened him with images of himself sprawled on the pebbly shore, having suffered some sort of attack, having collapsed from some internal disorder. He had woken up in the night, under a haze of stars, with his heart beating all over the place, and had lain there hardly daring to breathe, wondering if he should walk about gently or stoke the fire, do something practical to take away the dread of finishing in such a desolate place, faced with his own nothingness. He had faced so many dangers in his job, but this was worse. This was internal.

Death had chewed at him in Katmandu, swallowed a morsel and then moved on, leaving him lame. He did not want Death to take the rest. But neither did he want to retire, say, to Cornwall, shooting moody studies of abandoned tin-mines. He did not know what he wanted to do. He would like to dream the answer, he had thought, staring up at the star haze. He would like to sleep on it and wake up with the answer.

He had nodded off, finally, and dreamt of the glacier, hearing it snap and groan and move, inches at a time but swiftly over so many years, erasing everything in its path. He had woken at dawn, shivering, with the pony silhouetted blackly against the first flush of light, apparently enormous in its quiet animal patience. He'd scrambled out of the sleeping bag, his limbs frozen, shocked by the change in appearance of the distant, towering cliff of ice, catching the first rays and flashing them back in his eyes.

He had buckled his foot back on and walked to the edge of the lake and forgotten everything but the pebbles slicked softly by the water, over and over and over. He had not felt lonely, then.

Sitting with the others by the stream, listening to their banter, he marvelled at the ability of the human soul to shift from level to level, ascending and descending as in some massive lift of glass – for nothing of that sense of wondrous solitude had survived even as a taste; it was already a recreated thing, like a painting or a poem, losing in the process its essential wordlessness, its lack of utterance, its fullness more like that of an empty sky still replete with light.

'It's a bit parky, isn't it?' said Anthony. 'I think old Clive there's ready to go.'

'I'm fine,' said Clive. 'I'm just fine.'

That evening they were in a bar in the small town on the peninsula. Although most of the locals were sunk into themselves as if their mechanisms no longer worked, the strangers revelled in the warmth and smoky comfort of its humanity, drinking too much after a long and tiring hike through clean air. Clive suddenly remembered what else had happened in his dream. He had killed Tobias (with a knife, he thought) and raped Steinn. Not Anthony, but Steinn. He told no one, embarrassed by the disgust he felt even now, thinking of Steinn flailing under him. The fact that Gillian had been clocking Steinn all day set Clive wondering, as the others chatted and giggled, if he was jealous of Steinn. No, he decided. He was not in any way keen on Gillian. They were just old mates from university, and Anthony and Tobias were Gillian's mates from work. The construction of a new road had been delayed by angry *huldufolk*, Steinn was telling them. All the mechanical diggers had packed up, someone had died from a fall. The road had had to be rerouted. This led to more witty quips about folk hidden in unlikely places.

'Nice to have a good laff, in't it, Clive?'

'Aye, Anthony. You have me in stitches.'

'I'll have you in trousers, if that's alright by you.'

Clive blushed through their laughter, but his face was already red from the wind and the sun. Clive looked across at Steinn, the guide's upper lip shiny with beer, and smiled to himself. Anything is possible, he thought. He should simply have travelled on his own, faced his fears, got to know the pony as Stevenson got to know his donkey. The animal didn't even have a name. The room swam pleasantly. If Angie was still around, he'd be almost happy.

'The pony should have a name,' he said, loudly, interrupting Anthony's account of his earliest affair with a boy at his school who had subsequently been killed in a car crash.

'Sorry?'

Gillian looked cross.

'The pony should not be anonymous,' he added, stumbling over the last word, which came out as 'anomynous', but which he couldn't for the life of him correct.

Gillian smiled. 'But it has got a name,' she said.

'Derek,' said Tobias.

Clive looked at him. 'Derek?'

The three of them – Anthony, Gillian and Tobias – exploded into laughter. Steinn had gone off to buy another round. Tobias began imitating Peter Cook, but not very well: fumbling through the *I'll tell you the worst job I ever had* routine. Maybe even Steinn was in on it, although he would never have heard of Peter Cook, let alone of Derek and Clive. Dudley Moore, perhaps.

Clive felt as if a great secret had been revealed – not the secret of the name, but the secret of his relationship with the others. He knew before they explained that they had called it Derek in his absence, that they had talked of Derek and Clive in his – their – absence; that this had been a joke, a running joke, in the eighteen hours he had been away. Explaining it to him as they were doing now was unnecessary, it was as if he had heard it all before. It humiliated him. The dark bulky figures at the other tables turned menacing, their flat faces staring glumly at the merry group as it made its noise: bobble hats perched on unruly hair, boots on the bare boards providing a sort of drumbeat to his emotional execution.

Derek!

'Quite a task because Jayne had a big bum and they were very big lobsters,' Tobias was quoting, with his finger in the air.

He could either laugh along with it, as he had done once when surrounded by rebels in Sierra Leone, or take umbrage and sulk. It was a calculated decision, to sulk.

'Steinn,' said Gillian, when the guide had returned with more beers, 'what is the pony called?'

'Seltjarnarnes,' said Steinn. It sounded like sea breaking on black lava.

'Yer what?' laughed Tobias.

'What does that mean?' Gillian asked.

'Where he come from,' said Steinn. 'A place by Reykjavik.'

'How dull,' said Anthony. 'Once you know.'

'A place for the *huldufolk*,' said Steinn. 'Very big power.'

'Good evening, ladies and gentlemen, I was born in Sutton,' said Tobias, in an E. L. Wisty voice, leaning drunkenly forward, 'and I have a very important announcement to make, I am dead, I have passed on to pastures new—'

'Hello, Sutton,' said Anthony. 'And I'm Stoke Poges, and Gillian's Melbourne, and this is . . . ?'

He waved his hand towards Clive.

'Out on the Morar moor,' he said, into his glass.

'You never are,' said Anthony. 'You're not Scots. You're about as Scots as my left foot.'

'At least you've got a left foot,' said Clive, before he could stop himself.

'Oh look, I'm sorry, I completely forgot—'

'I don't care,' said Clive. 'Barnstaple, if you have to know.'

'Hello, Barnstaple,' said Anthony, genuinely sorry from the look of it.

Clive stood and limped out after the conversation had turned. He could take a joke, he thought, pissing into the glimmering northern night. The stars were hidden behind banks of wild cloud, vaguely luminous beyond the streetlights. He could see the wink of a television over the road, could hear the canned laughter over the whistle of the gusts that came and went and that smelt of the Arctic and of seas you could walk on.

Derek.

The glacier had definitely moved. He would buy a proper horse and ride off wherever his fancy took him. He would stay on after they had gone back home and ride off wherever his dreams took him.

Right now, however, his stump hurt, hurt like knives. New prosthesis: supposed to be lighter, state-of-the-art. Chafing him, blisters rubbing where the straps met the skin. But he'd adapt to it. Or it would adapt to him. Trekker! Something small and misshapen ran across in front of the houses and the television blinked and flickered, sent its grey light in spasms over the unlit room he could see between the open curtains.

He limped gingerly over to the window and peered in. The room, with its out-of-date furniture, was empty of people. He imagined sitting inside on the fake leather sofa with his legs stretched out and his feet whole, then turning round to see a white face peeping in like a corpse come back from the dead. His breath was ghosting the window, however, so he was still alive.

Soon after the operation, he'd taken a break with Angie in the south of France. It was very hot. They'd passed an antiques shop in Arles and seen this giant marble foot, probably classical, broken off at the ankle. And Angie had said, after they'd chuckled at it, 'If only you talked more, Clive, it'd be easier.' And he'd said, 'Easier for whom?'

'Everyone,' she'd replied.

Now he smiled. Thinking of Angie and that giant marble foot with its perfect toes. When the little girl came into the room, opened her mouth in surprise and then waved at him shyly, he waved back. She was smiling, and so was he. He pulled faces and made her laugh. The wind was whistling in the guttering above his head and so he couldn't hear her laugh, but he could see it clearly enough.

ABANDON

I

It had never once occurred to him that dying might be pleasurable. Without the solace of faith, he had anticipated the final weeks of weakening powers with some fear, just as he used to be fearful of going to bed up the long stairs as a child, shielding his night light. But when the time came and he was installed in the hospice, confined to the wheel-chair, he was amazed at the way it had all turned to simplicity, as if a very elaborate machine had been swapped for a carpenter's tool, its handle polished with use, its blade precise and functional.

'Any more tea, Jack?'

'No, thank you very much, Carol.'

'Anything interesting in the paper?'

'Oh, the usual stuff and nonsense, Carol. *I* don't need to worry about it, at any rate, do I?'

The nurse tut-tutted smilingly and moved on. He was only pretending to read the newspaper. George Brown had resigned as Foreign Secretary; the Stock Exchange had closed; Enoch Powell spoke eleven languages and read a book a day. He himself had no desire to read. He was content with two things: watching the emergence of spring through the glass doors of the lounge, and appreciating the young nurses: nurses like the lovely almond-eyed Carol or the waif-like Pooma. Youth had never seemed to him more extraordinary, as if it was a phenomenon only just discovered. Likewise the dappling of flowers on the lawn and under the great trees – crocuses, daffodils, anemones – seemed like something new and unique. Death was not winter, to him (nor to his old friend Bruno, but for other reasons – Bruno's heaven being a ridiculous perpetual summer), since death led to nothing further. Corporeally, of course, it was a return, a feeding, which was why he had asked not to be cremated, despite his sister's rejoinder that ashes were very good for roses, filled as they were with potassium (and good for lawns, too, if spread thinly before rain). But spiritually, or mentally, Jack considered any elaboration a fiction.

And amazingly his fear had not yet declared itself; he was climbing the stairs to the unmeasurable darkness, yes – but the pictures on the wall, the views of the twilit road through the landing windows, the very patterns on the runner and the gleam of its brass clips, were as the contents of Aladdin's cave. He now felt sorry for those upon whom the end came unexpectedly, as with both his brothers in the trenches. He had always envied them before, even though he had survived physically intact.

2

She'd read somewhere – maybe someone's poem in the local poetry club, which she attended most Wednesday evenings, returning on the last bus – that sleep was a cage of dreams. Her dreams had bent the bars, in that case. Colours swarmed into the wrong places, as did whispers and words; actions materialised very suddenly in front of her and were as quickly swept away. There were brief terrors during the tea-breaks, as if masked monsters or psychopathic criminals were heading for the staff sanctuary in which the nurses moaned or giggled about nothing in particular, relishing their hold on life, their vivid presence (most of them were very young, as if at a certain point the job called one away into another existence). The untamed beasts of her sleeping hours were prowling where they shouldn't be, and these were the first signs, like pawmarks she had forgotten the hunter's word for.

By the standards of the most senior of the visiting doctors, Richard Godley, she was the prettiest of the bunch. She knew this because he had told her. Only her hands, apparently, disappointed him, being stout and discoloured from the endless parboiling and soaping demanded by the strict standards of hygiene (there had been some sort of scandal a few years back, an article in the local newspaper, relatives threatening court action). He had flirted with her over dying patients or down the long corridor punched through to the new extension, but she had always stood firm against him, finding him repellent.

She had started reading yet another of the romantic shilling paperbacks from the hospice library, only to find that its setting was a hospital, its heroine a nurse, and its villain so like Dr Godley that it had made her laugh.

She found a kind of comfort in her less terrifying visions. Snatches of song and sudden wafts of perfume made her wonder whether the vast house was haunted. Constructed by an industrial baron some hundred and fifty years before, on the site of a sixteenth-century manor and in view of his mills' chimney stacks (smoking until a few years ago), it was forever within earshot of a raging torrent that, they were told, fuelled the opening shots of the Industrial Revolution. When a visiting lecturer gave a talk on local history at the chilly church hall, she had put her hand up and asked if there were any ghosts in Talbot House. Someone behind her suggested that if a hospice did not have ghosts, nowhere did. She added, so softly that the lecturer had to bend forward to hear, that she had meant rather more ancient ghosts.

A young man in front of her laughed and turned round and stared at her. Yes, the young man turned round in his seat and stared at her and she all but shrieked.

It was precisely the face that had appeared in her dream of the night before.

She had pressed herself fully to its lips and the sensation had been lovely, surviving the touch at dawn of the starched pillow against her cheek. Even the faint roar of the torrent in the clough, the snores of Pooma (her roommate from Bombay), the smell of mothballs in the drawers and the unpleasant aroma of the kitchens two floors below had not quite extinguished the luxuriance of her dream. It had clung about her all morning, its details forgotten while the rest remained hovering about her as if a tall wardrobe existed in her brain that led, as in the children's story, to a fabled land. Now the wardrobe door had opened at its own volition and just as abruptly slammed shut, the young man grinning at her as if wishing to fix his face on her memory for ever.

That night, when she tried in the warmth of her bed to recall his face, she failed to. She knew it was young and reasonably handsome, with a mop of blond hair, but that was all; he had left before the close of the lecture during a garbled question from the floor, and she had followed him with her eyes until he was concealed by those seated behind her. His jacket had frayed patches on the elbows and his trousers appeared to have holes in them. She had wondered what this young man was doing in a sea of grey heads and remembered the kisses and caresses in her dream.

Now she hugged her frayed teddy bear, Freddie, tightly to her breasts. The smell of Freddie's furry head was comforting: milk and biscuits, the stuffed insides of old sofas, the oats she would give her father's horses when the farm was still running up on the moor, even the sea that had delivered Freddie to her (a gull dropping him mysteriously at her bare feet one day on the beach at Scarborough, her mother clapping her hands in delight, a train puffing past under the rim of the hills) . . .

She fell asleep while Pooma was still murmuring her prayers.

3

He would position himself near, but not too near, the high glass doors, thus commanding a view of both the room and the garden. Fearful of hogging this view, he had his wheelchair moved to one side, though no one else was noticeably interested in the world outdoors. There he could watch the birds busy at their work, the gardeners at theirs, the plants pursuing their own dumb and intricate ways and the trees gradually burgeoning into leaf. Most of all he appreciated the weather: generally cold and wet, its subtlest gradations were not lost on him, and the odd burst of sunshine came as a heavenly elixir, the dew-drops sparkling first thing in the morning when the room was silent and empty and the garden full of noise and activity and the dull ache of his dying was not yet risen to his eyes. The dew was spread for a king to walk upon, though he never came.

That he had no idea what this was all for, for what purpose it was designed, struck him as the height of abandon: in all our human designs, he reflected, we know why we are doing such and such, for whom or for what we labour, but in the grander scheme of things we are lost, ignorant, fired only by some obscure desire to stay alive and generate copies of ourselves. Nature seemed suddenly to offer him a vision of complete luxury, just as he saw its workings as mere ruthless striving to reproduce and be. Seeing this fusion made him smile, and as if in response his body quivered and burnt almost deliciously, like a pressed tooth. The others heard him grunt and looked up from their newspapers, games, meditations, some of them plugged by their ears into transistor radios brought by their relatives; he engineered his face back into a smile and nodded, beaming at each of them in turn.

'Is he daft?' he heard one of them ask, a deaf old man whose shout must sound like a whisper in his universe. 'Is he daft?'

It occurred to him during these last weeks that the medicaments may well be intoxicating. At night − when vague shadows flitted beyond the door of his room, its upper half put to glass and discreetly blurred with lace − he wondered whether this gift of happiness and wonder wasn't, therefore, a simple matter of drugs, of chemicals awash in his twilit brain. So he asked the doctor if the drugs might have this effect, in the way morphine did. Dr Godley chuckled in the patronising way of his profession and said that it was a bit late for Jack to become a hippy, he would have to grow his hair a lot longer before he was eligible for LSD. (Jack had, in fact, almost no hair at all.)

'I can always bring you one of my son's Beatles records, Jack,' Dr Godley grinned. 'Awfully groovy, you know.'

So Jack was not much the wiser − although, as an after-thought, Dr Godley told him (in a serious voice) that at least one of the ingredients of the medicinal cocktail was, in certain cases, a 'depressant'. Jack did not like this information and vowed not to ask any more questions of a technical nature. He heard the faint roar of Culdean Water and remembered how in Africa he'd had to cross many a rope bridge over a raging torrent, and how it was only when an old timer told him tales of folk plunging to their deaths when a rope, rotted by the humid air, declared itself done that he had been assailed, each time, by a choking fear.

It was really quite extraordinary, this almost visionary sense he had been given, and he wondered whether he should record it in some fashion, if only for his children. But as soon as he tried to scribble something down, his hands scarcely able to hold the pen level, he felt the wonder shrivel up and die; he felt the inadequacy of his terms, the paltri-ness of words when faced with the multiple universe and his own particular multiplicity of wonder, like a many-petalled rose that was unfolding ceaselessly in his heart. He thought of his heart when he wrote 'heart', a flapping, dila-tory organ swathed in blood, and saw how the part of him that reduced the world to its merely physical particulars was stirred by the act of setting his feelings down, as if blundering about in a magic glade.

And yet how particularly physical the glade seemed, as he stared day after day into the garden and the grounds beyond, his view finishing on the clough's steep wall of trees where Culdean Water, its pour always the colour of tea from the peat on the moors, was raising shreds of mist. He remembered passing this place at fifteen, on a midnight hike in 1906, well before the trenches claimed him for their own. The air was hazy with smoke, then, and smelt sulphurous. Now, some sixty years later, he knew how to understand.

Even the first trembling fly on the glass, its waxy wings tested on the cool air, jolted his sense of amazement yet further down some long and private walk.

4

That Richard Godley was rumoured to 'help' some of his patients to their final sleep was well known even to her, and if the nurses watched him carefully it was not with the intention of catching him at this nefarious activity, but to confirm its reality. There were lacklustre discussions in the tea-room over the merits or otherwise of such final easing – some taking the view that the dying were like infants and they the midwives of death (these tended to be of a religious bent), while others professed themselves appalled at an activity tantamount to murder, seeing all sorts of possible ramifications (greedy or vengeful relatives backhanding doctors, and so forth) that, to those of a more didactic or philosophical mind, belonged inside the world of the cheap novel.

In her dreams that night these discussions became the cawing or crying of birds, and Godley (with his crisp beard and salt-and-pepper suit) a kind of gamekeeper, prancing among them with a large shotgun. His war had, apparently, been a good one – that is, he had emerged from Tobruk with a decoration. When she saw him, one afternoon about a week after the lecture, walking towards her over the lawn with exactly the same gun in his hands, she heard again the growl of the liberated beasts her sleep's iron bars had somehow let out.

'Just culling, my lovely,' he said. 'Too many pigeons.'

His eyes wandered over her face as if seeking a target. She had not heard any shots from inside the house, but the grounds were large and partly wooded. Looking up, wondering what to say, a large bedsheet folded over her arm, she saw how very red the sun was, as if full of blood, through the bare tops of the furthermost trees.

'Are they really such a nuisance?'

'You want me to spare them?'

'I don't know.'

'Would you care for a stroll? We could discuss books. I hear you like books. I hear you write. Don't you go to the poetry club? I have spies.'

'I have sheets to put out.'

She eyed his gun briefly. Yes, it was the same as in her dream the week before, down to the polished wooden stock.

'I promise I will keep it cocked, my lovely,' he said, following this up with a guttural chuckle that made her blush. The dying folk no one loved (except the younger children, who tugged at their relatives' hands thinking they might lie in this amusing way for ever) were as much at his mercy as she was, she thought.

5

There was nothing amiss with physicality – even the kind of brutish sort you had to face each day, each night . . . and here his nose wrinkled at the slight odour of fetor and decay that lingered in the lounge, emanating as from some general miasma, some bog into which, like those ancient sacrificial victims in prehistoric Denmark, they were each of them sinking, their bodies already half peat, their blood dark with its waters, until the surface rose over them and all that was left was a black pool under clouds. It is not physicality that is wrong, that leads one astray (here he imagined Bruno in glory, shedding the taint of existence in some heavenly wash that whitened the earth-blotched soul to something altogether unnatural), but the fight one has with it. He watched as a gardener heaped dung from the next-door stables into a barrow, the load steaming in the chilly air. All morning the dung was scattered over the flower-beds, its dark ochreous matter lovely in the sunlight, shot through with gleams where the unmashed straw still showed.

His daughter had brought from home his old trench binoculars, which allowed this sort of detail to leap into sight, as well as giving him the power to roam without moving. When he was allowed outside for the first time – muffled from the cold, which to him had seemed a fresh, joyous sensation in its teasing bite – he had found himself overwhelmed as on a great sea, and requested that he forego his planned daily 'walk', terrified that this engulfing would sweep away his wonder. A small battle had ensued, in which the advantages of fresh air had prevailed over his own 'agoraphobia' (Dr Godley's term), and he now ventured out with his eyes half closed, like a painter, greatly amusing whichever nurse was pushing him.

The lidded blur of the landscape was sufficient, and allowed him to appreciate – and with as much joy as the view from the lounge – the touch of the air, the smell of the earth, the sensation of rough movement over paths as the wheels of the chair grappled with the vagaries of gravel and stones. It was not his eyes that were needed out here; the lack of an edge, a frame, made them too free, the landscape encroaching on him from every side, swivelling into view from every angle, the utter terror of its spaces grounded not in prolixity but in anarchy. Anarchy is not abandon, he reflected; abandon is beautiful, anarchy is ugly. Abandon is surrender, as I am soon to surrender to death, surrendering also all my memories. Anarchy is wilful and destructive, egotistical and raw, making a sound like those rooks there, battened to the tree-tops.

'Would you like me to tuck your blanket in for you, Jack? You look a bit shivery.'

'No, thank you very much, Carol. I'm quite alright. I'm really quite alright.'

6

As they walked over the vast lawn, chatting about books, she found herself drowning mentally in the fug of Dr Godley's personality, as strongly repugnant to her as the wafts of pipe tobacco his breath gave off every time he turned his head towards her, yet unable or even unwilling to wrestle herself out of it. He was all of a piece – his bristly suit, his beard, his polished brogues, his voice, his opinions on current affairs, his bright-red, brand-new Triumph Spitfire that gouged the gravel or spat it at your knees. His waxy face was neither youthful nor too old, but poised somewhere in an eternal middle age that suggested he had never passed through any other stage of life. Against this certainty she felt herself flake into pieces as easily as the bark of the large birch that stood sentinel over the benches in the courtyard, not even the starch of her uniform helping her there.

When he took her – seized would be too strong a word – around the waist, too far off from the house to be properly visible, and sought to press his mouth upon hers, his other hand burrowing under her uniform, fingers scrabbling at the elastic of her underwear, a thumb making a stab at entering the muff of her privates, the scream she gave off broke into the hundreds of rooks it frightened into flight from the tops of the great elms beyond, and with this sound went the last vestige of control. She flung the sheet over his head, pulling him down by its edges into a crouched position, her arms strong enough after a year of nursing to take avantage of his surprise.

She ran, and he ran after her, tangling himself in the sheet like an awkward ghost, turning the sheet into a toga that hugged his body and felled him with one wrong footing while she fled to the nurses' quarters.

He lay there on the grass, his fury and surprise exaggerated, if anything, by the cotton that gripped his features and made his face resemble the plaster moulds of the dead at Pompeii, screaming in their agony – though Richard Godley's agony was that of shame, and came out rather muffled.

7

Positioned again by the glass doors, the binoculars in his lap, he saw how without memory life is anarchic and spiteful, how life today wrought terrible destruction on memory, filling the space it left with stuff and nonsense. The television blithered in a corner, turned up too loud, and for the first time it bothered him even after he had removed his hearing-aid. It was the afternoon news, and the word 'guerilla' kept repeating itself, and he imagined gorillas in khaki in the jungles around Saigon. The television had been broken when he first arrived and a man had come about a week ago and mended it as one might mend the broken statue of a deity, and now as it flickered like a shadowy, poisonous thing in the corner of his joy he considered whether he might break it purposefully, whether he had the strength to sabotage it in some way – passing through his knowledge of such things culled from a lifetime in advanced electronics, then sinking into scenes from his past, his work, the laying of the lines in Africa, the research project in Newfoundland, the dull routine of the Manchester years in which he had, nevertheless, formed the technical basis for all hybrid computer systems (increasingly in use on assembly lines, according to the reports he had read right up to the day he came to the hospice). He was wearied even by the thought of it. His life had been almost too long.

What, he reflected, had this sick, tired old man granted to the world – what new horrors, what dreams turning into nightmares, what little gifts? Their minutiae snaked into a thousand branches, themselves branching out into further possibilities as a twig snakes through the seasons and hardens into its life, leafing its growth. Why, he thought, training his binoculars on a nearby tree, do leaves look like lungs? Why do those new leaves on the ash appear to be coaxing the air into them as they quiver or lie still?

With the binoculars he could shut out the shadows of the crazed, flickering eye the other old men were clustered round, and he roamed over the garden in peace, catching birds pulling worms on the lawn, looking forward to the nightingales said to nest close enough in the shrubbery to be heard mid-summer from everywhere in the house. He did not like considering his working life; already it seemed to him a shrivelled thing, like the shell of a caddis fly, imitating exactly his form, his being, but not *of* that being, that life he was now discovering. As for his children's visits, they were almost a distraction, though he loved to touch their hands and kiss their cheeks, stroke the flesh that was part of his long-dead wife, the blood blended with his but her eyes in them both, their warmth and suffering, their unhappinesses; feeling the blood beat at their wrists with the tips of his fingers, listening to them without complaint or even bitterness.

His old trench-observer's binoculars swayed onto the high, far-off treetops of the clough, where rooks were swirling suddenly as if disturbed by a great wind, and then crept down to focus on a nearby winter rose. Behind the rose, at the furthest distance of the lawn, lay the edge of the woods where something moving caught his eye. He fumbled with the focus, and saw that someone was running, pursued by a white phantom. It was as if he himself had coaxed this scene into being, the figures so blurred and distant as to be almost imaginary; the pursued figure and the wriggling, white horror were like mythic figures providing, despite their tiny size, the disturbing subject of a vast painting. Greenery hid them before he could adjust the focus precisely enough to bring it out of dream. He waited, though there was nothing but the shadow of the woods, brushed here and there with the first blossom of spring.

He lowered his binoculars and closed his eyes, disturbed in some way he could not describe, even to himself.

From that moment on (and it was as if he was watching it happen from the outside, helpless), his feeling of joy and abandon withered. Remarked on by his visitors in the last week of his life, right up to the very last minutes of consciousness, his sinking into the blues was regarded by no one on the staff as the least bit abnormal, but the inevitable result of the fading of his essential powers.

8

'Did you kick him in the you-know-whats, Carol?' asked Pooma, whose sense of propriety was only equalled by her lust for titillating facts.

Her roommate shook her head.

The sun had been discoloured and the rooks had taken away her screams. She was poised on the edge of a great discovery: death was neither sleep nor awakening but the total defeat of both. She had studied the moment the last breath was not repeated — they all had — but the stiffening yielded no more than the carrying on. There was no actual instant, in fact. Life was, she thought, rather like the great marquee they had put up for the annual fête on the lawn and which she had watched being taken down on the Sunday, its slow collapse like that of an airship's she had seen in a documentary a year or two before. Life's collapse begins at some indefinable point and continues until the last peg is packed away and the lorry driven off out of the gates, or possibly until the trampled grass springs up again. The point is, one could not know where life ends and death begins, only that death spares nothing, not one morsel.

She ran these thoughts through her head over and over again, cutting deeper grooves in her consciousness and feeling her body under the nightgown with her hands as if to reassure herself of her own physical presence, straying long enough over her soft muff to drown herself frequently in a torrent of intense pleasure which encouraged sleep (of a deeper kind) rather than shame. The dead strode through her dreams with enormous confidence, trailing their soiled raiments and fouled sheets, stinking of discarded parts, babbling like excited children about to receive a treat.

Soon these too strode out of the cage of her dreams and into her waking days.

Dr Godley died in his Triumph Spitfire on a dark lane one late night in July. He reappeared in the corridor as she was carrying a chilled glass of milk to a patient some three weeks after the death notice had been printed in *The Times*. His face was gaunt but otherwise unharmed, though he trailed his fingers as if something had stamped on them.

'Let me tell you,' he whispered, as she stood quite calmly with the tray steady in her hands, waiting for him to depart, 'let me tell you, it is awfully cold in here, awfully cold.'

'I'm sorry, Dr Godley, I can't help you there,' she said, keeping her back very straight. 'It is high summer, the nightingales are singing and all the windows are open.'

They stood together and listened; even in the corridor they could be heard, the nightingales, by the dead as well as by the living.

THE ORCHARD

He was never quite sure of Lucy. She would sometimes approach him like a bear wanting a hug, ready to crush him. At other times she would manifest herself as a harridan, yet a gentle one, all smiles behind the torrent of vituperation. They would make love easily, at least twice a week when he was not working late, and the twins came with no undue difficulty. After their birth she developed complications and there were no more children: he had hoped for a daughter. There were no other women, though he had considered several, and her affairs were only in his mind. Their holidays were desultory but relaxing, filling the car with shells and sand and the fragrance of sun oil, filling his mind with memories that had as much to do with his own childhood as the immediate past. One day they decided the house was not quite big enough and they moved after five weeks, 'like lightning' as she put it. They moved into a house near Henley with Jacobean panelling and an orchard next to a crumbling garden thick with bracken, nettles, liverwort in the damp corners, a muddy pond with a concrete frog on its bank green with algae. She was happy, he was not. There were woods around it which in fifteen years' time, soon after they were gone under something of a cloud, would be cut down and replaced by a large commuter estate of forty well-appointed residences, thus depriving the house of its cosy isolation. During the time they were there they knew nothing of this, as one does not know what might happen in an hour's time, let alone the far future. They believed the old battered house with its leaking roof and crumbling garden and ill-tended orchard would be slumped in its verdant solitude for good, and that their life would go on there for ever. He cleared the garden of weeds and cleaned out the pond, but all this took longer than anticipated and he was tired of the luxuriance, the greenness that crept back in lolloping stems and broad, unnameable leaves. It was like a story-book picture, one of the complicated illustrations in the children's glossy book of fairy tales from which he would read to the boys on his free nights, emphasising the voices. Out of the greenery glared these pink and red eyes, denizens of the woods beyond. They walked these woods each Sunday and Lucy would thank God the trees were here, despite the mud underfoot and the miasma of rotting leaves between the mossed trunks. He imagined himself somewhere dryer, more exotic than Buckinghamshire, and wondered if he should have accepted that post in Dubai. He would dream at night of hills of sand, hills rolling on and on under a burning sun and their damp house in the middle of these hills, surrounded by a grey cloud of mist in and out of which the boys played, the garden and the orchard still rampant somehow.

The repairs to the house prevented them from going on holiday to the sea one year and he spent the two weeks fending off the twins' demands in the orchard while he worked on the trees, apple and cherry and plum, a book on orchard-keeping kept open by a stone, its pages rippling in the heat. He knew it was the wrong time to prune and cut but did it anyway, convinced that the trees were tough and sinewy enough to take it. He was impatient to see the orchard fruit properly, finding its rows of gnarled and twisted boughs the most beautiful place on the property. But after he had cut it in the ruthless way the book recommended at another season, the place was no longer beautiful but maimed. He had maimed it. He rarely went into the orchard after that, leaving its long grass to the boys. He went in once in the early autumn to spray it against a disease which contorted the leaves and made them swell like peaches, the spray catching in his throat and making him feel peculiar for a few days. The spray dripped off the swollen, twisted leaves like milk. He did this again just as the buds were breaking, at the recommended time. Half the trees did not leaf at all, or leafed only on one or two branches. He had killed them, it appeared. They were too old to take all this drastic treatment, Lucy suggested. He shouted at her then, perhaps for the first time in their marriage. She never stopped talking, he shouted. She never stopped telling him what was what. He crashed away into the undergrowth at the far end of the garden – a part they had decided to leave wild after reading an article in the newspaper's gardening supplement – and left her crying by the old sink outside with its green stain like a grass snake, its broken pots on the side, the hung fork above it webbed with cobwebs that no one had touched since the day they had moved in.

Her mother died and she inherited a large sum with which they renovated the house from top to bottom and cleared the garden once and for all, drastically. He felt he had made a desert of it from which he might start again. The new house – it was like a new house, though its spirit was very old, as was its clean repointed brick – stood up now in the cleared garden as it must have done five hundred years before, proud and defiant. This was what they told themselves. The twins were away at boarding school and the orchard was torn up to make a tennis court. Lucy had hated her mother and felt now that she had been rewarded for all her years of endurance. She looked out upon her property and felt even happier than she had done when she had first arrived; she felt she could breathe. The air was lighter. The sunlight came through undisturbed. She wondered about Douglas. He would not play tennis – they had rowed about this – or entertain the idea of her friends playing, so that she was stuck with the ball-cannon when the boys were away at school. He had been happy to lose the orchard, or at least he had accepted the idea in good grace. He spent more and more time walking in the woods without her since their bad row about the tennis, which she had lost. He could be very stubborn and had threatened her with divorce. He had let her build the tennis court – an expensive all-weather variety painted green – only to cripple the use of it, for she had imagined tennis parties during the week, the sun winking upon jugs of lime cordial, husbands far away in their offices or cars, the wives talking and talking. Laughter. She knew that Douglas's attitude was a kind of grief, he was in mourning for the orchard and by the next summer he would be fully recovered, the hedge would have grown around the wire fence a little, the court would have settled into itself and would look less raw and absurdly new and she could enjoy her tennis parties. Meanwhile she played the ball-cannon alone, adjusting its pitch and angle as recommended in the manual, notching up the speed. They had purchased it second-hand from the boys' prep school, but it worked impeccably. Sometimes it frightened her. She would have preferred Douglas or one of her friends. Gradually after hours and hours on the court she came to know the ball-cannon's characteristics, adjusted herself to its manic repetitions, its speed and clockwork character. She improved her game considerably and beat her sons hollow when they returned from their new school for the summer holidays – despite their sudden spurt of growth, their broad shoulders, the hint of facial hair that the sun caught. They were very surprised. Douglas was surprised, though he failed to show it. She seemed so much younger, he thought. He sat on the court's edge and sipped white wine, watching her from under a peaked cap. He remembered his sons squealing tinily between the orchard's trees as if it was both yesterday (or even that morning) and also very long ago, decades or even centuries. This made no sense, he thought. Behind him the house stood as if on its own, tender shrubs and the odd sapling manfully sprouting from a circle of mulch in the new grass, everything labelled in case they forgot what they were. The new grass was so tender that the boys had been instructed not to play on it, but they no longer played, he noticed. They played tennis and they played their music or their computers in their rooms, but they no longer rolled about the garden, scuffing it. His daughter did not exist but he imagined her anyway, he imagined her playing between the trees of the ·orchard and riding her horse along the lane or even through the woods, ducking the lower branches and trampling the wild garlic. She had blond hair and a winning smile and called him Daddy. He smiled and stirred the ice in his wine. One of the boys had told him languidly that it was barbaric to put ice in wine, and he had flinched not with embarrassment but with grief at the loss of the modest child he had once known. Now Lucy was playing both boys at the same time and they were getting angry because she was too good for them, running about the court in her white tennis skirt that he found sexy, its hint of virginal innocence and health strained at by the flesh within, the sweat and the sharp smells of effort, panting and grunting. One of the boys came over to him and thrust the racquet in his free hand while the mother was shouting out not to be a bad sport. Douglas got up and walked over to the vacated spot and waited. He was reasonably drunk with wine and sunshine and his own secret thoughts. He thought of the spray dripping off the leaves like milk and the red and pink eyes in the undergrowth. He thought of the hung fork webbed with cobwebs and how he had wanted to ask the builders to conserve it, to work around it, but in the heat of the moment he had not dared, it had sounded ridiculous. They had ripped out the sink in a matter of minutes and taken the fork off its hook without a moment's thought. The pink and red eyes had vanished. The fork's wooden handle had crumbled into powder. He gripped the racquet and told his wife to serve. She looked very pleased and he felt this pleasure run through him like ice. He had not played for years and he missed the ball. His son groaned and told his brother to come back, but his brother had already left the court and was walking towards the house over the tender new grass. The wire-frame door swung shut.

'Aren't I good enough?' Douglas asked.

His son smirked.

'Of course you are, Dad.'

A pang of love shot through him now when he saw how vulnerable the boy was, how ready to be afraid of life. It was his turn to serve and Douglas did so, lobbing the ball so gently over the net that it was certain to go in but it somehow missed the line. The sun was hot on his neck. There was no shade on the court. Of course, he thought, Lucy must have her tennis parties. She must fill the place with her affection, her friends in their white sports outfits must fill the place and talk. He served the second ball and it struck the top of the net and bounced the right side. An aeroplane groaned in the sky, throbbing westwards. He served again and it was alright, Lucy returned it gently to him and he struck it back hard in a pale imitation of his long-ago prowess when he could slice the ball so that it skimmed the net to drop abruptly the other side as if on a wicked thread. Now the ball bounced off the cannon standing at the back and leapt up high as if alive. He watched it curl against the blue sky, the sky of a desert in Dubai, of his possible other life, while the others squealed with laughter. When the holidays were over the house would again be empty of the boys and he and Lucy would find it much too quiet. A few months before, under the same conditions, waiting for their weekly phone call from school that was not coming (as if they had been forgotten), he had emptied a bottle of full-blooded red on the white carpet between the white leather sofas while Lucy was playing the ball-cannon under the new floodlights: he had watched the wine splash upon the whiteness – tipping it out for a reason he could not explain even to himself – and the stain had remained for good like the faintest of echoes where so much else had fallen into silence.

PRESERVED

I was working on a dance. This was the Philip Glass era and
the music was ambient, repetitive. It was by a composer I
won't name because I have grown to hate his music. I forced
myself to like it back then because there was no choice; it
was the future, and the future often turns out to be fraud-
ulent when it arrives.

My cousin Saul lent me his house in Tuscany for three
weeks to work on the piece. I wanted the choreography to
be plain, simple, with sudden odd eruptions from a much
more primitive era. But the music did not give me a story-
line. There was no rootedness. The commission came from
a major international dance company, operating out of
Stuttgart. (Later it was amalgamated with what my friend
Hector called the Rhine Gang.) After fifteen years in
California, I thought this job would reintroduce me to
Europe.

The big old Tuscan farmhouse was divided in two. The
other half was owned by Saul's best friend from the Jersey
POW camp days, Ivor. Right now it was empty, but I knew
from Saul that the two halves mingled on the paved terrace,
which was covered by wisteria and looked out over the lawn
and the woods to the hazy coast, where Shelley was washed
up. This was April, and the weather was very mixed. The
wisteria had not yet flowered but there was blossom on the
apricot trees. I lit a fire in the upstairs room and it was very
cosy. The cool and the wet were welcome after San Francisco.
I was thinking seriously of settling back in Europe. I had

this presentiment of catastrophe – maybe the quake, maybe nuclear attack (this was the 1980s, remember). I had lost a lot of friends to AIDS. And I'd split up with Angelo after he sold the flower shop. Either way, I fancied keeping my head down somewhere in Europe.

On the third or fourth day the other half was suddenly filled with noise – a group of friends, from England. I appreciate young people. Youth is important to me. I regard myself as a young man in an old man's body, and even that body amazes people with its supple elasticity. It is not just the exercises: it is also the meditation. To transcend, daily, one's cares for fifteen minutes is to smooth out one's skin. I pin my soul on the washing line and let it billow and freshen. Except that no one has a washing line in the States.

I introduced myself on the terrace. They were three unmarried couples. Mark was with Jill, Lucy was with Oliver, Jamie was with Tamsin. Tamsin was fine-boned with a dancer's long legs, but she had never danced (I asked her).

On the second evening they invited me to supper. At least, Lucy did. Lucy was gushy and kind, although I wasn't sure even then how deep her kindness went. She was the best friend of Ivor's niece and had well-bred looks and a comfortable, plumpish body. Oliver was tall and stiff, as if he had never gotten over being head of his public school. He had made two mistakes: he had brought shorts and he was wearing them. Jamie was smooth and narrow-eyed, a trainee lawyer with extremely expensive shoes. He had been kicked out of his public school for a reason no one would divulge. They were all training to be *something*.

I sat at the end of the kitchen table with Mark and Jill. They seemed the odd ones out – Jill plain and scholarly, Mark what my mother would call 'rough at the edges' and with dark colouring. He spoke with a pronounced northern accent. He was a botanist, he told me – a palaeoethnobotanist. He sat through dinner in a bright orange cagoule: their half of the house still had a chill in it. His eyes were almond-shaped, with long black lashes. He had a delicate nose on a big face.

'Macro- and microstructures of fossilised horse dung, stratifications of peat bog samples, pollen, charcoal, rhizopod analyses,' he said. 'That's me. 'Ow do.'

'Hello.'

He was from Wolverhampton, which he called Wolvo. He told me about his childhood. He and his parents would drive out to the Clee Hills for picnics in the family's old Austin, his dad smoking Senior Service and singing 'Oh What Will Mother Say?', the boy in the back under a trouser-press with big rusty wing-nuts.

'Big enough to take on ten thistles and a butterbur,' he said. 'Champion flower presser, I was, as a sprog.'

I smiled. I liked the way he spoke, even though it was loud.

'Mum would try to get me to count the telegraph poles so Dad'd pipe down. All I could think of were flowers, though. Smell of the earth they popped up out of. I loved to take my trowel and dig, even back then.'

'A nut, even back then,' said Jill.

Jill was his first girlfriend. She had been a fellow graduate student in the Department of Geography at Birmingham. She had short hair and contact lenses that troubled her, but a makeover might have made her pretty. Her thesis was about the influence of water levels on the siting of acid-tolerant species in the oligotrophic habitat of the raised bog. His thesis was on the characteristics of peat humification in relation to dead plant material.

'You can see how we're made for each other!' laughed Jill.

Mark said: 'We worked together as assistants on Lindow Man, just after he was excavated.'

I did not look impressed enough, although he waited.

'You don't know Lindow Man?'

'Spider Man, but not Lindow Man.'

Lindow Man, they told me, was found in a bog and dated from the pre-Roman era: the only British bog body of any significance. Although squashed and distorted, the only face from proto-historic Britain. Sensitive as lichen. A sacrificial victim. Mark had worked on the contents of the preserved stomach.

'Same as if you were to drop off the twig now,' he said, 'straight into a peat bog. If I were to cut you open in thousands of years' time, it'd be all spag and tomato bits.'

'Thank you, Mark, that's a nice thought. But I guess I'm pretty well preserved already.'

I couldn't finish my meal. As they were talking, I felt a familiar excitement. I knew that my dance had found its rootedness. My dance would be entitled 'Bog Body', or just 'Lindow' – it would be a homage to Lindow Man.

A couple of days on, Mark told me how his mother had disappeared.

We were at the end of a good supper and he had drunk a lot of the local Chianti. We all had; we were outside and the candles were flickering in the warm spring air. The others were sharing jokes about their crowd back in London – old school pals, mostly. Mark and I sat apart from the others on wicker chairs. He looked very fine in the candlelight, despite (or perhaps because of) his lumpy sweater, which had dried seeds and grass caught in its knit. I dread using the term Lawrentian, at least in public, but he did make me think of the young Alan Bates – if you changed the nose.

'They had a big argy-bargy one day, out on the Clee Hills near Trablow Moss. My hands were black. I was digging up this burst football out of a boggy patch, taking no notice of their nonsense. The burst football was soft and light. As black as my hands. Some folk reckoned that Mum had an accident, fell down a gorge or into a bog. Others say she had another man, in Goole. At any rate, she stomped off over the grass and never came back from that day to this.'

'Goole?'

'So they said. I've never been there. Maybe I should go.'

'That's terrible, Mark. I mean, that she never came back.'

'Hardly remember her,' he shrugged. 'Auntie May brought me up, after Dad went off to the nut-'ouse. I kept the burst football until Auntie May chucked it one day, saying it was mucky. Which it was, because I'd never washed off the peat. I felt a bit upset, to be honest, though I didn't say a thing. I didn't say a thing about how I hadn't dared clean the peat off it, just in case it was something else and not a burst football.'

'What do you mean, Mark?'

He grinned, most attractively. 'What does a bog-preserved head feel like?

'Actually, I have never felt one.'

'A burst football. Kind of soft, like.'

'I don't know. Does it?'

He nodded, and threw his head back to empty his glass and I saw the movement of the strong muscles in his throat.

Jill was not like Mark; her father was a judge, her mother a top research chemist. Her northern accent was an assumed overlay.

'She's only took me on to show them she's different,' Mark snorted, watching the others giggling with her. 'Her mummy and daddy looked at me down their snotty noses and I gave them a lecture on macrofossils and bleached vegetation layers.'

I laughed. I offered him some more wine. I wanted him for myself.

'This is my first time abroad,' he said. 'I've seen the cliffs of Mingulay from a fishing boat, walked the Pennine spine, stood on Ben Hutig in a March gale, but I've never been abroad. Jill wants to educate me. She wants to wean me off packet curries and freeze-dried beef stews. But a Vesta curry consumed on the edge of Barra in a salty headwind, after a good hike up and down Heaval, with a 'nana for pudding – that's pure magic. It's all context, is life. Like palaeobotany.

Without context, nothing means a thing. Nothing is but what it's removed from. I'm pissed. My skull's a boiled turnip.'

'Mark, I think you're a very profound person.'

I felt I had been preparing for this all my life.

The next evening I cooked them homemade lasagne. I used their kitchen (it was bigger – Saul was no cook) and every available surface was covered in long strips of fresh wholemeal pasta, lightly floured.

''Ow do,' said Mark, 'so this is where Dr Mengele ended up.'

'Do I look like Dr Mengele, Mark?'

He studied me. Something happened in the space between our eyes.

'Give or take a few years,' he said.

'Do you think of me as old, Mark?'

'Any road, I reckon it's better out of a packet from Tesco's.'

'You haven't tasted it yet. You'll be won over by the taste. Now you're sitting on it.'

'Bloody hell. What's it doing on the chair?'

'I can hardly put it on the floor, can I?'

'What's for pudding?'

'Zabaglione.'

'Sounds like someone throwing up in *The Godfather.*'

'Where are the others?'

'Reading literature upstairs.'

'Do you not appreciate literature, Mark?'

'I don't have a flash haircut.'

'What has *that* got to do with it?'

He leant against the door and folded his arms, watching me roll the last splat of pasta.

'Jill said to me, just now, "Whatever you do, Mark, don't ring your Auntie May from here."'

'And what did you say, Mark?'

'I said: "I don't need to, love; I've given her the number."'

'You're a very witty young man, Mark. In fact, you are one of the funniest guys I have ever met.'

'You think I'm an oik, don't you?'

'That's not what I mean. Your wit comes completely naturally. It's the same with certain dancers. They dance completely naturally. Training them is almost a shame.'

'Are you a Yank, in fact?'

'No, I just sound it, to the English. To the Americans I sound English. I've been over there now about fifteen years. San Francisco. I'd like to show you San Francisco, one day, Mark. Would you be so kind as to pass me that strip, without tearing it? Thank you. That's very kind of you.'

The farmhouse was near Lucca, a town I had never visited, although my friends said it was their ideal of what a town ought to be – unlike most towns in the US which had been taken over by barbarians and Macdonald's. In those days I was not left-wing, but a libertarian with a mystical streak, and my choreography was thought to be inspired as much by Gurdjieff as Martha Graham. This was not altogether wrong, although I was drawn deeply to Tao Buddhism. I tried to think of the space a body occupied and the space it did not occupy at the same time; a little like an artist who defines a limb by shading in wherever the limb is not. I was also influenced by jazz and free expression, which was big in San Francisco then. I was experimenting a little with Native American music, too, although I got into trouble for that, later.

I tried to explain this in the car to Jamie, who was impressed that I had heard of The Cure and Joy Division and that I had used some Brian Eno in my recent work (for New York).

We located the supermarket just outside the city walls and had a lot of fun finding stuff. There was a pack of what looked like ordinary lawn grass under the cling-film and we laughed at it.

'You could make a fortune out of this in the States,' I said.

'You could get the neighbour's lawn clippings and label it *Hand-Picked in Tuscany*. I know places in San Francisco that do that!'

I was going down rather well, despite being old enough to be their grandfather. Mark, however, did not like the supermarket. The bright lights seemed to diminish him.

'Here's the offal,' he called out, at the meat counter.

'Keep your voice down.' Jill's whisper had an edge of hardness.

'Faggits and pays, faggits and pays,' he chanted, laughing. I had realised by now that he was playing a very elaborate and ironic game.

It was a Monday. Every interesting church was *Chiuso*. It was like the Stations of the Cross, I said. I liked the town, though. I could see what all my friends meant. Aromas – coffee, vanilla, parmigiano, prosciutto – passed us down the narrow streets like a reward for being alive. The shops looked as if they had not changed for a hundred years. Everyone was effortlessly glamorous, pale gold rings, tawny gold wristwatches against brown skin. Lucca's charm was its medieval walls, their grassy breastwork where we walked for an hour. Sheer wealth had something to do with it, too. In spite of this wealth, they had knocked down very few old buildings. There was a sense of pride in the past.

'On the other hand, I like Berlin,' I said. 'I lived there once. There is absolutely no nostalgia in Berlin. I have been to East Berlin recently, for a show we gave, and I can tell you that when the Wall comes down that city is going to be a place of very interesting energies.'

'It might never come down,' said Jamie.

We looked at the great, fat medieval wall, with tufts growing from its brick.

'One day for sure it will look like this, but not nearly so pretty,' I said. 'It's a matter of patience.'

'Then capitalism will flood into every crevice,' said Jamie, the reflex socialist.

'The Italians move so well, don't they,' I pointed out, to change the subject. 'They are easy with themselves. The Anglo-Saxon race is awkward and aggressive when it moves. I am generalising, of course.'

'I hope you are,' said Mark. 'Watch this, you lot!'

He danced. There, on the wide grassy ramparts. The others found it embarrassing. Mark, imitating a ballet dancer! *Stop showing off, Mark. Mark, you're a total prat. Take him home, someone.*

An elderly German group stood watching as if he were part of the mystery and charm of Lucca.

Which he was, of course. His large, bearish body moved through space much more interestingly than anyone else realised. He appeared captivated by his own performance; its jokiness spooled to an end but he carried on. Perhaps it went on for only a minute, but for me it stretched on into infinity. He had a charge in him that was astonishing – a slow heaviness that his fake effeminacy made gracious, despite everything.

I was tired of taut, trembling professionals and their regimens and their tendon checks. This was something fresh. I had forgotten my camera, and tried to take mental snapshots to be transferred to paper the minute we got back.

A boy loses his mother on the moors. As a grown man, he dances her back – but she returns as the bog queen, as Lindow Woman, and drags him down into the wet and the dark, preserving him with her for ever.

Jungian, mythic, earthy: I was very excited.

We did a quick tour of the villa's grounds that evening. I enjoyed their company and I believe they enjoyed mine. I was something novel to them, no doubt: a seventy-one-year-old in denim who did Tai Chi on the lawn each morning and whose leather jacket had a little pink badge that said: *I Ride Tough*. If the swimming pool had not been empty and it had been high summer I would have dived straight into it every morning.

These were not people who had seen the world, unless it was through a smart hotel's glass. I lie: Lucy had done a year's voluntary work in Zimbabwe. She'd had a black boyfriend. But then, so had I – for a few months in 1962. It taught me nothing more, over and above the heartbreak when he left, than having a white boyfriend ever did. Karl was cute, that's all, and thought the Black Panthers were the bottom of the heap.

The swimming pool's emptiness was depressing. Looking down at its bared concrete, Mark pointed out the fieldmice: one living, one dead. The living one was cuddling up to its squashed colleague in the deep end.

'Maybe mother and child,' said Mark.

I watched his face, but it gave nothing away.

He was making notes in the failing light. We descended some overgrown terraces, past old twisted olive trees, and came out in a wooded gorge full of twilight birdsong. The others were making a noise and Mark asked them to be quiet.

'Look at Oliver's knees,' said Tamsin. 'Goosebumps.'

'Keep off my knees,' said Oliver.

'*Shut yer gob,*' Mark ordered.

'What are we listening for?' asked Jamie.

'It doesn't matter,' said Mark.

The house looked tiny up above. We went in and out of the trees, in and out of the pewter light. I asked Mark what the trees were.

'Ash, oak, some false acacia. A few manly curved specimens of *Pinus pinaster.*'

'Golly,' I remarked, 'that sounds enticing!'

He smiled. I thought his glance at me was full of shared meaning, but it was twilight. He was collecting the *Pinus* cones, putting them in his knapsack. I envied him.

Now and again he would stop and make little notes in his book. When we got back to the house, I asked to look at the page he had filled that day:

Generous quantities of ragged robin, ivory-fruited hartwort, blue bugle. A flaming yellow scorpion senna on edge of coppiced beech-wood. Picked a mouse-ear hawkweed, a giant catsear, and a fat rough hawkbit for the squeeze-box.

These were spread out on the table, ready for the press.

'They are very beautiful names, Mark,' I said. 'This is a poem.'

His writing was meticulous, and the other pages included very fine coloured sketches.

Jamie said, prodding the flowers, 'Surprised you're interested in dandelions, Mark-o.'

Mark went into the woods the next day, with a pair of binoculars that he called 'm'twitch-can'. I offered to accompany him, and was hurt a little by his refusal.

'No one ever stays still or shuts their gob for long enough in woods. It's a good damp wood with lots of boggy bits in its rift where the stream runs, but woods always take ages to recover from a human being's arrival.'

'I see your point, Mark. Never mind.'

I worked on the dance in the top room, but not in my usual way. Usually, I make sketches as the tape of the music runs, try to find the visual narrative, the negative spaces around the bodies, work out what forces are in play and where they are happening in the given area and only afterwards do I use dance notation. Really, I am giving my imagination a walk. This time, however, I found myself miming the narrative with my own body. I could not begin to fix it on paper before I had propelled myself through it physically and psychically, working with the Tao.

Except that the Tao was not flowing. Something else was flowing, something much thicker, much thicker. Silt. I frightened myself, feeling this thick, dark stuff working its way up my body to my neck as I danced very slowly and clumsily, just as Mark had danced on the ramparts. I was not dancing:

I was trying to find a way out. I was working out of my own labyrinth in which all the exits were closing. I felt *deathly*, actually. I shrank in the sticky cold bog waters.

I sat there, afterwards, for about an hour, thinking.

I was deeply in love. But there was absolutely no sign that Mark even knew about it. It never once occurred to me that he might find me in any way repellent, at my advanced age. He felt lonely, that's all, and I firmly believed that I was the one to relieve his loneliness – maybe by unlocking the rest of him. You can be lonely to yourself because the rest of you – the interesting you – is locked away. There was a grace to my desire.

He and Jill never touched. Jill was an irrelevance. Sweet, but an irrelevance. Mark needed to be liberated, just as I had liberated Alain and Hector and Kurt.

All dead, now, of course.

Jill's Mini was still out of action. Oddly, I am rather good at mechanics – something to do with the mechanics of the body, with the way I dissect movement and then rebuild in my choreography – and I offered to take a look. None of the others – Mark included – had a clue. Mark was Green and went everywhere by bus or bicycle back home. ˙

The engine had a faulty connection to the battery. I made sure it stayed faulty, although a quick spurt of de-greaser would have solved it. It wasn't quite sabotage, it was more passive than that.

So we drove back into Lucca, and this time Mark rode with me. He rode in the back, and Jill rode in the front. He kept very quiet. Jill was fretting about the Mini. I told her we should wait until the handyman called Paulo, whom Saul and Ivor employed to keep the house and garden in trim, called round again. We could ask him to recommend a mechanic. You could not trust any old mechanic.

We climbed the well-known tower with trees growing out of the top. Hundreds of steps, but I was first out onto the roof, closely followed by Mark. These youngsters were not fit, I can tell you.

Tamsin popped breathlessly into view several moments later, but I had had time to ask Mark what type of trees these were.

'Holm-oaks. Ilex to the Romans.'

'I like that word, ilex. It occurs in poems.'

'Do very well in drought. But now and again they need a good lot of rain, good heavy rain. A good soak.'

'Maybe that's why the holm-oak is a symbol of rebirth.'

Mark looked at me. I get vertigo and was beginning to feel giddy up there. This is why I never went skiing with Hector in the mountains.

'I thought you didn't know what trees these were?'

'I don't, Mark. My knowledge of Mother Nature is strictly mythic.'

Jamie was last up. Tamsin suddenly started having a panic attack by the low wall and clung to Mark's arm, pressing it against her pretty breasts. Jamie took her round the waist and she let go of Mark's arm and started to breathe normally again. Once, on the unwalled top of the Pont du Gard, I saw a strapping German youth reduced to tears and had to lead him gently back. We started a relationship that lasted nearly four years. I even moved out to Berlin, to the workers' district called Wedding, living with him in a near-windowless basement flat about 500 yards from the Wall. I was very happy, despite the damp and cold and the couples screaming over the babies. But that was long ago. I never mastered German.

'The trees looked bigger from below,' said Oliver, as if he had been defrauded.

'Most things do,' I said.

Mark pointed to a little red beetle on one of the oak-leaves.

'A kerm,' he said. 'Made into an aphrodisiac by the Greeks.' He looked at me. I blushed.

'You see, I'm not just a pretty face.'

Tamsin, who had recovered well, laughed.

'What's so funny?' asked Jamie, who rarely smiled below his expensive haircut.

'Mark makes me laugh, actually,' said Tamsin. 'Nice to make people laugh, you know.'

Jill had noticed. So had I. It was quite obvious to me that I now had two rivals for love.

We were all shivering on the porch that evening when Tamsin said she had the gift of foresight and held Mark's hand.

'Gosh, there's so much in there,' she murmured.

'And a 'nana spare for you, our kid,' said Mark.

Her bone structure in the candlelight was perfect, so like a dancer's. It was very unfortunate.

'Really an awful lot,' Tamsin insisted.

Jill said, 'You do surprise me, Tamsin.'

'Oh come on, Jilly, that's not fair,' said Oliver, completely seriously. I thought at first he had said 'that's not far', on account of his accent. I began to dislike him, despite his youth.

Tamsin released Mark's hand, her eyes glittering with a perfect flame.

'Gizzit back,' Mark joked, lunging for her hand, accidentally touching a breast.

The topic of conversation was work, during supper. Oliver and Jamie were trainee lawyers and Lucy worked for a charitable organisation for female prisoners. Tamsin worked in an interior design shop. The conversation turned to credit cards. Lucy had gone with her mother to Liberty's and spent a fortune the previous week. Oliver said he was afraid to admit he got all his shirts in M & S. Everyone (except for Mark and myself) catcalled and whistled.

'Lucky I was never faced with that problem up in Wolvo,' Mark said. 'No M & S.'

Lucy looked surprised. 'There's no M & S in Wolverhampton?'

'I don't know,' said Mark, 'but I know there are two D's in Dudley.'

I now guess that Mark had skilfully set up that well-known northern joke, but at the time I thought it utterly sponta-neous. The others groaned politely.

I steered Mark onto bog bodies and Lindow Man, for my own professional purposes. The body's skull was pliable in the peat. Enzyme-induced degradation and microbial coloni-sation had resulted in the rapid and almost complete putre-faction of all his internal organs except the stomach. Jill chipped in now and again. Only Tamsin looked interested over the tagliatelle. I had the feeling that Mark was not going down so well with the others.

Mark did the washing-up (which he called 'clattering the crocks'), I dried. He had a smell about him of old barns and it was delicious. I was telling him about my love for animals and the concept of the Tao when the telephone rang. It was for him.

'Oh no, it'll be his Auntie May,' Jill whispered to me. She was putting the plates away.

''Ow do, our kid,' Mark shouted. 'Line's good. You can talk normally, Auntie May. Yo'am OK, then? And the chrysanths?'

The others went silent, which I considered a little rude. The following is an honest account of what we heard Mark say, in a broad Black Country accent.

'I *brought* us a pullie, course I did. No, don't fret, the Mafia's more down south. She *is* hanging on to her handbag, like it's got money in it. Oh dear. Oh dear. Oh *dear*. It might just be indigestion from bending over. Well of course you'am famished if you don't eat yer pays!'

When he came off, everybody (except Jill and myself) looked as if they were trying to blow up invisible balloons.

'Auntie May sends you her love,' Mark said to Jill, picking up the scourer. 'And she hopes you're hanging on to your handbag.'

Then the others exploded, snorting and giggling and saying

sorry all the time. Jill looked cross, not with the others but with Mark. Or with the others *via* Mark. I hoped Mark would walk out into the night, giving me an opportunity to follow him, but he did not. Instead, he carried on scouring the dishes with his back to them and it was ten minutes or so until the mirth subsided.

I lay on the high, old, country bed and listened, not to the difficult piece I was meant to be choreographing, but to my faithful old tape of the music of *Lawrence of Arabia*.

I worked very hard on the dance – the ebb and flow of it. The spatial mathematics kept snagging on my desire to do something bold and dangerous. I could not conceive of the mother-figure – the terrifying, Lindow Woman figure, the revenant who enters on the sudden, deep throb of the synthe-sised second movement – in any way that either convinced me or would convince that exacting European audience. I knew the company had a date in the Roundhouse in London. Its vast, converted railway turntable-shed was both wonderful and hellish to work in. You needed gouts of revolutionary surprise to match it. I needed a Larionov to design our set, but there were no Larionovs left.

Then I realised what was wrong. Lindow Woman had to be danced by a man. It was so obvious. Lindow Woman would dance as Mark had danced on the ramparts, like a man pretending to be effeminate. It would be both a warrior's dance and a perverted, dead thing that ghosts dance. Mark told me they thrust the victim down with the aid of a forked stick. The goddess they were sacrificing to was Freya.

'Freya must have been a cruel goddess,' I commented.

We were sitting on the lawn. The sun was out and it was warm enough. I was reading a book written by a friend, about his time with the Druze of Lebanon. Mark was scan-ning the woods below with his 'twitch-can'. The others were 'resting'. It was just after lunch. He had emerged from the house alone. The book was indistinct in my hands: my friend had been ambushed by the Druze, but I was reasonably sure that this incident was exaggerated. Lebanon is complicated. I got extremely hurt by a Lebanese boy, once.

'How do I know, I wasn't there,' Mark said. 'It's not my field, at any rate.'

'But let's face it, she was a goddess with an appetite.'

'If you say so.'

'How can you not agree? She was hardly the Virgin Mary.'

'We don't know enough to say.'

'She rode in a trap driven by a pair of cats.'

Mark lowered his binoculars.

'How do you know that?'

'I am into mythology. Like I told you, I've read P.V. Glob.'

'Things have moved on a bit since his day. He did a lot of conjecturing. I stick to what I know. Data and analysis.'

'Mark, that is not what makes the world go round. That is like analysing the grammar without appreciating the contents. You are capable of more than that. In fact, Mark, I believe you have a great hidden force in you. I've been watching you. You're holding yourself back. You're a little frightened, I know, but you are very much holding yourself back.'

'From what?'

He looked sullen and a little afraid. I fixed him with the gentlest and most intense of stares, but my heart was galloping.

'From where you really want to go, Mark. You are a very special person. There are not many people in the world with your kind of energies.'

'I don't know about that.'

'I do. It's a question of belief. Of believing in yourself. I think you lost that the moment your dear mother disappeared.'

'What the hell has she got to do with it?'

'Everything, Mark. Just about everything.'

'Everything and everything, amen.'

'Yes.'

'On yer bike,' he murmured.

He raised his binoculars to his eyes and swivelled and looked at me through them.

'Oo, a loriculus.'

'What's that, Mark?'

'A blue-crowned hanging parakeet.'

I was wearing my blue denim sun hat. I laughed.

'Mark, you are really the most amusing person. And brilliant with it.'

He lowered his binoculars again.

'You're pulling my leg,' he said.

'No, I am not.'

'What are you after, mate?'

I did not blush. Maybe the sun was too hot on my face. 'After, Mark?'

'Yeah. You'll be offering me a piece of cake next. Or a nice big 'nana.'

I laughed again, although I felt queasy with disappointment.

'The trouble is, Mark, you feel threatened by compliments. I have met many men like you, who feel threatened by compliments. Let me be frank, Mark. You are punishing yourself, because you feel guilt about your mother. I have welcomed my seventieth spring, I have seen the blossom grace the blue air seventy times, as a good friend of mine put it in his poem, but my own mother is still alive. She is ninety-three. I escaped her by moving to California. You never escaped your mother because she was dead and ghosts never go away.'

Mark was not looking at me. He was listening, his head slightly to the side, the tendon taut in his brownish neck.

'Buzzard,' he said. 'Hear it? Like a short-circuited seagull.'

He remained staring out, saying nothing more. There was the faintest high-pitched mew that was, I guessed, the buzzard, and there was the silence between us which was very graceful.

★

We went on some interesting visits together, during those two weeks. Leonardo da Vinci's house, for instance. Paulo had come and unfortunately he was good with cars: he laughed when he found the dirty connection. At the very last minute I suggested I accompanied them in the Mini. I really did want to see Leonardo's house.

Jill drove. Mark made Formula One noises the whole way. He claimed it was the only way to keep the 'char-a-bang' going. Jill got very irritated. It rained when we got to the village and Jamie blamed Tamsin for not warning him to bring his smart raincoat. I was upset to see Mark and Tamsin exchange knowing looks. The farmhouse museum had models of Leonardo's contributions to human progress: the tank, the machine-gun, the mounted limb-slasher. I told the others that he was said to have said, 'I'll do anything for money'. Lucy spent twenty-three minutes choosing a 'Leonardo' T-shirt while Oliver grumbled in the café. I was enjoying myself: I felt back in my twenties and the sky cleared and everything shone in the wet.

'Look,' said Lucy, at last, 'it's got his backwards-writing on it, just what I was looking for.'

'In German,' I said. 'And very explicit.'

'Oh, Christ in heaven,' she moaned, looking at it.

'What does it say, go on, tell us,' Tamsin urged, wriggling in her seat.

Lucy held the T-shirt up for me to read. I don't know any German, beyond the very basics. I pretended to mouth what I was reading. I pulled a face.

'My my,' I said, 'I didn't know that was physiognomically possible, even!'

I made them laugh. I was their boon companion. Meanwhile, my feelings for Mark were written in invisible backwards writing on my heart.

That evening everyone, including me, drank too much. They were going to Florence the next day, but though I wasn't actually invited, I couldn't have stood another long car trip. Instead, I told them to watch out in the Uffizi for the Virgin's robes, which were very sexual.

'They are red and they have folds in them like labia, in which there is often her finger resting. This is not masturbation but penetration. It is the finger of God. It is to show how God penetrated her in a divine way, with his spirit.'

'What a load of crap!' barked Oliver.

'That is precisely what Veronese said to the dirty minds of the Inquisition when they interrogated him about his Virgin's robes, painting by painting.'

They laughed, even Oliver. I was holding them in thrall.

'Was it subliminally unconscious or subversively deliberate?' Jamie asked, revealing a sharp intelligence behind his languid manner.

'That is a very good question,' I said. 'I think all great art is the fusion of the conscious and the unconscious. You know that you don't know what you show. It's the dreaming time of the wakeful imagination.'

I had never thought of this before. I felt I was coming very close to the heart of creativity but I was one glass of Chianti short. Mark's eyes glistened in the candlelight, but he said very little for once.

Lucy especially drank too much and told me on the terrace, while she was locking up her side of the house, that she thought she was totally worthless. I was not locking up; I was enjoying the night, the stars, the early nightingales, and feeling good about the way the dance was going and that faint delicious pain in my heart. The wine was swaying in my head. I told her to sit down next to me and we talked. I was like a grandfather to her, she said, without meaning to hurt – or maybe only subliminally meaning to hurt. I'd have preferred it if she'd said I was like an uncle. Her grandfather died when she was two, she strained to remember him. She looked much more attractive in the one candle I had kept burning. She had this quiet, interior expression that fought against her love of society, her good breeding, her English manners. But it never quite made it through, that was the thing. Zimbabwe had been too great a shock for her, it had operated at a level so much deeper than dinner-parties, or even Christian good works, that she had disturbed her equilibrium. This is what I suggested, anyway – quite erroneously, I now recognise. She was just a snake tongue under the powdered sugar.

'You're a very good man, Jack,' she said. 'I'm not a good person.'

'You have this idea of goodness that's been handed on to you,' I said. 'That idea is to do with the status quo keeping power and privilege. The powerful people – your parents – decide what is good and what is bad. It's like a papal decree, you know? You are questioning that idea with your innate energies, with your heart. The heart is always truthful. You have to stretch yourself in life, go further. A lot further. There's a kind of zero point, a neutral position from which you start out, and that zero point is maybe where you are now, because it's a lot to do with recognising that you are not satisfied with where you are. And you are interpreting that as worth-lessness. You have to change your criteria, Lucy.'

'You are clever, Jack. I *think* I know what you're saying.'

She had this strangely diffuse face – large teeth, plumpish. I have no great memory of it. Her eyes were soft and a little dull, as if she didn't have to bother to look at anything prop-erly because it would all be there anyway. I search to recall her precise appearance, but she was all about the impreci-sion of comfort. As I was carrying on like some California shrink, reassuring her in our mutual haze of drink and night air, I thought that she was probably right about being worth-less. There *was* something futile about her and there always would be. She already looked about forty-five. At forty-five she would look as she did now, and everyone would think she was very well preserved. And then, out of the blue, she asked me if I was gay.

'I fall in love very easily,' I said. 'I have fallen for girls, too.'

'Half-and-half, are you?'

I smiled. 'You know in *Spartacus* how Laurence Olivier as Crassus has that scene with Tony Curtis as his slave Antoninus, massaging his master's back, and how Crassus says that some men like snails and others prefer oysters, and after Antoninus says he likes one or the other, Crassus says he likes both snails and oysters? I believe they cut that in the official version, but I get to see the full version in special cinema clubs in San Francisco. Does it bother you if I say I like both snails and oysters?'

'No. One of my closest friends is gay.'

'That's good.'

'I really hate snails and oysters, in fact.' She laughed.

'I hope you're not talking metaphorically, now. Actually, I am not really bisexual,' I added. 'I have never fallen for a girl in the same way I have fallen for a boy. I have an innate adoration for the human body and the heart inside that body, but my love for a girl would always be brotherly.'

'Hi, brother,' she laughed, raising her hand.

I took her hand and held it.

'Lucy, take charge of your own life.'

She blinked back tears.

'Oh, it's all so boring, my little life. I haven't even seen *Spartacus*, it's more Mummy's generation. She had me when she was nineteen, she's not even forty-five and amazingly glamorous, still. I wish I was someone like Mark, who's so directed, who just doesn't bother about pleasing anyone else.'

I realised my hand had flexed involuntarily, tightening on her fingers.

'Mark?'

'Yes. He's so completely selfish. It must be nice not having to think about behaving properly, or ever wondering whether everyone's happy around you.'

'You think Mark is like that?'

'Well, haven't you noticed? Of course you have, you're

just being frightfully diplomatic. I've noticed how nice you are to him despite the fact you're obviously *incredibly* irritated by him, like we all are. Except Jill, of course. He so puts on his northern accent thing, he doesn't really need to. He makes such a point of it.'

'Well, it's where he comes from,' I said, a little astonished. 'The Black Country. That's how a lot of people speak in that area, like Texans in Texas or whatever. I had a north London suburbs accent, once. It's been layered over –'

'Yes, but it comes and goes, have you noticed? It's so self-conscious. Oliver's going to hit him, soon, and as for Jamie . . .'

'Oh, but I don't mind Mark,' I said, feeling quite upset. 'Why was Jamie kicked out of his public school, by the way?'

Lucy laughed.

'For organising a hike,' she said.

'A hike?'

'No, I mean a heist. I'm incredibly thick, by the way. I don't know how I made it to Cambridge.'

'A heist?'

'There was this Gainsborough painting in the Common Room, an enormous painting worth a fortune, and the door wasn't even locked and there were no alarms or anything. He claims he was approached by someone in the town and then the police got onto it and somehow found out that Jamie was the inside chap, or whatever they call it. It was something to do with the IRA, in the end.'

'That's very impressive, Lucy.'

'And now he wants to be a lawyer,' she said, softly. 'He's Oliver's best friend. A bit arrogant, though, isn't he?'

'Jamie?'

'Look, *re* Mark. Can't you say something to him, like you've said things to me? It's not to do with any working-class or lower-middle-class thing, either. I've lots of friends from very ordinary backgrounds and strong accents and everything. It's just to do with a total lack of consideration for anyone else. He never lifts a *finger*. Like a fifteen-year-old.'

'He did the washing-up that time,' I said, but she ignored me.

'I can't think how Jill stands it, though she's not got much choice of men, I guess. And Jamie reckons Tamsin's gone on him – Mark, I mean. That's not what she told me! OK, he's a bit of a hunk, but he's such a nerd with it. Jamie's always been incredibly possessive. I knew him at Marlborough. He was just the same then, except then it was boys. That's strictly hush-hush, by the way.'

I looked at Lucy's round, shining face and wanted to tear it up, the way you'd tear up a magazine photograph. I let go her hand and stood and wished her goodnight, gently, giving nothing away. Oliver called at that very moment from the top floor, where Ivor had made what he called the Music Room, with a Bang & Olufsen stereo and some antique leather chairs. I could hear, as Oliver called down for Lucy, the strains of a Rossini opera through the open window.

It struck me that pretty well everyone was falling for Mark, in their own way. We would start to tread on each other's toes, very soon. I recalled something La Rochefoucauld said, about friends getting disgusted in the end with friendship and devotees getting disgusted with devotion. As I went up to my bedroom in my half of the house, wishing we didn't have to share a terrace, the thought came to me that maybe people who loved living could get disgusted by life.

'I want,' I said to Mark, 'to ask for your help. I want you to dance for me.'

He snorted. He had breakfast crumbs at the side of his mouth.

'I'm serious. Between you and me, Mark, I'm an important choreographer, I'm very well known, and this dance I'm working on is going to be famous. You have inspired this dance. It's going to be called, 'Lindow Woman'. Just that.'

'There wasn't a woman.'

'There is in my version. It's art. Listen, this is serious. When you danced on the walls of Lucca, it was very interesting. I want that way you danced, that precise way, in my show. Will you dance for me again? Because in my show,' I went on, seeing him grow uncomfortable, 'it's the bog woman who dances like that, and she's not a great dancer, it's primitive, she has masculine movements, she's very heavy and she's all about fecundity and death and preservation. But I am going to have this danced by some brilliant classical dancer – a man, by the way – but he's going to have some very precise movements to follow, I am going to key them all in very tightly. So what I have to do, Mark, is get you to dance this thing just the way you did on the battlements there and I will just write it all down, just everything you do, and maybe not change very much. It's the bog dance. What do you think?'

'We're out to the beach today.'

'All day?'

'Hoping to.'

'No one told me.'

Mark looked at me just for a second and then shrugged. I felt hurt, left out, as I did over the Florence trip. They didn't want an old body around on the beach, showing its sagging flesh. Then it struck me that even in the sun it wouldn't be quite warm enough to strip off on the beach. There would be a fresh breeze.

'I'll tell you what,' I said, 'I'll take you once we've done this thing. I'll give you a lift to the beach.'

'It has to be today, then?'

'I'd prefer that. If we put it off to tomorrow it'll rain or something and I want to do this outside. And then we'll never get round to doing it. This is always happening to me. You have to seize the moment. *Carpe diem*. It's to do with creativity, all that thing – obeying the flow.'

He nodded. He was in a curious, quiet mood. The others were fiddling about in the kitchen or getting dressed: they ate breakfast in their night clothes, all except for Mark. Jill appeared from the kitchen, stepping through the French windows with a sour look on her face. She threw some crumbs on the lawn.

'Thanks for helping, Mark.'

'I'm discussing art,' he said, wobbling his head deliberately, his wet, almond eyes catching the sun shafting round the side of the wall as if it were spying on us.

I chose the field below the empty pool for the dance, mainly because it was out of sight of the house, hidden by trees. I explained to the others exactly what I was doing, and Jill and Lucy wanted to come along to watch and then go along later to the beach. It was a difficult moment, but I insisted that Mark needed to be alone, that they would disturb his equilibrium, make him self-conscious. Jill looked even sourer than usual, but Lucy concurred and they all went off in two cars around mid-morning.

It was certainly a beautiful day, with that russet Tuscan light playing over everything as if it were eternally so, as if there would never be a winter again or even a dry summer, as if maybe there never had been. It was a mythological light. This started me talking to Mark, as we made our way down to the field, about how each of us has a personal mythology. We each of us write our own myths, with their own gods and magic totems, made up of quite ordinary elements, such as a long-ago meal, or a cheap bracelet someone gave you when you were eleven.

'It's a continual narrative,' I said, deliberately soothing his nerves by talking, because he seemed quite jittery. 'We all have to construct our own narratives, give our chaos some shape and form, kind of contain the energies in the same way a river-bank does, a river that curves and wriggles, goes wider and thinner, has its own beginning and end. A river really has its own beautiful story to tell and that's the essential river of life, Mark. Your mother, for instance –'

'What the fuck about my mother?'

'That's interesting. That's the first time I've heard you swear,' I lied. 'I respect that.'

'Respect what?'

'You not swearing and then you swearing. Fuck is good. Fuck is very good. I'll keep off your mother, right now.'

He laughed, which was a relief. I felt I was disturbing his mask, getting somewhere beyond it. The grass was tall on the way down and he kept pointing out flowers, including orchids. There were a lot of different flowers I would never even have noticed. I felt my throat constrict like someone on their first date.

We found a spot where the grass was low and I sat myself down on a log, looking out for ants. There were small thistles in the field that Mark said were a few weeks earlier than in England. It was the balmy coastal air. So he kept his sandals on, but I insisted he take everything else off down to his underwear. He was very obedient. He expressed no dismay. He seemed in a trance, almost. I had expected resistance, but then I realised that at heart he was a small boy, it gave him this poignancy and vulnerability under the bluff exterior and the jokes; he was missing his mother.

He was wearing Y fronts which seemed on the frayed and loose side. His chest was hairless. He reminded me of the David of Donatello. Or of Tony Curtis in *Spartacus*.

I made notes. I told him to move just as he did on the walls of Lucca but he could not manage this at first. I'm very used to this with students, and I had him loosened up pretty soon and then he was doing his proper thing – he was moving with that weird, heavy effeminacy. It was very potent. The pale auburn light played on his flesh, his muscles moved under the skin, I felt incredibly happy. I felt lifted out of my own flesh, my own tiredness and age and mortality. I wanted to live with him. I wanted what was left of my life to be spent with him. And every week or so he would dance for me.

There he was in the field, almost naked, dancing for the gods and for the earth and, ultimately, for his mother.

It was a terrible shock to turn and see Jill standing on the slope behind me, looking down on us.

Mark saw her at the same time. Maybe I called out in surprise, or maybe she had only just appeared. It was an ugly moment.

I rose to my feet, trembling a little, clutching my notebook. I wanted to wipe her away at that second, erase her from the earth. A terrible admission. But the way she stood there with her arms folded, nodding slowly as if she knew it all, was so very negative. I would have had to raise my voice for her to hear, as she was right at the top of the slope, but the truth was I couldn't think of a thing to say.

Mark just stood there, limp, gleaming with sweat and breathing heavily. He must have been dancing for longer than I'd thought.

Then she went off.

I put my arm around his shoulder − it was very wet − and thanked him.

'Bloody hell,' he said. 'I thought it was a ghost.'

He was trembling. He had danced himself into a trance state.

Realisation rose in me: Jill was the mother, conjured from the other world. The son would dance the Mother dance, in the guise of Freya. The mother would look precisely as Jill had looked, plain in her tight, modern dress and contact lenses, and dance something so minimal it would be almost motionless. Dance with her arms folded. With her arms *folded*! I was brilliant. The Germans would love it. And the Roundhouse −

'She didn't go to the beach,' I said, interrupting myself. 'That's all.'

The little demon of the mother would be jealous of life, of the life principle. I told him to get dressed, squeezing his shoulder with my arm.

'Mark, I feel like hugging you, you are so wonderful.'

'Piece o' cake.'

'May I hug you?

'No. I'm all sweat.'

'I don't mind.'

'On yer bike.'

'Why?'

'Let me get dressed, OK?'

'OK, Mark.'

He was pulling on his shorts. It was barely warm enough for shorts.

'I hope it was for the dance, and not just for thrills, mate.'

'Thrills?'

'What are you doing? What the fuck are you up to with your hand?'

'I am relaxing your lower muscle, Mark, that's all. Touch is not —'

I'm not sure, looking back now so long after, whether he did hit me, in fact. He might have pushed me. It might have been a self-defensive thrust with his arm or elbow. At any rate, I fell over. I fell over pretty hard and put my hand onto a thistle. It was extremely painful; the fat head of the thistle took my weight and the prickles dug into my palm. I yelled.

Mark did not shout at me, or say anything at all. He finished dressing and then walked off. He looked back once. I got to my feet, nursing my hand and swearing. The pain came in bizarre pulses. Shock, I guess. I was both outside the pain and inside.

I had my dance, but nothing else. All that was left to me was the rest of my life, diminishing unto death. I saw no one for two days, keeping myself to myself, pretending to work hard in my half of the house. I heard them, but did not see them.

True, it rained fairly hard for those two days, as if we had broken the sunlight itself with the dance. The guttering dripped and everything flowed and trickled. I listened to music and read and ate simple meals of pasta, feeling close to despair. I hit my face on the side of a door, stumbling to the bathroom in the middle of a night, and in the morning I had a black eye. I was already bruising easily, by then.

Once, it sounded as if they were arguing, and I sat there alone in my dining room at Saul's heavy oak table, wondering why humanity was so fallen and complicated.

Another time two of them – I don't think more – were making love. I heard the sounds through the wall, which made me realise what a bad job Saul and Ivor had made of the division. Maybe it was Mark making Tamsin moan. There was a pause, then the girl's moans would carry on until the next pause, as though they would never get there. It aroused me, anyway. I wrote a copulation scene into the choreography – something fairly savage, what François would have called 'the hurtsome number', which froze and then restarted to the rhythm of what I could hear. (It was cut, eventually.)

Lucy came round while I was having breakfast in the kitchen. Her eyes were red. She wanted to talk. I made her coffee. I'm good at making coffee.

'Look,' she said, 'things are *so* awful.'

'Things?'

'The whole hols, they've gone *completely* pear-shaped. Mark said our dinner – the one Ollie and me cooked really carefully last night, that took about three hours – made him think of the "one time his Gramp cooked during the gastroenteritis epidemic of '65", ha ha, and went on about 'nanas for pudding again, and Ollie got really silent and tense because every time Mark says "nana" he wants to hit him, then there was an argument about wine consumption – who was paying for it and so on, and Jamie got drunk and so did Mark and somehow they got into this stupid sort of pretend fight and Mark said Jamie's fist was like a bannock-cake, whatever *that* is, and Oliver tried to separate them and got a finger up his nose but nothing serious and then I said we should all cool off with a midnight swim and Mark said,

"There's no water. And that's not a joke." And Jamie said, "Eeh oop, by gum, we're so fucking *boring*, us botanists —" trying to be northern, you know, and Tamsin said, really terribly serious, "I wish you'd all stop being so nasty to Mark." You realise she's not all that bright, she got one-and-a-half O levels in art or *carpentry* or something. And she added, "It's not fair." And there was this huge long silence when you could have heard a feather drop, let alone a pin. And then Jill said, "Yeah but I think Mark can handle it, Tamsin. If he can handle old queers fondling him, he can handle anything." I'm sorry, Jack, but that's what she said, in that fake prole voice of hers. I thought you ought to know.'

'Queer is not a term of abuse,' I said. 'Old, maybe, is.'

'Anyway, you'll be pleased to hear that Mark told her to shut up. "*Shut yer gob*," he said, like he does in the woods. And Jill burst into tears and ran out of the room. I said it was awful of Jill to be rude about you, Jack, and Jamie said it wasn't surprising, you were obviously . . . and then Oliver asked Mark if it was true, had you, you know, with Mark . . . ?'

'I never got past first base,' I said, looking at her steadily.

'Oh,' she said. She started to redden. 'I defended you,' she said. 'I thought it was just frightful gossip.'

'Oh no. It's like they said about the GIs. Oversexed and over here.'

'I see.'

'Lucy, don't be all English and disapproving.'

'I'm very open-minded, actually. You didn't know me when I was a snow bunny. I screwed three instructors in the same week.'

'Well, we are really loosening up today. That's good.'

'You can screw the bum off whoever you like, actually.'

'Thank you. Who said that you meet your fate on the very path you took in order to avoid your fate? Prosper Merimée, maybe. No, it was La Fontaine.'

Lucy blinked. 'Anyway, the point is, Jack, Mark said

something really weird and irrelevant, after Jill had rushed out of the room, even considering he was so pissed. He said, looking at Tamsin: "I'm going to live in Ireland with Tamsin and work on the Irish bogs."'

'Really?'

'What happened to your eye? Did Mark hit you?'

I laughed.

'Jesus, no. I walked into a bar and said ouch.'

'I've got Rescue Remedy—'

'It's OK. I bruise when I'm not even touched.'

'Anyway, Jamie nearly pissed himself after Mark said this thing about Tamsin – which was better than hitting Mark. And Tamsin said, "What's so funny, Jamie?" And there was another silence and then Mark said, "That got you all worried, didn't it?"'

'Mark, be careful,' I said, as if he was in the air around us. 'You're going to break a lot of people's hearts.'

'You think so?'

'I do.'

'Not mine, I can tell you.'

'Sure.'

'Certainly not after he started going on about all the pubescent girls found preserved in Irish bogs. They're mostly clothed, he said, with plaits of thick red hair that went on growing and really long nails. And after a while these pubescent girls crumble to dust in the normal air and that really they shouldn't ever be exposed. It was just *so* weird. *Incredibly* creepy. In fact, Jack, I'm scared. He's got *really* dark eyes. You know about his mother?'

'He has very nice eyes. Almond-shaped, like on a Greek vase.'

'You know about his mother?' she repeated.

'I don't care about his mother. Because we'll never know the truth of what happened.'

Lucy looked disappointed. I couldn't stand her being in the house any more. I couldn't stand the house any more, as a matter of fact. It was damp and cold after the rain. I rose to my feet and I said, 'You know I'm leaving tomorrow?'

I should have been staying another week, officially. I wished I could leave today, but Paulo wasn't due to call round until tomorrow. I would sort out the key and leave.

She shook her head. 'That's a shame. It's been *terrifically* fun, having you around. We haven't even noticed your age. You're so *wise*. What's wrong with your hand?' she asked.

It was still red and swollen from the thistle, like a scarlet fever patch on the palm.

'Oh, just the mark of Cain. An allergy to life.'

'What's happiness, in your opinion?' she asked, at the door.

'It's feeling low and you're walking along the city street when suddenly a lovely girl or a lovely boy, depending on your sexual proclivities, gives you a very nice and very personally directed smile because, way back, she or he did your hair one time. And he or she has remembered you.'

Lucy said, 'Oh. I thought you'd say something deep and philosophical.'

'I just did, Lucy.'

The dance was performed in Stuttgart and was a reasonable success, and then it toured for six months and is revived now and again in unexpected places: Vilnius; a deconsecrated church in Lincolnshire; high-school festivals in Canada smelling of sandwiches. Mark's dance was performed by the company's leading male, Emmanuel Angelich. He did his best, smeared in the Bog Woman's terrifying darkness, masked and naked and clumping about, watched by Jean-Claude Wieck as the little demon of the mother with folded arms. But it was always like a parody, the Bog Woman dance that had possessed the son. I saw the golden field in Tuscany and felt the spring breeze on my cheek and smelt the sweetness of Mark's body and wanted to weep each time I watched from the director's box because my hand would start to hurt and I knew it was the darkness rising again, as it always did.

My mother died aged 102. The same year, 1994, that Mark stepped off a ledge backwards, admiring a flower in the Spanish Pyrenees. I do not know how high the ledge was, but it was high enough. Neither do I know the name of the flower.

I had not even said goodbye to Mark. He was out checking on the flora and fauna when I left. I sneaked away, closing the car door softly and keeping in first on the track until I'd left the house behind. Only Lucy was waving from the top window, although I'm sure everyone knew.

I stayed in California. Each time I went to the barber's I would remember what I'd said to Lucy, until I no longer had enough hair to bother going to the barber's with. I couldn't stand the barber's, actually: right from being a kid, back in Southgate, I couldn't stand the prickle and itch of the cuttings down my neck. My mother would always stroke my bare neck and shoulders and back with a cool wet flannel, afterwards, while I craved to tell her that it was even worse at the bottom of my spine, under my belt. It was worse than ants. As a grown man I would always have to have a shower after and a change of shirt and even pants because it was still worse down there, the itch of the fallen hairs. So there was one advantage to growing very old.

When they restored *Spartacus* to its former glory, I went to see it alone, the light flickering over me in the front row. I sometimes believe that this is all I am, now: a cinemagoer, waiting there in the dim light for the final darkness to close over me after the crucifixion of the slaves.

And a slave to love is all I have ever been.

YOU NEVER

Those who knew Stuart were aware of a past murky with acts not altogether run-of-the-mill. He had returned home from his time in Africa (where, it was supposed, he had been a mercenary) to find his mother dying and his sister in pod by a man she would not identify. The mother had died, the sister had settled in the far north of Scotland with her child and an oil rig worker who was not the father, and Stuart had inherited the house.

The house stood back from the leafy road, pebble-dashed and modest, behind a low screen of spindly Lawsons, and gradually sprouted accoutrements that pointed to days spent fiddling with electronics in the spare bedroom. No one visited Stuart and he rarely stayed elsewhere; yet on Tuesdays, Thursdays and Saturdays he was always to be found in the bar of the nearby Cap and Bells, treating the immediate world as if it was his bosom, his lifelong companion, his mess-hut.

Those regulars who drank alongside him – he was generous with his wallet – liked him, but only within the confines of the setting. He had a damaged mouth; that is to say, something vicious had left a badly stitched scar that ran from the corner of his mouth to his ear, giving his face a lopsided look.

At regular intervals – at least once a week, when he was more in his cups than other nights – he would tell the stranger next to him at the bar that he had 'killed a hotsy-totsy in cold blood'.

No amount of probing would reveal any more information

beyond the fact that, as Stuart had apparently been a mercenary, such things were bound to happen and that it had
happened in a far-off country. John, the barman, ventured a
theory (in Stuart's absence) that Stuart had shot an unarmed
'native' in somewhere like South Africa, thus confirming for
most of those present the essential harmlessness of the act
Stuart had long ago committed. No one could find out what
'hotsy-totsy' meant, because it was Stuart's invention and he
wouldn't say anything more.

'It's what it means,' he would say, and sink into silence.

After his evening in the pub, Stuart would walk fairly
steadily home and boil up some packet soup – Knorr's, generally tomato – to which he conceded a knob of butter. With
the natter of the bar circling in his head behind his deep-
set eyes, he'd finish the soup and wash up. All of these actions
– the walking home, the boiling-up, the spooning to his
damaged mouth of the soup, the scouring with the all-but-
bald brush his mother must have bought way back in the
fifties – were performed with a slow and satisfied rhythm.
There was an air of triumph to it. The whole had been
conceived and successfully executed. Then he would don his
headphones and ride the airwaves, homing in on the ships
or the jet aircraft or the local firemen dealing with something nasty like a road accident, before turning in.

He'd had women, he'd had a lot of women in Africa, a
lot of bibis for baksheesh – but not what he would think
of as an affair, let alone a steady woman. This bothered him
only when he watched some sentimental series on the box.
He'd got no plans to set up with anyone; nor even, at sixty-
one, to indulge in games. His vigorous twenty-five years as
a paid fighting man struck him as price enough for peace;
he enjoyed the sunshine through the windows of the sitting
room (not cleaned in his mother's absence), and would
succumb to the touch of its gold on his face and sit for
hours as impassive as a Buddha, much as a cat does on the
arm of an easy chair, feeling no guilt about it. He seldom

even walked, as the countryside around the town did not attract him, flat and bald as it seemed after the forest and the mountains and the bright red earth.

Preferring to entice the world in, he worked long hours on constructing short-wave radios of various types. He erected a huge metal mast in his garden, kept in place with wires and cables, as well as other antennae perched like skeletal birds on the roof. He communicated with other hams now and again, even in good old-fashioned Morse, but was more the listening sort. Aside from the firemen, whose morbid jokes he found amusing, he was particularly attracted to military planes, which posed a challenge he could rise to, unscrambling their coded intercourse or simply keeping them tracked.

The local airbase was close enough to walk to – he had no car – and he hovered regularly in a concealed part of the perimeter fence with a portable scanning device that enabled him to home in on the cockpits. He had his old ground-sheet from Africa days to keep the damp off: speckled with mosquitoes, its thick green canvas reassured him. His magic carpet, he called it.

He considered bringing along a member of the East Anglian ham radio club to which he belonged. The members were mostly much younger than he was, young enough to have been his offspring, and he hesitated for some time before asking Rob, a pleasant enough youth of about seventeen or eighteen with fur instead of a moustache, if he would consider a trip that Saturday to the airbase.

Rob was enticed by the illicit air around the enterprise, and agreed with enthusiasm. Thus it was that the two, armed with cheese rolls and a couple of Alinco scanners (Rob's being the more powerful and expensive, surprisingly), crept up between the firs to a point where the high electrified wire gave a view of the runway but was not covered by a CCTV camera: the observers were happily concealed in shade. Stuart unrolled his groundsheet and the two sat on it like happy infants on a mat. Rob didn't know it, but the groundsheet's smell was of the thick green Congo air gone bad.

They had an excellent time with the apparatus, eavesdropping on some very dirty banter between pilots (delivered in a US drawl Rob was reasonably skilled in imitating), and falling upon their rolls in high spirits. As they sat on the canvas, feeling the soft lumpiness of fir needles underneath, and chattily shared what was mostly technical data, Stuart noticed that Rob's chin had a 'button' in it, similar to his own. He indulged in the fantasy that Rob was his son, receiving in the process a recognition of loss, of what he had lost by certain actions and decisions, that was almost equivalent to a physical blow. He continued the conversation haltingly, all but overwhelmed by the thought of the days that still lay in front of him, shorn of satisfaction or triumph.

The American jets roared close over their heads, crushing him further, but he took hold of himself by concentrating on what Rob was now telling him.

'They sent me the US version and the cellular frequency was blocked. So I sent it back and then a UK-friendly version came back without the SMA rubber-ducky earphone and the memory-skip was faulty, so I sent that back with a rude letter and they sent me this DJ-X2000 instead, so I wasn't complaining then, was I?'

'UK version?'

'Of course. And I didn't know whether it was a mistake or them feeling a bit manky about their customer relations!'

Rob laughed so the button in his chin disappeared, and Stuart smiled in his lopsided way. Rob talked older than he looked, he thought.

'It's got a 2000-channel memory,' the teenager said, with his mouth full of chocolate bar. 'And an audio descrambler.'

Stuart pulled a face, showing admiration rather than the envy he felt. His model – the model Rob had originally ordered – had only 700 memory channels and could not decode scrambled signals. Rob was telling him how his ultimate dream was to be the one to locate a missing plane with his mobile RDF equipment, picking up the ELT signal, but for that you needed a few wild mountains and East Anglia was not exactly the place for wild mountains! He paused in his natter to pour some tea from his thermos and offered Stuart a cup. Chilled by the easterly wind, Stuart accepted: he had dropped his thermos on the kitchen floor the day before and the interior bulb had shattered. As the steaming tea was being poured, Stuart's hand jerked and his forefinger was splashed. His yelp was drowned in the roar of the jet fighter landing beyond the perimeter fence, and Rob apologised.

Stuart told the lad not to worry, it was his own fault, and he did not even blow on the scalded knuckle. He brought the cup to his damaged mouth and blew on the tea instead. Rob asked him if he was sure he was alright and Stuart said yes, he was fine.

Then he said, with a little snort: 'My trigger-finger.'

'Bang bang,' laughed Rob.

'I killed a hotsy-totsy with it. In cold blood.'

Rob nodded as if unconcerned. 'Hotsy-totsy?'

'An enemy soldier. My word.'

'What enemy was that, then? In the war, was it?'

'*A* war, Rob. Got what it deserved, it has. My trigger-finger.'

'Oh, I wouldn't think that. War is war. That lot are going over to drop bombs on A-rabs,' said Rob, pointing to the fat planes in the hazy distance beyond the hangars.

'They don't need to talk like that,' said Stuart. 'Always watched my tongue, I did. Personally. You've got to keep it respectable.'

Rob asked him again if he was alright, and Stuart nodded, noisily sucking at his tea.

'Butterflies,' he said, after a moment, his mouth trailing steam. 'Thousands and thousands of butterflies.'

It was not even as if Rob was the kind of son he would have liked – the boy was thin and pustular and had a voice right up in the nose – but it was very pleasant sharing a passion with him and how much more pleasant would that sharing have been if he had also shared his blood, sprung him from his loins. The young man had not heard the comment about the butterflies, he was already donning his headphones because a plane with an unusual profile had appeared, at some distance, to the left of the main hangar. Stuart watched him locating the correct frequency, shifting the rubber-duck antenna and straining to pick up whatever the crew were saying. Rob's face was all a-twitch with concentration, his pursed mouth like a girl's ready to have lipstick applied to it; Stuart imagined this face as the flesh of his flesh, the result of a carnal union between himself and his imaginary wife, who would be big-buttocked and well-endowed in the top storey and extremely blonde. Was such a union carnal, or did carnal only apply to an illicit or an improper embrace? At any rate, he was filled with affection for young Rob, at that moment, and his eyes welled with tears because the soldier he had killed was not a man but a brat of eleven or twelve, wielding a rusty panga and drugged to the eyeballs.

It was the shots that had raised the butterflies. When he tasted the Congo, as he was now doing, the taste was of blood mingled with the rust of the panga's blade. He had been squatting down in the forest, answering the call of Nature, taking care the ants weren't having a snack of his behind and that his SMG was to hand. The razor-sharp panga had come out of nowhere and slit Stuart's cheek to the teeth at one blow, knocking two of his molars clean out. His scream had raised the butterflies in the forest clearing. Or maybe it was the shots, immediately after. The kid was running off and dropped as if he'd tripped, butterflies all round the space where he had just been. Blood welled about Stuart's teeth and mingled with the sweat collected in his collar-bone. The top of the brat's head was blown off and the brains were spilled out like pink cauliflower, but he still looked peaceful, lying there with his mouth open, as kids do when they're asleep.

'A few years back,' Rob was saying, 'I had my two-meter radio on 145.550 MHz and picked up the Mir Space Station chatting away as it went over. The Mir bloody Space Station, all in Russian. You could hear every word, but fat lot of use that was. Now I can't even find this one and it's about two feet away. What do you reckon on the frequency?'

Stuart had hidden his face in his hands because he could not for the life of him control himself. His shoulders shuddered and he made tiny whining noises, like a poor signal. Rob turned round and stared, open-mouthed. He removed his headphones as if to see better, so that they sat either side of his neck and made it look even thinner. Over Stuart's muffled whines the headphones sounded like silly girls tittering.

The following week, in the pub, the talk was of why no one had thought to check on Stuart when he hadn't turned up either on Tuesday, Thursday or Saturday. John said he'd been run off his feet, Tony Wilson had had no idea that Stuart hadn't been in on Tuesday and he himself wasn't around on Thursday, if they recalled, and Geoff Eastley reckoned it wasn't their business anyway.

'Post-traumatic stress syndrome,' said Tony Wilson, who was a systems manager and read the broadsheets. 'Now we'll never know.'

'Never know what?'

'Whom he killed in cold blood. His hotsy-totsy or whatever.'

'Darkie, wasn't it?' said Geoff Eastley, a Tesco supervisor who liked to stir things up. 'Out in Bongo-Bongo Land.'

'I thought you'd personally employed that deaf Jamaican girl?' said Tony, touching the cream on his Adnams and sucking his finger. 'You bragged about it enough.'

'So?'

'I wonder what it's like being dead?' said John.

'Cold,' said Tony.

'Cold blood,' laughed Ron Crashaw, who had just come in after a few days' repping in Scotland and was rubbing his hands as if it was winter outside.

'That's an unfortunate joke, Ron,' said John.

'Stuart's done himself in,' said Geoff Eastley.

'Has he now? Cripes. How?'

'It's in the *Daily Excess*,' said Tony, unfolding the *Daily Express* at the right page. 'Picture of Stuart looking a bit more handsome. Read all about it.'

'You never,' said Ron.

There was the picture of Stuart, blurred and very youthful, togged up in military wear. The article was entitled DOG OF WAR MYSTERY DEATH IS SUICIDE, CONFIRMS CORONER.

'Well well,' said Ron, shaking his head as he read it. 'You never. It all goes on when I'm away. Pills, was it?'

'Slit his wrists,' said Geoff Eastley. 'The fire boys found him in the sitting room in a pool of blood. Read it to the end.'

'Like a Greek tragedy,' said Tony.

'And now we'll never know,' said Ron.

'Know what?'

'Who exactly he did in. Did he ever say anything to you, John?'

'Nope,' said the barman, waiting for Ron's Guinness to settle. 'He just went on about having butterflies or something.'

WANDERLUST

His wife and children no longer even asked him when he might be coming back. He left without warning and he returned without warning. The essence of freedom is self-ishness.

He would be standing by some strand in, say, faraway Sweden, gazing out at the bright scintillant water of the Baltic, and he would deliberately think of his family, allowing feelings of love and loss to well up inside him. He would have to sit and weep. It was a selfishness that gave him atrocious pain; consciously setting instinct against itself, nature against nature. One day it would spark into revelation, he knew.

He slept in barns and building sites and woods. He began to lament the passing of the horses. No one wept for them. Occasionally he would slash the side of a car with his knife.

Dogs were no substitute for the hundreds of thousands of horses. He hated dogs.

The great forests of France were infinitely welcoming, as were the barren heights of Romania. He avoided others on the road, as weathered and ragged as himself, with their tragic tales of lost families, their spite and drunkenness.

The fact is, he loved his wife and children more than he could say.

Sometimes he would formulate his journey thus, repeating it like a charm as he walked on his blistered soles, mapless, not knowing where he was heading for: *Selflessness lies the other side of the selfish impulse, as bones lie the other side of flesh; I am stripping my own flesh to find my bone.*

If this did not satisfy him, then he would think of himself as a small boy, with a small boy's innocence. Living on his wits, yet bewildered. He would talk to trees, feeling his words absorbed by every leaf as his hands rested upon the bark; or plunge deliberately into the coldest of rivers, the shock seeming to pain his very lungs and turn them into frosty wings. As he lay on the grass, naked, in some lonely region whose name was probably unknown to him, memories of his wife and children and the ache of his loneliness combined in exultation like sacred music rising in some cathedral of stone and glass to the furthest point of the firmament, and he would cry out in near ecstasy and sorrow, almost fulfilled for good, almost ready to die upon such a moment, upon such a cry.

Europe turned around him as a wheel turns round its hub – he appreciated this. How many were the wheels that turned invisibly around the myriad other souls that made up the world? How did they mesh unfailingly like some great complicated machinery, turning beside or within or above each other in the populated areas? How did they not snag and grind?

Death came and removed a wheel with careful fingers, or sometimes many wheels at once, whole handfuls of wheels – but the space was quickly restored, filled again with the turning cog-like encrustations that passed for an individual life.

When he returned home, each time he would feel the teeth of his wheel snag on the wheels of his family – his children most of all, since their demands were on his soul, his capacity for love and affection. He brought them strange presents found on his travels – quite ordinary objects that spoke to him of a stage on his journey, fielding their disappointment in something as banal as a worn toothbrush or an empty tin of shoe polish with tales it engendered, glimpses of the life he had led for those months away. The great house and grounds would look smaller – but his children, grown inches taller since he had last seen them, pointed to something achieved, for they were all still alive and thriving on the simple gruel of time. Only his wife looked worn, though he presumed she must have indulged in lovers; he did not allow himself to care.

His notes accumulated: he had a tiny study at the top of the old tower, where he would spend most of his waking hours resurrecting his travels. Imagine, he wrote, a pilgrimage without a centre, without a destination; which route must one take? The choice is endless, infinite – I proceed only where my feet take me, this way, that way, to the left or to the right. He enjoyed writing, but it was not a craving like the other thing, the actual movement of his feet on the ground, the passing of trees and houses, the unknown itinerary of food and movement and drink and sleep. And he would again leave his family waving and weeping on the familiar driveway – seeing his mother in her furs standing there in the guise of his wife, a hooded car around him instead of the open air, school's loathsomeness beckoning to him instead of the endless road, the hills, the heights. Then he would know that his self-ishness was good, was a possible key to understanding when everything else had broken in the lock.

And when he grew too old even to attempt to depart, long after his children had left home, long after his wife had succumbed to the early senility that left her trembling in a chair in the front sitting room, he took to walking very slowly and steadily along the furthest perimeter of the grounds in an attempt to establish the precise configuration of his wheel. It had grown almost unwieldy in its extent. He could feel it strike Mongolia, St Petersburg, the wave-tops of the Atlantic ocean far beyond St Kilda – and even, on a clear day, the heights of Iceland with their furry gauze of smoke and mist.

Its extent worried him, at times, until he burnt his notes on the upper lawn in a conflagration that, he was sure, had been felt as a warm blush on the earth-facing flank of Pluto, the coldest and farthest of the planets, and thus the nearest to his heart.

IS THIS THE WAY YOU SAID?

The profoundest way of feeling something is to suffer it.
Gustave Flaubert

Jonathan had spent ten years writing this novel and had sent it blind to an editor called Eddie – Eddie Thwing (Marion thought this was a great joke and that if you put it in a novel it would be like calling your heroine Fiona Crumpet). Eddie was quite young and glamorous, apparently, but then anyone in the publishing business was, to Jonathan and Marion, quite young and glamorous. In the three months between sending the novel and the extremely favourable reply, something very bad happened to Eddie Thwing. Neither Jonathan nor Marion knew about this, but most people in the publishing world did. It happened on a holiday in Greece and it was the worst thing that could happen to anyone. Eddie lost his kid, Ed, in a tragic accident the details of which no one was quite certain about, except that it involved the sea. Ed was not yet three. Eddie's wife, Holly, was recovering from the loss down in Sussex, where her parents owned an isolated and very old farmhouse. Eddie was back at work, looking a bit strange but holding his own. His reply to Jonathan Lewis, although brief, was every writer's dream. It said the book – entitled *New Demons* – was gripping, dark and dangerous. It concluded with a desire to meet the author at his earliest possible convenience (although, being a glamorous editor, Eddie hadn't put it like that; he'd written, 'Let's meet. Very soon. Give me a ring.').

'He sounds nice,' said Marion.

'Yup. Nice and relaxed. Not frightening.'

'Well done, you.'

'I had this feeling. Something was driving me on.'

'It's called faith.'

'And you've put up with me.'

'God knows how,' said Marion. 'I guess it's being blinded by love.'

They were drinking champagne. This felt very extravagant. Jonathan was fifty-three and had been a peripatetic drama teacher in various knotty schools for the last thirty years, while Marion was a self-employed weaver. They had very little money and fewer illusions, but they did live in Brighton, moving there when property was still tatty and affordable back in the early 1980s. If their tiny house was a couple of floors higher, they'd see the sea.

The world had not gone the way they had expected it to go. Jonathan had started his novel on his forty-second birthday – February 27, 1994 – and finished it on his fifty-second. In the week he had started it, President Clinton won a $6 billion order from Saudi Arabia for passenger aircraft, the Vatican attacked Benetton for using a dead Croat's blood-stained clothes on their publicity posters, and Pilkington Glass announced it was planning to float half its Australian business. Jonathan knew nothing about any of this, although it was of great importance on one level. This level was not Jonathan's. Neither (back then) was it Eddie's, who was just starting out as a junior editor in J. C. Laurence and Company – a small, academic publisher based in a house of many crooked floors in Soho. Almost immediately, it seemed, he had left Laurence for Jansen House, a new, aggressive group in South Kensington run somewhere at the back of it all by the Americans. Within two years he was in charge of reviving an obscure Teenage Fantasy imprint called Act uP, renamed Luxor and headed, under his control, for a more sophisticated literary readership. Fantasy with Brains was the house motto, and the strategy was wildly successful in a very competitive market.

SO WHO'S DUMBING DOWN?
[Photo of Proust in bed, reading the latest Luxor]
Fantasy with Brains.

When it was revealed that Prince Charles was a Luxor fan, taking a pile up to Balmoral, success was royally sealed. This much Jonathan Lewis knew, only because his friend Dave, an improvident bookseller with connections, had told him. Otherwise the world of education and the world of big-time publishing were not even in the same ball-park, if that was the right expression. It was certainly the one that occurred to him as he delivered the novel's six hundred pages by hand to Jansen House. He was used to shabby, Victorian, prison-like buildings lined with glazed brown tiles to the neck-high window-level and smelling of wet jumpers and bleach and onion crisps. Here he was in a converted boiler-factory where clouded glass met clouded glass and the scent of proper coffee made the world beyond the hammered-steel curve of Reception feel both brainy and sexual. Posters of an erect wooden penis advertising a 'steamily brilliant, spine-chillingly cool' novel by one Sophie-Anne Witlock made him think of the graffiti he had found this morning on the classroom blackboard. He had never had his own classroom, of course. His fate was to teach drama in spaces cluttered with desks and chairs and cupboards, only rarely being able to use the gym (if gym there was), because gym was for serious stuff like Sports.

He had started out bouncing like a rubber ball with enthusiasm, believing – like all his TIE colleagues back in the seventies – that theatre-in-education would change the world. He was a kind of Jesuit in loose, Japanese-style togs. He went to mime school in Paris, took courses in London from visiting Kabuki masters and Polish disciples of Grotowski and even learnt how to whirl like a dervish. He was an itinerant performer on the alternative theatre scene for a time. As part of his social programme of deep change, he took teachers' training at Goldsmiths at the age of thirty-one and then grew older and tireder pretty fast. It no longer seemed so exciting to use a chair as a car, or a rag as the billowing sea, or your body as the world. Certainly not to the kids – less and less his cup of tea, remedial rather than redeemable, most of them overweight and overtired, their 'self-expression' consisting of being on the job or out on the piss or just staring blankly, chewing. His classes were mostly confrontations steered artfully and wearyingly towards compromise. Then a fragile girl he had taught to whirl like a dervish ended up doing it obsessively at home and finished in a mental home for a year. (That was a bad time, when Marion had a miscarriage; then they moved to Brighton and Josie was born a year later.) None of what he did was going to make these kids into celebrities, that was the trouble: that was their main aim, to be rich and starry. That's what 'drama' and 'theatre' meant to most of them, and faffing about with chairs and rags and masks cut out of magazines felt like a deviant activity. Now, standing in Jansen House on a damp October morning, with the dolled-up receptionists taking calls and greeting visitors as if they were in the headquarters of the World Bank or some five-star hotel, not a ship of literature, Jonathan felt a thrill in his belly that was, he realised, precisely what his pupils must feel when dreaming of being famous and on the box.

His package had disappeared behind the counter. Ten years of work, his best years (in many ways) sheathed in a Jiffy bag addressed to *Eddie Thwing, Luxor Books* (he wasn't sure whether to put *Edward* Thwing, but Dave had said an emphatic no-no, stuff like that put them off before they'd even opened it and anyway it was unpronounceable). Now he couldn't leave, like a dad delivering his child on the first ever day of school. The roof of the ex-boiler factory soared to blue-tinted skylights over the lobby area, although the rest had been divided into floors. There were some *Star Trek* easy chairs around a scatter of the day's papers on a low teak table, and he loitered near them without sitting down, feeling shy and uncomfortable but reluctant to hit the streets again right away. The people who came in and out were taller and smarter than he was used to, like a species of confident bird, with the exception of a few short, disgruntled types – in shapeless jackets or parkas and with untidy hair – he assumed were authors. A fat man in a shiny black coat, looking like a walking aubergine, was royally greeted by a posse of suits. The author is king, thought Jonathan, but these ministers hold all the reins. Everyone looked as if they knew the place, had known it for years, and he imagined himself as one of them, his name in lights or whatever was the publishing equivalent.

New Demons, *a dark and astonishing tale of time travel, possession and searing love, has burst like a neo-Gothic Harley Davidson into the sleepy hollow of literate Fantasy.*

Or words to that effect. He was improvising off the posters. Everything was extraordinary, amazing, wonderful. He hadn't heard of most of the authors, but the few bearing familiar names seemed to him like gods, merely because their words were printed and in the shops. A few were Luxor, with very cool images that went against the grain of the usual pizza-coloured Fantasy type: they were like hyped-up ECM album covers. His secret was that he read very little Fantasy literature. His literary guru was Mervyn Peake, who hardly qualified as a Fantasy writer at all. Apart from various obscure Russians, he avoided the field. That, he felt, was his strength. The strength of an outsider. There was a lemon-yellow Citroen 2CV in the lobby, as if some eccentric woman author had parked it there, and a little stall of shiny apples you could help yourself from. He took five.

Marion wanted to know how it had gone, from behind her vast loom in the sitting room. (Jonathan worked in the box room, when Josie wasn't back from Politics and Philosophy at Durham.)

'I gave it in, that's all.'

'You didn't see anybody?'

'Well, he didn't come out and thank me personally for the privilege of offering it to him.'

'No need to be like that. How am I supposed to know how it works? I could never understand why you didn't try plays.'

'Plays? You really think I'm going to be part of that scene?'

'What scene?'

'The theatre scene. Bunch of incestuous hacks and gays and self-serving stuck-up Oxbridge pseuds. Or all three.'

'Mike and Dennis are gay. Mike went to Oxford. They're our best friends. You sound more and more like your dad.'

'Look, we've been through this so many times, Marion. I've written this bloody novel as an act of faith. I don't care if it's published or not. I had to write it, that's all.'

'Of course you care if it's published.'

He did care, he cared very much. Time had reared up in front of him like a deadening wall and turned everything futile when he was about forty-eight. His body, maximally exercised once for mime work, was showing signs of strain in the joints. The specialist doctor told him that mime, like ballet, made the joints too loose. The *clic* caused arthritis, eventually. The kids he taught were getting worse and worse. Culture was sloshing about in Lottery money but it all felt somehow impoverished after the glory days of the sixties and seventies – merely a wing of the commercial palace whose other wing was War.

New Demons said all this, but in a parallel world that was, Jonathan recognised, full of his own little traumas. It had been an act of therapy, far cheaper than visiting a shrink, or even banging on about it all in the Fox and Hounds, his old sporadic haunt (now a transvestite bar). Marion was Penelope during this long odyssey, in which Jonathan had been more difficult to live with than he would otherwise have been. Or maybe not. Marion recognised, waiting for him to finish

– to come symbolically home – that without the novel he might have been completely impossible.

Even with the trainee Post Office workers (an hour of 'communicational expression' every week at the college), he'd had somewhere to escape to during their total lack of participation, their bewilderment, their mask of abuse. The novel was a quest, both literally and metaphorically, but it was also a refuge. Tapped out on a 1950s Adler, it had been painstakingly transferred to disc on Dave's advice.

'On the other hand,' Dave said, 'if it's really good then that authentic, back-of-the-cupboard look will give it prestige. But it'd have to be really good. Otherwise it's slickness time.'

Then there was the waiting. Dave had said that very few people got taken on from unsolicited manuscripts, that most people made it through contacts, being someone's kid or lover or sex-slave or just squeezing the right hooter at the right parties. Jonathan reckoned this was jealousy on Dave's part, as Dave's poems had been rejected by everyone but *Decoys*, which was in fact Dave's own magazine, run off on an old roneo machine that had belonged to Brighton Town Council. His poems were long torrents of abuse, with confusing Dada-style typography. And Dave's second-hand bookshop, Fastidium, was so quiet that the most exciting event of his day was the bus stopping opposite. Jonathan had no idea how Dave Reynolds kept going, especially as he couldn't resist buying up books by the carton-load, adding to the tottering walls that made the two rooms into a labyrinth, something out of Lewis Carroll – or Mervyn Peake.

'Books aren't meat,' Dave would say. 'They don't have sell-by dates on them.'

'They do in Waterstone's,' said Jonathan.

'Waterstone's don't sell books,' Dave pointed out. 'They sell units of stock.'

It was Dave who first told Jonathan about Eddie Thwing. 'Is Thwing his real name?'

'Absolutely, guv. There was a Sir Robert Thwing who led a proto-Marxist revolt back in 1230, stealing corn from the fat foreign monks and giving it away to the poor.'

'How do you know so much?'

'I read what I don't sell.'

'But you don't sell anything.'

'Exactly. Ah, there's the bus. The most exciting thing that's happened this morning.'

'I've come in.'

'You don't bloody count. Eddie Thwing does count. He comes in here when he's down for the Festival, thinking he's going to find a signed first edition of – well, *Ulysses* or something. I deliberately give him the impression that I wouldn't know it if the first folio or the torn-out page from that Robin Hood ballad turned up. He never goes away a disappointed man without spending a tenner on paperbacks, ha ha.'

'So you reckon I should give him a try, do you? Seriously?'

'Nothing to lose. If you're a genius, he'll spot it.'

'But I'm not a genius. I'm a clapped-out drama teacher who's wasted his spare time on this stonker of a piece of drivel and I'm stupidly proud of it.'

'I'm always amazed at how well you understand yourself, mate.'

'It's called self-expression, Dave. Running your tongue over the site of the trauma.'

Dave nodded knowingly.

'No harm in trying, is there? I'm still trying. How's the lovely Marion?'

'You won't believe this, Dave, but she's got a big order from this vegetarian shoe shop in Duke Street.'

'A what?'

'Vegetarian shoe shop. Shoes made only from vegetable material.'

'Not dhal, I hope. Imagine if it rained or you walked through a puddle and your trainers were made of dhal.'

Jonathan and Dave looked at each other and cracked up, spilling a pile of old green Pelicans spotted with dirt. The funny thing was, Jonathan and almost everyone else in Brighton believed that Fastidium didn't go with Dave's shop, because they didn't realise that it meant Disgust.

Eddie went on holiday that summer to Andros, the Hampstead of the Greek islands. That's to say, it was relatively unspoilt by dint of the fact that rich Greek-Americans, fat with ships and trade, would build their plush villas on land they made sure was untainted by development and then spend half the year there. There was also an excellent modern art museum facing the sea, full of Matisse. Eddie did not usually holiday with his family, he was too busy, but Holly had insisted. Holly came from a wealthy dynasty of lawyers, one of whom had married an American writer called Felicity Keen who was very popular for about five years in the 1930s, penning a series of satiric detective tales set mostly in the world of the silver screen. That was Holly's grandmother, and it was Holly's lifelong task to restore Felicity Keen, or 'Buggles' to the family, to her rightful throne. Three of the tales were published in one volume by Virago in 1985. Holly had spent the interim in battling to find financial backing for a projected film of one of the tales, set on a set and weaving a real-life poison murder into the celluloid equivalent. Eddie had met her at a publisher's party six years ago and they got serious within minutes. That is, he fell for her instantly and they both knew that this was it from the very first second. Eddie was married and so was Holly, but neither had had time for kids and their relative spouses were deep in affairs themselves. Holly vaguely worked on the edge of the book industry as an authorial assistant, and had recently spent many months collating an exhaustive index for a history of poaching. They had clocked each other over the drinks and babble for about an hour; now they were together by the quietest window of the club's function room. The club was called Tidings, with one wall given over to a slowed-up projection of a seventies porn film – an installation by Marcus Kent, apparently.

'You wouldn't believe how many fields the subject touches,' Holly was now saying to Eddie. This was the second thing she'd ever said to him. The first was in response to his question, 'What do *you* do?'

'Poaching.' She had smiled. 'Anything you want to know about medieval forest laws.'

Her eyes glittered at him and his own glittered back, with vague writhing mounds of flesh reflected in them. It was extraordinary. They were both being more than flirtatious. The usual level of flirtation at this kind of shindy was unserious, a game, mere showing off, mapping the bounds in safety, a response to exhaustion and free lashes of drink. Authors peered about, bewildered, like moles dragged from their holes, and got embarrassingly drunk in a ciderish way before being sent back down again for another two or three years (or, in some cases, for ever) while the partying carried on overhead. The author at this one – it was, Eddie had to keep recalling, this author's launch – was the equivalent of one of those rattly little hire cars, if you were playing that comparison game. He wasn't (thank God) Eddie's bod, but one of the young and spotty hopefuls in Jansen House's purebreed literary stable, Peter Mapes Ltd, run by the immaculate David Roach. Mapes's sales were undetectable except for their youngish star from Newcastle, Benny Irish, whose *Jam Sandwich* (and equally filthy sequels) sold millions and kept the rest afloat. Eddie hadn't read the launch novel, set in a dilapidated Sicilian casino and featuring the slow torture and murder of at least three well-hung Albanian fieldworkers ('terrifying', 'blackly humorous'), but it was, by all accounts, a winner, as long as they could hide the author (a part-time English lecturer at De Montfort University, Leicester) from sight. The author was also by the quieter window, and Eddie was keen to get rid of him. Eddie had big shoulders (he was

a former rugby man) and simply edged the man out, casually, knowing that no author ever imposed him or herself on
these occasions unless drink made them excitable. The author
went off to join his parents (Eddie could tell they were his
parents by their air of obsequious anxiety and the fact that
no one else was talking to them), and Eddie and Holly were
alone together.

'You're not Canadian?'

'Do I sound it?'

'Maybe.'

'Jesus. I'm not even American. I'm English but I was
brought up in Washington until I was ten.'

'Your father?'

'Diplomat. Actually, he was a spy. Kind of. I'm not supposed
to tell you this because he's still alive but he was in the secret
service.'

'Spying on the Yanks?'

'Of course not. He kept going off to places like Bolivia.
He was in Bomber Command,' she added, casually. 'I mean,
originally. Forty-one raids. He raced cars for the RAF.'

'How glamorous,' said Eddie. Perfect profile, he was
thinking. She told him that her parents had a very old farmhouse in Sussex, that they were in their seventies but still
rode horses. Eddie's parents were a tax inspector and a
hospital clerk respectively, but he didn't tell her that. Anyway,
they were both dead, or as good as (his mother was in a
home, completely ga-ga). Holly also told him that she had
nearly made the Olympic alpine ski team in 1984. Eddie
was nodding slowly, in love for the first time in his life. Or
that's what it felt like. She had long silvery earrings and a
fringe gelled into fine claws over her forehead, which he
really liked. Holly didn't generally tell strangers all about
herself, but Eddie kept asking questions, bent over her with
his big shoulders so that she had to retreat slightly onto the
broad window-sill. It was as if he was hiding her from the
rest of the room. She hadn't even mentioned Felicity Keen,

which was probably just as well as Eddie had never heard of her.

'Don't you hate these things?' Holly said, looking past him at the crush of bodies and the slow-motion licking of a nipple beyond. She didn't want to tell him that she knew all about him and what a bastard he could be, excused only by his uncompromising brilliance, but he'd have guessed it anyway. Everyone knew about Eddie Thwing, 'the swinger with a lisp'. She was surprised to find he didn't have a lisp, in fact. Within a few days she knew much more about him and he knew much more about her, the planning side of all this aided by the fact that Jansen House owned a flat in Earl's Court for the use of visiting authors or bigwigs from the American parent company and that the author booked in for that week had been hospitalised following a car crash in Argentina. Within three months, both spouses knew about the affair but had put up little resistance, although Holly's husband (Neil, a failed screenwriter with nothing to commend him but his work with violent female prisoners) threatened to kill himself. Eddie's wife, Jill, had already left him the year before for another man, a drunken, wealthy landowner who shot ducks on his estate in Norfolk, but Eddie had refused to co-operate out of self-confessed spite. Now he was phoning Jill about the divorce.

'I want to come back to you,' said his wife, unexpectedly.
'Bad luck.'

Because Holly was rich, Eddie was very relaxed about the nitty-gritty of the divorce agreement and his wife caused little trouble, resigning herself to duck-shoots on the Alde and local charity work. Neil moved to Costa Rica. So it was that, six years on, Eddie and Holly were in the three-star Pension Keti on Andros with their little boy, Ed. Holly had refused the chance of a villa.

'I want full board. I want just to totally *lounge*.'

Eddie had brought along some work, but not much. Holly had given up the Felicity Keen film project after some fifteen years of trying, but was still in touch with her old contacts and would check over likely manuscripts for cinematic potential. Eddie had decided finally to tackle Proust on Andros and had therefore brought along only three manuscripts to read, one of which happened to be Jonathan Lewis's *New Demons*. Holly was attracted by the title. Eddie could tell her nothing about it, since he hadn't even rolled off the rubber band keeping the six hundred pages from turning into chaos.

'It's a bloke who's worked ten years on it, but then they all say that. The lonely genius thing. What it usually means is that they're too self-deluded to know they're crap.'

'The saving illusion,' said Holly, who was five years older than Eddie.

'Life is a noisy stay in a brief, garish hotel,' Eddie quoted, as inaccurately as ever. The Pension Keti was, like all Greek hotels, noisy: the bare tiled floors and walls made every room an echo chamber, a little nightmarish. It was also surprisingly hot, given they could see the waves breaking on the beach by a lift of the head from the bed. It would be so easy to go mad here, thought Eddie, like in an Antonioni film, staring up at that bloody fan going round and round. He'd have preferred the Outer Hebrides, in some ways. The sand made the floor slippery and Ed kept falling over. Somebody next door was playing some truly gumby Greek pop which, behind the white noise of the waves on the sand and the revolving fan, shifted into something that could almost have been Blur as he was drifting off. Siesta time. Relax. He wished he had, after all, brought along some hashish, but he hadn't dared.

'Who said that?' asked Holly, after a long time which might have been seconds.

'Conrad.'

'Are you sure he said "a brief hotel"?'

'Yeah.'

'Ed, don't do that.'

Ed was shaking the bed. It was after lunch and too hot

to be on the beach. Ed was very fair, taking after his father. He had exactly three hours of life left, but no one knew that. Maybe even the fates didn't know that. Or God. It was one of those things.

'How's the Proust?' Holly asked.

'Not started yet.'

'Proust didn't believe in love. He thought love was a selfish need to be loved.'

'OK,' said Eddie, who was drifting off deliciously.

'Are you listening?'

'Yeah.'

'Maybe he was right. Ed, please!'

Holly stroked Eddie's arm, then Ed's fair gossamer hair. Ed clambered back off again and was doing something under the bed. She hoped the floor was dusted under there, that there weren't scorpions.

'What do you call for 999 here?'

'Why do you want to know that?'

'Because you should know it.'

'We're in a hotel, sort of. They'll deal with any emergency.'

'I wish I could just lounge. I need a really good book,' said Holly, staring at the white ceiling. 'I always bring all the wrong books. That book on Greek gods is so fucking tedious. It's supposed to be amazing, but it's just tedious. I don't get it. So many of these fucking books are just tedious and pretentious. I can't get anywhere past page thirty-three. It's always page thirty-three.'

The sun was sneaking in through a broken slat in the shutters and striking her face via the mirror. If they opened the shutters there would be a sea-breeze, she could hear the breeze in the bushes. But then the sun would be hot and Ed would get burnt. She wished Ed was not called Ed, but Eddie had insisted. His father and grandfather were Edward. It was a Thwing thing. She had wanted Sam. Or Henry, even.

'Anyway,' she said, 'I don't care about the Greek gods. Everyone's so hung up on them. They're a bunch of prats. I can't believe there are duvets in the cupboard.'

'It gets cold here,' murmured Eddie.

'How nice,' said Holly. 'I'd love to come when it's cold here. I'm basically a cold-loving person. I mean, I don't like cold per se but it means you can snuggle up.'

'You forget,' murmured Eddie, 'the damp in the cold.'

'Yeah,' said Holly.

She sighed and closed her eyes.

'I guess I'll have to try one of your fucking manuscripts,' she said.

Ed said 'fucky' several times, from under the bed.

'I've told you before,' murmured Eddie, from his delicious half slumber, 'not to swear in front of the kids. He's only two.'

'My father always did,' Holly said.

'He was in Bomber Command,' said Eddie.

'It's only words,' Holly added, after a long time that again might have been a split second.

'Fucky fucky fucky,' said Ed, banging something on the tiles.

Jonathan and Marion were playing Scrabble. He had placed a K on the end of GIN and the word he then made, slowly, like someone descending a ladder – KNIGHT – ended on a Triple Word Score.

'Gink is not a word,' said Marion.

'*Colonel Blink, the short-sighted gink,*' said Jonathan, totting up.

'Eh?'

'The *Beezer*. The best thing in it.'

Marion picked up the dictionary. She found it after *ginglymus*.

'Sorry, it's slang.'

'Rubbish.'

'It says it here. US slang, in fact.'

'I don't believe in slang. The term's a hierarchical imposition, a mode of oppression to keep the elite in power. All utterance is expression, you can't ghetto-ise bits of it.'

'Crap. It's the rules. No slang.'

'You've got to give it to me. It's crazy. How many times do you use six letters in one go? This is genius, the best since I added a T to ERROR and landed on a Triple Word Score with TEAZLE.'

'Terror and teazle aren't slang.'

'There's nothing about slang in the rules.'

'Everyone knows you can't have slang or foreign words.'

'Anyway, I don't believe in rules.'

'Grow up, Jonathan.'

'Why?'

She put her head in her hands and started crying.

'OK, have your bloody gink.'

'What have I done?'

'Nothing. I dunno. It's probably the menopause.'

Jonathan looked at her for a moment as she blew her nose. Her hair was fulsome and frizzy and grey, streaked with henna. She had pouches under her bright blue eyes. There was a furry quality to the skin around her nostrils and on the flange of each cheek. He remembered her in that circle of African drummers at the unelectrified Ecology Festival at Glastonbury back in '76, incredibly beautiful, with long coppery hair down to her waist and a bright yellow cheesecloth shirt and huge clay bangles from Peru. Her eyes closed and calmly beating the African drum between her feet, over and over, and he joining her with a little drum he used in drama classes (his itinerant theatre company, Red Solstice, were running a workshop up in the main tent), and letting the rhythms weave in and out of his body, the energies accumulating into a spirit bubble that held them in a kind of transparent calm that might have been ecstatic if it hadn't been so overpoweringly stable, as if the whole universe was running to their intricate beating and the other drummers grinning above their flexing, ebony-gleaming chests and shoulders and the silk cloth at each of her wrists wriggling and shining and the drum nestled like a pool between her long red Indian-style skirt, and she just keeping her eyes so closed and calm.

That was love at first bloody sight, mate.

And now she was getting old, poised on the edge of being truly and properly grey and tired and old. Sometimes, over her loom, with her head-scarf on to keep her hair back and her mouth pursed in concentration, she looked like one of those toothless old crofter-crones in sepia photos of St Kilda. He was almost annoyed with her for letting herself go, until he looked in the mirror at himself and saw that it was time that had decided things, like a spiteful make-up artist, a giggling boy-god armed with a set of Leichner pencils and cotton-wool pads and tweezers for all the harmless hairs, the hairs you wanted to keep.

'It doesn't matter,' said Jonathan. 'We'll say you've won.'

'Is it tomorrow you're seeing the editor?'

'Yeah. I'm quite nervous.'

'Put the crystal in your pocket, it'll help,' she said, sniffing.

'Yeah. I think so.'

He really did love her. He breathed in deeply and breathed out again to dilute his pissed-off feeling about the Scrabble. She was everything to him. They had probably known each other on the Great Plains, in Sumeria, in nameless prehistoric caves. Some of that was in *New Demons*, but always subject to the story. The one great advantage Jonathan had over his writing peers (not that he fully realised this) was that for thirty years he had been dealing in suspense, the art of keeping the audience in thrall. Story. Story, you lot. How are we going to shape all this into story? Where's it all going? How's it going to end? Not with a knife or a gun or a shot of cyanide, OK? This is not a computer game, this is life. And he would give them very tight structures and methods within which to improvise, to play. He had evolved from free expression to something very disciplined, intricate, effective. Otherwise, as he said, it was like playing squash without walls. It was a pity, in a way, that so many of the kids had gone butthead. They were like permanently soft cement that could not be shaped: too much water. Too many knocks. Too much contamination.

He put his glasses on, peering over the rims at the love of his life.

'Let's at least finish, my sweet. You're winning,' he added – although that was only because he hadn't yet finished his turn.

'Don't do that,' she said, 'with your glasses. It makes you look about ninety. Don't for God's sake do that in front of this editor guy tomorrow.'

Eddie, Holly and Ed left the hotel about six, with the edge well off the sun and the heat pleasant. It was a short walk to the headland, where the beach ended and the rocks began. The beach was empty, this end. It amazed Eddie, how few people there were on these sandy beaches. There was no airport on Andros, that was probably the reason. Ed ran up and down in front of them, his little legs blurring as he kept his steps short and scuffed up the sand in clouds until he hit the wet part nearer the sea. He was really concentrated on this running on the sand; it was the feel of it, the warmth and the softness and then the cool, harder, wet part nearer the sea that made slappy noises. Holly was carrying a beach bag with three towels, a snorkel, a mask and all six hundred and thirteen pages of *New Demons* in its Jiffy, as if it couldn't be split into lighter sections. Amazingly, she had already got through almost a hundred pages. She had started in bed at three o'clock that afternoon, and hadn't been able to put it down despite Ed's repeated fucky fucky fucky and refusal to nap.

'Oh, this is good,' was all she'd say. 'This is good.'

Eddie probed, but apart from her saying that it was such a change to read something not trying to be clever and pretentious, he got no further. He hadn't even glanced at the first page before bringing it to Greece. At one point, waking up from his siesta, he had looked at it lying there on the bedside table her side and felt a touch – he was surprised by this – of jealousy. He would have a go at it when she was finished, not before. Maybe this was the big one. The punters were stupid enough these days to follow the herd; you could turn a small success into a massive roller-coaster if you pulled the right strings. Everyone was reading the same four or five books. The rest were nothing. One of the four or five books that everyone was reading could be *New Demons*. But then, he thought (rolling over and feeling horny against Holly's warm thigh under the sheet) he thought that about twenty times a month.

Then they had gone out.

Just before he woke up, however, he'd had the weirdest dream. He and Holly and Ed were waiting for the Tube, only the Tube was designed like the Paris Métro. It was somewhere central – it could even have been South Ken. Holly and Ed got on the train but he missed it because the safety doors, the type the Métro has, closed too fast. He watched the train go off and said, 'It's OK, I'll get the next one,' only he couldn't quite recall where they were supposed to be getting off. All he knew was that it was close, just a couple of stations on. He got on the next train and within minutes daylight was flooding in, as happens on the Met Line out to Amersham or Chalfont St Giles. He started to panic, but the train kept on going. He left it the first place it stopped at, which turned out to be Uxbridge. Uxbridge! The blue enamelled sign over the platform said *Uxbridge* and there were trees and the air was fresh. It was, in fact, Uxbridge in the forties or fifties. He was way out of London, and he wanted to cry. He was incredibly frustrated and angry and this woke him up and there was a tiny circle of wet on the pillow.

Now he was making for a quiet cove on a Greek island with his family and it was nowhere near Uxbridge or South Ken. He wanted to walk the wide dirt track that ran up to a little white church or hermitage on the topmost point of the headland. This headland was one claw of the crab-like bay, and was completely uninhabited. He couldn't work out why he'd ended up in Uxbridge rather than Hemel Hempstead, which was where he was brought up (although he pretended he was from Cornwall, where his mother and father had met and their family had gone for their holidays). He also wanted to snorkel, see some exotic fish. He hadn't snorkelled for twenty years, but had a vague idea that fish were only to be found around rocks. The sea was calm despite the wind that had picked up, a wind that Andros was quite famous for. They liked the wind because it kept the heat down. Yesterday it had been so strong that the plastic chairs in front of the Pension Keti had ended up in the pool (the pool was small and looked as if it had been made single-handed by the round-bellied owner over many years). Eddie hoped, out loud, that the wind wouldn't pick up too enthusiastically, as it had been fairly dormant over siesta time. Holly wondered, just as they left the last of the sand and joined the dirt track, whether it might not be better to stay on the beach. Ed certainly wanted to, he was pulling on her hand and saying, 'Wanna stay on de beach, where we goin'?'

But his father was striding ahead, now, as fathers do. The dirt track was wonderful. It had been beckoning for days, they'd even tried it once before but Ed had been sick as they set out, from too much sun or olive oil. Eddie'd had enough of the beach and of taking Ed to see the donkeys and of taking Ed to see the shops and of generally not striding out to see what lay beyond the brow of the hill the dirt track disappeared over. He could see the track appearing fitfully among the headland's rocky brown slopes of scrub and he could see the tiny white-and-blue spot that was the church or hermitage and wanted to get there because he assumed the track was there for the church. There was a snazzy, half-built villa down to the left, dominating this end of the beach, with glazed blue tiles all over the classical temple porch and nothing on the roof, but that was it. Beyond it was wild. He was striding out. He could hear a wail quite far behind him, Ed's wail, then Holly's cry. He felt a prickle of concern and turned round. He'd gone quite far ahead and was standing almost out of sight from them on the corner. He felt a delicious sense of solitude, for those few seconds. He could just walk on and forget them, but he wasn't that sort of selfish prick. David Roach would no doubt have organised a whole fortnight to himself on Andros, hiking every day on his own while his Suzie struggled with the six small Roaches back in Islington, and then he'd have come back and told everyone how he'd communed with nature as well as read the whole of *Pamela* and *Clarissa*, or was it *Clarissa* and *Pamela*, because David Roach was immaculate and he had iced tea for blood and life for him was easy and extraordinary, he was a fucking star. But Eddie Thwing was not that sort of selfish public-school prick in whose mouth a warm Jaffa cake would not melt. One day Eddie Thwing would tell the world about Roach and his toyboy from Doncaster, but not yet. It would make him even more of a star, in the current climate.

Holly came up panting, apparently telling Ed about the extraordinary, amazing, beautiful fish that Daddy was going to show them. Ed looked absorbed in these fibs. His mother looked at her husband as if he was not quite honest in some way. She looked appealing under her straw sun-hat, her long blond hair bunched up and glowing. He anticipated tonight in bed, stirring under his boxer swimshorts. She shook stones out of her sandals.

'Are you sure?'

'Sure of what?'

'That this is the way you said we'd've had to have gone, to get there?'

'Yeah,' he replied. 'It's the only track. Those other things are paths made by animals.'

'Anmuls!' shouted Ed. 'Fucky fucky anmuls!'

'Ed,' said Holly, feebly. 'The church looks too far,' she added.

'I can go to the church on my own,' her husband said.

'I think Ed might be anticipating something else,' she pointed out.

'I can go snorkelling and then nip up to the church.'

'Nip up? It looks further than you think.'

Her superior age was showing through, this always annoyed Eddie. She'd shade into his mother, or his elder sister. At work he was king, at least on days when he didn't come into contact with Jansen House's top brass. Even then he felt king, although he had to act obsequious: the top brass were rubbish, they didn't even read books. In fact, Harry Turner, the mad Australian Chief Exec, hated books. Actually hated them, like the Ryanair boss hated planes. At work Eddie was king but at home he felt more like Prince Philip.

They walked on. Eddie couldn't stride, he had to go at the infuriating pace of an under-three. They passed some goats on the slope next to them. Ed stopped and stared, hand in his mouth. The goats were hobbled, a thin hairy rope went from each foreleg to each back leg so that they couldn't jump or even walk properly.

'Poor things,' said Holly.

'I dunno,' said Eddie, 'better that than falling off the cliff. Or being stuck in some factory farm. Apart from that they're free, aren't they? Free range.'

'When were you ever worried about factory farming?'

'I'm not. I'm just seeing it from the goats' point of view.'

'*String*,' shouted Ed, pointing. 'String on de legs!'

His shout was so sudden and piercing that the goats wheeled away, scrabbling up the slope as best they could, like old folk with arthritis.

Ed laughed his loudest, uncontrollable, under-three's laugh.

It sounded cruel and mocking. The goats surveyed them from the outcrop they'd somehow scrabbled onto, either curious or terrified: it was hard to tell.

'Down there,' said Eddie, a couple of hundred yards further. The church had dipped out of sight, now. He pointed down to where the sea was swelling and rolling gently against several slabs of rock, slicked wet by the spray that occasionally shot up behind them. It looked deep there: the sea went from the colour of a peeled broccoli stick (Eddie thought of this spontaneously) to indigo, to dusk, to an eventide blue around the slabs. The sun shone golden on the flat rock surfaces. The only blemish was a curious whirl of white plastic bags and general flotsam a little way out, forming a near-perfect circle in front of a sea cavern, on top of which the continuing headland beetled in the shape of an aircraft carrier's prow. It was all rather nice, and was easy to get to: a little scramble down through scrub and some loose stones like scree.

'Looks good,' said Holly. 'Things to sit on.'

'It looks deep by the rocks. There'll be lots of fish.'

'Fish fishie fish!' shrieked Ed.

'Ed,' said Holly, 'do you always have to shout? You can say it quietly.'

'Fucky fucky fucky!' screamed Ed.

'That's enough!' Holly snapped, pulling him up short by the arm.

Ed started to wail again. Eddie was watching all this like a distant god. Everything was so complicated and sticky. Holly's arse was sticking out below her T-shirt, clad only in the Lycra swimsuit, which was a new one, very brief – too brief for Greece, they reckoned, so she wore the other one for the beach. It barely hid the cheeks. For that matter, it barely hid the cleft. She was bent over Ed, whispering into his ear. Eddie imagined, looking the other way, kneeling over her in bed and spurting onto the cheeks in their sliver of Lycra swimsuit. That would be very nice. Ed's wail had subsided into a sort of fissile moaning. Holly was worried about him, in fact. His speech was behind the others in the Montessori school he attended on the days she was working, and the teachers wondered about his behaviour. They didn't call it 'behaviour', as such, they just went on about his 'inter-action with the others', which made it sound worse. He hit the girls and made them cry.

'He's too young to know what he's doing,' Holly had said. 'They're so big on this guilt trip. They look at me like it's all my fault.'

Eddie felt very detached from all this. Ed would pan out. The early draft that would end up wonderful, amazing, extraordinary. Unique.

'I do want a bit of time to relax,' said Holly, as they were making their way down to the flat rocks. Not a single sign of modern civilisation in sight. Apart from the swish of their canvas beach bags against their legs. Their sunglasses. Their sandals were OK, they could be Greek, though they let stones and tiny thorns in, between the toes. The sun was glittering on the water, on the gently rolling and heaving sea as it kissed the rocks.

'You mean now? Or generally?'

He so wanted to get up to the church.

Jonathan wished their house was two floors higher, or that he could construct a wooden lookout tower, like a light-house, from the attic. On clear days you could see it from the loo (a thin sliver of silver or green or grey or blue, flashing or not between two buildings), if you stuck the little mirror out on the end of its pole. Knowing this helped, even though the pole and its mirror were gathering dust in the corner, these days. It was like hanging on to hope.

The seagulls were awful. They drove him mad. He'd loved the sound of them for about two days, until he realised you couldn't switch them off and they didn't take weekend breaks or even, apparently, emigrate to warmer climes.

He was in Dave's shop, trying to forget tomorrow. Tomorrow he was meeting Eddie Thwing. Perhaps it was the name, but the whole thing didn't sound real. He'd phoned up Luxor and expected a secretary, but apparently they didn't have secretaries these days. Eddie Thwing himself had answered. Jonathan had anticipated a fulsome, hearty greeting, but instead he got something much more like the surprise response he was always using in his drama work. For instance, he'd give a secret instruction to one student to play the boss in the interview impro as low status, and tell the interviewee to play it high status but never *ever* higher status than the boss. The students had to cope with the unexpected, the surprise, they had to keep adjusting as if they were – well, playing a squash game. Light on your feet, you see? Then, when it came to actual reality, Jonathan Lewis was still in Drama Course for Beginners, Lesson One. It was shameful.

Eddie Thwing hadn't been rude, just cold. In fact, when Jonathan gave his name, there was a little silence. That silence was like the floor giving way. Jonathan realised that the guy on the other end of the phone, who'd answered the phone so abruptly but who had confirmed he was Eddie Thwing ('Speaking, yeah?'), had temporarily forgotten who Jonathan Lewis was. Jonathan Lewis, the author of *New Demons*! In his own little pre-performance scenario, Jonathan had imagined the line, 'God, hi, yes, look – it's an amazing book! What can I say? Fabulous! Let's talk! Come and have lunch!' He'd thought that was quite realistic. Instead, there was this silence. Then Eddie Thwing had said, uncannily, as if he'd forgotten the rest of his lines:

'Come and have lunch.'

But it was said in a strange way, as if someone had given the secret instruction to Eddie Thwing to act as if he was on Death Row.

'Thank you, thank you very much,' said Jonathan, like a little boy. Over-grateful.

'Wednesday?'

'I teach on Wednesdays.'

Pratfall. Real writers don't ever say, 'I teach on Wednesdays.'

'Do you?'

'It's OK. Wednesday's fine. Sorry. I thought it was Thursday.'

'What?'

'Don't worry. Wednesday's fine. I'll come up on Wednesday. To London. What time?'

'Lunchtime. About one. You know where we are? Jansen House?'

'Of course.'

'You like Japanese, I presume.'

'Well, yeah, I don't meet many personally, in fact, but obviously I'm very influenced by their theatre, and the teachings behind it – Noh, Kabuki, y'know? In fact, I can see you've picked up on that in the book – all that stuff on the open flower, that energy being kept open just above the navel, that's straight out of Noh, and I did keep my own flower open all the way though the actual—'

'I meant food.'

'Oh, oh yes. Anything! Fish and chips! Anything! Really! Except meat. I'm vegetarian.'

Silence.

You are such a wally. As if you've been told to play the lowest status possible, and then some more.

'I'd forgotten you were in Brighton.'

'That's fine. I mean, it's no trouble. Shall I bring a copy of the manuscript?'

Silence. Perhaps sighing.

'No. See you lunchtime Wednesday. One o'clock. Just give my name at Reception. So fish is fine, then.'

'Fish is great.'

'I'm glad.'

Before Jonathan could reply, Eddie Thwing had rung off.

'The thing is,' he said to Dave, who was fiddling on the

computer in the cubby-hole at the back of the shop, 'he didn't sound very welcoming.'

'Of course not,' said Dave. 'He's a hard man. A cool man.'

'So?'

'You can't be hard and cool and slobber over somebody simultaneously, can you? They're all hard men and cool, up there. We're not cool. We're soft. They're high fashion, we're not. They have the stage, we're busking it on the street outside.'

'Give me the street any day,' said Jonathan.

'Whatever,' said Dave, 'they are the Fat Controllers. You know what Gramsci said—'

'Actually, Dave, I don't want to know what Gramsci said, right at this moment.'

'OK. How about Thomas de Quincey?'

'No.'

Dave gazed into the computer screen, his beard (like a maritime captain's, stained with pipe juice) catching its shifting glow on the silvery highlights. There was a character in *New Demons*, called Snarlsbitte, entirely based on Dave. Snarlsbitte was Lord of the Redemption Library, where you could borrow another life. If you went past the loan date, you died. Snarlsbitte was not evil, however. He was merely doing his job. Dave had once worked for Sussex County Library. Long, long ago.

And Snarlsbitte was important. The crux of the plot was when Gail Goodfellow, a distant descendant of Robin Goodfellow (prankster, but genial), found a book had been slipped into her bag that was due in that day. On the flyleaf was stamped, *Property of the Redemption Library*. And above the author's name – it was *A Midsummer Night's Dream* – was scrawled: *To gorgeous Gail, with all my love, Glottis Glossarist*.

As if somebody had slipped her a curse.

Somebody with a very strange name.

★

'Eddie?'

'Yeah?'

'What do you know about Lewis?'

'The island? It's in the Hebrides. The Outer—'

'No, daft punk, the author. Of this. God, you've got such a short memory.'

'Not much. Nothing, in fact. Except that he took twenty years or something. Don't make me think about work, my sweet.'

Eddie had only now got the mask to fit. It had a fantastically irritating strap that was rubber and refused to budge under the buckle because, when you pulled it, it just stretched. The snorkel was bought in a cheap-white-trash shop in the bijou village where their boat had come in, the other side of Andros, and was luminescent pink. It had been vaguely meant for Ed, but of course he was too young to use it. Eddie had tested it by lowering his face into the water over the edge of the big black slab where Holly had spread the towels and was already reading and then the water had lifted up unexpectedly as if somebody had tipped the seabed and he'd come out choking. In fact, it was psychologically hard to breathe through your mouth underwater, it went against instinct. The water was oddly cold. He guessed that was the wind, that the violent wind of the day before had cooled the surface or maybe brought some deep, cold currents towards the island. He didn't know much about the sea. In fact, the sea frightened him. He'd imagined diving off the slab and impressing Ed, who was now sitting on a towel and watching him intently (fed by propaganda about the amazing fish Daddy was going to bring up), but looking down at the slippery, easy subsiding and lifting of the water surface, the huge weight of it and the cold and the way you couldn't see far into the dark blueness when you were up close (though from further away, from the track for instance, it was quite translucent), put Eddie off the whole idea of going in. He was even afraid of the fish, of the possibility of meeting something big and nasty, of a big shadow looming out of the cloudy blue haze of underwater distance. He was, he knew it, pathetic. He was slightly overweight, too. His stomach folded like dough over the top of his swimshorts and his bosoms were a little exaggerated. On top of everything else, he was very white. A red tide-mark at his neck showed the phantom presence of his T-shirt, while a patch of discoloured skin on his midriff, like the beginnings of some hideous disease, indicated a lack of thoroughness in the suncream-application field.

That was the trouble with exotic, glamorous, beautiful places. They made you feel a berk.

'Daddy goin' in de water. Big fish.'

'That's reet, son,' said Eddie, in a ham northern accent. 'Down in t'pit.'

'Don't be long, will you? Ed'll only start screaming.'

'Oh, but look, I've got enough air for about three hours.'

'What?'

'Don't put pressure on me. How can I relax? This is a kid's snorkel. Do you really think I'm going to be *long*?'

A sudden spurt of foam followed a hollow, gulping noise the sea made in the underlip of the slab. The spume in the air reached Holly.

'Oh God, it's got the pages wet.'

'Wheee!' cried Ed, waving his arms in the air, spots of water on his face and his fair hair a little wet.

'I think the wind's getting up,' said Eddie, shivering a little. 'You'd better move back a bit further. I don't normally bring manuscripts near the deep blue sea.'

Holly shifted back on her haunches, the text in her arms like a baby.

'Keep an eye on Ed,' said Eddie.

'Come and sit next to Mummy,' said Holly. 'Daddy's going in the water.'

'Fish! Fish! Fucky fish!'

Eddie waited for the swell to reach up a few inches below

the level of the top of the slab and then put his foot on a
flat protrusion of rock underwater and pushed himself off,
wincing at the cold. The water pushed him back with
alarming force and he struck his shoulder on the slab, grappled to hold it, was sucked off again and realised that the
only way to counteract this helpless toing-and-froing was to
swim as hard as he could. It was surprisingly easy, once he'd
realised that. The swell was only powerful if you were a
passive cork in its grip. But if you were active, you were the
king. Now that was a lesson in life, already. After a few
minutes of thrashing further out and some salty spluttering
with the snorkel, he'd got the hang. The mask no longer
filled up with seawater when he put his face under, and the
silence, the roaring silence, was no longer like death. He
gripped the snorkel with his teeth and breathed calmly and
slowly, hearing his own breath as a loud sigh, like someone
labouring in a lung machine. He swam with his face down,
feeling the massive movements of the water playing about
his body but not dominating it. It was all willpower, he
thought. The rocks, quite close under him, suddenly fell away
to a kind of Grand Canyon of a gorge that gave him vertigo.
The real shadows were down there, it was like the earth had
split to something prehistoric and there were the fish,
hundreds of them, nothing overtly spectacular but silvery and
blueish and bright-red-spotted and in shoals that slipped past
like silk scarves or flocks of starlings. Oh, this was so inspiring.
He was on his own. He was all on his own and he was
living. At last he was living. This was adventure. The gorge
fell away to his right, he was being moved from it without
even knowing it, maybe he was way out now and Holly was
scanning the horizon. He lifted his face and was surprised
to hear the hiss and slosh of water on rock so close: he was
a few feet from the same slab, but on the other side. He
could hear Ed prattling on and Holly grunting her replies,
though they were hidden by the edge of the slab. He lifted
his mask and spat and he could see the canyon through the

water, a little shallow rift in the bed, nothing at all. Nevertheless, he was exhilarated. Or perhaps because he knew he wasn't in danger after all, that down there everything just seemed great and dangerous and spectacular, he felt exhilarated. The wind cooled his head. He adjusted his mask and went under again, Ed's prattling spliced into a silent roar.

'Can I visit you in California?'

'Ha ha.'

'You never know. It can happen overnight. Look at J. K. Rowling. Joseph O'Connor.'

Jonathan felt, in fact, strangely confident that this might well happen to him. It was crazy, really: he was so hard and embittered when it came to certain aspects of life, but there he was being a stupid teenage fantasist, dreaming of wealth and fame.

'Dave, let's face it, it'll be published and after a couple of years of total neglect, it'll end up here, buried without honours. I mean, look at all this lot. Every one of them was someone's lovechild. A lifetime's work.'

'Six weeks, in a lot of cases.'

'Yeah, but not all of them. In fact, your shop's really depressing. All these bloody novels. What a waste of ink and paper.'

'And all disintegrating. Yellowing. Tanned, as the collectors call it. The process of disintegration has already begun. You know why? Because British publishers are too mean to make their paper acid-free, unlike everyone else in the world. Hurts the profit margins. Costs about a penny for every book. So they print on lavatory paper. In two hundred years' time it'll all be a big flaky heap of autumn leaves. That's what's called long-term thinking, or caring about literature.'

'That's bad. I'd thought it was to do with the environment.'

'Economics, mate. You tell your jumped-up editor about it tomorrow. See him squirm, I don't think.'

'I don't reckon it's up to me to tell him that, Dave.'

'No, you're compromised now, aren't you? No resistance now, eh? Blank walls, dumb people. Isn't that what you called that show you did with those reform kids, back in the glory days? *Blank Walls, Dumb People?*'

'Thanks for remembering.'

'Good show, that was. And don't go in with your pony-tail. That world laughs at men with ponytails.'

'Seriously, Dave?'

Dave sat on his stool and stroked his beard and looked down at his feet, his awful *Save Her Knockers* mug cradled in his large hands. No one had come into the shop since Jonathan had been there – over an hour. It had started raining and the passing late-afternoon shoppers grew blurred and distant through the glass of the bay window, on their way to everywhere but in here. Rain suited a cemetery, which is what this was. But there were no mourners, even.

'It's not bad, your book, mate,' Dave said. 'I guess they'll love it, however much of a prat you are. Just remember, however, that they're hard bastards. If they offer you money, make sure it's a lot. Get an agent, as hard a bastard agent as you can find. You've got to meet them on a level playing-field.'

'I'd never have believed you'd have said something like that, Dave.'

Dave looked at him. His watery eyes were smiling. That's the only way you could tell if Dave was smiling, because of the great and fulsome mask of beard.

'Unsavoury. That's what the world is. Write that on your wrist so you don't forget it when you're in there among the gang.'

'Si, padrone. Un-sav-ou-ry. Now, how do you spell that?'

'Like *fastidium*,' said Dave.

'Alright?'

'Yeah. Very alright. Good. Very very good.'

'You looked like a basking whale.'

'Shark. Basking shark.'

Eddie was towelling himself down. His ears were semi-blocked, they kept opening and shutting like a trapdoor. Holly still had her head in that bloody manuscript, lying on her belly with her feet in the air, as if she was tanning their soles.

'Where all de fish, Daddy?'

'Amazing. They're down there. Lots of beautiful fishy-wishies.'

'Don't talk baby, Eddie. Or he'll never learn.'

He got down on his haunches to Ed's eye-level. The wind was cold when it blew onto his wet hair and damp shoulders.

'All the colours of the rainbow, Ed. Blue, and red, and silver. Little teeny-weeny ones, and huge great big ones, about the size of a car. Really huge and all white with sharp teeth.'

Ed's mouth was wide open. Holly didn't react. This annoyed Eddie. She only surfaced from that manuscript to tick him off. The thing was, their literary tastes were different. But it had to be said that she was a useful barometer. She was closer than he was to the mythical average reader, probably because she was a woman: the average reader was a woman. And Holly got a First in English at Oxford and went to Yale for a year, whereas he was a poor Second at Durham. So she knew what she was talking about. She wasn't dumb. Neither was he, of course. It's just that he had played too much rugby and screwed too many lovely lonely girls. You can't do everything, in life.

'Wanna go!' Ed cried, reaching up for the snorkel.

'That's only for daddies,' said Eddie. 'When you're a big boy—'

'Wanna go now! Wanna see de fishie-wishie wiv dem teef!'

'Out of the question,' said Holly, without lifting her head from the page. Her swimsuit was really very brief; she lay stretched on her tummy on the towel and her naked back curved to the sling that actually disappeared into her cleft, either side of which rose her solid buttocks into which he would like to rub the Mediterranean aromas: lavender and thyme and rue. Slowly. And then some more. God, he really wanted her right now. Ed was banging him on the thighs, tiny hands slapping his wet thighs on which his hair was laddered by the water. Ed was shrieking.

'He's tired,' said Holly. 'He didn't have a siesta. He's gone fradgy.'

She turned the page. The wind kept lifting the pages and she'd had to placate them with the end of the beach bag and her hand. If Ed wasn't around, he could just have taken her like that, a way negotiated past the Lycra slip of swim-suit and then right in, inside, into the heat – while she was reading, her attention irresistibly drawn from that bastard text, her breath growing deeper, her sighing and giggling turning into tiny shrieks of satisfaction, his hands finding their own way under the Lycra to the breasts and their secret lovely knobbles—

'Wanna goooo! Fucky fucky fucky!'

'Eddie, for God's sake do something!'

Not even lifting her head.

'Ed! Stop it! Listen, I'll go back in and get some nice pebbles, OK? Now stop it!'

Ed gripped one thigh and bit it. Eddie staggered back.

'He bit me!'

'Ed, that's very naughty! That's what he does at school. You see? I've been telling you.'

'We've got an animal as a kid!'

'Don't say things like that in front of him. It'll give him a complex.'

'It might help if you actually – participated, Holly.'

'What?'

He swept Ed off his feet and slung him over one shoulder and danced about with him. Ed shrieked with joy. Or maybe anger. Or maybe both.

'What do you mean, participate?' shouted Holly over the noise. The sea struck the slab with great force and sent up another white shock of spray.

Eddie stopped dancing about with Ed. Just held him on his shoulder. Ed had gone still. The little naked body was warm on his shoulder.

'You don't think I participate?'

'It doesn't matter, Holly. Forget it.'

'I just take a few minutes off after a whole fucking afternoon of it while you were snoring next to me—'

'I don't snore and you were reading, actually.'

'Oh, I'm not allowed to read now, am I?' Holly shouted. 'Who looks after him all those evenings you're partying and out on the piss?'

'I'm not out on the piss. That's work. I hate those bloody parties but I'm obliged by my work—'

'Eddie, you love those parties. Are you going bald, or something?'

'It's the water. Anyway, Erika looksh after him very nishe,' Eddie pointed out, in a bad Estonian accent, trying not to get really cheesed off with his wife.

He'd had a brief crush on lovely young Erika, this year's au pair, and had made an approach after too much booze following a big launch one night when she'd come in late at the same time as him – but she'd told him, very calmly in her broken English, that she would tell Mrs Thwing if ever he touched again at her bosoms.

'Erika has most evenings off, my darling,' Holly growled. 'Haven't you noticed? Ed's dribbling down your back. Ed, that's not nice.'

Ed had gone quiet because he was watching his dribble – a surprising amount of it – snake down his father's broad back, and was liberally adding to it from his mouth while his parents were talking. It was foamy, and sparkled in the sun. This would be one of the last observations he'd ever make.

'Thank you, Ed,' said Eddie, putting him down. 'That's to make me go back in, isn't it?' The dribble was a tepid tickle all the way to his swimming shorts.

Eddie did go back in and saw the Grand Canyon loom once more beneath him, the rocks dotted with ruffs of sea anemones that might have been nasty; he heard again the rueful, epic roars of his breaths as the fish shimmied and swayed and sped away, his own hands as unreal out there in front of him as a reawoken corpse's, pale in the water and faintly menacing. A stretch of sand yielded, just within reach of his fingertips, some flat, silver-streaked pebbles. He brought them out, the sea pushing at him as he left it.

'These are nice,' he said, shivering in the gusts of wind but feeling sexy and good after the water. 'These are like fish. Very valuable, Ed. Very precious.'

'Vallible,' said Ed, taking them from him.

Ed sat down on the towel and placed the flat pebbles in front of him.

'Dees are mine, Daddy,' said Ed. 'Vallible. Look, Mummy.'

'Don't get my pages wet, honey,' said Holly. 'They're great. Silver and gold. Don't put them in your mouth, they might be chokeable.'

'Vallible,' said Ed.

He's a great kid, really, thought Eddie. He's my kid. Our kid. The sun shone on his kid's hair and turned it golden and the wind moved it like gossamer.

I'll play with him a bit and then I'll make for the church, even if I don't reach it, thought Eddie, making a little house of the pebbles, feeling a pulse of love for his kid, enjoying the air on his freshened-up body. I just need half an hour on my own. I just need half an hour of quality solitude to have in my battery and to draw on when I'm in that fucking place called Jansen House and dealing with fucking account-ants and fucking authors and fucking London in general.

'Look, Ed. A palace.'

★

Jonathan didn't know South Kensington at all well. His fifteen years in London had been mostly spent in places like Catford, Hoxton, Whitechapel, bringing art to the people, fighting on the front line of social deprivation with his body as the only weapon. In those days he was toned up, flexible, he'd actually work out every day with exercises honed by Japanese monks many centuries back. When they moved to Brighton he was disappointed by the pebble beach; he'd imagined trying out his Japanese exercises on sand, like the Japanese themselves, making them ten times as hard. These days he felt stuffed, in the full-up sense, with disappointment, with the way in which everything had got worse. That's what his father, an ex-Army transport supervisor with a limp, would always say: everything had got worse. Even mime had gone so out of fashion it was pretending to be dance.

Jansen House was off the Old Brompton Road and Jonathan was sitting in a fug of quiche in a café run by noisy Italians called Cuppa 'n' Crust, opposite. He'd arrived much too early, being a drama babe, but that was OK. Jansen House seemed smaller, the second time round. It must have been an upper-class boiler factory, from the look of it, as its brick was a luscious glazed yellow and there was fancy ironwork above the windows. Amazing, he thought, what used to be found in the posh centre: market gardens, saw mills, water-works, boiler factories. *New Demons* conjured that era, as if someone contemporary was tripping on all the English past. Elizabethan bear pits, Victorian urchins, gas-fired automobiles and nineteen twenties clothes. After the theatre company had broken up, he devised a one-man show which anticipated the novel, mingling old fairy tales with East End stories. It even had a week's run at Battersea Arts Centre, at the end of which he felt he was on the threshold of fame. He received a nice review in the *Daily Telegraph*, of all places, but that was it. A smug bastard with an earring came up to him after the last show and said, 'I liked the story, but like most other people I hate mime. Drop the mime, man.'

Jonathan had loved mime too much to drop it. He decided that mime subverted consumerism and a society of manufactured images. It empowered the spectator and cost nothing. It took film millions of dollars and hundreds of people to create scenes he could whip up with nothing but his skilled body. Mime was, in fact, dangerous to the status quo. It was more dangerous than words on the page, which also created something out of nothing, out of thin air. But the prejudice against mime, fuelled by the mediocre shits who made money out of manufactured objects and images, had won. He hadn't performed in years, though he still taught the techniques among the other stuff: what the kids called the 'moon walk' went down well, for instance, thanks to Michael Jackson.

'Jonathan Lewis. I've got an appointment with Eddie Thwing. I think I'm slightly early.'

The receptionist gave him a security badge and told him to wait. He ought to have been teaching today at a couple of schools where the kids no longer yelled *Shut y' cake hole* but *Fuck off wanker* and the drama lessons took place in the canteen. But he'd phoned in sick (Marion had phoned for him, in fact). He felt vaguely guilty, letting down the kids, who wouldn't get a replacement teacher in time, but maybe they'd enjoy the sudden freedom, maybe they'd have some life-changing experience in that idle hour of theirs, their breath smelling of marmite, the air full of chip grease and mushy peas.

The thing is, you never know what life may bring. Surprise yourself. Don't rely on the old excuses.

He sat straight in the terrible sci-fi mauve chair, stretching his vertebrae that were beginning to feel the strain of thirty years' physical theatre, flexing his fingers automatically into a hand ripple, keeping his flower open, the energy uncoiling and flowing through the flower. He'd left the ponytail as it was. Marion had insisted. 'Take you as you come, that's what they've got to do.' As if they could be pushed about. His nerves told him that this was not possible. The boiler-factory feel.

Among the people coming in and out, the smart, the clever, the cool, he recognised the living version of a portrait on one of the bigger posters: fleshed out, older looking, her hair no longer dark. The portrait could have been a decade out of date. It was the same with actors. Everyone always looks older because the demon Time is prince. The author looked lonely and small in comparison to her poster, where she was a feline goddess in moody black-and-white, like a bad pastiche of Lauren Bacall. He had definitely heard of her: Anita Barry. Marion had read one of her books on that holiday in Wales where, when it didn't rain, the mist made everything disappear up to the first few cows next to the cottage. Anita Barry came down and sat opposite him. He nodded and felt a fraud. She must have been rather beautiful, once: now she seemed suburban, elderly. She had a twitch, too: a little spasm of the neck. A faint whiff of spirits saddened the air between them.

'Like Death Row,' he said.

He hadn't really meant to say this. It was a stupid thing to say. Inappropriate. It was nerves. She looked up at him sharply.

'I totally agree.'

'Great. Actually, I was joking.'

'Fellow author. I can tell because you look normal. Is that you?'

She was glancing up at a poster behind his head. He looked, half expecting it to be himself, by some miracle. A bloke in a chef's hat, well into his sixties, grinned back. He looked groomed and American. Larry Drake, *Everything You Were Afraid to Ask About Chefs*.

'I hope not,' he said.

She smiled grimly. There was the alcoholic's evil twinkle in her eye, but her mistake still made him feel (aside from the existential reminder that he no longer looked like a twenty-year-old) that he was in the wrong place. He was used to clapped-out staff rooms where ribaldry and depression battled for first place around a broken coffee machine and the air was full of smoke. He was not used to fencing with famous novelists. In fact, he had never met a famous novelist in his life, not informally. The odd playwright, yes. But they were different.

'Don't tell me you're an experimental fiction man.'

'No. Just fiction.'

'What sort? I'm supposed to know you, am I?'

'No, I don't think so.'

'You can't be a beginner, not at your age.'

He didn't know what to say. She was eyeing him like one of the dark witches in *New Demons*. There were five of them, they all shared a house in Eltham and worked in Westminster in the typing pool, turning government into a frenzy of nonsense by planting auto-suggestive spells in papers and reports.

'Anyway,' she went on, her white hair awry, 'we all love to ruin our lives, don't we? I've completely buggered mine.'

'Oh dear. That's quite negative.'

He was thinking: I can tell Marion, when I get back, that I met Anita Barry and had an intimate chat with her.

'It's not negative, it's honest. I used to be scrummy, according to the men. Now look at me. And you were a mere boy when we first met.'

'Sorry? We've met before?'

'Haven't we?'

'I don't think so. Maybe.'

'What's your book about?'

The plastic bag was between his feet. Marion had insisted he take it in a plastic bag rather than his work bag, which was covered in dated political stickers. They'd chosen, from the kitchen drawer, a British Museum Bookshop bag with a discreet Lewis chess-piece on each side. It was hardly a fashion statement, but Jonathan had realised he would be on a stage where every prop and item of costume would invite a judgement about him.

'Right. My book. Where do I begin?'

'Oh, I know, one of those. Well, I can tell you what mine's about in two words. Sex and money. That's all they want in this awful dump, anyway. I remember when mine were proper publishers, in a most delightful ramshackle building in Ladbroke Grove. Now it's like one of those airports. They'll be examining your luggage soon. Are you well known? I know very few writers these days. I stop at Henry James, and even he's a bit much. All we're doing is telling stories, isn't it?'

'I agree with that,' said Jonathan, warming to her. Like the subversive witches Emily Walnut and Janet Pitchfork in his novel, there was wisdom in amongst the spite and battiness.

'Well, no one else seems to think that, these days,' she said. 'It's all clever words. Decoration, I call it. Hiding the rot. Don't listen to me, I'm an old bat.'

'No you're not,' said Jonathan, blushing under her gaze. 'You're a famous author.'

'Know my work, do you?' she said, leaning forward expectantly, her face softening with grateful pleasure. It was pathetic and disturbing for Jonathan, to see how grateful she was, how expectant, with her black-and-white portrait beyond like a mocking double in its mane of dark hair.

Eddie was walking up the track. Holly had given him half an hour, which he could stretch to at least forty minutes. You couldn't get very far in a quarter of an hour, for God's sake. He'd never make the church, that was obvious. This made the church, or hermitage, or whatever it was, even lonelier and more enticing. He looked at his watch to time himself; he'd taken five minutes just to scramble back up the slope and walk a few yards along the track. It was ridiculous, how fast time went. It only went slowly in meetings. Every bloody Monday morning they'd have a planning meeting, these days. Strategy plotting, it was called: when they were told what to do. He'd make the right noises and then ignore it all. Luxor was successful because he was a maverick, but there was no room for mavericks in Jansen House. The Americans were shadowing their every movement. As flies are we to the gods, they kill us for their sport. Something about wanton boys, too. This is why he got a poor Second: inaccurate quoting. And the word drunken. As drunken flies? Christ.

He smiled. He realised he'd been staring at the ground as he walked. He could have been in Hounslow or somewhere, for all he was noticing the view. He looked up and scanned the horizon as he carried on striding. There was the Mediterranean, shining, glittering, not quite as blue as in the adverts, but still stunning. The wind had dropped and the early evening sun felt suddenly strong on his bare chest and neck. Maybe it could still burn. Surely not. He breathed the scented air deep into his soul, which stirred like an underwater anemone. Thyme, lavender and rue. Anise, maybe, like in California. Definitely wild thyme under his feet, in the middle of the stony track. This was good. This was quality time. You had to be alone to have it. Alone with the gods.

A sudden, dark chill seemed to touch his insides. He turned round. He'd cleared a bend and a high rock and could look down on Holly and Ed. Just checking. They looked very small together on the flat black slab, with the sea apparently still but its swelling and subsiding given away by the odd whiteness expanding and dissolving around the rocks.

He walked on further where it was quite steep and took a breath: he was not fit, not at all fit. Now the sun glittered on the sea around the rocks, and Ed's tiny figure was a silhouette in the glitter. He seemed to be standing up, quite near to the edge of the slab, but it was hard to see properly. Holly was lying down, he could make that out easily enough. Reading that bloody manuscript. He didn't like the idea of Ed being so near the edge, but even if he shouted down they wouldn't hear him. The sea was noisy down there, and he was too far away. From up here the sea was a suggestive, faint sigh. It didn't move, its blues and greens staying put like an abstract painting, and then the whiteness appeared, quite close to Ed's confused silhouette. Ed must be looking out for fish.

That was the trouble, Eddie thought, squinting to see through the glitter: I can't get away for a minute, I can't ever relax. I've got to let myself go, stop worrying. Trust, trust others. Trust my wife. Trust the gods. Or God. No, he didn't believe in God. But he still said to himself: *Dear God, protect my wife and son. Amen.*

And armed with a little glow of trust, he walked on.

'Jonathan Lewis?'

A large guy in a dark leather coat was standing there. Jonathan had rehearsed this moment, but he'd imagined being whisked up to the office by a flunky. He hadn't expected Eddie Thwing to come down to the lobby, for some reason.

'Yeah. Yes.'

'Eddie Thwing.'

'Oh, hi. Alright?'

Jonathan stood up awkwardly and the plastic bag fell over. The heaviness of the manuscript and its lack of spine meant that you could neither stand it up nor keep it solid, like a brick. Now it was half out of the bag. Eddie Thwing was looking down at it. Staring. The guy had dark rings under his eyes and he was smoking, although there was a *This is a Smoke-Free Zone* sign on the wall. Anita Barry looked cowed and wicked at the same time, as if a powerful wizard had entered. Jonathan's hand was stuck out but Eddie Thwing didn't take it; his left hand was in his pocket and the right was holding a cigarette.

'Hello, Anita. How're you doing?'

'How are *you* doing, Eddie?' asked Anita Barry, who had stayed seated but was close enough to place a hand on Eddie Thwing's arm.

'Fine. If you're into Fantasy.'

Anita nodded and then laughed uncertainly.

'I thought you couldn't smoke here,' she said, fishing in her handbag and breaking into a moist cough like a badly directed cue.

'That's the book, is it?'

'Yes,' said Jonathan. 'Rather heavy. But that's my fault.'

Jonathan had picked the bag up and it was dangling by his knees. The book had curled up like an animal. An otter, maybe. It stretched and distorted the bag.

Eddie Thwing didn't smile. A hard man, that's what Dave had suggested. Hard and cool and not looking in the best of shape.

'Shall we go and get a bite, then?'

'Yeah. That'd be great.'

Ten, fifteen years younger than him, probably. Yet Jonathan felt about thirteen. Dave had been dead right about the ponytail. Eddie Thwing's glance had just taken it in: a subtle moue of distaste, as if someone was blowing onto his face.

'Who're you waiting for, Anita?'

'David, *natürlich*. Out to lunch. Once a year, it makes us feel wanted. It's their job, you know,' she added, addressing Jonathan, who smiled wanly. 'Otherwise we'd go hungry in our little dens, wouldn't we?'

'I found eight Snickers wrappers in Roach's basket yesterday.'

'Dearie me.'

'It's OK. It's killing him slowly.'

Anita Barry laughed – she was lighting her cigarette – and collapsed into a raucous coughing fit, tapping her bird-like chest and trying to apologise. Her dark-maned double watched her from above like a disapproving daughter.

'Like these bloody fags,' she panted. 'Dearie me.'

'Let's go,' said Eddie Thwing. 'They know we're coming.'

Jonathan followed him out. People nodded at Thwing on

the shallow steps as they passed, their expressions oddly compassionate, as if the editor was fragile in some way. He all but ignored them. The pavement here was narrow and marked by Victorian-style bollards, which made it difficult to keep alongside him. Thwing walked briskly and Jonathan hung back just behind, a bit too dog-like. The long dark leather coat with its dangling belt was very smart and expensive, of that Jonathan (who knew very little about such things) was certain. He was wishing, clutching the plastic bag to his chest – weaving to avoid people coming the other way while Thwing didn't seem to need to – that he had never come. He wished he was in the evil-smelling canteen, where the class would be coming to an end over the clash of dinner preparation, rather than here, where he was not a comfortable fixture, or a fixture at all.

They walked for some ten minutes, in the end, towards Earls Court. The noise and the way Eddie Thwing kept on walking just in front made conversation impossible. Jonathan had dressed too warm and sweat started running down his ribs, as happened more and more when he was doing mime in overheated classes. They turned down a cobbled side-alley hung with pots of hanging ivy, off which was an even thinner alley leading to what looked like an old factory yard with a big closed gate at one end. They went up three steps to a metal door with, oddly enough, *Nagasaki* stencilled badly in black on its cream paint.

'The coolest place in town,' said Eddie, 'and the best sushi.'

Jonathan realised he must have looked as if he needed reassuring.

The entryphone crackled and Eddie said his name and the door buzzed. Eddie pushed it open and Jonathan followed him into what at first reminded him of a theatre's blackout curtains – that moment when you struggle to find your way off-stage, blinded by the lights and in a felty darkness. He groped forward until a further door opened to a dim, reddish light which turned out to be a bar with a few men playing cards around a couple of low tables: they were all, Jonathan presumed, Japanese. That was a good sign. Lounge music, the type that makes sense only when you're stoned, beat like a very slow heart. He wondered where the food was. Eddie was talking to a pallid girl behind the counter, which was black with little lights set into it, like stars. Jonathan's excitement was increased by the fact that he had never been in a proper club in his life – the type of club a lot of his students went to and endlessly used as settings for their impros. He felt he had begun to live. The men were looking up at him as if he didn't fit, and he tried to smile but they didn't smile back and he felt stupid.

The girl led them through a bead curtain beyond the bar into a further room where there were two wooden tables: one was of normal height, with soft chairs, and occupied by a harassed-looking Japanese man totting up figures on a calculator in front of a sheaf of papers. The other was a large, low table encircled by tatami mats. The walls were a warm orange, with fake candles flickering behind pierced steel. Dagger-eyed leather masks glared down at them: Jonathan had expected shinto or zen, a black-and-white purity of paper screens, but this was more samurai in Western trousers. There were no windows.

'Take your pick,' said Thwing. 'Back to the wall?'

'Anywhere,' said Jonathan, although he hated, it was true, having his back to other people.

Thwing took his seat on the mat, resting casually against the wall. Jonathan sat opposite him in lotus position, with nothing to lean against and nothing to look at but the editor and a malevolent leather mask above the latter's head. A young waiter came in and laid hot, scented towels in front of them. The Japanese guy (perhaps the owner) was snapping at the waiter: or perhaps it only sounded like snapping. Perhaps he was saying: 'You're doing a great job. I'm giving you a pay rise.' Then the man got up and came over to Eddie Thwing and said something softly in his ear. Thwing nodded and the man went out. Jonathan wiped his hands on the hot, sweet towel, taking his cue from Thwing. He wiped his face, too, which felt soiled from the London air. Thwing, who had not wiped his face, watched him.

'Happy?'

'Oh, yeah. This is great. Sorry, I was drifting. I hardly ever go . . .'

'What?'

'These sort of places. I guess you go all the time. They seem to know you here, anyway.'

Stop talking. Keep the patter minimal.

'I'm sick of it. Restaurant food. It all tastes like restaurant food. But today will be different.'

'Oh.'

'There's no need to look at the menu. I ordered this morning. It's a very special dish. Actually, it's under the counter.'

'Under the counter?'

'Because it's banned.'

Jonathan smiled. 'Laced with dope, is it?'

'I'm serious. They have a very special chef, here, who does a very special dish. It's extremely expensive. Have you ever heard of the puffer fish?'

'I think so, yeah. Blows itself up into a ball?'

'Yup. Fugu, in Japanese. It carries inside its liver a deadly toxin, twelve hundred times deadlier than cyanide. The raw flesh of fugu is a great delicacy in Japan. But it has to be expertly prepared, or the toxin shuts down your nervous system within half an hour.'

'Oh, great. We're not eating that, I hope.'

'We are.'

The waiter came up with a bottle and two small glasses and filled them in one flowing gesture without a drop spilt.

'Sake,' said Thwing. 'Fermented rice.'

'Ah yes. Sake.'

The editor said 'Kampai!' and drank his sake in one gulp. Then he slammed the glass on the table.

'Your turn. The toast.'

Jonathan hardly ever drank spirits, but a lot was at stake.

'Kam . . . ?'

'Kampai!'

'Kampai! Here goes.'

The sake was a crime to his throat, but a blessing to his head. It made him feel better within seconds. The waiter laid napkins on their laps and removed the towels. The napkins were starched white but soft and smelt of summery linen. The waiter whisked away their unused plates and it was all rather pleasant. Oh, much better than the canteen at Scots Avenue Secondary School! The puffer fish business was obviously a joke.

'Kampai!' sounded three more times. Thwing's hand trembled slightly when he put the glass down.

'Great place,' said Jonathan. 'Feels almost private.'

'A favourite of the Japanese mafia, the Yakuza. They're very big. They keep the Japanese economy afloat. Ours, too, probably. It's called Nagasaki.'

'I saw that. Very droll.'

'Poker and heroin and puffer fish. High stakes. A gambling den one side and the best Jap restaurant in town the other.'

'I'll skip the heroin,' Jonathan laughed.

'Keep your voice down,' Thwing growled, 'would you, please?'

'Sorry.'

Jonathan felt very good. This was real life. This was better than he'd expected.

'So,' said Thwing, staring at the glass. 'You're Jonathan Lewis. You're the author of *New Demons*.'

'That's me. I hope that's not a problem,' he added, grinning, feeling even better with the fourth sake keen and burning cold in his chest.

Thwing's eyes swivelled upwards and settled on Jonathan. The eyes were bleared, very tired, almost defeated-looking, but there was something fierce in them that seemed aimed at Jonathan personally. Of course it couldn't be aimed at him personally. This guy loved my book – at least, he called it 'gripping, dark and dangerous' – and he's taking me out to lunch. This is what editors do, he thought. They take authors out to lunch and the authors feel wanted at least once a year. That's what Anita Barry said. Out of their little dull dens into much more exciting dens.

'A problem?'

'I hope it isn't.'

'No, since you're here, in front of me. Before, it was a problem. Not meeting the guy who's . . . had such an effect.'

'Effect?'

'On your life.'

Jonathan felt a delicious heat in his belly. Ironically, it was all so like the celluloid crap he kept insisting his students avoid. This hard-bitten guy was about to say that *New Demons* had changed his life, it was that good. No, he'd said it. That's what he'd said. Ten years and this was it. This was the moment that made it all worth while: the struggle, the late nights, the clamp of despair and age. At the same time, he felt he'd wasted his life, coming in here and seeing what he'd been missing. The danger and the elegance. The sophistication. The fine, dark food of things.

'On your life? Really?'

'Really. A very big effect.'

'Well, what can I say? Glad you liked it.'

A slight frown.

'Liked it?'

'Yeah,' said Jonathan.

Eddie Thwing, the renowned editor, leant forward slightly, his hands folded on the starched cloth.

'How can I have liked it, when I haven't even read it?'

Eddie came to a gorge that ran straight down to the sea. Everywhere was dry and brown except for here, where a stream was still running and the sides of the gorge were green with bushes and trees. Those trees looked like poplars and there were tall rushes growing. He could smell the freshness, there was a magic about it: this is where the gods come, he thought.

He scrambled down to the stream, where someone had placed two planks as a simple bridge. A goat, hobbled like the others, limped away. A solitary goat. The scapegoat. He wouldn't mind being that goat, able to get away like that, from the others. No responsibilities. No typescripts. How many titles published a year? Three hundred thousand. A disease. They ought to have a moratorium, a ceasefire. No books for ten years. No authors.

The goat was looking at him. That same strange stare. Goat-god. Pan. Trouble, maybe. A gust swept up the gorge from the sea and stirred the leaves and swayed the rushes and Eddie thought of that wicked wind in, what was it, *Where Angels Fear to Tread*? That alien, southern wind of excitement and danger.

He shivered. The sun was no longer high enough to reach the gorge, it was lighting the rocks overhead but not the gorge. The sound of the stream was pleasant but seemed to mask a perpetual tumult of screams and tiny cries. This was the moment, sitting there on a patch of green by the stream in the shadows of the little gorge, that he'd look back on as premonitory or even worse – as the moment Ed was lost. Something telepathic, some intensity thrilling the air. Maybe the goat had felt it, because Eddie remembered it pricking its little ears and looking up, scenting something he couldn't. But right now he didn't know that, of course. He was enjoying the solitude by the lonely stream on the wild headland of Andros. Savouring it, despite the anxiety sounding underneath the music of leaves and water. That distant booming that must be the sea striking the rocks out there.

'You haven't read it?'
'No. But my wife did.'

'Oh, I see.'

'You see, do you? That's good.'

Jonathan was out of his depth. He knew it. He didn't know any of the rules. He knew the rules of his job, he even knew the rules of the proper theatre world – that, like film, it was mostly a family affair, an affair of blood and then an affair of sex, or luck, or class, or charm, or sheer brutal self-ishness and self-belief to the point of sickness and maybe, somewhere in there, talent – but here in this book world, he was out of his depth. The waiter had laid two pairs of wooden chopsticks. Jonathan was OK at chopsticks.

'I know you must be really busy,' he said. 'I mean, I wasn't expecting you to have read it. You probably have people to read things for you. I dunno, I just sat down and wrote it.'

'Ten years.'

'Yeah, I know.' Jonathan grinned, acting sheepish.

'You brought it along with you. That's good. Because I haven't got a copy.'

Jonathan blinked, like a clown who's been hit on the head.

'Oh?'

'The copy you sent me, it was thrown into the sea. Into the deep blue Mediterranean sea. Off Andros. Do you know Andros?'

'Er, no.'

At that moment the waiter arrived from the kitchen beyond the swing door with small plates on which raw flesh was curled or spread in thin fillets soaked in oil. Fish flesh. Fresh fish from the sea. You could smell the sea. Jonathan felt dizzy.

'Who did that? Threw it into the sea?'

'Take what you want. This is good. This is carved up while it's still living. In Tokyo, they carve it up in front of you. Alive.'

'Jesus.'

'No, it's very good. Have you never had it? They slice up the belly without touching the major organs. Technically the fish is still alive, just lying there with its belly sliced up ready to be eaten. This isn't the fugu, by the way. This is tuna and this one is halibut. This is just for starters. A sushi meal takes a long time. This is the best place in London. In fact, it's the only place that does puffer fish under the counter. I have contacts, I checked it out, I checked out the age of the chef, because it's like surgery: a young chef might not have the experience to slice up the puffer fish and he might make a mistake, despite his two years' training. A mistake would be fatal. The amount of toxin sufficient to kill you can be fitted on a pinhead. The toxin is called tetrodotoxin. I thought you might want to know that. Certain books can be fatal, too. The chef is an itamae. That's what they're called. The samurai of the kitchen. Actually, he's not the usual chef. An itamae has to be called in especially, when there's an order. He's the only itamae in London, as far as I know. But today, he's the chef.'

Thwing was looking at him, calculating the effect.

'Great,' said Jonathan. 'I'll try anything once.'

Thwing smiled. 'Once and for ever, maybe, in the case of puffer fish, if the itamae is inexperienced. But I checked him out. He's over forty. Here he is. Hello, Kaze.'

The chef, a small man with a smooth skin and greying eyebrows, gave them a little bow. He was grinning from ear to ear. He was eerily like the Kabuki actor who had taught Jonathan the gruelling exercises all those years ago, that you were supposed to do on dry sand.

'The fugu costs nearly £200,' said Thwing. 'That's one reason he's come out of the kitchen to see us. The other is to check that we're not the police or a hitman hired by some crazed smack addict of a Yakuza boss who thinks he's been cheated. Or maybe it's to see what we look like alive.'

Jonathan laughed, a little falsely. The chef laughed too, out of politeness. He had hairs coming out of his nose. Thwing offered him some sake. The waiter was hovering and the chef barked at him and the waiter came back almost immediately with a third sake glass. Thwing filled it to the brim.

'Kampai!'

'To fugu!'

'Kampai!'

'Very good sake,' said the chef, nodding. He had another.

'Kampai!'

'To life!'

'Kampai!'

'He'd better not have many more, if he's operating,' Jonathan suggested, the sake oiling his mind and converting his anxiety – for he realised the puffer fish was for real, now – to excitement.

'You once told me,' said Thwing, addressing the chef with a hand on his arm, 'that the fugu closes its eyes. Eyes close? The only fish in the world to do so. To close its eyes.'

The chef nodded. 'Cry,' he said. 'Make a noise – cry! Oh, sad. I sad when fugu kill cos cry. Fugu make sound like cry.'

'Here's to the end of sorrow,' said Thwing, filling the chef's sake glass to the brim.

The chef threw his hands up in protest; but Thwing declared, with an assured authority that Jonathan admired: 'Kaze, in this country, as you know, it is dishonourable to refuse a drink, once you are offered a drink. Dishonourable.'

Kaze gave a high little giggle and picked up the glass and called out, even more enthusiastically, 'Kampai!' Then he downed it in one go.

'Yeah,' said Thwing, once the chef had left them, knocking a chair as he went: 'Kaze Iwamoto is a master, a great sashimi chef. We're lucky he was available. They do it in front of you, if you ask. I didn't think you'd want to, being the guy you are.'

Jonathan almost found himself protesting.

'They use very sharp knives,' Thwing continued, 'and the tail flicks up and the mouth gulps, as fish do when they're out of their element, even as the belly is being sliced. It's impressive to watch. It indicates, obviously, that they haven't just defrosted the fish. I don't think they've defrosted it here, but you never know. As long as something's expensive enough, they can do whatever they like. I think they keep the puffer fish in an underwater cage that is hidden somewhere from officials, from the police. They sew its lips together: it has very sharp teeth. Or maybe it's frozen. Either way, you'll still get the effect.'

'The effect?'

'I call it the kiss. Your lips'll tingle and your tongue'll feel a little numb. That's the minuscule traces of the toxin from the liver, which they cut out, along with the testicles. You remember sherbet crystals, as a kid? Well, this is infinitely better, because it's dangerous. It's adventure. It's a thrill. It's even better than the first time you snogged. If you can't actually feel your tongue, you call the ambulance. Although by then it'll be too late.'

Jonathan nodded, a little anxious again. Eddie Thwing was behaving like a villain out of a James Bond movie. It was pure ham, pure drama queen – the slow delivery, the words rolling precisely off his tongue.

He clearly loved words. This editor.

This is some kind of test, Jonathan realised. An initiation rite. And at the end of it, you finished up like Anita Barry.

'But don't tell anyone that you've eaten fugu here. Or the place will get into big trouble, and it doesn't want trouble. It doesn't want to be noticed, even. In New York, of course, fugu's legal as long as the chef's a proper itamae. I ate it a few times when I was in Tokyo. In London, it's banned. Because no one notices,' Eddie Thwing went on. He hadn't once smiled, Jonathan realised, until now. Now Eddie Thwing was smiling. 'No one notices if food's crap, as long as they pay enough. It's the same with books. Except it's not to do with how much you pay, it's to do with how much the publisher pays.'

'The author?'

Jonathan was finding the sushi's rawness a little conspic-uous, if that was the right word. It filled his mouth with the sea, with harbours and sea winds, but he was used to that from Brighton. His favourite dish was a heap of tiny, fried sprats. The chopsticks were fine, he could handle chopsticks, although the effect of the sake made him want to giggle when the raw flesh slipped off before it got to his mouth. His knees were aching from the lotus position. His body used to be able to hold it for ages, no problem, but age was stealing in, and the tiny injuries from thirty years of mime were showing up. He didn't want to sort himself out, though, while Thwing was talking.

'The bookseller. The chains. What I call protection money. The publisher pays for the price to be slashed, for special offers like three-for-two, for posters and window space and all that crap. But it's decided on potential profit, not quality. And the punters are stupid, undiscriminating, so they follow the signs, follow the herd. Sheep, not goats. I prefer goats. They can be solitary. But the goats are hobbled. The stupid sheep read the same four or five books. The big booksellers lick their lips and are happy, because they're false. They're not selling books at all. They're selling product. They take your ground-breaking, amazing book to sell only after they've looked at the fucking EPOS figures and what that says about your previous sales. I call it the intelligence-saving device. It saves them having to think, to consider.'

Thwing helped himself to sake without giving a toast.

'Welcome to the glorious world of books,' he said. 'Where are you from, originally?'

And drank.

'Daventry, near Northampton,' Jonathan replied. 'And you?'

'Cornwall.'

'Right. Great. You know, you sound like my friend Dave. He runs a second-hand bookshop in Brighton. Typical second-hand place, you know? Chaos, you can hardly move. But he says what you're saying. The trouble is, he doesn't sell a thing. In fact, I think you know it. The bookshop. Fastidium.'

Eddie Thwing stared down at his food. The coil of fish on his plate lay untouched.

'So you ask yourself,' he said, almost murmuring it, 'what am I in it for? Why have I let this *disease* enter my life?'

He looked up again. It seemed that he was actually in tears. At least, his eyes were filmed over.

'I think that about every five minutes when I've got a class of thirteen-year-old yobbos,' said Jonathan. 'But you still persevere. Pays the bills.'

Eddie Thwing stayed staring at him until Jonathan had to concentrate on his food, serving himself to the final slip of rawness. He was talking in clichés, he was spewing offal. His mind had gone thin. This guy hadn't even read the book. So? Why *should* he have done? A busy man—

'She called the gods *prats*.'

'Sorry?'

'That was a mistake. It attracted their attention. The second mistake was yours.'

'Mine?'

'Yours.'

'Right.'

Jonathan shook his head slowly from side to side. 'Hey, I'm really lost. Sorry.'

He dabbed his mouth automatically with his starched white over-large napkin. This guy was looking at him with such malevolence. Maybe Thwing was having a nervous breakdown. Jonathan's father had got like that, with his war wound and his war memories from El Alamein and a bottle of gin a day.

'Sorry,' he repeated, feeling suddenly able to handle it, as he'd handled his father. (Don't search for logic in this. Go with it. Don't let it block itself, keep the flow going, we're not here to watch two dumb guys staring at each other, you lot.) 'As the Sufis say, "Lose cleverness, buy bewilderment". I'm bewildered. I'm bewildered most of the time, actually.

But I thought you'd taken me to lunch to discuss the book, which in your letter you said you'd liked.'

Eddie Thwing's eyes had drifted onto a point roughly where Jonathan's heart was.

'I hadn't read it.'

'No, but—'

'If I had . . .'

Pause.

'Yeah?'

'I wouldn't have taken it.'

'Taken it? You mean for publication?'

'To fucking Andros.'

'Oh, right. The holiday didn't go well, then?'

Eddie Thwing burst into laughter – if such a harsh, savage sound could be called laughter.

He didn't stay long in the gorge.

He checked his watch: five minutes, maybe. He scrambled out of the gorge and back up to the track. He'd been away fifteen minutes already: the next stretch of track climbed steeply to disappear over the brow of the nearest ridge. The church was hidden again. He felt like climbing up to the brow of the ridge to see what lay beyond, it was as inviting as any near horizon – although when you got there it was always the same old thing rolling away. And the image of Ed through the blinding glitter a few minutes back was nagging at him.

This was always happening, he thought, as he strode back: he was always thinking the worst because he read fiction all the time and even intelligent fiction of whatever genre relied on things going wrong, on tragedy and disaster. It was screwing him up.

He came to the bend that bordered the slope beetling over the unseen sea canyon below, way under his feet. The glitter on the water had shifted slightly, it was easier to see Holly.

No Ed.

He shielded his eyes with his hands and screwed them up, shuttering down the little twinkly stars of glare until the edge of the big slab loomed a bit clearer. Holly was reading, he could see that. He could see her in exactly the same position as five minutes back. But there was no Ed. This couldn't be true. His heart had hammered like this before, when Ed had run out into the road in Camden and a bus had passed between them and then there was Ed, on the other side, a mere toddler whom the bus would hardly have felt. And times before, before Ed. Was there a time before Ed? He supposed so.

This couldn't be true. He stayed looking, screwing his eyes up, waiting for his son to appear from behind the slab, or from behind Holly. He's probably lying down beside Holly, Eddie thought, but it was too far away to see and he was the wrong angle. He's probably just there. Christ. You can't even go for a little stroll on a nice Greek island without putting your arse in the highest gear. Insecurity, that's what it is. You're so intrinsically insecure, thanks to your mother faffing about over you in Hemel, in that little over-stuffed semi in Hemel. Eddie was talking to himself in a stage whisper, now. Where is he?

Ed! he shouted, waving his arm. Ed! Ed!

His voice got nowhere, flattened somehow by the open air, as if it wasn't in inverted commas.

He was breathing hard, now. He could see the sea whitening abruptly around the rock. Then he saw Holly move, get to her feet. Ah, she was getting Ed. He must have made his way behind, into the scree and scrub. Eddie wanted to laugh with relief. But Holly was shouting. He could just hear it above the sigh and sough of the water, a weeny little cry. She was echoing his shout. He was pretty certain she was shouting for Ed, too.

He started running down the track, feeling sick, feeling his whole body turning into a circuit board with the cover off. He was shouting *fuck fuck fuck* as he ran down, and then *Jesus Christ oh Jesus*. The details of the stones he was slapping through were very clear. He wished he was a stone. Or a goat. Then his right sandal strap broke and he found himself losing it and sliding his bare foot on the roughness of the track, dust clouds piling up like he was a motorbike, and limping back and cursing and then using his sandal like a flip-flop by trapping the thong between his toes, but this slowed him down and he had to hop and run at the same time and the sun was in his face.

But it wouldn't have mattered if he'd been able magically to leap from the bend in the track and swoop straight down onto the black slab where the water heaved and subsided and now and again thrashed into foam, because Ed was already four-and-a-half minutes under, already a pale underwater form among the beautiful swarms of fishes, his hair floating out like the frill of a sea anemone or the fronds of weed, already taken by the curious currents to the anonymous depths a hundred yards out from the slab on which loose pages were fluttering and Holly was screaming and screaming his name.

Something very dark was happening. He could feel it. He could feel it pulsing from this man the other side of the low, wooden table. He wished Marion were here. He felt oddly alone in this swirl of dark energy. Maybe this is what all authors feel. Real authors, not the fake ones. Very alone.

Eddie Thwing had stopped laughing and the plates had been taken away. He ordered a second bottle of sake.

'Fermented rice,' he said, again. 'The only thing to drink with puffer fish. The glass of rum before we go over the top. Kampai!'

The two glasses slammed down. Jonathan was aware of a little suspended animation about his own movements. His unsupported back hurt. He shifted from his strict lotus position into something approximate, rolling his ankle-bone painfully against the floor.

'Why did you write your book?' asked Thwing, all of a sudden.

The malevolence had been tucked away. That was good.

'*New Demons*? I can't say. I don't know. I mean, I do and I don't. I wanted to escape. Parallel world. I'm a drama teacher – physical theatre, mime, impro, situations. You know, trying to teach kids to be tolerant, open-minded, freeing them up. Not movie stars, or musicals, that glitter stuff.' He was moving his hands around too much. The editor looked on over his small and perfect sake glass, impassive, the neutral mask. Only the eyes disturbed. 'So what I was really – I mean, originally I wanted to settle for a story, y'know?'

Eddie Thwing nodded. He'd heard all this before, no doubt.

'Then the story – well, it went on and on. I kind of – escaped into it. The job, it's a bit – it kind of bleaches you out. Tough kids, tough schools, bad conditions, all that. It can be really heavy.'

'They say it is.'

'I don't know whether you have kids, but . . .'

'What?'

'I said, I don't know whether—'

'I heard.'

The editor's hand was trembling. There was a long moment of silence between them. The gamblers could be heard through the bead curtain – joking, or maybe arguing, with the chirrup of a mobile through the faint, deep suggestion of the music. The kitchen itself was silent until the swing door opened, and even then it was muted.

'Right,' said Eddie Thwing. 'Alright. Look, what I really want to know is . . .' He sighed, the kind of sigh that follows a crying fit. This poor sod is definitely having a nervous breakdown. Jonathan had seen it before, in the staff room. People crack up differently. 'What I'm trying to get to is the nub. The root. The half-past-two-in-the-morning root, when you still haven't got to sleep and you're thinking. Because you can't stop thinking. You've got a bottle of brandy inside you and it makes no fucking difference. Because you haven't found it.'

'OK,' said Jonathan.

'It's not OK. If you hadn't written anything, if you'd just stuck to your . . . humble position in life, and not reckoned like every other . . . fucker in the country that you could apply pen to paper and *write*, then I would not be . . . in my present position. Which is that of . . .'

He was searching for the word. His speech was broken-backed, with pauses for breath.

'I don't know,' mumbled Jonathan. This was really, really disappointing. The guy was panting, now, as if he'd run a long way. What was he – thirty-nine? Forty? Overweight. Out of condition. Off his rocker. I could just get up and leave, he thought, but something said no, don't do that. Cowardice, maybe. Not wanting to let the audience down. See this through, you lot. See it right through to the end of its curve where the crock of gold lies that is us, clapping and smiling.

'Which is that of a very . . . sad . . . broken . . . person. Y'know, she said to me –' He drained his glass and refilled it, still not touching his food – 'she said to me, *Is this the way you said we'd have had to have gone, to get there?* Something like that. And I remember thinking – this was on the way . . . up, onto the headland, on that fucking track . . . will o' the wisp . . .' He drank again, having clearly lost the thread.

Make the offer, guys. Keep it going. Don't block.

'Thinking?'

'I remember thinking . . . how amazing that sentence was. The grammar of it. The structure. The whole thing. She'd said it, y'know, without aforethought. The way you do. It's probably not even correct. Who cares? I have authors who can't spell, who can't spell *grammar*, Jesus Christ – but who cares? I don't. We have to punctuate for them. Semi-colons, y'know? Commas. And they think we're grateful.'

Jonathan nodded. The editor was rambling, drunkenly.

This was better. The vitriol had been appeased somewhat by more poison, like an antidote. He pictured his father spitting venom and then subsiding in front of *Z Cars*, the Gilbert's gin drowning him in slumber. Peace, at last. He shifted his body and his knee twinged.

'Yeah. Anyway, she said this, and I thought that, and this was all before. Like before the dinosaurs. Like before Hiroshima. Like before that kid in Iraq lost his arms because we blew them off. Y'know, I didn't care about him, when it happened. I never watch the news. Too busy. Don't go to the theatre, either. Too busy. Or cinema. But now I care. I mean, I'm cross about it. About all the kids in Iraq or Africa or wherever. The dead ones. And so she said that . . . before. And I can fucking *touch* it. Her voice. Her saying it. But it's lying on the other side, isn't it?'

The word 'touch' had left spittle on his lower lip.

'Before what, exactly?'

Jonathan knew what it was now: the poor sod's wife had gone off with someone else. An author, maybe. The affair uncovered. Wasn't that what Dave had said — that it was a world where everyone had affairs? And this guy, this famous editor, had been struck down by the knowledge. The sake was flashing pleasantly in Jonathan's body, all over, illuminating it from within.

The waiter came out from the kitchen, the man with the calculator apparently shouting after him. Or maybe having an argument with the chef, the master. The heavy swing door swung back and hid it all. The waiter, who had beads of sweat on his nose and upper lip, took their plates.

A long silence.

He would stab melons, plunge a carving knife into a great deal of melons over the days, but Eddie didn't know that yet, lying sleepless on the hotel bed in Andros. Holly had cried herself, with the help of her emergency tranquilisers, to some kind of sleep. Melons, because that's what Holly had said they used in films for the sound effect of a knife blade in flesh: it gives just the right resistance.

At this moment, however, he had not yet formulated what he was going to do to Jonathan Lewis; there was only a great, blurred rage. He couldn't see this from the hotel, but the pages that hadn't sunk had now joined the circle of plastic bags and other flotsam circling outside the sea cavern, the moonlight making it resemble a great O of foam. Glottal sounds of satisfaction came from deep within the sea cavern. Gulps of deepest pleasure.

Eddie would have liked to have made his way back to the rocks on the headland and studied that O, right now he would have liked to have done that. The moon was bright enough. He rose carefully, inching out of bed so as not to wake Holly, and stood in his pyjama briefs outside their room, on their little veranda. Ed's toy cars were parked where he'd left them, any old way, and this had annoyed his parents, you could fall over on them, but each one was at the end of a trajectory begun by a little hand that was now no longer able to do that, or anything else. It was no longer around. Eddie knew that, now. He was certain of it. He had been certain of it, if he thought about it, right from that moment he had first seen that Ed was not with Holly on the slab.

He had run down and cut his foot, because his sandal had broken, and he had limped onto the slab where Holly was just climbing out of the water, shivering, holding the bright pink snorkel.

'He's in there, he's in there, he's in there.'

'Jesus Christ it's OK this can't be true.'

'He's in there he's in there he's in there—'

'I'm getting him out, it'll be OK, fuck, it'll be OK, it has to be OK—'

The water seemed bigger and heavier and stronger: the sea-bed was on hydraulics and was tipping up and the sea was lifting and striking the slab with great force. But that's only the way it seemed: really, the sea was just the same as twenty minutes ago.

'Get him out, get him out. You had to go for your fucking walk, didn't you?'

She started screaming at him. She was a fury. She just stood there shivering and shaking in her minimal swimsuit and screamed at him, screamed at him about this little walk, this modest excursion of his up to the church, not even up to the church, just a stroll for a few minutes, it was terrible, the way she tore him apart as he swam about, dipping his head under, using the other pair of goggles that leaked because the better pair had gone. Little Ed had gone in with the goggles and the snorkel, he had gone in deliberately and Holly had not been aware of what he was doing. Or maybe he had just dipped his head in to see the amazing fishes and the white fish the size of a car with sharp teeth – Ed was a brave kid, plucky, that would have attracted him.

Eddie stood now outside their room watching the strips of foam now and again whiten in the moonlight on the sea beyond the sand, and the sea was beautiful at night, the moonlight glittered on it, softer than the sun, kinder on the eyes. He could make out the bulk of the headland, and the scents were sweeter than in the day, the scents of thyme and lavender and rue and maybe anise like in California. Then Holly had howled like an animal and – he had seen this from the water – she had lifted the manuscript and thrown it into the water. That was the worst thing she could have done to him, professionally speaking. It broke all the rules. For all he knew, it might have been the only copy of the book – some authors were that stupid. The pages snowed down and scattered themselves on the water around him. Fuck that, he thought. He dipped his head into the water again, always terrified of what he might see, but saw nothing, saw only the Grand Canyon with its silvery fish and its sea anemones, the strip of sand with its flat pebbles, the blue haze of distance before the goggles filled up. He even dived right down (he wasn't using the snorkel) but panic left very little breath in his lungs and he kept having to burst up again, half choking, the sound of Holly howling breaking over him like a reason for staying under for ever in the calm of fish and sea anemone.

He would really like to go up there in the moonlight and have one more look. Maybe Ed had just wandered off. Maybe he was snuggling up to the goat right now. Though the men had spent three hours on the headland, the shepherds and the hotel keeper's sons and the local police and the local drunks: fat men and thin men and boys who had shot up and down the track on their scooters. Even a few women went up, daughters and wives, and a couple of Germans and some Americans who were actually Greek.

'Ed! Ed! Ed!' they kept shouting, like a massive flock of seagulls. The whole headland had become Ed. The parents hadn't told anyone about the snorkel in the sea. Or the locals would not have bothered to scour the headland for him, to help them in their distress. They'd have known.

Even so, it had been embarrassing, causing such a stir: Eddie had actually thought that, momentarily forgetting what it was all about. None of it had sunk in beyond the shallowest level of his brain, unless you counted the wobbliness in his knees.

But before they had gone back and told everybody that Ed had disappeared and been given a stiff shot of something fierce the hotel keeper had made out of lemons from his lemon orchard, Eddie and Holly had had a fight. He had come out of the water, totally exhausted and weak with despair, and Holly had shrieked at him about the walk and Eddie had pointed to the pages floating or sinking around the slab – six hundred and thirteen of them – and said, 'And what about that? That fucking book? You weren't watching. You were in charge. You were totally deep in your fucking book.'

Her book, he had called it, shouting at her. Her book.

She had called him a bastard and leapt at him, slapping him with her hands, flailing, completely beside herself with sorrow and disbelief. He had nearly fallen off the slab, her nails took skin off his shoulders and chest, she was tough, she had almost made the Olympic alpine ski team, but he had controlled her, gripping her wrists, the ex-rugby player's strength finding itself again and teasing her down to the ground as she squirmed and flailed and bit. Prop forward, he had been, at school and university.

Then she collapsed, sobbing. Curled up like a little girl. As if someone was kicking her over and over. She knew. She knew Ed had not just wandered off to see the goats. The little palace of flat pebbles was still upright. Ed had added an extension. The pink snorkel from the trash shop had floated. Ed had not. The plastic snorkel had been retrieved. Ed had not. All this was mystifying and terrible to his father, standing at half past two or three in the morning, gazing on the sea in moonlight, wishing he had a cigarette. But a beautiful sense of Ed as part of the sea, like a sacrifice, came over him then. It was because it was Greece and the intensity of grief and loss had in it a diamond fragment of wonder, too: that you were part of the great cycle of life and death, of losing and becoming, of flux and change and renewal. It was the last beautiful moment Eddie was to experience for years, and mainly the result of his hypnagogic state of exhaustion and the moonlight on the calm Grecian sea: from then on in, it would be the dull bite of depression and the background boom of rage. That would be his grief. And drink.

The need to blame, too. Not the gods. There were no gods. And if there were, they were out of reach.

Your book is gripping, dark and dangerous. Let's meet. Very soon. Give me a ring.

Melons. He worked out for hours on melons.

Authors, he would grunt, at each stab. Authors.

But standing there in the moonlight, wanting to go up

onto the headland where (if this was, say, a Luxor novel) he would find Ed nestled, pale and shining, against the flank of that solitary goat by the stream, like a vision, perhaps real, perhaps not, Eddie was not yet over the abyss. He was in the shallows, still, and wanting a cigarette, as well; wanting things to be as they were the day before; wanting to have taken another way so as not to have got where he was right now, here, after all.

The fugu arrived on large white plates, the transparent slices of flesh spiralling like petals to a little heap of pockmarked skin in the middle.

'A peony,' said Eddie Thwing. 'Or a chrysanthemum. I forget which. That's surgery for you. That's beauty. That's art.'

Jonathan felt pretty excited. This strange guy from another world was going to a lot of trouble to impress him. He had to be impressive back.

'This is the deadly puffer fish?'

'Let's hope it's not deadly,' Thwing replied. 'Remember, if you can't feel your tongue, stop eating. Immediately. Mind you, it's too late by then. Thousands have died in Japan, over the years. A famous Kabuki actor, even.'

The waiter was hanging around by the bead curtain. He was like a bodyguard. It was as if they were scoring, or something. He looked anxious about it. The lounge music had stopped. Perhaps the bar had been emptied, for ceremonial reasons.

Two little bowls held a lime and some soy sauce. The petals were beautiful. He'd so wanted to be a master Kabuki actor, at one time. He'd considered going to Tokyo, but as with so much else he'd been a coward. Now what was he? He didn't know. He was bewildered. This was certainly better than Scots Road Secondary, that's all he knew.

He caught a petal in his chopsticks and put it in his mouth. It was good. It was very good.

Thwing hadn't yet touched his.

'She was caught up in it,' he said, suddenly. 'She told me that before she threw it into the sea. She couldn't understand why, it wasn't like her not to keep an eye on Ed. My kid. She's a worrier, you see. But you'd gripped her.'

Jonathan's lips were beginning to tingle. His tongue, too. It was the strangest feeling. In fact, it did remind him of his first-ever kiss. Sally McLeod. His heart started to beat solidly and rather fast. He'd thought the whole thing was one of those stupid style things, the latest rich-man's fad, that nothing would happen. But something was happening. He wasn't really able to concentrate on what Eddie Thwing was saying, that was the trouble.

'Alright, is it?'

Thwing's eyes were red.

'It's weird,' said Jonathan. 'My lips, it's like I'm – the Delphic oracle – or something. I feel I'm about to utter great truths.'

'That's just the poison. Don't kid yourself. Eat up, go on.'

'Are you sure it's . . . ?'

'He's a master. He's an itamae. That's cost Jansen House nearly £200. I ordered it two days ago.'

'I really appreciate it.'

'Eat up, then. You can stroke the lime with it. Not the soy sauce. That's sacrilege.'

Jonathan put each petal into his mouth one by one, spiralling down to the centre. The taste was of far-off lemons and pale seas. There was something like singing coming from somewhere, very Japanese, very pleasant. The waiter crossed over to the swing door and opened it a little and peered in. The singing was live and in the kitchen, very jolly, perhaps an ancient love song. It didn't seem to please the waiter.

'That sounds like the chef singing,' said Eddie Thwing. 'That's the sake. Poor old Kaze. He doesn't usually drink sake. But I do so like to loosen them up, these perfect, anal Japs.'

Jonathan smiled because it was a joke and his lips glittered with tiny stars, tiny terrible stars that had scattered